CW00536781

The
ASHMOLE
BOX

MICHAEL ANSON'S

The ASHMOLE BOX

An Apothecary Greene Procedure

PAGE D'OR
MMXXII

Page d'Or is an imprint of Prosperity Education Limited
Registered offices: 58 Sherlock Close, Cambridge CB3 0HP,
United Kingdom

© Michael Anson 2022

First published 2022

All rights reserved. No part of this book may be reprinted or reproduced
or utilised in any form or by any electronic, mechanical, or other means,
now known or hereafter invented, including photocopying and recording,
or in any information storage or retrieval system, without permission in
writing from the publisher.

The right of Michael Anson to be identified as the author has been
asserted in accordance with sections 77 and 78 of the Copyright,
Designs and Patents Act 1988.

A catalogue record for this book is available from the British Library

ISBN: 978-1-913825-58-4

Designed by Steph Thelwell
Typesetting and cover design by ORP Cambridge

For further information visit: www.pagedor.co.uk

Ad infinitum et ultra.

For Kit and Hughie, who'll be the finders of
the treasure in the days to come

Richard Greene (1716–1793): surgeon, apothecary and proprietor of a museum that attracted the notice of the antiquary and the curious of every denomination. Reproduced from Stebbing Shaw, *History and Antiquities of Staffordshire*, Vol.1 (London, 1798).

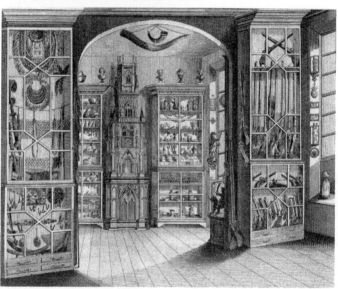

One of two surviving engravings of Richard Greene's Museum, Lichfield, published in *The Gentleman's Magazine* of 1788.

A
PARTICULAR, AND DESCRIPTIVE

CATALOGUE

OF THE

CURIOSITIES,

NATURAL AND ARTIFICIAL,

IN THE

Lichfield Museum.

COLLECTED

(IN THE SPACE OF FORTY-SIX YEARS;)

BY

RICHARD GREENE.

THE THIRD EDITION.

LICHFIELD:

PRINTED, AND SOLD, BY JOHN JACKSON.

MDCCLXXXVI.

(PRICE ONE SHILLING).

The title page of Greene's third and final catalogue. 1786. © The Samuel Johnson Birthplace Museum, Lichfield.

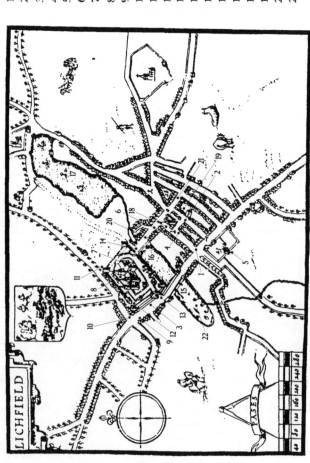

Adapted from Spede's map of Lichfield in 1610. A city virtually unchanged in the mid-18th century. Reproduced with permission from the National Monuments Record Archives.

1 Richard Greene's Apothecary
2 The Ashmole/Blomefield House
3 Erasmus Darwin's House
4 Samuel Johnson's House
5 The Friary. Michael Rawlins
6 Richard Neille's House
7 The Prebendary House
8 The Bishop's Palace
9 Doctor Milley's Hospital
10 The North-West Tower
11 The Bishop's Tower
12 Vicars Close
13 The West Gate
14 The South Gate
15 The Vivarium
16 Minster Pool
17 Stow Pool
18 The Market Place
19 The Guildhall
20 The Dam
21 Greenhill

Loyal and Ancient City

Spede's map of the City of Lichfield from the early part of the 17th century portrays an inconsiderable market town located beside a trio of large meres that separate its small quadrangle of streets from a Cathedral church set within a heavily fortified Close. It was the latter – the medieval walls, moats and two formidable gates – in addition to the singularly strategic location of the little city itself, that brought down upon it the three devastating Civil War sieges that were to utterly wreck 'this great fortress'.

By 1646 the Cathedral church was a roofless shell, its great steeple brought down by parliamentary artillery, its principal defences wrecked by the first use of explosive mines in Britain. So comprehensive was its ruin that wholesale demolition was considered by the Commonwealth parliament in the aftermath of the war. Its future was only finally guaranteed by The Restoration of Charles the Second, when Elias Ashmole – himself a native Lichfeldian, educated at the Cathedral School – led the petitioners for the resurrection of the great building at the heart of 'This Loyal and Ancient City'.

By the middle of the 18th century, its fortunes restored, and now a bustling agricultural and coaching nexus for the East Midlands, its renown as a cultural beacon had spread further still. What one of its most famous sons, the great lexicographer Doctor Samuel Johnson, described as 'a City of Philosophers' would, in fact, produce equally famous sons and a renowned daughter – from within its small ambit. Poetess Anna Seward – 'The Swan of Lichfield' – the precociously accomplished daughter of Canon

Residentiary Seward, presided over the city's formidable literary scene as hostess of her father's grace-and-favour residence, the superbly rebuilt Bishop's Palace within The Close. Her paean to Cook's *Voyages* of discovery was the first, prescient, public recognition of their historic importance.

Seward's equally formidable mentor, Doctor Erasmus Darwin, one of his era's most admired proponents of the natural sciences, provided a ready focus for the Midland's renowned Lunar Society – the intellectual power-house for the region's 'coming men' – the likes of Matthew Boulton, Josiah Wedgwood and Thomas Baskerville. Not a hundred yards from Darwin's stately house beside the ruins of The Close's West Gate was the birthplace of the celebrated actor-manager David Garrick, later the doyen of the London stage, whose reputation would bring even the great theatrical diva of her age, Mrs Sarah Siddons, to perform to rapturous audiences at the city's Guildhall.

Not least, in terms of his inestimable contribution to Lichfield's cultural and intellectual life for over half a century, though most certainly the least likely to occupy a uniquely stellar role in the city's fame, was an Apothecary named Richard Greene. Awarded an honorary doctorate in Medicine from the University of St Andrews for his outstanding services to that profession, Greene was, in addition, one of the leading antiquarians and pioneering museum curators of eighteenth-century Britain. In an Age of Enlightenment characterised by a small and select number of aristocratic aesthetes and collectors whose deep pockets and Grand Tours swelled the private collections that adorned their great houses, Richard Greene's Museum, in rooms above his Apothecary shop and accommodation in Lichfield's Saddler Street, were open to all for the price of a few pence admission.

From its beginnings in 1740, when Greene and his wife Theodosia opened their new premises, until its closure on Greene's demise some 50 years later, the collections grew to the extent that several full-page illustrations in *The Gentleman's Magazine* of the

1780s feature the unique assemblage of antiquities, curiosities, arms and armour, clocks, printed ephemera and, most particularly, natural history, that had drawn tens of thousands of spellbound visitors over the decades. Greene himself would become a regular and most eclectic contributor to the *Magazine*, encouraged by its sometime editor, his cousin, Samuel Johnson. That Doctor, born less than a hundred yards away from the famous stained-glass windows that would later attract myriad customers through The Apothecary doors, famously commented – admiringly if somewhat ambiguously: "Sir, I would rather have embarked upon the building of a Man-of-War, than undertake such a project."

The astonishing variety and, not least, the scholarly identification of the huge collection is preserved in prized copies of the three ever-expanding guide books produced by their curator between 1746 and 1786, still to be found in Lichfield's Johnson Birthplace Museum and in the Salt Library, Stafford.

Just as Richard and Theodosia Greene provide both *The Burning Zone* and the companion volumes *The Bishop's Grimoire* and *The Ashmole Box* with their intriguing central characters, so too do the magnificently eccentric catalogue entries provide a verbatim header to each chapter of the novels.

Prologue

Late summer, 671 AD. The geese and fowl upon the marsh-pool clattered past, heedless of the still, white thing at the edge of their domain. An occasional moorhen strutted, nodding, past him as water-boatmen bustled around this blue-veined obstacle to their endless regatta.

That first dusk, the mosquitos and the clouding midges swarmed and pricked but found nothing to their taste in the cool, almost waxen skin, settling for the dusty grass and water's edge to feast upon all that moved. By the second dawn, there were dewy webs in his fine grey hair – and one, in that chasm-spanning mystery known only to the spider-kind – that joined his bowed head to the waterside.

By the third day it seemed that all life had departed from the corpse-like figure in the shallow well, and yet it knelt as if in prayer, though breath and pulse seemed scarcely there.

On the golden evening of the third day, the scent of dog-rose hung in the breezeless air upon its closing moments as the dusk began to fall. As brightness turned to amber softness, and the wildfowl fussed and chattered through the reeds, a deep, shuddering breath seemed to well from deep within the half-sunk man as thin, pale shoulders heaved; a grey-haired chest expanding as if it would not cease until ribs splayed out through parchment skin. Wide-eyed and open-mouthed the figure swayed as if to fall, but then it stopped as if gripped – or cradled – by an unseen hand.

Three days and nights upon a voyage deep within – a place of ice and fire, of storm and thunder – in a place beyond all time, and time that never touched the waking world. And now, as the marsh hummed and clicked its way to dreamless sleep, wonder, first, and then a joy beyond all else came to the eyes of the kneeling man.

Above the reeds and watery mists of dusk, it seemed a light now spread, and sounds of many voices murmured in the evening glow – and joined – and swelled and rose together in a chord of rainbow hues, a harmony aching with such beauty that he shook and swayed in its all-consuming fullness. Three great points, upon three blades of gold that rose to flower in the falling light. Three spires that soared and shimmered in the western sky and then were gone.

Gone, as rainbows go, leaving only wonder in their place.

Gradually, the darkening marsh crept back into his eyes and ears. He flexed and stretched and moved at last to climb stiffly to the water's edge.

Now, feet planted once more upon the coarse-stemmed grass, he looked in rapture out across the pools, out to immense, grey woods beyond.

It was agreed; this place would have a great and glorious church to magnify and praise his Lord.

And then Ceadd slept.

(1)

Over the Fire Place: A Cast in Wax of the Face of a Child,
with Cherubinic Wings, in Card Paper, decorated with Festoons
of Italian artificial Flowers. Two Leverets in a Glass Case.

16th March, 1776. The wound was as bad as anything he had ever encountered. Intent, though, on not allowing his fury to distract him from the job in hand, he doggedly refocused his attention on the all-but-hopeless task. Splinters of bone protruded from the appalling cut, itself smeared and clotted with leaf-shreds, twigs and nameless filth. Had it not been for the untouched contents of his own hipflask, there would have been nothing in this sparse hovel to ameliorate the suffering man's agony before he passed into a merciful semi-consciousness, no longer aware of the Apothecary's best efforts to save the ruined leg.

As he picked and swabbed, pausing only periodically to slacken the makeshift tourniquet – his own leather belt – he thought on the vagary of fate that had brought him to this squalid bedside; its pallid, sweat-slicked occupant certainly dead by morning but for the quirk of fortune of a cast shoe and a lame horse in the lane beyond the peeling door. Not that there was any certainty of his survival now, Richard Greene thought, grimly. The mantrap had done its dreadful work only too well.

As a shuddering groan punctuated his reverie, he once again felt the black bile of anger rise in his throat. A trap contrived solely to spoil a man? To protect the privacy of land – and a covey of birds – at the cost of human life? Sweet Jesu, what has this world become?

He became aware of the silent, watchful presence, shadowed in the half-open door; a wide-eyed child clinging, fearful, to her mother's skirts.

"More water on to boil, if you please," he said. "Boiled – not simply hot."

She disappeared without a word; the child swept off before her. When she returned, hurrying with a chipped earthenware bowl held in apron-wrapped hands, some of its steaming contents slopped down – for all her care – and shot in dusted globs across the earthen floor. Seeing her dismay, he rose and took it from her with a smile of reassurance.

"This will suffice and thank you for it; I'll soon be done with cleaning him, and then I'll sew and splint him just as best I can."

"Will he..?" she began, her voice hoarse. "Can you..?"

"All that can be done will be done; you have my word. As to the rest, he will be in the hands of God. He's lost more blood than any man can afford, though that will be restored if he can weather the fever that is mounting as we speak."

As her eyes followed his to fix upon the livid colour burning in the pain-stretched face, he saw despair flood into her own pinched features, and reached out, instinctively, to place a hand upon her arm.

"Although I'll soon have cleaned his wound of all the dirt that can be seen, there is no knowing, yet, what foulness might have driven deep into the bone itself. Then, not least, there is the shock that he has suffered from this monstrous assault. That, in itself, can wreak its own grievous mischief. I shall return as soon as I may with what medicaments can ease him through the worst of what's to come; the rest, though, will be in your caring hands, and in the grace of God."

"But Sir, we've no money for…" He stopped her there.

"What has been done to your husband is a crime against everything I hold sacred. There will be no question of payment. I shall be passing on my way to Aldershowe, each day, for three or four to come, so it will be of little moment to stop off here and see how…"

Tears streamed down the careworn cheeks; thin shoulders shook beneath her threadbare shawl. "He's all we have," she whispered, eyes wide in supplication.

"He seems a sturdy one, this man of yours," said Greene, briskly. "Together we shall fight to pull him through. Now I must finish off, so if you please…"

He turned back to the twitching, sweat soaked figure on the truckle bed as she hurried out.

How in the name of all that's holy did you escape the trap at all? the Apothecary asked silently, though the answer came in simply looking at the awful damage to the calloused hands. It had been the blood, freshly pooled and beset by flies, that laid the trail along the sunken lane, right to this poor wight's door. Greene, footsore and plodding with his limping mare, had come across it as he turned the corner by the boundary wall that marked the eastern limit of the huge estate. Blood, slicked down the newly pointed bricks, had caught his eye and led it off along the lane that was his own way home. He'd heard the anguished sobbing then, even before she'd run, distraught, to beg his help.

Her man had somehow dragged himself this far but now laid sprawled across the threshold of his home. She'd had no idea who – or what – Greene was; she simply couldn't shift her ravaged husband inside.

It was sometime later, when Greene had finished what he could and was standing, wet from his ablutions at the pump outside, that he heard the dogs.

Some instinct made him grab his coat, his hat, and don them regardless of his dripping state, then clasp his bag and walk, unhurried as a strolling lord, up to the broken gate, his slight form blocking access to the weed-grown path. He was barely in time.

Two burly men, each with a slavering mastiff tugging at their short-gripped leads, skidded to a halt in front of Greene, managing only with difficulty to restrain the huge beasts from lunging past him down the path.

"Move, master; you've no business here," one snarled. "You'll not stand long in the way of this pair. I'll say it but once."

"I'll stand long enough, and firm enough, to know what business *you* have here, fellow," replied the Apothecary with every pretense of haughty authority. "And be quick about it, before your master hears how his creatures are set upon a man of quality going about his business. He will understand the price of lawless threats, if you do not."

Neither the insulting ambivalence of his words nor the tone of their delivery were lost upon the pair. Hauling savagely against both hounds, they opened space between themselves and the small but resolute obstacle to their hunt. For that was what it was, plain as plain, Greene knew, a hunt. Bloodhounds were not sent out to follow rumours.

Panting with the effort of restraining the scent-crazed dogs, though measurably more circumspect now, the foremost of the pair spoke again: "No offence meant, master, so now be a good gentleman and stand aside, if it pleases you. We've business here of a kind that'll not detain you."

"Do not…" the Apothecary's voice lashed back, so unexpectedly that both men flinched back from its fury, "…presume to tell me what my business is or is not. Tell me instead why you are here. And quickly, I said. I shall not repeat myself."

"It's him, in there, master; the poaching bastid that we've got at last. There's no mistaking it." He yanked on his great hound's leash. "These two don't make mistakes. He'll hang this time, caught red-handed with the trap marks on him, good and proper."

"The only mistake being made here is by you, and by God I'll see you hang for it if you offer violence – or worse – to the injured man within. As for these 'trap marks' that you describe with such relish, grievously hurt though he is, who on earth can say just how he came by such wounds? I am a physician and can do no more than guess, and guesses have scant value in a court of law. Did you see him in some trap of yours? Either of you that pursue him with such zeal? As for these hounds: show me a pair that will not be side-tracked by fresh blood wherever they might find it, and howsoever it may have been shed?"

He saw uncertainty flash through dull eyes and pressed on: "Unless I am mistaken, that fine wall yonder marks the boundary – the limit, do you understand – of your master's land?" Neither responded, glancing uneasily one to the other.

"That limit extends to any rights or usages in law which permit your master to exact what he would call justice upon trespassers or the like. Beyond those walls, you and your dogs are no more than warrantless ruffians, seeking to bully your way without a jot of law behind you. Your master may care dearly for his fish and fowl, but how much can he care for you, to place you in peril of your own lives and liberty?"

He had them, then. He knew it as he watched bravado ebb and shoulders sag, as neither man would look him in the eye. "Be off now, before harm's done for one who'll never share the blame. Go while you can, I'll say no more."

With his heart in his mouth the Apothecary forced himself to turn back towards the mean dwelling and walk away from the sullen, fidgeting pair with every appearance of self-righteous nonchalance. He had not the slightest idea of what more he might do or say if his bluff was called.

Not daring to look back, he heard the pair move off, shouting and cursing at their bewildered hounds, and thought he might expire from sheer relief. It was only then that he remembered why he had been hurrying home.

(2)

Third SHELF. An Instrument Case of Aegyptian Pebble, polished and mounted with gilt Metal. An Aegyptian Idol, from Grand Cairo. An Amulet or Charm, being a ring of Brass, found on the Field of Battle; near Bosworth.

Saddler Street, Lichfield. Theodosia Greene resolutely ignored the arrival of her panting, dishevelled husband until she had carefully wrapped the purchases of a particularly well-dressed customer of long-standing. When that lady, maid in tow, had made her august departure from the shop, she finally turned to her spouse with a tight smile that failed to get further than her mouth.

"They've been upstairs for the best part of an hour; alone, left entirely to their own devices. You knew I would not be able to leave the shop with both Tillett and the boy away. Is it how you would have wished this of all visits to begin, Richard?"

"Of course not, my dear," he replied hurriedly, seeing the genuine anger in the well-loved features. "I would not be so cavalier; but Samuel is family, after all. He will make allowances for the fact I was det…"

"He might, Richard, I shall not," she hissed. "Shall you make allowances for the fact of your wife being treated as if she were little more than a stain upon the wainscoting? 'Dictionary Johnson' he may be, but for all his repute and his mighty opinion of himself, I declare your cousin to be the least civil man I have ever met!"

At this stage, the Apothecary made the grave mistake of glancing nervously at the stairs and simultaneously placing a finger against his lips in a vain attempt to hush his wife. Unfortunately for Greene, though fortunate for the innocent bystanders who would normally be busily providing custom at this time of day, the shop was empty.

"How dare you shush me in my own place of business, Richard Greene! Scuttle upstairs and entertain your boorish visitor and his familiar, if you must, but as you obviously place so little value upon your own wife's sensibilities, you shall seek your supper elsewhere, Sir!"

Before he could even begin to frame a reply, the door opened to several customers, and Theodosia swept past him to greet them with her accustomed acumen. Miserably, he turned for the stairs to their dwelling and the museum-rooms above, the sound of his wife's professional chatter hollow in his ears.

Climbing past their apartment on the shop's first and second floors he hurried on up to the sound of murmured conversation coming from above. Brushing past the painted signboard at the stairhead, its expertly gilded lettering proclaiming the museum's many benefactors, he heard the portentous rumble of his cousin's familiar voice, raised now – he knew – solely for his benefit: "Here mark what ills the scholar's life assail, toil, envy, want, the garret, and the gaol."

"Juvenal," said the Apothecary, striding into the company of the two men, now turned expectantly towards him. "From the Tenth Satire, if memory serves."

"Dammit, Sir, you cut me to the quick. What of Johnson and *The Vanity of Human Wishes*? Am I to be denied authorship? What of my vanity, pray?"

"Here in my home, I would deny you nothing, Cousin Samuel," said Greene, all nervousness forgotten as he strode forward, hand extended. "I was simply applauding the excellence of the author's inspiration. You are most welcome." He turned to his cousin's companion, a bland-faced, pale man who had been witnessing the opening foray with a small smile of relish. "And your companion,

Mr Boswell, too, of course. Greene, Richard Greene, at your service, Sir."

The small, pouched eyes set in the gross, pockmarked features missed nothing as the two shook hands, before Johnson turned to his companion, saying: "He has said more already than he had to say for himself the first time he came to Clerkenwell. Cat had your tongue that day, Richard, and no mistake. Wondered why you came at all, in truth."

The unbidden memory of a small face haloed with golden curls upon a satin cushion clouded his unremarkable features for just an instant; she had been their joy for such a few, short, years.

"I was… out of sorts, as I recall, Cousin, though it was many years ago. We had recently suffered bereavement, though you may not recall it." A perfunctory nod was all that met his words as the big man's attention was already elsewhere. He had stooped, with a frowning squint, the better to read the neatly printed description set beside a heavy broadsword and a studded, circular shield.

"'A Highlander's Claymore and Targe left behind at Derby. 1745'," he read aloud, before turning to his companion and saying: "Your compatriots came this damn close, James. Derby's but a hop and a skip from here; no more than a few days' march to London, if they'd stepped it out."

"Indeed, Mr Greene," said Boswell, neatly sidestepping the proposition, "the Doctor and I saw more than our share of the relics of The Rebellion during our own sojourn in my homeland in '73."

"So I believe," Greene nodded in response, adding: "Would I be right in supposing that, as Lairds of Auchinleck, your people to be descended from the Earls of Mar?"

His visitor flushed with pleasurable surprise. "I am indeed, Mr Greene. It is a matter of great pride to us; the title was granted by James the Fourth more than two and a half centuries back. For my sins, I am the ninth Laird; though, with all due respect, our lineage is not a matter I would have expected to be of any great moment outside my native land."

"Och, he'll surprise ye at every turn, this diligent wee cousin of mine – a-pokin' here and a-pryin' there." interjected the Doctor, admirably straight-faced, though in a more than passable imitation of the Caledonian brogue. Greene laughed, delightedly: "I can see your northern progress was far from fruitless, Samuel. I greatly enjoyed your *Journey to the Western Isles of Scotland*. In fact, it has been a fixture on my night-table since its publication last year."

The large head nodded in appreciation. "Vestigial though their remains may often be, there survives such a trove of ancient Gael's treasures to make much of our own raggle-taggle past seem pallid and lifeless by comparison. For those with the eye and wit to seek it, there is a lost world out there, Cousin. It would entrance you, as it amazed me – and that…" – the fleshy lips creased into a smile – "…in spite of my oft-quoted expressions of aversion and distaste for all things north of the Border."

He had already moved on, prodding and peering at Greene's close-set labels with absorbed intensity. From gazing at a wall-mounted display of martial trophies, he turned back to the Apothecary, saying: "Seeing to what effect you have exploited this garret of yours, I believe I shall loan you the lance and dagger presented to me after my Abyssinian work. Frankly, I forget from whence or whom they came, but they will be quite the thing for your magpie-nest if you will have them."

Despite the somewhat barbed phrasing of the offer, Greene glowed with gratification: "That work will have been *Rasselas*?" The large head nodded. "The reading of it gave me far greater pleasure than its unfortunate subjects enjoyed," said Greene, remembering the catastrophic misfortunes of its characters journeying into Egypt. "In fact, the Museum…" – the slight emphasis was missed by neither of his visitors – "…can already boast several small Pharaonic pieces which your generous offer shall nicely augment. Permit me to show you."

With surprise, Greene became aware of an early dusk descending outside the Museum windows, the Cathedral spires grey spikes against the darkening sky. Conversation, critique and riposte had crackled in air redolent with the scents of beeswax and gun-oil as uncounted minutes turned to several hours. All three, it seemed, had been in their respective elements.

Consulting his pocket watch as his visitors pored over a shallow tray of ancient deeds in the ebbing light, he exclaimed: "Gentlemen, I had not realised the time! Due to the absence of our staff, the shop will be closed and, at last, my wife able to join us for some refreshment. I have been most remiss; you must be parched from all our dusty treasures."

Straightening to his considerable height, the Doctor consulted his own pocket watch and began: "Time has indeed overtaken us, Richard, so, with regret..." He got no further.

Greene, interjecting with a reckless authority that amazed himself, exclaimed: "Nonsense, I do insist! You'll take a cordial, at least. There was so little opportunity to converse with Theodosia when you arrived, she would be mortified if you were to leave without remedying the situation."

A certain sideways glance of approbation – underpinned with just a glint of humour – was not missed upon the Apothecary, as Samuel Johnson relented.

"Indeed, we must not neglect the niceties. Lead on, Cousin, do."

By the time that the street door finally closed upon the day's visitors, the initially frigid temperature of Mrs Greene's parlour had risen to a comfortable degree, as had the spirits and general humour of the lady in question. She came to him, smiling ruefully, and placed a soft hand beneath his chin.

"I am a fractious scold, Richard; it is I who deserve no supper. Forgive my ill-temper, I was fraught and harried well before our visitors arrived; it has not been the easiest of days."

With huge relief he took her gently in his arms, saying: "For me either, my dear; though there is nothing that calls for apology between us. I was detained by what I can best describe as an abomination – the victim of a mantrap, out by Walhill. Frankly, I was ill-prepared for any visitors, let alone our recent guests."

"A mantrap? Oh Richard, no. How is the..?"

"That can be discussed later, Theodosia, I have had more than my fill of man's inhumanity for one day, to tell the truth. To recount it would doubtless send me out of sorts to bed, and I would avoid that and the spoliation of such a memorable meeting.

Your opinion of Cousin Johnson and of *his familiar*..." – he grinned – "...would seem to have risen?"

She smiled in response. "In the case of the blameless Mr Boswell, my earlier opinion was a measure of my tetchiness. He is the absolute gentleman; bred to the bone; so widely travelled, too. Was his account of giving dinner to Captain Cook not enthralling? And Cousin Johnson..?" She paused, theatrically, as if pondering, before relenting, laughingly: "Who could have guessed that great Bear of a man to possess such a capacity to enchant? I see now that his mighty repute is not one jot overstated, Richard. In my entire life I have never come across such erudition, indeed, such raffish charm, when he's a mind to exercise it. And to think he was here, as family no less? Well, there's a thing! We shall order *The Dictionary*'s new edition first thing tomorrow, husband. I doubt that even The Close can boast a copy of it yet; I'll not be without it now!"

Greene suppressed a smile, revelling in his wife's delight. Only an hour earlier he had watched, intrigued, then frankly admiring, as the ugly boor of popular notoriety had transformed himself into the very personification of grace and artless charm, discoursing with genuine enthusiasm over Theodosia's accomplished floral paintings displayed about the comfortable room, and going on to laud the independence of the seemingly innumerable women of his chosen acquaintance.

"I fear though that the poor, dear Doctor has little idea that for all his inexplicable approval of our Miss Seward, it is most certainly not reciprocated," she said later; not – Greene suspected – without a certain arch satisfaction. "She has never forgiven him for his slights upon her late grandfather, and rarely misses an opportunity so to say."

Theodosia was referring not only to the *doyenne* of The Close and City society, but also to the young Samuel's purgatorial experience at Lichfield's ancient Grammar School, and, most particularly, to the harsh discipline of its headmaster.

"What was it the old rascal said of Hunter?" enquired Greene: "'He taught nothing; he beat us, so we learned' – was that it, my dear?"

"Words to that effect, indeed. Scarcely the sort of thing one wishes remembered about a deceased grandparent, Richard."

"Mm," replied her husband, sleepily. "Memorable is an adjective the good Doctor seems to have claimed as his own, for all that our Miss Seward aspires to the condition."

He snuffed the bedside candle and turned over to sleep. She moved companionably against him, warm through his nightgown.

"Just as I claim you as mine," she whispered to his neck. A snore was his only response.

(3)

ITEM:

In the Upper Drawer marked A Glass, stained from Herculaneum.
Tin melted in the Mines, Cornwall. Siliquastrum Gibosum.
Artificial Crystals. Flinty Nodules. And a curious reticulated Slate,
found over the Bed of Coal at Brown Hills Works, Staffordshire

19th March. By his third visit to the ramshackle hovel, the
Apothecary's worst fears were confirmed as the fetor of the
sickroom met him like a living thing. He had to steel himself to
approach its source, inured as he had long supposed himself to be
to the grotesqueries of the human condition. What the fever had
left, the septicemia was devouring; the virulence of its pace and
appetite unlike anything Greene had witnessed.

"There is but one choice left to me," he said to the terrified
woman, herself wasted and gnawed by her despair. "Oh no, Sir, not
the saw, I beg you! Anything but…"

"There is no remedy left to me but cutting, and that's as like no
remedy at all, I fear," he said, as gently as he was able. "Your man
has precious little left to fight another shock…" He took her hand,
the chapped skin and broken nails rough against his own. "…but
it offers one last chance. Will you permit me, aid me, even; at my
side, assisting? There's but little time."

She nodded her head in mute, grief-stricken assent.

"First, then," he began, "we must scrub hands, clean nails;
everything we employ must be as purified as can be contrived."

All briskness now: "Your Joe shall have as much poppy tincture
as I think he can take. Some sort of balance between mitigating
his pain and exploiting his remaining strength must be struck."

He realised he had been talking to himself; he could hear that she was already at the pump outside.

With a fortitude that Greene could only marvel at, she had not only managed to restrain and cradle her tormented husband while he sawed and sawed, but, in the stinking, blood-spattered aftermath, had collected the severed ruin of his limb and borne it out with all the gentleness of carrying a sleeping child. It was only as she came back in that she swayed, and with a gasping sob, collapsed across the earthen floor. When he'd brought her round, she lay back, blinking, on the rough-boarded settle that – save for the rope-strung bed – was the room's only furnishing.

"It's done then," was all she said.

"It is, my dear, and thanks to you, your Joe may yet revive. The wax-cautery I used will have less staying-power than pitch, though we used the best that was to hand. It did its job when needed most; at least the flow of blood was stopped. I shall replace its brief protection with binding as soon as I may, but until then, should he awake, he must not be permitted to move."

"*Move*, Mr Greene? Chance'd be a fine thing," she said, with such bitterness and anger he was astounded. "Lemman and Pearce 'ave done for my Joe, just like they said they would."

"Do you mean the two with the dogs? Outside when I was first..?"

"Aye, but *them's* the black-hearted dogs – not hounds as knows no better, Mr Greene. Lemman swore 'e'd do 'im in – my Joe – for tekkin' me. Pearce just followed like a fly to shite." She sank back with exhaustion, unable to continue.

"Is there anyone – a neighbour, a friend – who can come in to be with you tonight? A few nights perhaps, until we see how..?"

"Oh aye, there's an old biddy near the Lodge who'll come in for a scrap of baccy and a sup of Joe's sloe gin. We've not much else but that'll do the trick where kindness won't, you'll see."

He left her as the rain began, relishing the discomfort of a wet ride home compared to the bleak despair he left behind him in that forlorn and joyless place.

As he walked up from the small stable, through his garden towards the back door of the tall house, he paused for a moment to admire the snowdrops clustered round the sorry remnant of an ancient font, its hacked stonework still glistening from the recent rain. The relic, along with a variety of disfigured statuary and less readily identifiable lumps of dressed stone, were arranged around the narrow garden, itself now showing the tenuous greening of an early Spring.

Momentarily lost in thought, he was surprised when his housekeeper's voice boomed from above. Glancing up, he saw she stood at an open casement, in the process of shaking out a small rug.

"Oh, you're returned, Sir. Told him you were out, didn't I? So, he said he'd call another time. Had to see you, personal, he said. You might just catch him in the shop, though; said as how he'd pay his respects to the mistress on the way out. Busy on his way in, she was. No time to see him. Well, she saw him, of course, couldn't miss him; but couldn't talk, like, because she was busy. Still sent him up, though; must have thought you were above, even though you weren't."

Greene waved a hand in mute acknowledgement, knowing better – from long and trying experience – than to try deciphering the singular interpretation that the ever-bustling woman imposed on the events around her. As a cook, housekeeper and domestic treasure she was without peer, an opinion she would readily have shared; as a communicator of even the most basic minutiae of life at Saddler Street, she was a walking nightmare. When she felt especially harried or 'put-upon', attempts at elucidation usually resulted in the ever-more garbled repetition of the original statement, though now in the slowed-down mode she reserved for children or employers being particularly obtuse. There were times, they had discovered, when the only course of action was to ignore every word she said and simply pretend she wasn't there. The danger of that, effective in preserving one's sanity though it might sometimes be, only confirmed her in the conviction of her employers' deafness; hence the volume just broadcast from the upstairs window.

He hurried into the rear lobby just in time to see a tall, angular figure with an ill-fitting wig making his farewells.

"Lionel, hello!" he called, waving through, pausing to prise off muddy riding boots at the jack by the threshold and perform an undignified hop across the cold flags to where his indoor shoes stood waiting his return.

As the Reverend Blomefield stood waiting for the Apothecary to come through, he retrieved a large, sack-wrapped object from the counter upon which it rested.

"Ah, the Wanderer returns," he declared, in his best pulpit voice.

"And not before time, Richard," called his wife's voice from somewhere out of sight. "…I had no idea you'd even gone. The Liverpool Carter won't wait on you, you know. Not like poor Lionel."

(4)

ITEM:

The following Medals in Sulphur, gilded. Oliver Cromwell,
Sir Isaac Newton, Pope Clement the 12th. Benedict the
13th. Two Sons of the Chevalier de St. George.

Intrigued, though with wilting patience, the Apothecary sat across
from the clergyman he had known for so many years, knowing
that he was being played along. For several minutes, the gaunt
figure seated opposite him craned this way and that, admiring,
quizzing and commenting on a variety of the exhibits; anything,
in fact, rather than admitting to the presence of the still-wrapped
object that sat between them on the polished tabletop.

Finally, he relented, and with a grin that stripped the years
away from his face, exclaimed: "Patience being the virtue that it
is, today you have excelled yourself, Richard. I'd wondered if you
could be persuaded to explode!"

Greene laughed, replying: "The fuse was lit, Lionel; great age
has withered none of your pyrotechnic skills. So now, unless your
package contains a collection of your briefer sermons, put me out
of my misery for pity's sake."

Suddenly earnest, though obviously relishing the moment,
Lionel Blomefield removed the covering with a flourish, revealing
a fine, carved box, much the size of a family bible; that being
precisely, in fact, what Greene now expected it to contain.

"No, it is not," said Blomefield, intuitively, beating his old friend
to the punch with another grin, reaching deep within a pocket as he
did so, and continuing: "And if its contents are a mystery now, how
much greater will they be when you read this that accompanied it?"

As Greene reached out for the folded paper, he had time to glimpse a broken wax seal upon it before it was whisked away by his old, but more than usually trying, friend. Blomefield raised a mollifying hand to Greene's hiss of frustration: "The story of its delivery, first, followed then by its rediscovery." Greene groaned with resignation and sat back, bowing to the inevitable.

"According to our nicely painted signboard, one of my predecessors, *Harrison* by name, held the living of St Mary's from the early 1640s until well into the 1680s – no small achievement in itself – though he was, by the few accounts still extant, a man of some standing and substance. It was to him this box was sent, in May of 1692. Therein, however, lies the first problem."

"That being?" enquired Greene, wearily; understanding his allotted role.

"That being that the Reverend Harrison had, by then, been the late Reverend Harrison for more than twelve years."

"Ah," said Greene, with no idea where this was leading.

"You should now, perhaps, become apprised of this," said Blomefield, handing the paper to Greene with no further prevarication; "The subsequent problems arising from it will then start to become clear."

The Apothecary took the folds without apparent haste and pulled spectacles from a waistcoat pocket. He scanned the pages first: two narrow, grubby, ill-kempt sheets whose content – scrawled and blotty – promised little at first glance. He would realise within a dozen lines the extent of his misjudgment.

Brother Harrison,

Remiss in both my correspondence and felicitation
tho I have been these many months past,
I beg forgiveness of yr generous heart.
Accept now my greetings and a gift.
Gift indeed though it is meaned to be,

your tutored eye will plainly see
that which is concealed to be greater still,
though more as burden than as gift it could be descried – albeit
by some lesser man.

I should have chanced on none of this,
had not the Source of your own gift led me to it.
For twas he that led me to an ancient place
whose key – though it lies now in yr hand –
was cannily contrived by old Row. Lee.

For fear of peeping eyes and busy tongues I shall write no more
for you old friend shall read with ease my veiled meaning
I have acted not without honour in this matter,
but much lacking in courage and firm judgement
though it shames me so to say.
Mayhap as free agent which I never was,
you may straightway
perceive a way where I saw none.

As above, so below.
Tis perception wherein fortune lies.

For him that you will doubtless meet employ I pray your Best
Offices that he may be given the decent repose I could not
bestow.
From him that I believe you will surely come upon
I pray you ask a similar benison,
and his intercession for your true friend.

Elias Ashmole. at Lambeth.

Greene simply gaped. *Ashmole:* The historian of the Order of the Garter, Herald and genealogist, numismatist, epigraphist, connoisseur and lauded collector, one of the great names of Restoration England; the eponymous museum in Oxford, one of the greatest ornaments of his troubled century. He read and reread the letter several more times before finally looking up at his visitor.

Lionel Blomefield sat regarding the Apothecary with a mixture of amusement and intense expectation written across his bony features. "Well, did I exaggerate? Is it no more than the ramblings of a dying man, or is there something going on here that is passing me by in its entirety?"

"*A dying man?*" responded Greene.

"Indeed," said Blomefield, again fishing in his pocket. "Along with the letter, the counterfoil of a carter's receipt was inside the box when we happened upon it."

He finally retrieved what he sought and squinted at the crumpled note before passing it to the Apothecary.

"'May 26. 1692'," he read aloud. "'St Mary' – and some squiggle of a signature that is wholly illegible," said Greene.

"A churchwarden or some such, one imagines," commented the cleric, "whoever took delivery of the thing. Its only address being St Mary, Lichfield. Where else could it have been taken; Harrison or no Harrison? And…" he grinned once more, "…by some strange chance it was delivered on precisely the same day as his own funeral, so I have learned. Writing that and sending this must have been among Ashmole's final acts. It would have taken a good week to arrive."

More than one cog strove to engage in Greene's head.

"So, you came across this *where?*" he enquired, an unworthy suspicion taking shape in his mind.

"In the lumber-room above the church porch. The priest's room, as was," replied Blomefield, looking away suddenly as if he had anticipated the Apothecary's next question.

"And you came across this *when?*" Greene continued, in a voice of sweet reason.

"Er… less than… no more than…"

"How long have you been trying to work this out, Lionel? How long have you been keeping this to yourself, Lionel?"

"Scarcely…" Blomefield began, a scarlet blush betraying his embarrassment.

"And when did you finally have to admit defeat, Lionel, and say 'I suppose the only thing left is to take the wretched thing to good old Richard and get him to crack the mystery for me', Lionel?"

Blomefield capitulated, throwing grubby-cuffed hands up in mock surrender.

"My deceit has found me out! I've spent weeks poring over the damned thing without a glimmer of inspiration; and it's not as if the contents have helped one jot. Look for yourself. It is why I concluded that you would be the only man in Staffordshire who might perceive the slightest merit in them, Richard."

He shrugged and smiled disarmingly: "I had meant you to be a party to all this from the start, it's just that…" he tailed off, this time prompted by rather more than the theatrics of a moment past.

Greene continued where his old friend had left off: "…It is just that when we get so much as a sniff of the scent of the Secret, the Hidden, an inkling of something of value squirrelled anciently away, our better judgment turns to putty, whilst our highly regarded propriety is all too often left at the door? Just as I number myself amongst the Fallen, I am heartily relieved that clergymen are as prone to frailty as we lesser mortals, Lionel."

"Look, then – for heaven's sake – at what all the fuss is about," Bloomfield said, diverting attention from his obvious embarrassment by throwing open the lid and finally revealing the interior of the box.

"Oh, my word," responded Greene, peering in with rapt attention. "How very peculiar."

(5)

In the Center, below the PAINTING. An altar; the Antependium,
a fine transparent piece of Stalactite, from Derbyshire, with a
Margin of Black Italian Marble, both finely polished; upon
the altar, raised on three Steps, stands a neat Crucifix carved
in Wood and painted, eighteen inches high. This Crucifix
was taken from a Chapel belonging to the French near
Cherbourg, by a Centinal, belonging to the English Army.

20th March. "Traps, you say?" drawled the bedridden patient,
glaring up at the Apothecary with every appearance of fury at
his presence. Greene, unperturbed by the protuberant eyes and
irascible countenance he had come to know well over past months,
continued with his ministrations. "Damn things might be legal, no
denyin' that, but they're damn bad form all the same," concluded
the nightgowned figure of the squire of Aldershowe.

"Something of an understatement," murmured Greene, still
intent on the varicose ulcer he was cleaning, "when they are
intended to cause nothing less than crippling mutilation if not an
agonising death."

"Well, that's what I'm sayin', dammit, Greene. Damn bad
form whichever way you dress it up. Didn't like the look of the
man when I first clapped eyes on him – held some sort of showy
junket at the Manor shortly after he bought it: Bub and biscwits
to impress us all, fat chance! Like him a damn sight less now! It'll
be spring guns, next, I'll be bound.

"Won't be content 'til he's riddled a brace of lads out bird-
nestin', or some randy pair simply lookin' for a leafy bower. D'you

see, Greene, tenants and cottagers can be decent enough coves; keep 'em in line, by all means, but gentle 'em with the odd kind word and a light hand on the reins and you'll have 'em eatin' out of your hand – and not settin' a torch to your ricks! But traps? It's not as if there's a damn thing worth poaching up on Wallhill, not the way he's let things go. No way to run an estate, that, not in this day and age."

Equine similes apart, Greene found himself unable to dislike the bluff old countryman. For all his bluster and heavy-handed jocularity, William Strong'itharm was a well-liked landowner whose family had inhabited the rambling yeoman house for as long as anyone cared to remember, farming what had grown to half a thousand acres of prime Staffordshire arable.

Greene's visits, of increasing frequency given the aging squire's uncertain health, provided the Apothecary with what amounted to a month-on-month almanac of a life beyond the sophisticated purlieus of the little Cathedral city, often akin to a visit to another land, another place in time. So little of consequence had changed in the lives of the country folk – the largely unseen providers of all the staples of his city life – that those memories of plague and plenty, of image-breakers in a village church, or armies marching through the deep-cut lanes, seemed, somehow, more alive out here. It was, he often thought, as if their dusty shades had passed by only moments before, to leave a half-seen glimpse, the echoing of hooves around a distant bend. It was why, that morning, he had set out determined to discover more about the unseen master of Walhill, a comparative newcomer obviously more than prepared to leave his mark upon the land. William Strong'itharm, he knew, would be the fount of all knowledge where a neighbour was concerned.

"Liverpool money behind him, the bugger makes no secret of it," the patient growled, wincing from even the lightest touch to his inflamed limb. "Had the damn nerve to boast about it, too. 'Blackbirding' he called it, all tied in with some money-grubbing cronies of his in shipping."

He hawked and spat, noisily, into a chamber pot beneath his night-table, continuing: "What's it all come to, eh, Greene? When Gentry's up for sale to any jumped-up Johnnie Quickpence who'll buy and sell the Lord's folk? For I'll hear none of the old squit that says Negras ain't just that," he continued, accusingly, as if expecting Greene to protest. He, though, simply continued with his bandaging, content to listen to a man whose simple decency never failed to impress him.

"What's black hide but a covering for flesh and bone when all's said and done? One too many high and mighty fools have tried to tell me a coloured horse ain't worth more than pie-money; often as not had to eat their words when time came to settle up the wagers, though."

He pushed himself up against his heaped bolsters as the Apothecary began packing away. "Can't abide the crabby sort of narrowness that afflicts the likes of 'em, to tell the truth."

"From all you've said," responded Greene, "it sounds unlikely that philosophy – in any shape or form – enters into this. If Wallhill's present master is content to prosper from human misery, any consideration of its source or its scale can be neither here nor there. The only concern that slavers have for a life is when there's a price-tag attached to it."

"So, what's to do about this trapped man of yours? Will he live to tell the tale?"

"That," said the Apothecary grimly, "lies in greater hands than mine, Squire, though you remind me of the time. If I'm to see him in the light, I'll need to set off soon. I fear there'll not even be a rushlight left in that sad place, by now. They have so little it makes my heart bleed, to tell the truth."

"I'll not detain you, then," said the big man, levering himself gingerly from the high bed and testing his leg with care before placing his considerable weight upon it.

"You'll oblige me by taking a truckle, a ham-hock and a loaf or two with you as you go," he said gruffly, then seeing the mystification in Greene's well-fed face, he added: "Should they, however, prove too heavy a burden, you could drop 'em off somewhere on your way."

Greene acceded, gravely. "Indeed, Squire: though the spirit be willing…"

It was as if he had brought the sunshine with him, such was his reception at the cottage door. Though still gaunt and red-eyed with exhaustion, the woman – he realised to his surprise he still had no idea of her name – met him with: "'E'll live, Sir! I'm sure as sure can be! Joe knew me when 'e woke. 'Eld my 'and asked about our child, then slept agin. 'E's sleeping now, but proper like. The fever's gone, Sir, thanks to you."

Before he could even enter, she had seized his hand and squeezed it to her brow; he felt her tears of gratitude warm against it. "God bless you, Sir, for all you've done. Joe would 'ave been a deadman but for you."

He gently disengaged himself and made his way through to the bed in its shadowed corner of the cheerless room. This time no putrid fetor met him in the dusty air, and his rising hopes were all confirmed by the sight of the slumbering man, his broad chest rising and falling with a steady, reassuring rhythm, his brow free of the rancid sweat that had signaled his raging fever.

"'E cried out, sudden like, sometime deep into the night, Sir; I thought I'd lost 'im then. But it was like the badness left 'im like a bursting boil. I dosed 'im, just like you said I should, and then 'e settled after that, just like a bab."

"It seems we've both done well enough this far, my dear; perhaps now I've even time to learn your name. Forgive me but, 'til now, my mind has been on other things."

She smiled such a smile the tiredness seemed, for a moment, banished from her careworn face. "It's Agnes, Sir; just Aggie, to my Joe."

"Well, Mistress Agnes, tell me when you, and this little one…"

and he reached out a hand to touch the dark curls of the small girl clinging, as ever, to her mother's skirts, "…last had a decent bite to eat?"

She looked away unable to meet his eyes, mumbling a reply he could not hear.

"Well, just to prove that not all neighbours need be unwelcome ones, a friend has asked me to run his errand as he couldn't come himself." He bent to the child and said quietly: "If you were to come outside and see my horse, he has some things in his saddlebag we think you'll like. You could bring your mother, too."

"Your Joe will need most careful tending so that no infection gains a hold again. The broth will help to strengthen him, but sleep's the greatest healer given time. I'll be back within a day or so to dress the…" – he saw the naked pain behind her eyes – "…to dress the wound. We'll have him up before you know it, then we can do what's best for all concerned. We'll meet that time when it comes."

He took her hand: "There will be discomfort, no doubt, sometimes as much as he can bear, but we must draw strength from how much worse it could have been. Your daughter has a father, and Joe still has his life. Not so small as mercies go."

By the time he rode off into the lengthening afternoon, the smell of a simmering stockpot followed him to the sagging gate, and a bright-eyed child waved shyly from the open door.

It was only on the ride home that the Apothecary permitted himself to think about what awaited his return. He had risen early from a night of broken sleep, his tired head reeling from the boxful of mystery with which he'd been confronted the previous day, only to be plunged into his daily regimen of preparations, treatments, and then his rounds; no time to dwell upon the thoughts that set his pulse racing and his imagination working overtime. As he left the shelter of the hilltop copse and saw ahead the three graceful spires rising dark against the greening lands beyond, he realised that he had seldom, if ever, approached the familiar skyline of the little city with more anticipation.

(6)

On the left Hand the CHIMNEY-PIECE. An Head of
a Mitred Bishop, in Stone Alto Relievo, neatly carved,
formerly an ornament broken from the Cathedral Church of
Lichfield, by the Fanatics, during the Civil Wars 1643.

August, 1646. For all their dust and stain, the appearance of both
horse and rider spoke of quality. The fine bay gelding of some
eighteen hands – though lean from scarce fodder – carried a rider
whose travelling cloak revealed a crimson glimpse of silk lining
as it shifted about his hunched form. The horseman, so wrapped
in his thoughts that it seemed his mount must know the road,
managing little more than a nudge of his booted knee or a flick of
reins, to guide their ambling progress.

Above them, a squat tower on the wooded hill marked the
village of Shenstone. Soon now they would cross the Roman Road
and, from there, the last mile or two to Lichfield, to bathe, to bed
and blessed slumber.

Stiff with exhaustion and with a head fit to split from the
ceaseless loop of recrimination and self-justification that had
plagued his journey – the strict injunction of a week-old horoscope
that had forbidden courage had seemed to lose its first, unarguable,
power as each leaden mile of defeat and humiliation stretched
out behind his horse's hooves. The erstwhile Commissioner of
Excise and Commander of Royal Ordnance, riding away from the
surrender of His Majesty's Loyal Garrison of Worcester, burned
with the shame of waving comrades off to capture or to death.

He travelled now, God help him, under the terms of *Ye Generals*

*passes and portentions, whereby all persons not under the degree of
esquire are allowed to pass with three horses, with their armes and
goods properly belonging to them to be carried on their horses.*

He had left his books in Oxford, his conscience – by conspicuous
absence – at his comrades' final defeat at Stow on the Wold – and
his previously well-starred military expectations at lost Worcester.
Two days earlier, he had ridden forth from its battered walls, sworn
*never to bear armes any more against the Parliament of England or do
anything willfully to prejudice their affaires.*

How would he ever hold up his head, again? No answer
was forthcoming, though the question seemed to bear endless
repetition. He wished he could remove his head.

Such was his complete absorption that it took the second 'Oi!',
shouted from the irate, swollen mouth that glowered up at him,
to rush him back to the place and the moment. The mouth was
framed by a barred helmet, the helmet crammed upon a short,
foul-tempered parliamentary trooper grown desperate with
boredom and toothache.

It followed up with: "Tha deaf and soddin' dumb, or what?" A
question emphasised by a matchlock musket whose barrel jabbed
and wavered below him. With numb resignation, the rider looked,
carefully, down into the scowling face.

The intention he saw written across the swollen, lumpen
features could not have been more straightforward: it was the face
of murder at the crossroads in search of a solitary victim.

"Forgive me, my mind was elsewhere. It's been a long and tiring
road."

"Road from where, *maaster*?" Small eyes squinted through the
visor bars.

"Worcester."

Eyes glinted, narrowed still more, and then the musket barrel
was jerked up below the rider's chin, tilting back his head:
"Worcester's King's country, *maaster* – so whose man might you
be, now?"

With deliberate care, the rider slowly raised both hands away from his sides, reins dropped, palms open. "If you will permit me? The words of your generals should have some sway where mine will not."

"Mockin' me, are ye, *maaster*?" A dangerous, levelling motion of the firearm as the soldier stepped purposefully back.

"What I mean is that I bear a guarantee of safe passage – with horse and arms – vouchsafed by your own Colonel Ramsbottom, speaking for your own Sir Thomas Fairfax. Where is the mockery there?"

The resonance of quiet authority, and a subsequent scrutiny of a document held upside down but scanned with a knowing scowl, finally elicited sullen leave to pass.

"Whipped and trounced, eh, *maaster*? Well, don't stray off this road or there'll be hell to pay."

For the numbed Cavalier, hell had – in recent months – been paid for too much and too often. Elias Ashmole nudged his tired horse forward; to the place that he'd once called home.

A small GLASS CASE with folding doors. An Artificial Thorax in
Glass, by wich is shown Respiration; On the top, a carved Head.

20ᵗʰ March, 1776. The Apothecary ran his fingers across the
scratch-carved lid, touching fingertips to the deeper, more
emphatic carving of the coat of arms at its centre. *Ex Uno Omnia,*
in finely cut letters surmounted an oddly bare field containing no
more than a *fleur de lys.*

"From One come All? Comes Everything?" he said to no-one
in particular; feeling, once more, the flutter of excitement in his
stomach. He lifted the lid, to be met by the lingering smell of
beeswax and, beneath it, a musty note so faint as to be scarcely
discernible. Grinning to himself, he recognised the sensation of
the moment: he felt like a child on Christmas morn.

Within a formed bas-relief of purple velvet – its colour vibrant
still, preserved so long from light – a magnificent crosier-head
of obvious antiquity nestled beside two heavy seal rings. Beside
them, another preformed shape seemed to have been made to hold
a shallow cartouche or emblem – though in place of its presumed
content a scallop shell now rested, inexplicably, pale against the
rich plush. Ribbon-pulls, to left and right, indicated that this top
layer could be removed.

So perfect was its fit, the drawer lifted out with the just faintest
sigh of air, the smell of dusty age intensifying as it came away.
Within lay several pages, brittle to his touch, each covered in a
tight cursive hand, written in what was obviously some form of
cipher. Greene grimaced and set them to one side; these would

have to wait; he was no codebreaker. Beneath them, a somewhat smudged and gracelessly presented wood-block print of Lichfield Cathedral – at a cursory glance, a second-rate specimen accompanied by some florid dedication in Latin. Conspicuous by its absence, the Apothecary noted, wryly, was any translation, even though it would have been a work of such piddling challenge to Lionel Blomefield's considerable scholarship that it would have been the first – and least – of the challenges presented by the box. Well, he would just have to do it for himself, Greene decided with a degree of relish, realising as he did so that it was a decision that had apparently been made for him.

The printed image, in turn, lay above another: a final, more substantial sheet being revealed. It bore a drawing of a cruciform piece: jewellery, church ornament or a reliquary, perhaps? That was set above an enlarged version of an archaic inscription seen first in miniature, engraved on the object's base.

Greene squinted at the angular letterforms: *AA*, certainly; *S*, perhaps; then – something or other. He failed to recognise the fourth character. Might they be Greek? He would have to refresh his scant knowledge in that direction. So, little the wiser, he turned his attention to the awkwardly set text that accompanied it, composed of more closely written lines in a somewhat childlike print; these, though, immediately legible as a bible extract beginning:

When Jesus came into the coasts of Caesarea Philippi...

As he read through the compellingly beautiful prose, he was carried back to the rote learning of his school days and smiled to himself as memory took over.

...Thou art Peter and upon this rock I will build my church...

It was only as he reached the conclusion of this first long single paragraph that he frowned in puzzlement; the second part of the text, set gracelessly and in an apparently contrived form against it, was from no source immediately familiar to him.

Old Testament he decided, knowing he would have a laborious search ahead to find its source, and realising – to his own wry amusement, given their recent conversation – that he was reluctant to consult Lionel Blomefield on the matter. The information he might otherwise have sought from the cleric had, in fact, been singularly absent when first they had pored over the contents of the box together, the previous day.

No, dammit, I'll do this on my own, he thought, addressing the sheet once more. All that now remained to be examined was a rectangular cartouche set above a large empty space, and containing the two initials EA, set in the top right-hand corner of the sheet.

If that does not signify Elias Ashmole, I'll eat my wig, he thought, satisfied with that, if little else. The space below it, though? Why so much when the text is awkwardly crammed about the drawing?

"The reasonable presumption that all the written content of the box is the work of Ashmole's own hand…" he murmured to the empty room, "…surely must rule out mere clumsiness, though that at first seems apparent. Can one thus assume that the layout of the page – however odd – is in itself intended to convey some significance, perhaps?"

A call to supper brought an end to fruitless speculation, and the calls of domesticity saw him through to an early bed.

The Ashmole Box – as he now thought of it – closed-up and set aside, gave back little of the moonlit night that cast its pearly sheen across the old oak floors and glassed displays above. Whatever riddles it contained slept on, just as they'd done across so many years.

The morning brought a blustery day of showers and rolling clouds that scudded west to east and promised little let-up for the hours to come, though as the sheeting rain lessened for a while, Theodosia donned a hooded cape and sturdy overshoes, announcing that she was meeting ladies of The Box Club.

"You will of course have forgotten my arrangement, Richard," she said brightly, looking in on a husband busily sharpening his surgical implements. Seated at his workbench in the small back room reserved for private consultation and treatment, he looked up from his whetstone with a bewildered smile that confirmed her suspicion. "But as I see you are at home for once, you will attend to the shop door, won't you? I have lost all track of the number of times I have reminded you. It's become so stiff that customers will be starting to think we are trying to turn away their business."

"Well certainly, my dear, if I can but find the…"

"Time is one commodity that never seems in short supply, Richard; not when it comes to Museum business, leastways. The shop will not look after itself, as you well know, and Tillett and the boy will have more than their share to cope with whilst I'm out. So, you'll be a dear, won't you?" The question required no answer, and Theodosia departed in a rustle of skirts and the sound of a door being wrenched open.

"Today, Richard, for pity's sake!" her voice called from the shop.

Theodosia's appointment involved little more than a short step from the apothecary. Glancing up at the massing cloud, she hurried along Saddler Street to where the old Johnson house stood sentinel on its corner. Turning right into Breadmarket Street, she reached the front door of the house beside The Three Crowns inn just as the skies opened. Even in the short moment it took for her knock to be answered, she was drenched, the lashing rain obscuring even the great grey shape of St Mary's that loomed above the street, opposite neighbour to the tall house. As the maid helped her from her sodden cloak, the wispy form of Elspeth Blomefield hurried out to greet her.

"Oh, my dear!" she exclaimed, looking at the newly bedraggled form standing in a growing puddle on the stone-flagged floor. "We must towel you at the very least. You are soaked to the skin."

That Theodosia could well have done without the statement of the obvious, paled, instantly, into insignificance at the sight of the plump figure that was now emerging from the parlour beyond.

"Oh, Mrs Greene!" that young lady cried in mock alarm, "Has the Dam broken its banks? Are we to be washed away to Ararat?"

Not for the first time in their acquaintance, unladylike thoughts of physical violence flashed through Theodosia's mind, as she wiped errant hair from her eyes and then arranged a careful smile upon her moist features.

"Your concern, welcome though it is, is quite unnecessary, Miss Seward," she said brightly. "It is merely an irksome Staffordshire shower, not a biblical visitation."

Their hostess, sensing the *frisson*, turned back to the younger woman, saying: "Miss Seward be so kind to go back to my ladies and reassure them that Mrs Greene and I shall rejoin you all in a moment. I'll not have a guest in my house catch her death of cold."

As if on perfect cue, Theodosia sneezed into her gloved hand, shaking her head in sheer exasperation at her disarray in the all-too-composed face of the self-appointed doyenne of the city's cultural life.

"Of course, Mrs Blomefield. We shall long for your return," said that lady, bobbing away into the buzz of conversation through the open door.

As the two women ascended the fine oak staircase, Elspeth turned conspiratorially to her companion, and in perfect mimicry of her departed guest whispered: "Do we not long for an opportunity to catch a certain young woman unawares, on occasion; at something less than her perfect best?"

"She can be very trying," agreed Theodosia, "but what can one expect from the child taught to recite Pope and Shakespeare by the age of three?"

"And 'Paradise Lost' by heart, by nine," added Elspeth

Blomefield, with an eloquently raised eyebrow, leading the way towards a linen-press. "I think the loan of a shawl might be advisable," she said, "to ward off the chill."

"I think some piece of Richard's armoury might be more appropriate," sniffed the Apothecary's wife, "Less for the chill, but more for that we are about to receive. I rather fear that Miss Seward is at her most sparkling today."

"Oh dear," replied her hostess, trying, not entirely convincingly, to keep the anticipation from her voice. It was such a rarity that anything less than adulation was directed towards the Dean's exemplary daughter – or anything less than utter capitulation expected from that quarter.

"Shall we go down if you're quite restored?" she enquired, some moments later. Elspeth Blomefield knew that she was in the presence of an expert tactician, a force not to be underestimated. Precisely, in fact, what The Box Club required. The ostensible purpose of today's meeting, in as much as there ever was one, might, she fondly hoped, prove to be contentious.

Most of the dozen or so city ladies gathered in the comfortable parlour had been Theodosia's friends for as many years as she and Richard had been engaged upon their thriving apothecary business. She was now, though, of an age when that sort of arithmetic had lost any appeal it might once have had. That was the particular benefit of *old* friends, she thought, glancing around the well-dressed company; we all grow older in the most companionable way, having achieved a lexicon of familiarity and shared experiences that make for relaxation. Infinitely preferable – she had decided, long ago – to the exhausting cut and thrust of social intercourse that constituted *polite society* in the city's more elevated social echelon.

To that end she was studiously avoiding the dark, darting eyes of the younger woman who, today, was the club's guest, ensconced at the assembly's centre and assiduously captivating all about her. It was not that Theodosia Greene felt one jot inferior to their impossibly erudite young visitor, but simply that she had reached a time in her life when intellectual stimulation counted for rather less than warm and confiding friendships.

Whilst the Seward home – the magnificently rebuilt Bishop's Palace at the heart of The Close – was the focus for its own brand of ecclesiastical and intellectual exclusivity, denizens of the grander city houses – the Seppels, the Mountjoys, the Donegals – were so self-regarding in their inflexible insistence on *ton*, that their doors were resolutely barred to anything that smacked of *trade*. Unless, of course the trade be of such a discreet and advantageous nature it could be euphemised as *Merchant Venturing* or *Colonial Development;* the vulgar business of money-making being conducted as far away from one's own nicely appointed door as could be contrived.

Today, though, as she watched Anna Seward's effortless direction of the group's conversation, Theodosia had to admit that in as much as there ever was an explicit purpose to the Box Club gatherings, then the co-option of that section of Close society that looked to the Sewards for their prompting in all things philanthropic – and hence the opening of those purses for *a worthy cause* – was precisely that discreet purpose. The good offices of today's guest, at work in her natural habitat, were seen as the most effective means of achieving said purpose.

"It is surely no overstatement that Ignatius Santo is dubbed 'The Extraordinary Negro' ," their plump young visitor was saying – bringing the Apothecary's wife out of her reverie with a jolt – Miss Seward had, apparently, been holding forth for some moments. "One has only to encounter the eloquent clarity of his writing," she paused, looking enquiringly round the group before asking: "I am assuming, of course, that we are we all familiar with his journal excursions under the nom de plume 'Africanus'?"

A variety of noncommittal nods and averted gazes were her only response. A tall, auburn-haired figure, Margery Abbott, the widow of a prosperous city mercer, elected to reply for them all, saying: "I fear, Miss Seward, that whilst some of us may be aware, in passing, of this remarkable man's achievement in becoming the first of his race to gain the franchise, we can lay few claims to sharing your well-known currency in matters beyond our small sphere. Hence the appeal for your assistance in our newborn scheme."

The recipient of the neatly expressed compliment, dimpled, graciously.

Well played my dear, thought Theodosia, glancing admiringly at her old friend.

"No, please, forgive my presumption, Mrs Abbott. I had thought that with Ignatius Sancho's involvement in the London grocery trade, you might... he would have..." she faltered, visibly, suddenly aware of her own gaucherie in the present company.

"Howsoever we might try, our island is so packed with fellow shopkeepers we cannot know them all, Miss Seward," interjected Theodosia, lightly, continuing even before the rising blush could reach the round face: "Your Mister Sancho, though – author or not – can give the lie to all those gentlemen who regard his abused race as no more than a less-than-human commodity."

Their guest rallied magnificently: "Ladies, if there are means at my disposal, any of my small talents can be placed at your disposal in this matter; consider them given. I should explain, perhaps, that I require little or no persuasion regarding the matter at hand. In the currency of my acquaintance..." – she smiled graciously to Elspeth Abbott – "...I have corresponded for several years with a valiant clergyman on the Caribbean Island of St Christopher, one James Ramsay. At ever-growing risk to himself he has ministered to his flock regardless of either colour or creed." She now had their undivided attention.

"His taking of Holy Orders, some years ago, was prompted by an experience aboard the warship *Arundel*, on which he served as Ship's Surgeon. He was present at the interception of a vessel – a

Bristolian, I am ashamed to say – whose hold revealed more than a hundred dead or dying slaves. They had been confined in such hellish squalor it came close to forever destroying his faith in our humankind. It was this experience that marked a crossroads in his life.

"His sentiments towards the plight of plantation slaves upon his own and other Caribbean Isles, his constant efforts to apprise the greater world of their inhuman plight, have brought untold hardship as his lot.

"A situation now made so intolerable by the machinations and false complaints of Planters and those whose pockets are lined by that filthy trade, that he is being forced to abandon the good works that are his life. He may be sailing home, bloodied but unbowed, even as I speak. His voice, and that of others being raised where one might least expect them, will no longer go unheeded; they have the power of unassailable truth behind them. If sufficient groups such as this – newborn though it may be – can begin to raise funds, and perhaps even more importantly, comprehension, that will address the plight of the slaves beyond number who disappear into the maw of our colonies, then a step forward in our common humanity will have been made. It is a Christian duty; no more, no less. You shall have my unstinting support."

She finished to a patter of spontaneous applause, and a dawning reappraisal from at least one of her listeners. As the room dissolved into chatter, with the serving of light refreshments, Theodosia Greene waited her moment.

Before she could approach their guest, Anna Seward took matters into her own hands. Excusing herself from the group clustered around her, she came across to where the Apothecary's wife stood, gazing out at the brightening afternoon.

"No more Deluvian threats on the horizon, I trust?" she enquired, with a disarming smile.

"None I can foresee," replied Theodosia, matching her smile. "Thank you for coming today; an invitation from a coven of old biddies cannot be the most enticing proposition. You spoke most movingly." To her listener's obvious surprise, she placed a hand on the young woman's arm. "Your assistance will be invaluable."

Anna Seward knew a Declaration of Peace when she heard one.

"You are most gracious, Mrs Greene. I am only sorry we have not had more opportunity to know each other. Mr Boswell was fulsome in his praise following that most recent visit of his. I had not known your husband to be related to the formidable Doctor. My first instinct is to run and hide at his approach, I must confess."

"A sentiment I shared until recently, though," the older woman smiled, "until now his other engagements have kept him from our door during his few visits to the city."

"One might suspect that he feared the undoubted attractions of your husband's extraordinary Museum might offer a trifle too much in the way of *competition*, Mrs Greene. Our esteemed Doctor does so love to be the centre of attention. On this occasion, though, from what I hear, he was astounded by it all."

"It was most gratifying for Richard, there's no doubt," she said; her mind slipping back to Samuel Johnson's parting words: 'I should more readily have embarked upon the building of a Man of War, than to have considered undertaking such an enterprise'.

Even now she remained uncertain of *quite* what had been meant by that formidable visitor, so contented herself with a few more pleasantries shared amongst the ladies of the Club, followed by the departure of their guest.

As was their custom whenever the Club met at Breadmarket Street, Theodosia stayed on to chat when the others had left, enjoying a glass of Shrub and the opportunity to dissect the day's gathering. To her hostess's growing annoyance, the welcome tranquility was almost immediately shattered by the sound of, first, a saw, from somewhere outside the rear of the old house, followed by an insistent hammering that rapidly defeated all attempts to ignore it.

"It's Lionel," sighed the clergyman's wife, by way of explanation, before her words were followed by the sound of breaking glass and a muffled shout from outside.

"Oh, *drat* the dear man," she exclaimed, jumping to her feet and hurrying out. She returned, moments later, after the sound of her raised voice had carried through to her still-seated guest. "He will *not* be persuaded that half a guinea can be well spent on window repairs that at his age are quite beyond him – not..." she added with weary exasperation, "...that they ever were within his repertoire. He has never been the most practical of souls, but now, with the hours of retirement heavy on his hands, he will *insist* on making a confounded nuisance of himself in all directions. You should thank the Lord for Richard's industry, Theodosia; the Devil himself would have difficulty making work for those busy hands of his. I have never come across a man so constantly *occupied*."

Theodosia's response was an amused snort. "Busy with whatever takes his magpie fancy, he is indeed. When it comes to the humdrum, though, that is another matter altogether. Richard is a creature of enthusiasms, which is all very well if those enthusiasms tally – even occasionally – with one's own."

"And do they *not*?" enquired Elspeth Blomefield with, Theodosia thought, perhaps a mite too much interest.

"Oh, Lord, we rub along better than most," she replied, realising just how much she meant it, but continuing: "He can just be so *singular* in his attention, sometimes, especially with anything and everything pertaining to the Museum. I sometimes feel little more than a Relict to Antiquity when the blessed man lights upon some new fascination."

"It must be said that Lionel is, on occasion, no different, Theodosia. When he finally elected to take that wretched box to Richard – as he should have done in the first instance – I breathed a sigh of relief. It had become an absolute fixation to him. He even, on one occasion, brought Ashmole's ciphers to *bed* with him before I put my foot down."

"In Lionel's transfer of that most particular burden I fail to share your relief, Elspeth, as the wretched thing has become precisely that new *fascination* of which I spoke. What is it that our menfolk find so irresistible in the dry dust of ages? It is frequently beyond me."

Her companion laughed: "At least we might take comfort in the fact that our ever-increasing age should guarantee their ever-increasing fascination in *us*, my dear!"

They shared the joke, before Theodosia Greene enquired: "But why Lionel's particular interest in this old thing, Elspeth? Richard's I can, of course, understand, but I would not have expected such…" – she sought the word – "…*zeal* on his part.

"It must be over a year now since he retired. Did he not sever those ties with St Mary's then? I know you were mindful of his health and pressed him to make a decisive break."

"Ah, thereby hangs the tale, my dear," was the reply, delivered with a humourless smile.

"As we both know, the new man," she nodded towards the unseen bulk of the church outside, "is what Lionel describes as an 'all-too-new broom'. As you can imagine, it is not intended as a compliment. So, when that broom sweeps through the vestry, the cupboards, the parish chests and the like, the Reverend Smale is – in his own mind – disposing of so much lumber and would doubtless have consigned Ashmole's box to one of his frequent bonfires, had it not been for its obvious association with this, our house. Hence his 'gift' to Lionel.

"*Association?*" enquired the Apothecary's wife, "I fear you have lost me, Elspeth."

"Oh, surely, you knew of it? Has Richard never mentioned it? This house, number three Breadmarket Street, was the Ashmole home for generations. Old Elias was, most likely, born in the very room in which we towelled you down. He will have sat much where we are now, all through his younger years."

For some reason she could not explain, Theodosia felt a

distinct prickling in the hairs on the back of her neck. "What a small world we inhabit," she said, rising rapidly to her feet, to the evident surprise of her hostess. "I really should get home. Richard has been left to his own devices far too long for one day."

Shortly afterwards, rubbing a bruised shoulder from her unsuccessful negotiation with a rain-swollen shop door, Theodosia glared down at her utterly absorbed husband, a fan of stained, yellowed, papers spread around him on the dining table. He finally registered her presence, and looking up with a bewildered smile, said: "Back already, my dear? It scarcely seems a moment since you left. Is it still raining?"

(8)

On the right Hand the Shell Case. Part of the wooden Porch, situate in Dam-street, in the City of Lichfield, under which stood Lord Brooke, General of the Parliament Forces, when he received a mortal Wound in his Forehead, by a shot from the great Steeple of the Cathedral Church, the force (as Lord Clarendon expresses it) of which was abated by the Bullet passing through the above piece of Board. 22 of March 1643.

August, 1646. A late summer chill had fallen with the dusk and a small fire now burned in the upstairs parlour of the house in Breadmarket Street. The reflected flames flickered dully in the wainscot panelling and Elias Ashmole, slumped in a fireside chair, dwelt on the matter of Faeries.

By this his twenty-ninth year, the astrologer, antiquary, Captain late of both Horse and Ordnance, inveterate fortune-hunter and tireless womaniser, was still a dozen years away from his apotheosis at the King's own hand. The man who was to become Windsor Herald to the merry world of Monarchy Restored was, tonight, alone with his sorrow and his memories of this house, this street, in the distant land of childhood years.

An Irish piper, apple-cheeked and wrinkled brown, once set up with bread and ale outside the nextdoor inn, had woven airs and laments, jigs and reels, into a gliding, sliding meld of tune that had entranced the boy. Elias had been transported by the old man's tale of *Faerie* and enchantment. Lichfield, from ancient times a clearing in the great, Grey Wood of Mercia, had – he confided, with knowing certainty – been well loved by the Little Folk. Why, to this day, he could show the wide-eyed boy the gardens where they sometimes danced. Houses, too, just here and there, whose darkened windows sometimes gleamed with elfin light, if one could only glimpse it and believe.

Then, though, the flame-lit reverie was soured, as memories of yesterday crept back to blot out those of yesteryear.

Skirting the grass-grown humps of Roman *Letocetum*, his final approach to the city had revealed a prospect of desecrated ruin. Ahead, black against the still-bright sky, the Cathedral which had stood at the root and core of his early life lay roofless and derelict; the great spire, once its glory and its crowning grace, now no more than an imprint, an after image, in the eye of memory.

In recent months, his ciphered diary had recorded – in terse abbreviation – the deadly waning of the royal star. One by one the cities, the embattled manors and the tattered castles that had held for the King were falling: Oxford, Devizes, Basing House, Worcester, Lathom House – all gone. When, six weeks earlier, he had noted the newly transmitted intelligence 'Lichfield Close surrendered', nothing could have prepared him for his own entry into the decrepit, plague-ravaged wreck of all he had once loved.

Even less had he been prepared for the next and bitterest blow of that bleak homecoming. His mother had died of the Pestilence, three weeks earlier, in the epidemic that had claimed a quarter of the ravaged city's souls.

Sweet Jesu, he thought morosely, *if ever a place needed the dart of elfin shadows and the lilting echo of a faerie dance, it was this empty, aching, place.*

These dark musings were abruptly – and genially – interrupted by the bustling entrance of a large woman under full sail.

"Here's potage and new-baked barms, porter and my rabbit pie. D'ye recall my rabbit pie, Master Elias? You've been known to pick and poke at it, out of kindness, in the past?"

The dish in question would have broken the resolve of a fasting saint and Elias was match for neither its steaming allure nor the well-honed wiles of the family housekeeper. Tonight's laden tray of Ticknall slipware and the dull, infinitely reassuring gleam of old family silver was following closely on from: 'just a slice or two of my seeded cake', which, in turn, had followed close upon 'just a plate of gammon-ham and pickles' and all preceded by the breaking of a fast 'that any self-respecting young gentleman needs before embarking upon the hungry work of the day'.

Mistress Joan had become all too familiar with the wild-eyed exhaustion and the frayed nerves of fighting men during these past years of Garrison and Occupation, but the arrival of this hollow-cheeked, red-eyed spectre, late the previous day, had shocked her beyond measure.

The details of his homecoming were hazy in his mind: he recalled his horse being led away by a boy scarcely tall enough to reach its bridle, and being helped, unprotesting, to the porch settle where his buckled black riding boots were tugged off from legs numb with tiredness. Half asleep, he had obediently lowered feet into a large pewter bowl of near-scalding water whose liberal infusion with mustard had brought tears to his eyes and cleared dust-clogged sinuses for the first time in what seemed weeks.

She had brought him a bumper of plum brandy from a small keg, which, tucked away in an inglenook salt-cupboard, had somehow escaped search and requisition. Then, she had hovered above the slumped, dozing form she'd known so well, sick with dread. How to tell him? How to break the news of her mistress, his dearly loved mother? The answer to her unspoken prayer had suddenly arrived in the large, austere form of the Reverend Richard Harrison, Vicar of St Mary's, the church in whose shadow stood the Ashmole home:

"Elias, m'dear," he'd boomed, and pressed the young man back down when he'd sought to rise. "The lad ran across and told me of your arrival; it's a bad business and a sad time for us all."

Suddenly, intuitively, he'd glanced across at Mistress Joan.

She'd responded with a shake of nervous denial and helplessness. Drawn with exhaustion, Elias Ashmole had noticed none of the swift exchange, until, looking from one to the other, he appeared to register the absence of his mother for the first time. He had sat frowning, with the unvoiced question rising to his lips, when Harrison dropped heavily to his side, and placed a hand upon his shoulder.

"It was these three weeks past, Elias. She fell suddenly ill on the Wednesday and was taken, by the Lord's mercy, two days later. She suffered little and her passing was lovingly attended."

He glanced affectionately at the damp-eyed woman beside them. "I saw that all was conducted as you would have wished it. She will be sorely missed."

Elias Ashmole, unmoving, had stared blearily ahead, and then with enormous effort had seemed to drag himself back into the shell of his body. "Yes, I'm sure that... yes, you will have... thank you, but..." A great shudder passed through him as the first racking spasm shook his frame.

Pausing only to remove the bowl and wrap his feet, housekeeper and Vicar had quietly left him to his grief.

(9)

The DRAWER, B. A great number of ancient Deeds and
Evidences. Among which: No, 1 Letter from the Earl of
Nottingham, Earl of Suffolk, and others, to the Corporation
of Lichfield, for procuring from the Bishop the Fee Farm
of the Mannor and Lordship of Lichfield, for the Earl of
Essex, &c. Deliver'd to Mr Bailiff Ashmole 1604.

21st May, 1776. The Apothecary could scarcely believe his eyes.
There, from rest on a clump of wayside grass, a superb butterfly
– gold edged blue and umber wings spread to the morning sun –
rose to flutter ahead of him down the greening lane. He felt his
spirits soar in concert with its jigging flight, as if the weight of
winter days were sloughing from him like a cast-off skin.

Camberwell Beauty, he breathed to himself, racking his
memory for its classification. *Vanessa something-or-other,* was as
far as he got; he would have to look it up. Nothing, though, could
detract from the joy of the moment as he followed its wind-blown
progress out across the new-ploughed fields that stretched away to
Aldershowe. As he passed up through a stand of roadside trees, his
sharpened eyes caught the year's first sight of elm and beech leaves
uncrumpling to the brightness of the day.

"Of *course!*" he said, out loud, "It is the *twenty-first!*"

How could even the dullest clod forget that it was the first
day of spring? From there, along the winding lanes, it seemed to
the newly contented rider that the air grew sweeter, each breath a
tonic draught to soothe away the staleness and the flat, dull taste
of winter weeks and months spent cooped inside.

As he turned into the deep-set lane that led down towards his patient's peeling door, he paused to watch the rooks at work, off foraging to make repairs for weather-beaten nests. A wheeling dance of flying shapes, their wings black against the tumbled cloud. The absence of smoke should have warned him that something was amiss, but it was only as the broken door came into sight, its shattered planks like broken teeth against the darkened room inside, that he felt fear clench at his gut like a griping ache. He jumped from his horse, tossing its reins to tangle in the hedgerow by the gate, and ran down the brick-laid path.

Before he could call, before he even reached the threshold of the sagging porch, a voice croaked from within: "I'll kill you if you tek another step. *Stay off!* I've told you once and won't again."

"*Joe*? Is that Joe?" called Greene in shock and alarm. "I'm a friend; it's Greene, Richard Greene. *Joe is that you?*"

He was met by a sobbing cry of relief as the wild-eyed figure of Agnes rushed out from the shuttered darkness of the hovel, her hair a matted halo to her ashen face.

"Oh, Sir, it's you; thank God, thank God!" Before he could respond she had hurled herself into his astonished embrace, tears streaming down a face bruised with exhaustion.

"What in pity's sake is amiss, my dear? Calm down, I beg you, do. Just tell what has happened here." Releasing her, he held her at arm's length as she struggled to compose herself, her breath coming in shuddering gulps as she fought to stem her tears.

"They came last night, that pair of pigs again, and tried to tek my Joe. Stood outside, they did, both pissing on the door, forgive me Sir, they did. Both were in drink and when I wouldn't let 'em in, they kicked it in and would've tekken Joe. I cut 'im, Pearce or Lemman – don't know which, the first in through my door is all I know – and cut 'im bad, for sure. He falls down and t'other falls on top; that's when my Joe fired off his gun and frit them both away. Ran off and just left that behind." She turned and pointed to a blackened stain on the earthen floor visible within. "When us

heard you coming to the door, us thought they'd come again to…"
She looked away, trembling.

"But *Joe*?" began Greene weakly. "*A gun*? *Fired off*? How could
he..?"

"It's only an old rook gun, Mister Greene; bird-shot, no more'n
that. Scared off those yellow buggers, though; or else they'd 'ave
killed us both."

"So, Joe is..?"

"Oh, come in and *see* him, sorry, Sir. He's mending faster than
a Granny's stitch, all thanks to you."

If ever he had doubted the power of the human body to repair
itself, the figure propped against the threadbare bolster was its
living proof. Though pain had etched its mark deep into the
weather-browned features, the eyes that watched his approach
shone with a brightness that seemed to illuminate the shabby
room. The bedridden man propped his archaic fowling piece
against the corner by his head, beside the shawl-wrapped figure
of a sleeping child. Then, holding out a hand to Greene, he said:
"Didn't know it were you: I'd stand to thank you if I could, but
that will come in time; more thanks to you, my Aggie says. I don't
remember ought, and just as well I reckon, Sir. I owe you my life,
Mister Greene, Sir, and that's the truth. I don't know 'ow, but
payment will be made; you have my oath on that."

"Your thanks will do as a down-payment to be getting on
with," said the Apothecary. "It was only by the grace of God that
I stumbled upon you. I had never thought to play the Samaritan."
He turned to the silent figure at his elbow. "And now, Mistress,
if you'll boil up some water for me, I'll dress the leg while I'm
here."

Beside the prone man, a small figure struggled awake. Greene
smiled down at the wide-eyed child, saying: "And if you'd like
to go up and see my old horse hasn't wandered off, you might
just find a barley-sugar stick in his saddlebag. It is one the fairies
sometime leave there for any good children I might meet."

Without a word she scrambled down and ran off through the broken door.

"You know you can't stay here, not now, don't you?" he said, into the silence of her departure. Only downcast eyes met his question.

"The fact that those two *gentlemen* returned at all is proof that my words of warning had no lasting effect." He looked at Joe, who met his eyes this time, and said: "Whatever bad blood lay between you in the past, they'll have double the reason to hate you, now you've seen them off – and hurt them, too. You'll be in great danger if you stay." He watched as they exchanged miserable glances, but wondered, was there something else besides that flashed between them in the dim-lit room?

"This old place is all us own," said the gaunt man. "It was my Aggie's Grandma's house, gifted from the old boy as farmed at Seven Trees. Reckon she must've done more than keep house for 'im over the years if you tek my meaning. Anyroad, us've had it since my luck went bad. It was home to bats and mice the five years since she died, but nothing to be sniffed at when my luck ran out."

His wife, returning with a steaming crock, cut in: "Joe made good money with the test-diggers for the new canals. Until 'e hurt his back that is, and then they let 'im go wi'out so much as thanks and 'ere's a shilling for your pains."

"Oh, leave off, Aggie, do," he said, not unkindly, but obviously reciting a time-worn line.

"What use a digging-survey man as hasn't got the brawn to dig, no more? They're men of business, after all."

"So, you mean to stay here, come what may? You have no other place to go?"

"No, here's our place," he said. "Anyroad, betwixt us we've no kin to speak of, savin' some old aunt as Aggie's got, a milliner in Walsall town. No, us'll just 'ave to find a way to make it work. Reckon you can fit me up wi' a peg-leg like a sailor-man, d'you, Mister Greene? My Aggie'll carve it for me, given 'alf a chance."

The bleak humour was lost on the Apothecary, momentarily, until he looked from one to another and said: "Oh, ...*carve*, I see... I hadn't..."

"Sometimes a laugh is all a man can call 'is own, Mister Greene; don't take it amiss."

"Neither do I," responded the Apothecary, "though I can't see that anything to do with that pair is a cause for much humour. They must be vicious to the bone if they would fall upon what they believed to be a helpless household."

"You've got 'em both to rights, Mister Greene. They'd pluck the feathers off an angel's wing if they thought they'd profit from its pain." He reached out a protective hand towards his wife, saying: "Lemman would like nought more than the chance to spoil this lass o'mine, as 'e can't have 'er for his bastid self. 'E'll not cease in that as long as there's a beat of life in 'is black 'eart."

"But when did this begin?" asked Greene, appalled and intrigued in equal measure.

"It was back in the days when old Mister Beasley had Walhill, and I was little more than a girl, living here wi' my Gran," began Aggie, only to be hushed by her man, who continued: "Decent enough cove, old Beasley was. Brought me and a couple of my best lads in, to build an icehouse for him a few years back, now. He'd been a shareholder in Bridgewater's canal and must've got a good word on me and my special lads from Mister Brindley, 'cos right out o' the blue, the old boy 'as shipped us over 'ere to sort 'im out. Special rates, special conditions, sweet as a nut, if it hadn't o' been for Lemman and any little tick as could burrow into 'is stinkin''ide. Ganged up on us, right from the start; queered us at every turn, given 'alf a chance. Jealousy it was; black spite, too. Mischief every place you didn't keep an eye tight on." He hawked noisily and spat upon the earthen floor, before continuing: "See, Lemman had been apprenticed – sort of – to the old lad as ran the 'ole estate for the Gaffer; Beasley bein' too busy makin' money and a-spendin' of it, to 'ave the time to look after 'is own backyard, like. So, when old lad breaks 'is daft neck, out beaglin' or some-such, Lemman thinks 'e's goin' to be stepping straight into a deadman's shoes."

"Not reckoning on *your* arrival, recommended to the hilt?" enquired Greene.

"As you say, Mister Greene, as you say," he murmured, with a solemn nod. "To tell the truth, I could run that many rings around the idle sot, I gave no thought to all the ill 'e could do behind my back. And that was my first mistake."

"And your second was..?" the Apothecary enquired, guessing the answer.

"The second one was worst of all, Mister Greene; by Lemman's reckoning, that is," he said, looking up at his watchful wife, "I took 'is girl, and along with 'er – or so 'e thought – all the standing 'ereabouts 'e'd ever 'ad. The bastid wants me dead, alright; these past ten years 'ave softened not one jot o' that."

He hauled himself laboriously up the stacked bolster, grimacing at the pain of movement, but continuing: "...and now wi' that godless bastid, Hawson, a-lordin' it up on the 'ill, Lemman's gone and got the master 'e deserves. I figure they'll both burn together if there's any justice in the life to come."

"So, not a well-liked man – Walhill's new master – then?" enquired Greene, lightly, looking from one to the other.

The propped man seemed to consider his reply before he made it, and even then, seemed to speak with some reluctance: "That'd depend on 'ow keen a man might be on 'avin a master as believes 'e 'olds the power o' life an' death, Mister Greene," came the reply, straight-faced. "Awson beat a stable lad close to death, not a six-month back; lad was near crippled by the cruel swine. 'Ushed up though, usual-like: lad's folk couldn't afford to lose their place, could they? Not wi' things the way they are. That weren't first time, neither. Word is, 'e cut a footman all about the face for peepin' in on 'is goins-on behind closed doors. Awson an' 'is cronies all dressed up like them old monks o' days gone by, wi' masks an' all, doin' it wi' 'ores brung in from Brummagen. It's what bastids like 'im 'ave allus counted on, though; folks too frit to stand agin the master."

His wife looked away though not before Greene saw a shiver pass across her hunched shoulders. His reaction to the baleful words was not what might have been expected.

"Oh," he said, solemnly, "That hoary old chestnut is raised up again, is it? How very unfortunate. One might have hoped the world had outgrown that kind of vicious nonsense, once and for all."

(10)

A piece of a Cope, worn by Wicklif, now preserved in
Lutterworth, Leicestershire, given by Mr Mott. The representation
of an open Book, painted on a flat piece of Board.

August, 1646. Two deep and dreamless nights of sleep had done
much to restore Elias Ashmole's complexion if not his humour.
It remained a constant mystery to him that daily consultation of
the Horary whose stars guided his every move should insist, with
relentless good cheer, that he was in the best of spirits and enjoying
perfect health. It was not as if the roots of his dark humour were in
any way puzzling, though; such was his absorbed fascination with
astral potency and planetary conjunction that he felt, somehow,
that he must be betraying his predestination by feeling out of
sorts. As to questions of his health, he needed – in truth – to study
little more than his enthusiastic dalliance with Venus to ascertain
the cause of various embarrassments in the nether regions.

Believing that nothing could be worse than the initial shocks
of his blighted return, he resolved to renew certain acquaintances
in the city and The Close. He passed an agreeable morning with
an elderly cottager in Stowe Street who had served the family
in his younger days, and now lovingly tended a kitchen garden
whose produce marched in well-ordered ranks of fruit and foliage
down to the reed banks of Stowe Pool. They stood together and
gazed towards the Cathedral's desolate skyline. His eyes bright
with unshed tears, Esau Cotton recalled the day the spire had
toppled, speaking with the bright anger of a plantsman who sees
the wanton destruction of nurtured beauty.

"It'll break your heart, Master Elias, to see what they've done in there. What they didn't burn or thieve, they spoiled so's no-one could ever take pleasure in the Lord's House agin."

Later they sat in the backshoot's shade and drank early pressed apple juice, talking of past and happier times and the hope of brighter days to come. He parted from the wistful gardener laden with produce for Mistress Joan, agent – for today – in a long-standing commerce between the two that extended, he suspected, well beyond provisions and provender.

Calling then, by prior arrangement, at the office of William Groves, Notary in Law, Elias was relieved of his burden, as a junior clerk was dispatched to deliver the green bounty to the kitchen door at Breadmarket Street. Dispositions of property and title having now to be settled, the tiresome procedure was set in motion over a glass of execrable Madeira in the stuffy, fly-blown office looking down upon The Dam. Seeing his client's attention straying towards the distant wreck of The South Gate, Groves sniffed to the effect that Master Ashmole was 'indeed fortunate to have been a non-combatant in Lichfield's recent woes', adding that here, in this very office, they had seen cannon balls land 'not a score of paces from this very window'.

As Ashmole turned and looked at the pinched disapproval on the Lawyer's sallow features, the sights and sounds of war came swooping back: *the shell-pocked merlons of the Dover Point bastion he had commanded at Oxford, the blistering heat of his over-stretched guns on Worcester's walls.* The unbidden memories clawed behind his eyes: *high on the rampart walk that looked towards the Malvern Hills, a staggering companion's fall against him with a rover's arrow through his eye; the rats, the putrid stench of…* Enough!

He stood, abruptly, pulling a kerchief from a sleeve to wipe a sheen of sweat from his face. Then, with terse authority he rapidly presented Groves with a list of instructions and dispositions. Leaving addresses in landed Cheshire and the City of London, he departed in haste, giving the Notary much for later thought.

Escaping into the late morning sun, he joined the Reverend Richard Harrison for a companionable meal.

"I'll only come if you swear not to force food upon me," he had grimaced when invited. "Mistress Joan must intend me to leave this place on a sledge, for soon no beast will bear me."

The conversation was welcome in its levity, aided in no small manner by several bottles of an excellent elderflower wine. Finally, with the air of a man who can no longer contain himself, Harrison jumped – a mite unsteadily – to his feet.

"Elias, I have something for you!" he exclaimed.

The two had long shared a passion for *the remaines and mysteries of the Antients,* and when Ashmole saw what his beaming host placed on the littered dining-board, his eyes lit with delight. Grabbing it up he squinted at the damaged print and read aloud:

acta Capitularia Decani et Canonicorum Ecclesia Cathedralis Lichfeldensis a 10. Kal. Maii 1321 ad id Julii 1384

"But surely, everything perished in the flames when they burned the Cathedral Library?" he breathed, holding the treasured volume spread in his hands.

"Obviously not, as you are holding part of it," laughed Harrison.

"This is extraordinary," responded Ashmole. "I once held this very book as a lad. It's the oldest Act book of the Cathedral. We were shown it and many of the other treasures by Michael East on one of Chad's feast days. How on earth did you come by it?"

Harrison's good humour seemed to evaporate and he glanced, as if by habit, to right and left, though they sat alone. Voice lowered, he replied: "There's a corporal in what's left of the garrison in there..." – he nodded in the direction of the Cathedral Close – "...who is not averse to turning a quick profit out of what little survived from their *Godly Cleansing.*" His face wrinkled in distaste as he spoke the words.

"Do you mean there could be more from the same source?" asked Ashmole, unable to conceal his excitement.

"He would have me believe so," nodded the clergyman, "but frankly, Elias, it's a dangerous business having any commerce with one of that ilk; they'll sing you a psalm as they slit your throat – if there's a gold coin to be had for the doing of it. For all the pieties spewed forth from The Lower House, venery and vengeance are to be our new masters now, I fear."

"How is he to be found?" came the dogged response, but seeing the answering frown on Harrison's broad features, Ashmole added: "I shall take all due care, old friend, though I can assure you that an early death is not in my stars."

The frown deepened. "I pray that your astral dabblings do not endanger more than your health, Elias. There is an outer darkness to be shunned; never, ever, doubt it."

"The stars do not compel me, Richard, my will remains free. Oftimes, though, my eye can perceive glimpses of that hidden mechanism of life wherein lies harmony and greater laws."

Harrison regarded his companion thoughtfully, well aware that the years of war had seen a flowering of the 'Estate of the Sciences Mathematicall' in which Astrology enjoyed a tolerated, if ambivalent, respectability. Horoscopes were greatly in demand for predictions of births, marriages, deaths and inheritance. Indeed, there were many who would not set foot abroad unless their stars concurred.

Finally, his laughter broke the lengthening silence between them: "I'd rather that you cast your blasted horary than that I should cast a shadow on our friendship, Elias. I simply urge caution – in all respects." Ashmole smiled assent and the moment passed.

Harrison continued: "The man, Madden by name, is to be found in the small taproom at The Swan, most nights; though, in truth, it is not a place for those that value health."

Left unsaid was the painful fact that it was from the crowded squalor of the city's inns that plague had spread. For months they had been closed and shunned, but now – scrubbed and scoured to a state of tolerable filth, they were again open for business in a city struggling to return to a semblance of normality.

"He bears long scars on his cheek." Harrison crooked his fingers to describe the marks, continuing: "He should be approached with caution, for he knows all-too-well what will befall him if taken in the trafficking of loot – and idolatrous loot at that!" Harrison's grim smile failed to reach his eyes. Ashmole took leave and carefully wrapped his treasured gift in a borrowed cloth bag.

"He has at least one other for sure," were Harrison's parting words: "'written by a Frenchie', his eloquent description. But take care Elias… Take very great care."

ITEM:

Beneath the Cases, on the CLOSET DOOR. Two scalping
Knives, the Sheaths decorated with Porcupine Quills split,
and dyed, of various Colours. Maucassons, or Indian
shoes, ornamented like the pouches, and some of them
with Human Scalps, tanned, with the Hair preserved.

22nd May, 1776. "*A Hell-Fire Club*, Richard? Up at Walhill?"
said Theodosia Greene, her expression a mix of incredulity and
amusement; "The poor man must be deluded by his pain, or by
the sheer extremity of his experience, to imagine such a thing!
Everyone knows that all that horrid nonsense died an unlamented
death along with the likes of... – oh, what *was* the dreadful man's
name? – ...him, along with the so-called Monks of somewhere
or other, years and years ago?" Her fine features wrinkled with a
frustrated frown of concentration.

"He suggested *no* such thing, Theodosia," said Greene in mock
reproof. "He was talking only about rumours of some sort of
masked goings-on, involving Bartholomew Hawson's cronies and
some ladies of the night brought in for the purpose, so to speak.
Hardly fire and brimstone foolery of the old variety."

He added, smiling: "*Dashwood*, though, is the name you sought,
my dear, *Francis* Dashwood, Baronet, and sometime Chancellor
of the Exchequer, as I recall; and most certainly a gentleman
who should have known better. As to the proper demise of such
carrying-on, my own thoughts, precisely. Though it would appear
– if that poor wight, Joe, can be believed – that the lure of orgiastic
masked revels can still exercise its appeal to the jaded and depraved

palate. How though…" he narrowed his eyes in mock inquisition, peering intently at Theodosia across the remnants of a pie, "…did a carefully educated young lady of impeccably proper upbringing come to hear of The Monks of Medmenham and their unsavoury antics? Not a fit topic of conversation in a Croxall parlour, either then or now, I'll warrant!"

"Oh, don't be so stuffy, Richard!" she laughed. "Can you really believe that the very *nicest* young ladies do not crave just such tales? It is the very stuff of whispered confidence and girlish fancy. Why, one could imagine that without tales of the naughty antics of highwaymen and the unprincipled roguery of the Spanish Main, the nicer sort of young person would simply expire from ennui."

She reached a long-fingered hand across to lay upon his, saying, in mock appraisal: "You really do remain a complete innocent when it comes to the fads and fancies of all things feminine, do you not, my dear? It is why – as a good wife – my first duty must be to assist your better understanding of all the little ways to engage my interest and make me happy. It is the very least I can do, don't you agree? I should be failing you otherwise."

"Such a failure would be as unlikely as it is unthinkable, my dear," grinned her husband, rising from the table and coming around to place his arms about her shoulders.

The eyes of cornflower blue that looked up into his, had never lost the power to entrance him, and he bent to hug the bonneted head gently to his breast. A fleeting thought, unbidden and unwelcome, came to him as he looked down at the beloved woman who had shared so much of his life. A woman – and a life – he had once so nearly lost. *How fragile is the world we construct about ourselves; how easily sundered by thoughtless error or blind fate.* He hugged her closer while the moment passed, and then, his habitual good-natured self once more, said: "I really must endeavour to stop bringing my work to our table, Theodosia; It is both intrusive and unconstructive, and I beg your pardon for it." Now, though, it was her turn to respond.

"You, your work, your museum and your vagrant fancies are all but part of the whole to which I willingly bound myself, Richard. They are indissoluble even if occasionally infuriating, but I would – most times – have you no other way; so that is quite enough self-deprecation for one suppertime, husband. Tell me more about this Walhill business. I am agog and well you know it."

He relented with a quiet smile, saying: "Well, to start with my patient: I cannot help but feel there is far more to his misfortunes than meets the eye, Theodosia. Why poach behind high, well-guarded walls, inviting retribution from an established and already vengeful enemy, when the woods and fields for miles about could supply that meagre table any night of the week? What then, prurient fascination apart, would take our Master Joe back with the regularity his conversation has revealed to me? Sufficient intrusions to warrant the statement: 'there've been a dozen or more down there, with Hawson; most times; I've watched 'em lit down through the wood from the Manor to the Icehouse'."

"*The Icehouse*?" interjected Theodosia. "Indeed," Greene replied. "The one that Joe and his workmates dug for old Beasley, and which now seems to be doubling as a tucked-away hideyhole for whatever goings on can be credited to Walhill's new master."

"This man, Hawson; what is known about him? I've heard nothing mentioned amongst the ladies, or in the shop. He appears to have no commerce with Lichfield at all. Is that not in itself strange, Richard?"

"Let us not fabricate mystery were none need exist, my dear," he responded, evenly. "For one whose business would appear to be based in Liverpool and abroad, our little metropolis..." – he grinned, indicating the unseen city beyond their door – "... may well be proving far more resistible than we might chose to believe. If Walhill is fed and watered from elsewhere: Walsall, Wolverhampton, Birmingham even, and its master seeks his pleasures and his playmates – however nefarious – elsewhere, too, then why should he look to our small society at all?"

Theodosia was having none of this.

"Why would anyone of any breeding, any standing, cut themselves off from..?

"Why on earth should *breeding* and *standing* be qualities necessarily associated with Walhill's new master, my dear? The simple fact of sufficient wealth to purchase an estate is predicated upon neither. If Old Townley is to be relied on, the source of Squire Hawson's wealth involves precious few niceties."

"Richard, you are beginning to annoy me," she said, ominously. "Must the pith be dragged forth?"

"Oh, The Triangle Trade, apparently; but based out of Liverpool rather than Bristol, he says. Did I not make that clear, my dear?"

"Slaving?" she exclaimed, incredulously, "What? Here on our own *doorstep*? Richard this is abominable! Miss Seward must be informed! Why only this week the ladies of the Box Club have resolved…"

Unwisely, Greene cut in: "No, of course there is no suggestion of slavery here on our doorstep, Theodosia; it is simply, supposedly, the source of his…"

"Richard, in the same breath you have blithely informed me that in this very neighbourhood Satanic practices are being financed by the tainted profits of that vile trade and yet you prevaricate when pressed? What has become of your sense of perspective, husband? I am lost for words that you fail to share my outrage."

"I fail to share *nothing*, for pity's sake, Theodosia!" he replied, rather too hotly, "You are choosing to misinterpret my words. I too share your…"

"You shall share nothing more with me this evening, Mr Greene," his wife snapped, coming to her feet in a rustle of taffeta, "and neither shall you until your moral compass regains some fixity in your affairs. I fear you have become not only short-sighted but perilously detached in your outlook, Richard. You are seeing nothing beyond the end of your nose, it seems to me."

She swept out of their small dining room, leaving a crestfallen silence in her wake. The small man sat glumly for some time, pondering on the role of good intentions as paving stones, before rising stiffly to stand, coat tails raised, in front of the small fire, and surveying the resonantly empty room.

The box, he thought, brightening perceptibly. Moments later, to the sound of their incomplete meal being cleared by a muttering housekeeper, he climbed the stairs to the museum above, a lit candle lamp in each hand.

A benign calm seemed to envelope him as his ascent brought him into the first of the rooms, lamps summoning flashes and darts of light from innumerable surfaces of steel and shell, of crinkled old crown glass and polished woods. With a small sigh of satisfaction, he drew the weighty old box from its temporary resting place beneath a carved coffin-stool of much the same vintage and placed it upon the opened leaf of a side table that served him as office and workbench. Gazing intently at the closed lid, he watched the scratch-carving around its edge shift and waver in the candles' amber gleam. Incised scallop shells, and – as he knew – another, actual, shell within, nestling where something else should, by rights, have been. In general, an image viewed as the symbol most associated with pilgrims; in particular, as the token of medieval pilgrimage to the renowned Spanish shrine of Saint James the Apostle, at Compostella. That much he knew, but precious little else, he decided, staring once more at the spread contents in the spill of light.

Tonight, he decided to address himself to the dedication cartouche on the oddly rendered print of the Cathedral, which, as he peered at its fly-spotted surface once again, perplexed him anew. He stood, as if on an impulse and crossed to the stairhead and a small, curtained alcove whose shelves were crammed with what – to the untutored eye – at first appeared to be a haphazard, dog-eared jumble. The well-used volumes, pamphlets and monographs, notebooks and loose leaves had been assembled, however, with a logic entirely comprehensible to their owner, if to no-one else. As Theodosia had been known to observe on the various occasions when some new consignment of arcane publishing had spilled down the stairs themselves until squirrelled away by the harried culprit. The works had been assembled over a lifetime of collecting and represented the nucleus of all Greene's research, whether into china marks, gun-proofing, ornithology, mineralogy or any of the myriad highways and byways of human activity as represented by the ever-growing collection at Sadler Street.

With a small grunt of recognition, he retrieved a coverless, ink-stained pamphlet, and returning to his seat with it, held its contents to the lamplight the better to scan the scores of names and dates listed therein. "Got you!" he exclaimed after several moments' scrutiny, re-checking the name of the artist/engraver on the Cathedral print. 'Samuel Kirke, London, active between 1650 and 1665'. Of the engraver: *Ro. Vaughan* no mention. "Now that at least is fixed, let's see what you had to say for yourself, Master Kirke," he murmured, addressing the penmanship of the neat italic text.

In the minutes that followed the silence of the upstairs rooms was broken only by the sound of a scratching quill and incomprehensible murmurs from the absorbed translator, as line after line was set down, corrected, reshaped and reconsidered as part of the emerging whole. Finally, he had it down, almost to his satisfaction, and with it the dawning solution to another of the evening's smaller mysteries. "Of *course*," he breathed, speaking aloud to the slumbering museum. "That is why the drawing looks so wrong in parts: you had to make it up!"

Feeling a glow of accomplishment suffuse him, he sat back to reread the translated dedication, understanding how – if not yet *why* – it came to be present among the contents of the box.

Lo Reader, he grinned to himself as he read out the translated text. *So has T.F. wept for the Church of Lichfield depicted here in*

writing... He paused, pondering the word 'graphice'. Perhaps 'pictorially' rather than *'in writing'*, he decided, quickly amending his translation before continuing: *...than which the sun has looked on nothing lovelier in the English world, but of which, now, alas, the ruins splendid in...* er, 'damage? No, he decided: *...deformity...*

scarce survive. But so that it may be known to posterity in what form it once flourished, TF... Greene frowned at the indecipherable initials once more: *...offers congratulation on this monument to such a holy cadaver...* no, 'corpse'. He scratched busily again: *...set up at the expense of Elias Ashmole who raises up alive again a phoenix from the ashes.*

For some time, Greene sat, absorbed, by the possibilities presented by the signature initials TF, before expelling a pent-up breath and exclaiming 'Fairfax!' to the empty room. Thomas Fairfax, renowned commander of Parliament's armies, his apogee at the crushing royalist defeat at Marston Moor. Unlike so many of the driven zealots of his acquaintance, Fairfax had attempted to moderate the destruction visited upon ancient libraries and collections, saving those of Oxford and York from wanton plunder and destruction. Although virtually the master of the realm by the time of Charles Stuart's trial, Thomas Fairfax had become the exception amongst his peers in opposing the King's execution, before retiring from public life rather than further oppose the force of nature that was Oliver Cromwell. He had subsequently played a key role in the restoration of monarchy – even to the extent of providing his own horse for the newly landed Heir Apparent as he landed at Lyme Regis. Yes, Green mused, this was exactly the type of elder statesman whose approbation would have been sought and applauded by Ashmole in the furtherance of his own ambitions.

He sat silently mulling over what now lay revealed: At the time of Kirke's engraving – completed sometime, by necessity, prior to 1665 – the Cathedral Church had lain not only in complete ruin, spireless and largely roofless following the last and worst of the three sieges it had endured, but also, throughout the years of Cromwell's Commonwealth, had been under sentence of final demolition, such was its utterly ravaged state. Hence the sheer *wrongness* of much of Kirke's image: it had to have been a work of imagination, restoring visually what – in fact – would not be physically made good until the later years of Charles II restoration to the throne. The Apothecary recalled with relish the accounts of how on the first day of his appointment to the devastated See, the new King's nominee – the dynamic and ever-resourceful, John Hackett, a Doctor of Divinity from Cambridge – had begun the process of saving the ancient wreck by employing his own carriage team and servants around the shattered Close, joining them to embark upon the herculean and heartbreaking task of clearing decades of ruin with his own hands.

What part, if any, had Ashmole played in this? Greene asked himself; other than – perhaps – being persuaded by nothing more than a sentimental attachment to the place of his childhood schooling to pay for this undistinguished rendition of its former glories? It was no good, he decided: he would sink his pride to determine what, if anything, the infuriating Blomefield had discovered about *this*, at least. Had he not spent weeks to Greene's days in attempting to make some headway, and even admitted that he was awaiting an answer to various enquiries made to a friend in Oxford? He would have it out with the equivocating wretch, and the sooner the better, Greene decided; perhaps wisely in the present circumstances, though, making as little noise on his way downstairs as was humanly possible and letting himself out from the garden door.

(12)

An Organ, built originally by Father Smith, for the use
of the Cathedral Church of Lichfield, after its destruction
by the Fanatics, during the Oliverian Usurpation, when
no part of the goodly Fabric; fit for the celebration of
Divine Service was left, but the Chapter House.

August, 1646. Standing at the southern end of Bishop Langton's
great bridge, The Swan Inn – and particularly its northern
elevations – had presented an irresistible target for friend and foe
alike; for who held the city and who held the bridge had seemed
to change with bewildering regularity. At least, so it seemed to
the landlord of the battered hulk whose bad bread, rancid cheese
and watered ales had done as much as pike or grenade to thin the
ranks that tramped past his unkempt door.

Ashmole entered early and settled himself as best to scan the
passage and the yard. He held back from the small taproom, empty
as yet, and sat with his back against the stable wall on a bench in
the weed-ragged entry.

The afternoon had clouded in the north-west and as an early
twilight dimmed the sky, Ashmole saw his man. He entered the
yard with a hunched stride; a powerful and contained figure, but
one who bore the pain of old wounds. Without a glance at the
discreet watcher, he disappeared into the gloom of the interior and
its boarded stalls, from which came a clatter of pewter announcing
his service. Some moments later, as a burst of raucous laughter
and the sound of breaking crocks echoed from rooms at the front
of the inn, it became clear to Ashmole that passing trade would

be drawn to that cheery din rather than to the gloomy lair of his observation.

Walking unhurriedly across the yard, he entered a low, drab, room and was almost overwhelmed by the stale reek of damp and ancient spillage. Seated on a settle beside an empty fireplace, Madden – an upturned face with livid scars confirming his identity – glared in the direction of this unwelcome company. A slithering tortoiseshell shape tangled in Ashmole's boots and almost tripped him as he stepped down onto the cracked and greasy flagstones; it fled yowling from a well-placed kick. As he cursed and recovered himself, a voice from the fireplace said: "Need to watch your step hereabouts, Master," met with an answering chuckle from a lumpen, coarse-featured girl who leered from the room's bar-hatch.

"Your pleasure, Sir?" she said, with bored indifference.

"My pleasure is privacy – *now*," he said in clipped tones and tossed sufficient coin to conjure her rapid disappearance. She took one look at his eyes, scooped coins and slops into pudgy hands and slammed the hatch behind her.

As he turned back to the room's sole occupant, Madden was already on his feet, a saurian glint in his eyes and a black, needle blade held unwaveringly in each hand. The icy stare held Ashmole as Madden moved towards him, viciously kicking aside a bench that stood between them. Whilst space remained, Elias spread one hand, palm open, to his side as the other tossed a small leather purse onto the floor at Madden's feet.

"I know who you are, and what you serve, corporal; there is a token of the language that *I* speak. Have you the ears to listen, or..?" Suddenly a small wheel-lock pistol seemed to materialise in the hand at his side, "...or shall blood – *your* blood – be shed with gain for no man?"

In seven years of war, Madden had learned to read men's eyes. There were those he killed with ease, there were those he'd learned to please, and then – just occasionally – those he wished he'd never seen. This evening, looking into the eyes of Elias Ashmole he saw a level of detachment and chilling contempt that turned his blood to water.

"I believe you value coin as much as I value that which can be bought with it," Ashmole said evenly. He reached inside his cloak and then held the ancient book before him.

"I gather that you and your fellows may, perhaps, have graciously spared other such scraps from your *cleansings*, and are now disposed to profit from them. Am I correct?"

Madden was suddenly torn by conflicting desires: whether to rip this icy bastard's smile from off his face, or whether to fall to his knees and give thanks; for here, at last, might be the means – the brawn, the other pair of hands – for which he'd prayed. He could scarcely believe his luck.

Although it would mean returning to the place of his worst nightmares, the crush of darkness that haunted his every dream, this one, this cold whoreson bastard, could be the means he'd sought these three years past. The stiletto blades disappeared with uncomfortable dexterity to be replaced by a smile of equally chilling insincerity.

"Why Master, if it's a bit o' business you have in mind, you should have said so. No harm done, and all's soon mended, eh? *Ale!*" he bellowed at the blind hatch, which opened with suspicious alacrity. "You'll join me, Master; I've no doubt."

Ashmole stared into the calculating face. "Your certainty does you credit, corporal; if little else does." The other's eyes narrowed dangerously at the insult, though Ashmole continued unconcernedly: "But as you say, all's soon mended; so, to business."

Sitting warily across from each other at a stained table, Harrison's words were soon confirmed as it emerged that, yes, there was another book:

"Not perfect, you understand, Master, but good. In most parts it's not scorched."

Ashmole hid his revulsion as best he could and arranged

delivery. A price would follow when he could inspect the book, or what remained of it. They would meet, as if in passing, near where the parchment-maker's windmill stood – out by the Pool – at dusk next day. Ashmole, feeling suddenly tainted and lowered by this rank kennel and its unsavoury occupant, began to crave the open air and honest company. They parted wordlessly, each to their own thoughts of loss and gain.

A man less weary and preoccupied might have realised that his brisk homeward walk – and its destination in Breadmarket Street – did not go unnoticed.

Madden was in no hurry to return to The Close. It was garrison duty in name only. The war had moved on, and with it had gone the zealots and the divines, those hard-bitten, driven men whose passion scorched all about them. Those of his fellows that remained – a half troop from broken units – had little cohesion and less companionship. They were men old before their time, longing for little more than an end to this blighted war and a return to the humdrum dreams of hearth and home. If that return could be sweetened or hastened by a purseful of coin, then some small profit would have been won from the filthy shambles of it all.

When he had returned to the inn and finally spent up his coin on the rank apology for ale, and his half-hearted lust against a loose-box wall, he stomped ill-temperedly back across the causeway to the West Gate. A brazier burned beneath the broken arch of its barbican where lolling sentries, lit by its glow, glanced incuriously at him as he passed.

His boots sounding a hollow clatter in the tunnel of the Gate, he walked under the broken portcullis, askew in its deep-cut stone runnels, and emerged into The Close. The great dark bulk of the Cathedral Church which loomed above him signified no more than welcome shadow whose cover would guide his stealthy progress up and round the desolate enclosure. He knew precisely where his muffled tread would lead and would kill any man who guessed or followed.

Avoiding the open ground, he picked his way with familiar ease around the rubble-strewn shell of the Old Library, and around the tumbled spoil-heaps that the fall of the Great Steeple had rained down upon the nave and Chapter House. He glanced left and right and then moved noiselessly up the slope to the lightless ruin of the Bishop's Palace. He slipped inside its outer Court and stopped to listen. An owl and a restless chattering of woodpigeons in the nearby trees were joined by the distant sounds of the settling city across the unseen expanse of the Minster Pool. He sensed with practised instinct that he was quite alone and hurried through the ruins to the space beyond. It could no longer – by any stretch of the imagination – be described as a garden, but this desolation of bramble and nettled shadows was Eden to Josiah Madden; the promise concealed in its dark soil sweeter than any fruit yet dreamed-of.

Madden had been slow to heal from the dreadful injuries taken here, and the near-fatal fever that had followed them, though he at least had survived. How many of his mates had he seen sicken and die from even the smallest sword-cut or bullet-nick? At first, he'd lost count and then, lost interest, as the endless tedium of war ground on.

Never the most sociable of men, he'd become solitary and withdrawn, his fierce, darting eyes and dreaming moods setting him apart from what raucous pleasures the troops could always find. He had neither sought nor gained advancement – though who could have guessed that the single, simple, goal of his life was to return to this place and all he feared most in the world? For here there lay not only riches beyond a man's wildest dreams, but something more, besides; a thing to which he could ascribe no name, a thing that stirred a formless longing in his heart. Another man might have called it magic.

(13)

Between the Eastern and Middle **WINDOW**. Stands a Bureau, the Front of which is an arched pane of Glass; two Feet, nine Inches, by eighteen Inches, over which, against the Wall, hangs a piece of Wood, rudely carved, taken from the Roof of the Parish Church of Stone, Staffordshire, with the Letters, I.H.S. MCDIV.

22nd May, 1776. The Apothecary, arriving after dark and without prior appointment at the Blomefield's door, had been treated to the unusual sight of the obviously *déshabillé* mistress of the house rapidly absenting herself from his unexpected entry; though not before, Greene noted, a ferocious glare had mutely informed the young housemaid responsible for admitting him that there are times when a Master and Mistress are, *absolutely*, not at home to chance visitors.

"You'll have to excuse me, Richard," she'd called over her shoulder, busily enveloping herself in a shawl as she hurried away. "You'll find Lionel pottering somewhere outside. Look for his light and the sound of things breaking. You know the way."

Greene – having run the gauntlet of the kitchen's guardian deity who, judging by the hastily moved Jenever bottle from the kitchen table, had seemed even less prepared for a late evening visitor than her mistress – found his old friend on his knees beyond the scullery door.

Lionel Blomefield looked up, owlishly, at the figure of the Apothecary silhouetted against the light within. "Richard, is that you? Elspeth has not taken ill, suddenly, has she? What brings you out at this hour?"

"And a very good evening to *you*, Lionel," said Greene sweetly, looking down at the broken eggshells his unwitting host had been in the process of scattering around the neat parterres of the kitchen herb garden.

"I have come to intercede on behalf of all slugs and crawling things. Have you no pity to spare for those that can only nibble when our backs are turned?"

"*Pardon?*" replied Blomefield, clambering painfully to his feet, expecting to smell the alcohol on Greene's breath as he drew near. "Are you serious? Why on earth..?"

"No, of *course* I am not, you idiot," exclaimed Greene with fond exasperation. "I have – in the telling absence of assistance from alleged friends – completed the translation of the wretched cartouche on the wretched print in the wretched box. I need to talk to someone about it, and you, more's the pity, appear to be the sole candidate."

"Oh, Richard, I do know exactly how you feel, believe me. Why do you think Elspeth insisted..." – he stopped himself, before hastily continuing: "Why do you think I passed the damnable thing on to you in the first place? I thought my head would split asunder if I had to spend another moment on its puzzles." He placed an earth-stained hand on the Apothecary's shoulder and said: "We both need a drink."

"I really do assure you, Richard," said Blomefield, both seated now in the soft candlelight of the small parlour at the top of the stairs, "the reply to my enquiries from Oxford arrived only this afternoon, coming to my attention only after supper. By then it was too late to..." he stopped, seeing the harried impatience on Greene's features. "Perhaps you'd share your translation with me first, Richard? You have such a way with these things."

Though obscurely pleased with the compliment, Greene snorted and said: "We both know full well what it says, Lionel, even though I might have been spared the fag of having to make my own translation…" He let the sentence hang, meaningfully, before continuing: "So simply tell me what more you know about the *why* and *wherefore* of the thing."

"Well," replied his host, squinting at the letter in his hands: "It appears that Ashmole had achieved considerable eminence even by the time of the print's dedication – before 1660 would seem to be a reasonable stab at a date. So much so, that he was not only in a position to approach Charles the Second with a direct petition to fund the saving of the Cathedral, but also to have said petition listened to and acted upon. His loyalist credentials were beyond reproach and he'd obviously been building most assiduously, if discreetly, on them throughout the years of the Commonwealth. *My man at Oxford* quotes here from Ashmole's own letter, preserved as part of the huge archive of his papers."

"At the *Ashmolean*, of course," nodded Greene, half to himself. "Where better to look?"

Blomefield ignored him and began, portentously:

16 June 1660.
This morning Mr Rawlins of Lichfield tould me that the
Clearke Viccars of the Cathedral Church had entered the
Chapter House and there said service; and this when the
Vestry was the only place in the Churche yt had a roof to
shelter them. This very afternoon, I, having an opportunity to
waite on the Kg, and being in his Closet, tould him that the
aforesaid remaining number of poor Clearks Viccars
had assembled in the aforesaid place, and there kept their
Canonicall houres and prayed for his Ma'ty which he
was pleased to heare. Upon further, I acquainted him
with the desolacion of the place, wch he much lamented and,
said that he had been informed that Winchester
Cathedrall had exceedingly suffred in these late times
and that they had turned it into Brewhouses,
Malthouses, etc…

"…and again…" said Blomefield, pausing for breath:

July 18 1660, Mr Dugdale moved Dr, Sheldon to become an instrument for the repair of Lichfield Cathedral; and proposed that the Prebends etc, that were admitted should part with one-half of their profits towards the repair of the fabrick, which would be no great burden to them; and by this example the gentry would be invited to join with them in some considerable contribution. NB. I find this method succeeded accordingly.

"So," Blomefield continued, looking up from the pages grasped in his liver-spotted hand, "one way and another, we appear to have tangible proof of Ashmole's very active concern for the poor old place, albeit from some distance." He grinned wolfishly across at the Apothecary, adding: "My correspondent then goes on to say something that, by happy coincidence, would appear to have particular relevance to at least one of the other items in our box." Greene restrained himself, enduring the theatrical pause with saintly resolution, until Blomefield went on: "An item recorded in one of Ashmole's own early catalogues notes, and referring to 1646 – the time of his brief return to Lichfield towards the tail-end of the First Civil War – makes unabashed reference to the decidedly shady purchase of two books, *A fine Crosier head of great antiquity* and *Divers ancient Episcopal relics.* However uncertain the source of the latter, he could identify the crosier as having been looted from the tomb of Bishop Scrope. Its discovery, and that of a silver chalice since lost, had apparently sparked off a veritable orgy of smashing and looting, so Ashmole was told – by its actual *discoverer,* if that's to be believed: a shadowy figure referred to simply as 'the corprl'. The crosier is absent from the Oxford collection, I am informed, so it is a perfectly reasonable assumption that we are now in possession of it."

Once more, the Apothecary politely ignored the possessive pronoun, sitting for several moments in thought, before asking:

"So, Lionel, what does all this add up to? Apart from dating our crosier head to the late fourteenth century – which was about old Scrope's time, if memory serves?"

"Ah, you have me there," Blomefield admitted ruefully, though with a most mischievous smile, adding: "apart from the fact that *you* would now appear to be in knowing possession of what a court of law would describe as illegally acquired goods stolen from hallowed ground. Are you superstitious by nature, Richard?"

(14)

Within the Table in the middle of the ROOM. A pair of
Kid Mittens, embroidered with Gold, worn by the unfortunate
Mary Queen of Scotland; purchased at the sale of the late
Eben. Mussel, Esq; of Bethnal Green. Gloves worn by King
Charles, 1st. given by Mr Kemble, father to Mrs Siddons.

24th March, 1776. Favourite interludes in Theodosia Greene's week
were the local rounds undertaken on Richard's behalf – calling
upon those favoured lady customers whose conditions required a
certain sensitivity, most properly catered to by the female partner
in the Apothecary. And, not to be underestimated, the fact that
the visits presented the opportunity to leave the endless bustle
of the shop with its constant demands upon her many skills; she
being the ever-capable presence behind the polished counters with
a word for everyone, not the least of them. For many years now,
it had not gone unremarked by the small city's medical fraternity,
that Richard Greene – 'little more than a druggist by rights', as he
had once been sniffily described by an ill-informed and patently
envious new arrival on the Lichfield stage – enjoyed an unusually
professional status, counting more than one bishop, a raft of senior
clerics, several members of Parliament and a notable collection of
the county gentry as loyal patients.

His wife understood, only too well, the social tyrannies that
ruled the lives of a certain proportion of City and county *Quality*,
whose attitude to tradespeople – such as the Greenes – usually
extended to little more than a brief, patronising acknowledgement
on those occasions when the services of one of Lichfield's *proper*

medical men could not be called upon. Knowing that the nicely framed Doctorate bestowed by the University of St. Andrews, for 'most distinguished services and the greater ornamentation of his profession' had hung for many years past in a discreet corner of her husband's private consulting room, was quite sufficient for them both.

So, it was with her accustomed poise that Theodosia Greene had been welcomed into several of the grander dwellings within The Close, that morning, dispensing medicaments, advice and gossip in equal parts before leaving the confines of the ancient walls by the old West Gate and turning into the busy street that led up towards the Stafford road. She had paused only briefly to check whether the fine venetian windows that characterised the opulent frontage of the Darwin house were still shuttered.

The fact that they were, meant that the Doctor and his large family must still be holidaying in Derbyshire – a fact she would report back to Richard who, she knew, had some pressing reason or other to seek out his old acquaintance and consult on whatever it was that men consulted upon. It, like so much else concerning her husband's vagrant enthusiasms, was likely to remain a mystery to her, she knew.

Then, arriving at the timeworn steps down to the almost subterranean doorway of Dr Milley's Hospital for Women, she had reached her final call of the morning. The oak- timbered Alms Houses nestled below Beacon Street, looking across the bustling thoroughfare to what was left of the dry moat and the old Close wall beyond. Its crooked timbers and old red brick bestowed a particular quaintness to a building now sandwiched between the grand town houses that, in recent years, had risen to left and right. Dr Milley's, she thought, had the look of some fading elderly relative crouched down, asleep, in a favourite chair. In answer to her pull, a bell jangled somewhere distantly within, and it was several moments before the grey, nail-studded door creaked open to admit her.

Founded by charitable bequest in the early years of the previous century, the venerable, tall-chimneyed refuge provided a snug home of unimpeachable propriety for a dozen elderly residents living out their twilight years. This, not surprisingly, was one of Theodosia's most regular ports of call, and she was on familiar terms with all but one of the occupants of the tiny dwellings: a new arrival who had yet to call upon the services of the Apothecary. Today would shortly change that.

She was admitted by the small, diffident figure of the warden, a widow of middle years who was responsible for the day-to-day running of the Hospital, though in general, as Theodosia knew, her charges tended towards a fierce independence and a high regard for their privacy. Mistress Ames nodded her visitor into the dark hallway with her accustomed air of harried preoccupation, and left Theodosia almost immediately to her own devices, knowing that her visitor needed no guidance in the warrenous passageways between the dwellings.

It was as she ascended the stairs to the landing that she heard the unmistakable sound of breaking glass and a muffled cry of distress. It had come from behind the closed door of the Hospital's tiny chapel. She hurried across the landing and threw it open.

Revealed on the polished boards was the sprawled, ungainly form of a tall woman surrounded by a scatter of daffodils, broken glass and a large, spreading puddle of water. A rug, rucked and pushed off to one side of the small room, was the obvious culprit.

The angular face, tight with pain and shock stared beseechingly up at her: "Oh, thank *heavens* you've come," the prone figure gasped. "I'm such a fool, not to be trusted alone these days."

Stepping forward in the hurry to her side, Theodosia skidded in the spilt water and would have fallen herself had she not somehow managed to grab at a thick curtain hanging at the doorway, which, in turn, was wrenched away from its fastenings and collapsed, in a welter of pole, brass rings and dusty fabric, almost taking the staggering woman with it. For a second both exchanged fraught glances before exploding into helpless, pained, laughter.

Moving to the other's side, the Apothecary's wife looked down into the pale features of the woman. "Is anything broken, do you think?" she asked, peering with concern at the awkwardly bent leg beneath the prone figure.

"I don't think so," she gasped, struggling to turn and move her weight from it, "but my gavotting days may well be behind me."

Some moments later, and by the time that Mistress Ames appeared, Theodosia had managed to help the victim to a bench beside the low altar-rail and was examining her stockinged ankle with professional detachment.

"It's a nasty sprain," she pronounced, having elicited a gasp of pain from the seated woman when she attempted to rotate the injured foot, "but there appears to be no other harm done."

At an audible sniff from the wide-eyed warden, now gazing in proprietorial disapproval at the shambles spread across her floor, the seated figure added: "Apart from to Mistress Ames's housekeeping and my dignity, that is."

"Least said, soonest mended, Miss Beasley," the warden replied, the tight-lipped admonition of her tone depriving it of any conciliatory intention, as she stooped to retrieve the now-sopping curtain from the floor's disarray.

"I shall of course make good the damage," the seated woman said.

"Of course," the warden agreed, "and now perhaps, Mrs Greene, you will be good enough to assist me in getting Miss Beasley back to her rooms, to avoid any further… *incident*."

When, some moments later, that door had been reached and the lady safely deposited on an easy chair in her small parlour, the warden left them with a frowning nod and the air of someone who has been diverted from some task of vital importance. She turned back in the low doorway to add: "Perhaps you might bear in mind that, unless by special arrangement, the chapel flowers are replaced, as required, on a Friday, Miss Beasley."

The figure in the chair gave a weak wave and sighed with relief as the door closed behind Mistress Ames.

"Dear God, what have I let myself in for?" she enquired of Theodosia. "Our warden has missed a promising career in the Yeomanry, by the sound of it."

Theodosia laughed, replying: "You have seen Mistress Ames at her inconsiderable worst, I fear. She really does do a very acceptable job, most-times, and is liked well enough for her pains. One does, however, threaten the order of the Hospital at one's peril, though it must be said that the poor, dear lady has only the best interests of 'her ladies' at heart."

"You seem to know her well?" the other replied, "yet you are not one of my fellow denizens, apparently?"

Theodosia explained the reason for her chance presence at *the incident*, and the two women exchanged introductions with an easy informality.

"But you are not from hereabouts?" enquired Theodosia, mildly puzzled. "Forgive my curiosity, but I had always thought that Doctor Milley's was open only to ladies with very *local* credentials."

"Oh, absolutely," replied her companion airily, "though the fact of a girlhood spent no more than a few miles from here, added to the considerable benefices showered upon local good works by a well-meaning but spendthrift brother, seemed to swing the Court in my favour, so to speak." She paused, looking around the tiny apartment with theatrical disdain: "Though the Lord only knows why I bothered."

"Oh, there are many ladies hereabouts who would give their eye-teeth for such an apartment," replied Theodosia, earnestly. "For those that find themselves single and in…"

She barely stopped herself, but her companion cut in, laughing,

"Oh, do not fear to say it, Mrs Greene: …*and in straitened circumstances*… for I most certainly qualify on that account! Though, lest you cast me as some feckless flibbertygibbet, I should add that those circumstances are not of my own making."

"My dear Miss Beasley, they rarely are," responded Theodosia, in all seriousness, "To be at the often less-than-tender mercy of Mankind is a woman's lot, more's the pity. You are far from alone." Seeing, then, the look in the other's eyes, she added hastily: "Oh, do forgive my presumption! We have only just met and here I am pontificating on private and personal matters which are not one jot my concern. What must you think of me?"

She made as if to rise but was immediately restrained by a pale hand laid upon her arm. "No, please, it is I that should apologise. It is just that…" she seemed to falter before continuing: "…it is just that having been largely deprived of close company for some considerable time, I was unprepared for your acuity."

Theodosia felt herself blush at the compliment, as her companion continued:

"Will you take a glass of cordial with me, Mrs Greene? I do believe we might become good friends."

"Well," she responded, "I should like that very much, but my husband…"

"Your husband is a most fortunate and obviously discriminating man who will probably find a way of coping with your absence for a further half hour," she suggested, smiling.

"If you would be so kind, you will find glasses and a decanter over there, within arm's reach – as is everything else here, it would seem."

Their laughter was absorbed by the ancient walls.

"I shall of course call upon the good lady when I can find the time, my dear," said Richard Greene some time later, as they shared a lukewarm tureen of soup ordered at short notice from below, by way of an early supper, "…though it sounds as if you did all that could be done by your timely intervention. Sprains benefit from nothing more than prolonged rest, in my experience."

"And from the application of the comfrey-balm I promised you would take, Richard," she said sweetly.

"Indeed," he replied with a grave smile, tacitly acknowledging a master tactician at work.

"And what is the name of this lady that so pressingly requires the ministrations of both the firm's partners, may one enquire?"

"Oh, did I not say? *Beasley*, Miss Beasley. She grew up hereabouts, so I gather. There is something familiar about the name, I have to say, though quite *what* eludes me, Richard."

"There is indeed, my dear. There is indeed," her husband replied, thoughtfully, before wiping his mouth and excusing himself from the table.

"I shall probably not be back before you leave for the play, my dear. I trust you will have a most agreeable evening."

Before she could question him as to purpose or destination, he had clattered off down the stairs. Several moments later she watched his small form striding towards the stable at the end of the long garden. Words from earlier that day returned to her, as she saw her husband pause, stooping, to admire a clump of early tulips near the tack-room door: 'To be at the often less-than-tender mercy of Mankind is a woman's lot, more's the pity. You are far from alone.' *There are exceptions to every rule*, she thought, smiling inwardly as she left the room, hurrying out before her approaching Housekeeper came upon the unfinished soup.

(15)

In large DRAWERS marked with numeral letters. No.1.
A Miscellaneous collection of Articles from the Island of
St. Vincent, sent by Charles Ashwell, Esq; viz. The Eggs
of a Land Snail, lately discovered at Tobago. Coral from
Barbuda. Sea Weed, or Coral in its first Stage. Sulphur
gathered from the Mouth of a Volcano at St. Lucia.

Walhill. 25th March, 1776. "I believe you to have not been frank
with me, Joe. Tell me if I am mistaken," said the Apothecary,
watching the surprise, then the guilt, spread across the raw-boned
features of the man propped against the coarse bolster. The sunken
eyes darted towards the watchful woman at the Apothecary's side.

"*Tell him*, Joe. Tell Mr Greene all of it. We owe him that, and
more besides." His wife, her voice little more than an urgent
whisper, hugged the wide-eyed child ever closer.

"I meant no wrong, Mr Greene. Not with what I did, nor what's
not been told to you. It's all got tangled in my 'ead, is all – that an'
just not knowin' what to do, not knowin' what's for best, like."

"Show it to him, Joe. Mr Greene'll know. He'll not blame you
for what you did."

With what seemed to the Apothecary as numb resignation, the
wasted man nodded, "Fetch it bab, we should've done it sooner."
She rose and went to a small bread-oven set into the wall beside
the fireplace. Reaching deep inside she removed a cloth-wrapped
bundle and, returning to the bedside, handed it to her man.

Making no move to unwrap it, he spoke levelly to the
Apothecary. "You'll recall I told you what brought me and my lads

'ere in t' first place, Mr Greene?" The listening man nodded, saying nothing, watching as a vein worked in the gaunt neck, the face above frowning in concentration as Joe continued:

"It was in seeking out a best place for the Ice 'Ouse dig the old boy wanted, that I came across summat strange – not what you'd 'ave a right to expect, in the middle o' woods, like."

"And what was that?" encouraged Greene, seeing the difficulty his patient was having in getting the first words out.

"A bloody great piece o' dressed stone – almost broke my ankle on the bugger when I stumbled on 'im in the ferns. Alone, I was, not another soul up there that day. The old boy 'ad the lads out mendin' fences, off on t'other side o' the woods – no-one there, but me."

Greene nodded, patiently. "It was when I took a closer look an' dug about a bit to see 'ow big the bugger was, that I saw it was a step – another one right there beneath it, like. Both worn as worn could be."

Greene was now leaning forward, silently willing the halting speaker on.

"I 'ad my pole and all my gear, but 'adn't thought to even start on testin' the ground where I was – too many trees an' roots about, and not an easy walk from either lake or 'ouse to make it worth a spit. On wrong side o' the 'ill, like."

"How so?" asked the attentive listener, thinking he already knew the answer.

"Why, for an Ice 'Ouse to be worth the trouble o' diggin' the bugger, it 'as to be close enough to water to haul the ice out, and close enough to the 'ouse to get it there afore it melts," Joe responded with strained patience, as if talking to a child.

"Of course. Silly of me," replied Greene. "Continue, if you please."

"Well, I started pokin' round a bit, then, further from the steps I'd found, and only nearly lost my bloody pole, didn't I? – and that's as true as I'm standin' 'ere, Mr Greene. Pushed it down and down in soil as soft and sandy as you'll ever find – and it almost fell right out o' my hands. I knew I'd found an 'ole and then some, I can tell you. Couldn't work it out at all."

"So, what did you do then?" enquired Greene, eagerly. "Inform your employer what you'd found? Start to dig it out?" Judging by the expression on the other's face, the Apothecary knew he had struck a nerve.

"No to the first bit, yes to the second," he murmured, sheepishly. "...fast as I could, to tell the truth." He slowly began to unwrap the small bundle.

"There were about a dozen steps in all, deep enough but lost in the softest soil, just like I said. An' right beside the place I'd found 'em, a big old bugger of an oak had toppled in the gales and wrenched up soil all round its roots. Reckon it might've bin the fall as showed up that old step in first place, see? I must've dug two hours, three perhaps, before I got down to a sort o' floor. Looked like what once 'ad been some kind o' doorway 'ad fallen in and got all choked wi' roots and every kind o' shite, beggin' your pardon, so I could see the only way to pass 'im would be to do a proper job – wi' props an' all."

He finished unwrapping the grubby bundle and held out its content to show the Apothecary. The dull gleam of white gold was given back from the spread palms. Greene felt as if his heart had risen to his mouth. He gasped at what lay revealed.

"That's when I found 'im," the other said, "jus' lyin' in t' muck, like 'e was a-waitin' on me to pick 'im up."

The casting was as fine as any workmanship that Greene had ever seen. The modelling of a dying Bull seemed to possess a vibrant inner life, so perfectly had the ancient craftsman rendered the taut musculature of the powerful haunches, the jutting pizzle, the down-thrust, short-horned head protruding from the thickly muscled neck, the raised fore-hoof about to paw, to rip, the plinth on which it stood.

"It is *absolutely* magnificent, Joe. I've never seen its like," breathed Greene, mesmerised, unable to take his eyes off the superb sculpture. "It's Roman, without a shadow of doubt. I'd stake my life on its being what is called by scholars a *Tauroctony* – the image of the slaying of the Bull of Mithras, the god of soldiers."

And then he had it: *Letocetum!* How could he have failed to make the connection? Forgotten grass-grown hillocks down below Walhill, the ruins of a Roman station on Watling Street, the ancient road to Wales. Where more likely place to find a shrine, a temple to the Legions' god? He thought he might burst with excitement.

"This is an *incredible* find, the luckiest I've ever come across. The value of the bullion apart, it's worth a small fortune to a collector of antiquity, but then you must know that?" He stopped, suddenly, peering closely at areas of damage around the fallen bull, an awful suspicion dawning as he did so.

"Joe, was this how you found the piece? It lacks a number of its proper elements – they seem to have been crudely cut away from it." The suddenly averted eyes gave him his answer. He began to feel physically sick, but managed to continue: "There would have been a dog and a snake reaching for the bull's blood, if I am correct?" He looked below the superbly modelled torso of the animal to where a deep gouge was apparent beneath the bull's pizzle: "And a tiny scorpion here?"

"Of course, too, the figure of the God, Mithras, himself – all that remains is what is left of the arm holding the sword he has plunged into the creature's neck."

"Us 'ad no choice, Mr Greene," came Joe's miserable, whispered response: "I cut off all they bits you've said – melted all but one of 'em in an old shot-mould, bit by bit, like, and passed 'em now and then to an old Jew in Walsall. 'E didn't give a toss for ought but the metal – said the silver wasn't quality stuff, but gave me proper coin, instead. It's 'ow we've lived all these months past."

"*Silver? Not quality stuff?* But Joe this is…" He got no further.

"All I know is, Mr Greene, that for all 'e might be worth, me findin' 'im 'as brought me to the state I'm in today. I've been that 'ungry to find the rest of what's down in that bloody place, I've come this close to losin' my bab 'ere, my little'un, and lost a leg, besides. That's not what I'd call good fortune, Mr Greene. I reckon as 'ow that old bull god – or whatever else the bugger is – 'as brought nought but ill-fortune in 'is wake, to me an' mine." Tears glistened on the pallid face as he raised a coarse grey sheet to wipe his shame away.

The Apothecary scarcely recognised the voice as his own as he blurted out the words that followed: "Then that ill-fortune shall end right here and now, Joe, I'll swear to that! It is worth far more than you might imagine, more, perhaps than I can afford, but if we can fix upon a price, either I'll buy him outright, or, failing that, know a collector who surely will – one whose pockets are a sight deeper than my own. One or other of us, though, can surely release you from whatever curse you fear the old bull bears. You'll have enough to move away and make a fresh start free from all the baggage of your life round here." He turned, wild-eyed with excitement, to the silent woman in the shadows by his side. "What do you say, Aggie? Can this not be the way forwards for you all? To make a life anew, free from the fear of Lemman and his ilk?"

He saw a welter of emotions conflict in the bloodless features framed by lank black hair, her eyes darting to her man as if for some prompt or support.

"Only my Joe can have the sayin' o' that, Mr Greene, but I reckon 'e'll only tell you what he's kept on tellin' me."

"Which is?" prompted Greene, mustering all his patience to control his own excitement.

"Which is I've got unfinished business, Mr Greene – no more or less'n that. Not just with that scummer Lemman and his mate, but wi' what I know's still in that 'ole up there, just waitin', like it 'as been all these years." Suddenly, unaccountably, he seemed to redden with fury, glaring at the Apothecary as if he were the fount of all woes: "It *owes* me, does that bastid 'ole – twice now it's tried to see me off, the second time it almost did it, too!" Suddenly there was no stopping the torrent of words: "I've seen inside a way, though, dug a way through where the fall 'ad blocked it all, through to the place my pole fell through, a place wi' pictures made o' little stones made on the floor, but further in it all 'ad fallen years ago, on top o' more steps down. I saw enough to know, Mr Greene, but couldn't..."

Greene interrupted, in spite of himself: "So *that* is where you took the hurt that's kept you from your work, isn't it Joe? Not off canalling with Brindley after all, but digging your way to a treasure-store you think to be hidden in the Walhill woods? How many more lies would you have told me when all I've sought to do is..." Before he could finish, Joe's wife cut in:

"It's all he's thought about these two years past Mr Greene," she blurted out, tears starting down pallid cheeks. "Every hour of every day, waitin', schemin', crawlin' through those bloody trees whenever 'e thought 'e could get away wi' it."

She turned, red-eyed, reckless in her grief, her voice mounting, the pinioned child beginning to squirm in fright on her knee: "You *know* it's true, Joe, an' God 'elp me I've 'eld my tongue for long enough. It *can't* go on, its driven sense clean out of your 'ead, you know it 'as." The prone man gaped in obvious astonishment at his wife's fury, as if this were an emotion he had never seen before.

"But bab..." he began, all anger fled, helpless confusion flooding the narrow face. He got no further.

"Don't *but bab* me, Joe Crede, I've 'ad enough *but babbin*' to last me a lifetime! You lie there, spoiled for good an' all, and tell this good man you've unfinished business? There'll be but one thing *finished* hereabouts if'n you don't unblock those clagged-up ears o' yorn and listen to Mr Greene! We'll *never* get a better chance to leave all this behind, why can't you see that? Why *can't* you see?"

She fell, sobbing to her knees, the child, suddenly released, standing, dazed and frightened beside her, looking at her mother with pleading eyes that filled with tears. Appalled by the naked intensity of what was unfolding around him, Greene rose to his feet, moving to raise the distraught woman, but being waved back, angrily, before he could assist her.

"D'you *see* now, Mr Greene? D'you see just 'ow it is? There's no 'elpin' us, not with 'is nibs and 'is *business.*"

At that, her husband lunged across the threadbare blankets on which he'd lain, desperately attempting to haul himself upright on his single leg.

Whether it was to comfort or attack the furious woman Greene could not tell, but he would have fallen had the Apothecary not grabbed him beneath both arms and held him in a fierce embrace – the only way to stop the flailing man from bringing them both down on top of the weeping woman.

Shocked by the sheer physicality of the rank-smelling embrace, Greene held the staggering man only for a moment more before setting him back down upon the narrow bed. The look of pleading, helpless, desolation that met his gaze, hit the Apothecary like a physical blow. He had seldom seen such utter hopelessness in human eyes and it shook him to the core of his being.

"Please, *please*, both of you!" he exclaimed, turning from one to another. "I had no intention of coming between you, you must believe that. I act only out a desire to help you in the best way possible. You must believe that."

"No man could doubt it Mr Greene, not seeing what you've done already," murmured the gaunt figure, suddenly deflated like a spent bladder. "It's all the things I've *not* done, these two years past, that's brought us to this state. But it's *eaten* at me, Mr Greene, like a worm deep in my gut, a worm as can't be stilled unless it gets what it craves. I just 'ad to go back and back agin to try to get at what's down there." He held out his scrawny arms towards the weeping woman and their child, "But not for me, not just for me – but for all on us, we three, and that's God's honest truth, I swear it on my bab's life, it is."

Greene looked at the mute pleading in the other's eyes and knew the truth when he saw it. Coming to his feet, he said: "We all need pause for thought on what's been said here today. Whatever your decision might be – and that must be for *both* of you to decide – I will still give you whatever help I can. One way or another we will get you back on your…" He stopped, feeling suddenly helpless and foolish as he confronted the picture of misery before him. A feeling of impotence threatened to overwhelm him. He knew he had to leave, to get some air, some distance from these tortured souls. He turned back though as he reached the door:

"My offer stands, as the one sure means to move your life along. I can only pray you reach the right decision. I'll return as soon as I can, though. You can count on that." He hurried out, savouring the gusting breeze that met him as he climbed the path to the gate and his ever-patient mare grazing on the wayside grass.

He trotted away, down the deep-set lane, his head reeling with the image of the small golden marvel, burned like an after-image behind his eyes, with the anguished words resounding in his head: *a place wi' pictures made o' little stones made on the floor, but further in it all 'ad fallen years ago, on top o' more steps down. I saw enough to know that Mr Greene…*

Knowing already, in his heart, that the resources of shop and museum were as stretched as a prudent man could permit, he began the mental composition of a letter to Sir Ashton Lever, describing the golden bull. If he could not afford the true value of the miraculous find, then here was a wealthy man, a kindred spirit, who could. One way or another it had to be acquired, saved from the melting-mould. In his absorption, he had no reason to look back as he hurried away between the hedgerows. Even had he done so, he might well have failed to see the figure crouched deep within the shadow of the backshoot wall.

Only when the sound of the horseman's departure had faded off into the blustery spring afternoon did it detach itself from concealment and melt away into the ragged cover of the overgrown orchard at the hovel's rear. As the rooks chattered high in the windblown trees and the first of the rabbits ventured out into the last of the sunlight, it might never have been there.

(16)

An Order, signed by King Charles 1ˢᵗ, to the Inhabitants of the City of Lichfield, to bring in their arms, and etc. Dated at Wolverhampton 17 of October 1641. Allegations against Sir Richard Dyott, by the Committee, for the County of Stafford, for attending his Majesty at Edgehill. Dated 1645.

Late August, 1646. He walked in the Lichfield Minster church among the graves, many of which were open, and saw many carcases. He then came upon one, surrounded by children, which he thought to be his wife's. Their playing feet kicked mould and earth down into the open tomb so that, briefly, it covered her before sinking away. He looked down upon her face which was much withered and stooped to kiss her. Suddenly, her eyes opened and amidst the sound of screeching, terrified children, Elias Ashmole lurched awake.

Shaking and wet with sweat, he recognised the nonsensical dream that had come to plague him since the second day of Christmas at Worcester. His beloved Eleanor had been taken five years earlier – he in London, she with child at her family home in Cheshire. Again, now, he had arrived at this house in Breadmarket Street to hear news of crushing sadness, again a loved one had died alone and left him with the gnawing ache of his inadequacy.

If nothing else, the desolate resonance of the night's dreaming steeled his resolve. Today he would face what he had postponed until now and dreaded still: the return to his much-loved Cathedral and its treasure-store of memories.

Prodigious early days at the city's Grammar School had been

followed by his happily spent adolescent years as chorister and instrumentalist at the Cathedral. There, the Organist, Henry Hinde, had taught him the virginals and organ, whilst Michael East – 'Batchellor of Musick' – was his tutor for song; cultivated years that were rounded in courtly fashion by dancing lessons from Rowland Osborne.

At that light-footed master's side, he had learned *The Oulde Measures* and many more besides – all of which were to stand him in effective stead in the tireless pursuits of his later years. For the most part, his tutors were now dead or in their dotage, but the memories of those carefree, soaring, years were held glowing within him.

The prospect of seeing the ruin of all that they – and he – once loved so dearly, had held his gaze averted from the northern skyline, and his feet from the way to the broken walls of The Close. Now though, he resolved, he would go to lay his dream to rest and, doubtless, shed a tear for childhood's end, for his departure from Lichfield could not now be long delayed. Business on behalf of his in-laws at Smallwood in Cheshire, the ongoing pursuit of a certain Lady Mainwaring, and the gathering in of the personal tatters and shards of his present life were all, once more, of pressing importance to the mercurial man, now that the physical exhaustion of his recent ordeal had begun to ebb.

His entry into the devastated moonscape of The Close was predictably awful. Shock gave way to fury, fury to tears, then those to an awful, numb acceptance of a loss that could never be made good. Everywhere that his appalled gaze fell he could see that the hacked mutilations completely precluded casual violence and spoke instead of a calculated zealotry that turned his heart to ice.

The scale of damage to the encircling defences could come as no surprise to one all too familiar with the effect of ball and grenade upon bricks and mortar, but the wanton spite to which this poor, dear, old place had been subjected, pierced him to the core. He wandered – clambering as often than not – about the hills of rubble that littered the once-pristine precinct, his gaze passing from gaping frames of traceried stone to yawning gouges in the ruined floors, from frost-bitten, rain-stained sandstone to charred and splintered timbers. Instinct and reflex guided his feet through the desecrated shell until he found himself standing in the void of what had once been his favourite place.

The little chapel at the top of the stairs had been his own quiet refuge, over which the glorious sounds of the great church at worship could wash and eddy as if coming from another dimension. Here had been where the old saint's relics were sometimes displayed, and here was where a special tranquility had reigned. Now, dead pigeons or some other feathered, rotting things, stank in the doorway, and daylight lit the roofless, naked walls with banal cruelty. Every pock, every stain, every charred joist and beam mocked his memory of how this place once had been. He stepped out onto the filth-strewn floor and looked about him.

The stone tracery of the west window had largely survived, but the rest… What could have done this? A mortar shell, perhaps – the destruction was from the roof and shattered vault downwards. A trick of the light drew his eye to a single remaining stone-carved face that grinned back from the smoke-grimed wall. There was a mocking irony in its eyes that struck a strange chord within him as he saw that this sole survivor from the image-breakers' spite was Old Jack, himself. Jack in the Green, the Green Man. Gob-full of foliage, the ancient carving so beloved of the Masons' craft still spouted its timeless message. It was as if Ashmole heard the whispered words: 'Take it or leave it, like it or not. The seed is the secret, the secret is the seed'.

Your time has well and truly come, thought the morose man, for are you not sole Lord of this sorry place now? Here where lichen, grass and bird-sown bramble creep and burrow to your whim?

"Not much to see, eh, Master? Or, perhaps, too much?"

The mocking voice cut through his gloomy reverie and he whirled to where Josiah Madden leaned, at ease, against the ruined doorway. The grinning intruder raised a hand in mollification to forestall the furious retort he could see forming in Ashmole's eyes.

"Saw you coming in and thought to save my weary legs a walk tonight. Thought to show you a mite more of what you fancy, besides, if more than just book-reading be to your taste?" Instantly, the acquisitive heart of a born collector quickened.

"What have you to offer? Is it here now?"

Madden nodded, and spat expertly at a large spider that scuttled past his boots. With a jerk of his head, he indicated the broken-roofed stables near the South Gate. "Meet me in there when the hour strikes and bring your purse. It is better we're not seen together here."

Without waiting for a response, he turned and disappeared, the sound of his boots receding as he clumped down the stairs to the Lady Choir below. Ashmole consulted his pocket watch and then went to the doorway, its narrow balcony beyond. Across from his vantage point the disembodied legs of a well-remembered statue – Saint Christopher bearing the infant Christ – still stood sentinel above the vestibule to the Chapter House. Once more, he felt a tear spring to his eye; it was these fragments, these ruined traces of all he remembered that were so much worse than a complete absence could ever be.

The faceless, handless lumps that remained seemed like the mutilated messengers of horror and despair, sent back to mock those who had waved them off to war.

No bell had struck from the Jesus Tower these three years past, but the distant knell of St Mary's carried the hour across the Minster Pool. At first, Ashmole thought himself alone when he entered the cheerless dereliction of the stables. An elusive whiff of ancient saddle-soap and polish still clung to the whitewashed walls, though fodder – and every other combustible material – had long since gone.

Madden stepped, grinning, from a loosebox further down the narrow building's length and beckoned. Spread like a huckster's market-show, a small jumble of items were displayed on a spread cloth. Before Ashmole could stoop to examine them, Madden drew a small volume – battered, discolored, but intact – from his jerkin. Ashmole reached for it. Madden jerked it back. "Brought your purse, have you, Master?"

"I'll talk payment with you when…" – his eyes narrowed – "…and *only* when I see what you have scavenged." His fixed stare and cold enunciation were met with a shrug of reluctant surrender. The main part of the volume, once past the charred covers, seemed to be comprised of a dozen or more of the *Speculum Historale* of Bishop Vincent of Beauvais. Ashmole knew it of old.

If nothing else were to come of the day, this alone was well worth a deal of squalid commerce. In tacit acceptance he set it to one side, then crouched to view the pickings displayed on the cobbled floor.

"There's gold and silver, both, but I'll sell all or none, Master. The choice is yours but make it quick."

"Your *gold* is but gilt on this," retorted Ashmole, prodding a crozier head with feigned casualness. "These two are gold, but the stones are of no account." He held out two ancient rings. "These buckles may be silver but of less than middling quality and this…" – he weighed a medallion-like object in his hand, its inscription clogged with grime – "…whilst silver too, is better than the buckles." A little candour seemed no bad thing, as Madden nodded in agreement with the evaluation:

"You know your gee-gaws, Master, that's for sure. So, shall us now see if you know how to count your coin?" He bent swiftly as if to rewrap the bundle, glancing over his shoulder, the question on raised eyebrows.

Quite shortly it was done. For Ashmole, the metals at no more than a breaker's price – Madden having no regard for their obvious antiquity and the book: the price of a pair of Haymarket whores and a chop supper. For Madden: the price of enough liquor and soft company to convince him of a deal well struck and a young fool easily parted from his purse.

"One question."

Madden looked warily at Ashmole as he weighed the wrapped bundle in his hand.

"Did all this come from one place or many dark holes?"

The corporal shrugged: "The one only. The hole's still there for some unwary fool to tumble in and break his neck. Though it is not just *any* hole – but a *bishop's* hole, no less!" he smirked and turned away, though, as he did, a thought seemed to strike him. He paused and seemed to arrive at a conclusion. When he turned back to Ashmole, there was none of the sardonic mockery that usually lit his eyes. He said levelly: "Is a certain neat and proper house in Breadmarket Street a safe and private place where business of a serious kind might be discussed between men of good will?" Ashmole was dumbstruck: first, that Madden knew where he lived, but more, by the straight and level intensity of the questioner's gaze.

"I stretched my legs and strolled awhile when last you took your gracious departure." The mocking smile flashed once more and Ashmole flushed with angry embarrassment – that he had been followed had been the last thing on his mind.

"Do not reproach yourself, Master... *Ashmole*, I believe, yes? When I have a mind for a quiet stroll and stretched legs, none are *meant* to know as they've got company."

Despite himself, a small smile crept onto Ashmole's lips at Madden's barefaced admission. Something just a little like respect played, new-found, behind the young man's eyes.

"What *private and serious business* might there be between such men as you describe?"

"Business enough for a closed door and no passing eyes, Master Ashmole, and that's for sure."

Scarcely believing his own actions, Ashmole agreed to the

undreamt-of rendezvous, silently reassuring himself that he would be on home territory for an *entente* known to none but the two of them. They left separately, having agreed that Madden would come to the garden door an hour before midnight on the following day.

Neither could guess that what he would bring to that sleeping house – and the cost it would exact – was to change more lives than theirs that night and echo far beyond their years.

(17)

In a Glass case, on the left Hand of the before-mentioned frame of SHELVES, against the Wall. A Madagascar Batt, the Wings when expanded, measure twenty Inches. A Concave and a Convex Mirror, ten Inches diameter, in neat circular Frames.

2nd April, 1776. With Easter fast approaching, business at the Apothecary in Saddler Street had been brisker than ever, though Greene puzzled once more at the quirk of human nature that regarded the imminence of short holidays as the time to commence panic-buying of all that might conceivably be required to see one's family through a prolonged siege rather than through the lesser crisis of shops closed for longer than one day. As it happened, and given the nature of their business, it was a rarity that the Apothecary failed to open, albeit briefly, on such holidays, for the dispensing of medical necessities and attention to the inevitable, unforeseen emergencies that also characterise the human condition.

This year, though, Richard Greene had promised himself at least two days uninterrupted respite from the daily round, and – to that end – was attempting a degree of forward planning that was rapidly coming to resemble the logistics of a military campaign.

"But if I am prepared to begin my rounds at first light, why should any patient find that unreasonable, Theodosia?" he asked in the vain hope that an increasingly harried wife might agree with any part of his would-be strategy.

"Because quite simply, Richard, the number of amenable customers and easily satisfied patients can be numbered on the fingers of one hand. You of all people, husband, must know that, having – over all the years I have known you – bent over backwards to give such a degree of service, if not downright *indulgence*, to all and sundry, that now they will accept nothing *less*. You have only yourself to blame."

With that exceedingly back-handed compliment, Theodosia Greene had returned to the business of overseeing that week's dispatch of nostrums and toothpaste for collection by the Liverpool Carrier.

"And another thing, Richard," she called, some moments later, from the vestibule beside his Consulting Room, "I have asked you repeatedly to renegotiate the price of our licorice-root and our peppercorns from those thieves in Bristol. Despite the fact that we are certainly their major customers in the Midlands, their oil of capsicum has all-but tripled in cost over the past twelvemonth and we shall shortly be *giving* our toothpowders away, if you do not take some sort of stand with the rogues. Must I attend to everything myself?"

By then, however, blithely unaware of the harangue, the Apothecary was already on his way to the Darwin house and a meeting postponed for the several weeks of the family's absence from the city. They had returned some days earlier, though a lingering throat infection had kept the Doctor to his bed until now. With its scribe obviously now on the road to restored health, his recently delivered note had read:

> *Kindly bring prescription for effective respite from womankind and ravening young, soonest. E.D.*

This morning, bright with the prospect of a rapidly warming season and the approach of a clement Easter weekend, Greene found himself walking with a new spring to his step, and a cheery word or a wave to his many acquaintances in the busy streets. This, today, was an Apothecary determined to let no arcane distractions of an antiquarian nature divert either his attention or his determination to bring outstanding business nicely up to date, the better to properly enjoy said distractions at his fullest leisure over the coming holiday; a hope that he had decided not to share with a wife already talking of outings and family visits. So, this fine morning, to the business in hand: for a Doctor feeling sorry for himself, he had the very thing. He tucked his parcel more firmly beneath his arm and hurried on.

"D...D'you take me for an *Assassin*, G...Greene?" exclaimed the corpulent convalescent in a hoarse stutter rather than in the booming mode which was his usual trademark. He had been staring in mock alarm at, first, the apparatus the Apothecary was in the process of setting up between their chairs, and then, back to the resinous, red-brown nugget on his own outstretched palm, shaking his pock-marked head as he turned back to his busy companion.

"You'll be t...telling me you've got the Old Man of the M... Mountains, himself, p...pickled and stuffed in one of your Curiosity C...Cases, next!"

Greene grinned in response, knowing that even after their many years of acquaintance the formidable Darwin took endless pleasure in baiting him in regard to the Museum. He finished filling the glass reservoir of the hookah to his satisfaction before standing to regard his handiwork and replying:

"What I can promise you, Erasmus, is even more of the hallucinatory experience you so remarked upon from your experiments with *Digitalis Purpurea*, but with none of the more regrettable side-effects. If your reported two – or was it three – days of seeing the world in nothing but shades of yellow impressed you to the point of foraying into verse, we might reasonably expect nothing short of an Epic from today."

"The digitalis certainly p...produced *epic* effects all its own," growled Darwin. "Quite apart from the Xanthopsia you describe,

I d…did not manage a solid s…stool for a week."

Something seemed to amuse him at the recollection of this experiment with the deadly foxglove: "Mind you, Withering had the w…worst of it – almost brought the soles of his b…boots up, with the vomiting, day in, day out. Damn near lost the poor old f…fellow."

Greene smiled at this account of one of the Doctor's more potentially lethal experiments, knowing the odd mixture of camaraderie and competitiveness that characterised the often stormy relationship between the two erudite men.

"Right, Erasmus, are you game?" enquired Greene, standing back and regarding his handiwork with satisfaction.

"Once placed upon the lit coal, a moderate sucking upon this mouthpiece carries the smoke down through the water-bowl and thence to the smoker. The cooled inhalation can do nothing but good for that throat of yours."

The large head bent forward to sniff at the contents of the spread hand once more. "It smells damn spicy to m…me, Greene. I am not going to p…puff up like some over-seasoned Nabob, am I?

"Assuredly not, Erasmus," responded Greene. "I have used this Egyptian hashish in my preparations for a number of years now. It is a sovereign remedy for neuralgia and sleeplessness when ingested in controlled quantities, and a well-proven analgesic, particularly for the treatment of both the numbness and the severe muscular pain associated with dropsy and strokes. It also possesses the considerable advantage of having none of the addictive properties of the poppy – though its, shall we say, *visionary* aspect is scarcely less potent in my experience."

"P…Persuasive as ever, Richard," said the big man affably: "but that's what makes you such a damn' g…good shopkeeper." He watched for the expression on the Apothecary's features and laughed uproariously as he detected the flicker of annoyance that touched the round face.

"Lord forgive me, but I do love to t…tease you. You're just so d…damn' rewarding!"

"The Lord may well forgive you, Doctor Darwin," responded the small man, with an ambiguous smile, "but, beware, there may well come a time when *I* do not!"

"Nonsense, my dear fellow. Do we not know you for the m… most *equable* of men, imperturbable to the last? Your g…good humour p…puts us all to shame."

As the Apothecary shook his head at the sheer dexterity of his alarming host, Darwin clapped his large hands and croaked: "Let intoxication c…commence! And if the drifting shade of old Hassan-I-Sabbah should visit us, we shall b…but dream him and his ruffians away!"

By way of response, Richard Greene simply handed Darwin the silver mouthpiece at the end of its flexible tubing and said: "Do not inhale until I say so, and then only moderately. This is not a substance to be underestimated. Ready?"

The room's longcase clock, unnoticed until now, seemed suddenly to become louder by the tick, and Greene drifted back into the moment, only gradually becoming aware of the well-appointed room. Beside him, the bulky form of Erasmus Darwin was lolling in its large chair, the oversized head turned towards the wall as if viewing something of compelling importance. After what could have been fleeting seconds or many minutes, it turned, and the voice of its owner spoke as if continuing a conversation interrupted only an instant earlier:

"Withering will simply not be told. The mind of *any* young woman of the middling kind is not one whit inferior to the male of our species, and neither is her capacity nor her *right* to be fully conversant with all things amatory to be denied. How should it be that a healthy young creature should be excluded from a frank understanding of any normal aspect of the reproductive process? Is she not an inseparable component of the process? Withering will *insist* that wordy euphemisms are the only suitable means for discussion of sexuality, indeed, he seems to positively shrink from the Linnaean mode in its entirety."

Finally, the bemused listener understood the gist of the Doctor's monologue, knowing from earlier conversations that Darwin, wearing his Botanical hat, had recently – and with hectic enthusiasm – embarked upon a translation and study of the works of the Swedish naturalist Gustav Linnaeus, most particularly that trailblazing botanist's mode of plant classification.

That author's identification, Greene knew, of the stamen with the male *membrum virile*, and the pistil with female genitalia, formed the basis for a towering thesis of familial relationships, extramarital affairs and even deviant sexuality within the botanical universe; a thesis that the extraordinary Doctor had embraced with all his considerable energy. Hence, the Apothecary was only mildly confused – a normal condition in Darwin's company – when the Doctor continued:

"I see it now. How could I not have come upon it sooner? The work shall be narrated by The Goddess of Botany herself, in the form of a didactic poem wherein I shall dramatise the representations of each of the eighty-three species of plant, whilst interspersing the whole with dialogues on the nature of poetry itself. There!" he exclaimed, "That is settled. Are you hungry, Greene? I am suddenly peckish. Perhaps you'd be good enough to ring for something. I am told I must not over-exert myself."

The Apothecary, still in the process of gathering scattered wits about him, suppressed a smile. *Not over-exert myself?* Why, the mental acuity he had just witnessed would have turned most brains to porridge with the effort.

"I shall indeed, Erasmus. Some bread and cheese would certainly not go amiss." He stood, looking down on his seated companion. "So? No ill-effects?"

"From what, pray?" replied the Doctor.

"*Cannabis Sativa?*" replied Greene, patiently.

"Oh, that! Why none whatsoever, apart from a sensation of mild relaxation. Can't see what all your fuss was about, frankly," said the Doctor, waving a hand dismissively. "Do ring for that refreshment, there's a g…good fellow."

It was only sometime later, as the Apothecary made his way back through the bustle of the afternoon that he realised he had entirely forgotten one of the main purposes of his visit to the universally well-connected Darwin. His enquiries into the new owner of Walhill would obviously have to wait.

Crossing the Vivarium and pausing to admire the fleeting shadows of the fish beneath Bishop de Langton's great bridge, the bell from the Jesus Tower struck the hour, and with a sinking heart, Richard Greene realised the time.

He stood for a moment, undecided whether to hurry back to the myriad uncompleted tasks of an absentee day, or to make a break for the open lanes and a carefree Romany life beneath the open skies. He hurried home.

(18)

In the upper part of the window, of the Inner Museum, in a frame Glazed. An artificial Leek of Silver, with the Coronet and Motto, of the Prince of Wales, embroidered, and ornamented with Gold and Silver Spangles, worn at Court by a Person of distinction, on St. David's Day March 2d, 1765.

19th April, 1776. The invitation for Theodosia Greene to take chocolate with Miss Seward was as welcome as it was unexpected. The pleasurable anticipation was then enhanced in no small measure by her encountering the angular, immediately recognisable form of Miss Beasley, stooped against a chilly breeze, apparently heading in the same direction on the blustery morning.

With her accustomed brisk efficiency, the Apothecary's wife had decided to drop off several prescriptions on her way to The Close, not least to make certain that a particularly fetching new outfit might be appreciated by as many of her more demanding customers as could be contrived. She had not been disappointed, a fillip much appreciated in the absence of any flicker of approbation from an increasingly preoccupied husband.

'I shall be gone for five or six days and we shall have mashed rat for supper on my return', had been her parting words, to which he had smiled a vague smile and waved her off, returning at once to the jumble of papers spread across their dining table.

He would shortly have to be taken in hand, Theodosia knew, wearily accustomed to the periodic, all-enveloping reveries to which he was prone. She would have to fall back upon a well-honed repertoire of shock tactics to shake him back to what passed for normality in his frenetic double life. She was the first to delight in the extraordinary success of her husband's museum – a venture now so acclaimed and well established that it had become a commonplace to welcome visitors from far and wide whose often considerable journeys were made with the sole intention of viewing the astonishing cornucopia he had assembled in the upstairs rooms in Saddler Street. But, oh, what a price they both paid for it, she sighed to herself. Either one of her husband's driving passions – be it Medicine or Museum – would *more* than suffice for most men, but not hers.

No, she thought, crossly, *not for Richard. The confounded man is only content if he is juggling, dipping, ducking and diving every hour of every day. I am married to a human gadfly.*

So absorbed was she in her tetchy thoughts that she might have failed to spot Miss Beasley gangling across the freshly cut lawn towards the Bishop's Palace.

Her call, and a wave of her basket, halted the tall figure in mid-stride, who turned and peered shortsightedly in the direction of the greeting. Theodosia caught up with the squinting lady before she had properly recognised her rapidly approaching figure and was gratified by the beaming smile of recognition she finally received.

"My dear, *what* a surprise," exclaimed the wind-blown woman to the breathless newcomer, "Could it be we are summoned into the same August Presence? We are *both* in Sunday-best, by the look of us!" Theodosia laughed at the arch expression on the quizzical face and replied.

"Most likely, yes. Chocolate and best behaviour?"

"The same," replied Miss Beasley, linking her arm, "though now we can make a two-pronged assault on The Citadel of Intellect. Thank heavens you've come!"

"How do you come to know our hostess?" enquired Theodosia, both striding, heads down, against the wind that cut across the huge expanse of the Minster Pool beyond the broken walls.

"Oh, we go back *years*, my dear. I dandled her on my knee well before she could recite the Latin Poets in their entirety." Theodosia laughed: "She really could, then? It's not just hearsay?"

"Lord, *no!*" replied her companion: "She would be genuinely terrifying did not a heart of pure gold beat within that plump breast. I sometimes think the term 'prodigy' was coined on her behalf. She is redoubtable in every sense."

Before Theodosia could question her companion more fully, they had arrived at the imposing door of the Bishop's Palace and been ushered into the stone-flagged hall by an attentive servant who relieved them of their coats.

The ample figure of their hostess limped out to greet them, a buzz of conversation coming from behind the double doors open in her wake.

"You know each other already, I see. How splendid!" she exclaimed. "Are you both chilled to the bone? That wretched wind whistles through every nook and cranny of this great *barn*. There is a fire burning in the library." She indicated the room from which she had just emerged, continuing: "Though poor Papa swears it will bankrupt us, ever to heat the house properly. Shall we go through?"

The company, of around a dozen men and women, turned at their entrance. To Theodosia's surprise, Elspeth Blomefield stood among them. Her friend gave a small, slightly disconcerted, wave, as if to say: *Don't start getting annoyed. I didn't mention my invitation in case you'd not received one.*

In the split-second's glance that passed between them, Theodosia's unspoken reply was: *As I, too, failed to mention mine to you. We shall call it quits.*

She waved in return, by then recognising the imposing mass of Erasmus Darwin closer to the fireplace. The rest were strangers.

Introductions were made, and Theodosia found herself in conversation with a lawyer from Derby whose name she had already forgotten by the time that refreshments were served. The arrival of the delectable beverage served steaming and glutinous in fine china cups proved an effective icebreaker in the small gathering, and, amidst general expressions of appreciation and indulgence, she was able to move on to the more congenial female company of the misses Seward and Beasley, laughing at some shared reminiscence over by the room's soaring windows.

"I'm so glad you could both come," said their hostess, with simple warmth, "especially in the light of your message, Mrs Greene. I was determined we should talk at the earliest opportunity. Certain… shall we say *enquiries*… have been put in hand concerning the person in question, though little enough seems to be known about him."

"Known about whom, may one enquire?" boomed the voice of Erasmus Darwin. "Do not, p…pray, tell me I have a rival for your affections."

Despite the intrusion, Anna Seward laughed delightedly at the heavy-handed compliment, replying: "Doctor, dear, how could you suppose such a thing? Do I not sit at your knee with perfect deference in all things poetic and sublime?"

Pleased, obviously, in return, by the neat response, he said to the others: "Are you aware of this young lady's recent triumph at Batheaston, in the renowned salon of Lady Anna Miller, no less?"

The young person in question dimpled with embarassed pleasure, and her angular guest said: "Tell us, do, Anna. I had no idea you have been travelling far afield."

"Well, yes, if the West Country can properly be considered *afield*. My small triumph entailed the placing of one's poems, by invitation, into an Etruscan urn, from which they are taken and read to the assembled guests by some unfortunate gentleman who has not the least control over what he must deliver. Those are then printed and bound in the form of an annual journal circulated amongst the equally unsuspecting." She laughed with every appearance of modesty.

"It really is something of a pot-pourri, if truth be told, though one must admit to a certain gratification on receiving the encouragement and occasional approbation of those whose regard one values."

"Hear, hear," said Theodosia, with rather more emphasis than she intended, adding hurriedly: "The more that the achievements of our sex can be celebrated, the better, as far as I am concerned. Though, of course, you do come from a literary background, do you not, Miss Seward?"

"Indeed, I do, Mrs Greene, just as *these* very rooms were the cradle of inspiration and encouragement of both your own dear Doctor Johnson…" – Theodosia prayed that she would not flush with pleasure – "…and the immortal Garrick. Both had the supreme blessing of Gilbert Walmsley's early patronage, although…" – she could not suppress the frown that creased her plump, pleasant feature – "…of late, I gather that the Doctor has been less than generous in his opinion of our small city's cultural standing in the world. I regret he has been reported as employing the term 'back water' in our regard."

"Which is as untrue as it is uncivil," rumbled Darwin, "though of little surprise, coming from Samuel. A mite too over-pleased with his own celebrity on occasion, is our *Doctor Dictionary*."

Theodosia, at his side, was suddenly beginning to wish that her familial tie to that other Doctor had not been quite so publicly acknowledged by their hostess only moments earlier, when Anna Seward interjected with mock sternness:

"For all that I have foolishly prompted this, I shall hear no more word spoken against our absent friend." She placed a hand upon Theodosia's arm, continuing, in a decidedly conspiratorial tone: "If truth be told, one doubts that even the pyrotechnics of Vauxhall Gardens can compare with the mercifully rare meetings of our *two* Doctors, my dear."

She smiled disarmingly at Darwin, before continuing: "To say it makes for a *combustible* mixture would not be to overstate matters."

Erasmus Darwin snorted, humourously, and indicating he

would replenish his chocolate cup, stumped off. Both Theodosia and her companion regarded their hostess with renewed respect.

"Do you work with lions, too, my dear?" enquired Miss Beasley, quietly, staring after the corpulent figure.

As the guests circulated around their small group, it was a time before Theodosia had the opportunity of reanimating her interrupted conversation with Anna Seward. During the half-hour or so that elapsed, the Apothecary's wife found herself in conversations ranging from the alarming deterioration of the colonial situation to the imminent prospects of a fine day's steeplechasing out beyond the city's racecourse. Not being sufficiently conversant with either topic to provide anything more than a ready ear and the occasional nod, she regained Anna Seward's company with a degree of relief.

Their hostess required no prompting: "The coincidence – if such it can be called – of our Box Club topic and the intelligence transmitted by your husband is not insignificant, Mrs Greene, of that I am quite certain, for I believe that there are tides in our affairs whose ebb and flow we ignore at our peril. To have such a creature – if not yet in our midst – but virtually cheek by jowl, is not a prospect I shall tolerate. Whatever else may occur, I shall employ all my best offices to make certain he is not received anywhere which has regard for the opinion of decent people."

The earnest speaker had failed to notice Grace Beasley's rapid approach as that lady seized the opportunity of breaking away from the lawyer's droning monologue on the merits and demerits of turnpikes. She had come to stand, guilelessly, behind Anna Seward's shoulder, sharing a grin of release with Theodosia. Joining them, she inclined her head, conspiratorially:

"May one enquire, most indiscreetly," she asked, *sotto voce*, her eyes bright with mischievous interest, "the precise nature of a crime so heinous that it merits consignment to Lichfield's outer darkness?"

"The man is a slave-trader, Grace, is that sufficient?" replied the plump woman, with no trace of her earlier good humour, "and, as chance would have it, he now occupies your late brother's house: Walhill, your own childhood home."

The pale eyes seemed to widen, and the angular jaw dropped, though the effect was far from comical.

"Hawson? You are referring to Bartholomew *Hawson*?" she hissed.

Eyes turned towards her, but she appeared not to notice. Before replying, Anna Seward, alarmed at the sudden transformation of her guest, took her by the arm and in company with Theodosia walked her to the comparative privacy of the large room's far side.

"My dear, are you quite well?" she enquired with concern

"*Quite well*'? No Anna, scarcely. I had not dreamt to hear the name of that vile man, here of all places."

"But why…?" she began, her soft features drawn in perplexity.

"I hold him directly responsible for my brother's death and my own penury. Sufficient reason to loathe the very name, I believe?" Her smile was a corpse-like rictus.

"But my dear, surely poor Humphrey died as the result of…"

"…*a fall whilst beagling*?" came the humourless retort. "No, Anna. That was a convenient fiction. The poor, weak man hanged himself from a Walhill tree."

It was her listeners' turn to gape.

"He had been cozened into cards whilst in Liverpool on business," she continued, "In drink, he scarcely had the wits he was born with. The process – for that is what it surely was – took a number of visits to that port, over a period of some months, but time by time, game by game, he was drawn into Hawson's snare like a lamb to the slaughter."

They listened, incredulously, scarcely aware of the low buzz of conversation that continued across the panelled expanse of the large room.

"He won quite handsomely at first, of course, but then, to the poor dear man's surprise, his luck began to change. And then he began to lose and lose again. You can imagine the dreary inevitability of it as well as I. So, that 'run of ill-fortune' continued until the day that he came home, so I am told, a broken man. He had lost it all: the stocks, the bonds, the money that our Father left, all well gone by then. So, what was left to gamble but the Manor itself? He hanged himself next day, presumably while he still owned a rope to do so."

Tears shone in her wintry eyes as she concluded: "The accident was a well-respected fiction, maintained by decent folk who had fond memories of a decent man."

Their hostess's plump face had paled, visibly, during the recounting of the tragic tale.

"Oh, my dear, I am so sorry," she whispered, glancing almost beseechingly at Theodosia as if for corroboration of her raw emotion.

This is so far removed from your accustomed world of poesy and aestheticism you scarcely have the vocabulary to express your own reaction – even to yourself – do you? thought the Apothecary's wife, not unkindly, though with a piercing insight into the hermetic world of the Seward household.

Suddenly, alarmingly, the vitality seemed to drain out of the tall, angular woman: "Oh gracious, I really think I must ask you to see me home, Mrs Greene. I really feel quite…"

She would have crumpled to the floor had Theodosia not seen exactly what was about to happen. She stepped forward and grasped the fainting woman firmly beneath her thin arms, even as their hostess rushed to support.

"Perhaps if you could send for the chair-men we passed on our way in, I can do as Miss Beasley asked of me, when she is able to move," said Theodosia, breathing with the effort of manhandling the still comatose form to a nearby window seat.

By then surrounded by the concerned company, jostling and craning to see the source of the sudden drama, Anna Seward had to clear space sufficient to minister to her stricken guest.

Help was summoned, smelling salts were applied, and within moments Grace Beasley was staring groggily around the concerned faces with a mix of embarrassment and annoyance, wiping eyes, red-rimmed and streaming from the stifling pungency of the salts. She accepted a glass of water and turned to the concerned plump face hovering above her, weakly waving a long, bony-fingered hand:

"Do send all these kind souls away, Anna. I fear the sum of their attentions and your wretched salts will see me off, otherwise."

As if the incident had signalled the end of the gathering, the assembled company was wrapped and hatted only moments later, expressing thanks to their hostess and condolences to her recovering guest as each made their departure. Informed that a sedan chair was waiting in the hall, Anna Seward oversaw Grace Beasley's installation, as Theodosia was helped into her coat by a maidservant.

"Well, what a to-do!" she said, watching as the chair was lifted out through the Palace doors.

As the bearers waited on the gravelled court for Theodosia to join them, Anna Seward placed an arm lightly around her shoulders, saying: "It is most reassuring that you are able to accompany poor Grace back to Milley's, my dear. I should have gone with her, otherwise. Might your husband look in on her, too, do you think? I really am rather concerned. That was, I fear, more than just a passing vapour."

"He will, of course," Theodosia replied. "In fact, might you send one of your people to summon him from Saddler Street now? I agree that there is cause for concern and will be loth to leave Miss Beasley alone until he has seen her."

"You are kindness, itself, my dear. I only regret that we are parting on such terms. I look forward to your company in more congenial circumstances."

"As do I, Miss Seward. Thank you for your hospitality. We must speak again soon."

As the Canon Residentiary's daughter stood, waving after the retreating chair and its striding escort, she thought back to the day's extraordinary denouement.

Coincidence? No, that was most certainly not the word for it. As the doors closed behind her and she re-entered the claustral comfort of the great house, she found herself pondering on the paucity of language.

(19)

ITEM:

A Crucifix in Copper, formerly gilded, twenty eight inches
high, weight, four Pounds, twelve Ounces; it has a Socket
to fix it upon a Staff, in order to be carried in procession
before the Host, by the make, and rude workmanship,
it should seem to be above four Hundred Years old.
Presented by Sir Ashton Lever of Alkrington, Knight.

September, 1646. A Hunter's Moon lit the well-tended garden,
its walls clad in late-flowering clematis and rambling rose, an
espalier with fruit soon ready for picking, its branches stretched,
like bones, against the mellow brick. There was already a keen note
of autumn to the night, and Ashmole was glad of his good cloak,
drawing it closer about him as he waited in the shadow of the
darkened house. The gentlest of taps, an expectation of immediate
response implicit in its lightness, sounded on the boarded gate.

"All are abed, so it will be well to leave your boots by the door,"
said Ashmole quietly. Madden grunted assent, though the levering
off of heavy dragoon boots was no small task for a stiffening back
and a sagging paunch.

They moved inside and entered the stairwell of the house, its
dry, fragrant air, redolent of care, all at odds with a world gone
mad. By tacit consent they trod carefully up the three doglegs
of the stairs and turned into a small parlour at their top. It was
warmed and lit by a low-logged fire which had scented the air
with the tang of woodsmoke and damp; the smell of seasoning
cut short by scarcity and need. The soldier looked around at the
simple comforts of the room: a walnut armchair, leather-backed

and slung-seated, its thick cowhide dully reflecting the fire's red heart. A joined stool beside it, set with a dark, squat, bottle and a trencher of nuts and cheese. A table, its gate part-open, stood against the wainscot panelling, its top covered with plans and written sheets.

Rushlights had been prepared, unlit, and a large candle set in its brass stick, short-stubbed from use, ready to light the strewn table. A small, high-backed settle was set at an angle to the fireplace where the basket's low glow and small jetting flames lit the surround with occasional highlights, dancing upon the blues and whites of tin-glazed tiles.

"A very proper home, Master Ashmole. You are a fortunate man."

Elias, abashed and somewhat disarmed by Madden's obvious sincerity, murmured words to the effect that he was but passing through this, his old family home, and that now, as a long-term resident in London, the old place had been well kept during his many years of absence. Seated now, by the fire, Madden accepted a glass of dark wine which glowed ruby in the light. He sat, straight-backed and not a little tense as Ashmole lowered himself into the chair and raised his own, small, glass.

"To your health, Corporal Madden."

"Aye, and to our *wealth*, also, Master Ashmole," responded the soldier with a solemn nod. For a long moment, silence reigned and the fire hissed and rustled, small lights, small shadows dancing in the room.

"The floor is yours," said Ashmole finally. "And here's a man of good will to listen to your proposition. Pray…" He invited explanation for this, the strangest of trysts, with a wave of his hand.

"Let me first show you a poor, ruined, thing that was once perfect in my grasp," Madden began, "though it has lain in wet and dark, spoiling, these three years past. You may even know something of it, where in truth I do not. I show it as a token of all

I have to tell and – mayhap – to share."

With that, Madden reached inside his coat and passed a crumpled leathery rag across to Ashmole, who accepted it and knelt in the firelight for a closer look. He stared and scanned, turned it over and back, then moved to the table to light the large candle from a fire-kindled spill. Once its flame had sputtered into tall, bright, life he brought it to the stool and set it down beside the untouched cheese. From a pocket appeared a small scrying lens of polished glass which he moved rapidly across the ragged scrap.

Stained with mud and smudged by damp and mildew, a tiny world of iridescence curled and danced around the letter A, foliated jewels and sinuous beasts and serpents twined and played in luscious growths of flower and foliage, whilst a small remaining trace of uncial script hung and flowed across the scrap of ruined page.

A memory of joy, of youthful rapture almost too bright to bear, flashed through his mind as he recalled the first, unforgettable, time he had seen such marvels; the day – the very first day – that the great gospel book had been opened to the choir-school boys. It had been a winter's afternoon of lashing rain, of winds that sought out every nook and crevice of their stony rooms. Hungry, as ever, tired as usual and hoarse from antiphon and psalm, Michael East's shivering charges had been led to the library where he told them he would warm the very cockles of their hearts, a task that would be accomplished, he said, 'with the work of angels'.

The great gospel book had been lifted from its fleece-lined box and laid before his suspicious and distracted class. Then it had been opened.

For Elias, the wind died, the rain ceased, and the itch of impetigo fled away, as the magic, writhing world of ancient enchantment glowed before him in all its illuminated splendour. He had never forgotten that moment when the awful power of beauty broke over him, engulfing his every sense, claiming his heart and soul for the rest of his days.

Not since then had he felt so moved – for here, once again, was more of the same – *and yet not the same* – as had overwhelmed him on that far-off day. He had come to know and love the book's magnificent gospels: Matthew, Mark and – in part – Luke, through the swirling beauty of their pages and the cool perfection of their scribe's hand. And yet this, the torn fragment that he held now in the flickering light, was from a page he had never seen. He had known for some years that the great gospel book had not perished in the zealots' pyres, but had been spirited away and was safely hidden, still. None asked by whom and none asked where; its safety alone was all that mattered: a small beacon of hope for a future day, still so distant that few scarce dreamed of it anymore. But *this*, held now in his hand, defying grime and mildew, from whence did it come? From what could it have been so wretchedly torn? Madden had sat quietly, sipping his wine and missing no flicker, no nuance, of Ashmole's rapt absorption. He had been right: this was his man. This was his time.

"It was the day that Rupert's moles thought to burrow in and pay us a visit," he began. "We, too, thought to dig some holes…"

"Listen!" An urgent hiss.

"There's nought to hear, so what's..?"

"*Listen*, you whoreson dolt! *There*! There, again." This time, the dull thud of a pick, a chink and rattle from somewhere far below, was unmistakable. Helmet cast aside and an ear pressed to the dew-slicked grass, Madden looked up with a feral grin.

"The bastards are mining in from the moat. That's why they've been keeping our heads down since daybreak."

From first light, a hail of fire – musket, canister shot and lethally silent arrows – had kept the sentries low on the northern parapet. A particularly heavy barrage had been directed at the lofty vantage of the Bishop's Tower which scanned the deadly marshes of the northern and eastern moat. Suddenly it all made sense: the foul-smelling reek of mud and privies that had become more evident as each day passed. *The pox-scabs had been draining what little there was in the moat – they would be coming from the north!*

"Call the Officer, and get the lads, *quick!* And Timms…" – the retreating figure halted in his stumbling rush – "…keep your noddle down or you'll be joining Jones and the boy."

That morning, a ragged hole smashed between his eyes had done for Trooper Jones: a shattered jaw and whimpering, bubbling agony for the powder-monkey pinned by Royalist sharpshooters from up on the Beacon Hill. That image of the grinning, black-faced boy whose smile had been shot clean away, was all the reminder that Timms needed. He crawled away with arse-in-the-air caution that might have seemed comic in another place, another time.

Within minutes, the Duty Officer had called the Garrison Commander, and a cloaked group knelt as if in silent prayer, listening, in the shadow of the northern ramparts.

"There's one coming this way, something further down towards the Vicars' Close and, I am informed, another further west," growled the colonel, between the bars of his heavy siege helmet. "Now we'll have 'em, lads! Well done, Corporal, I'll not forget this."

Madden's grin of self-satisfaction was short-lived, when his officer snapped: "Well, are you going to stand there like a bunch of simpering maids? *Dig!* All of you, *now!*"

Hooded lanterns were all they could hazard on the relays of sweating, silently cursing troopers as they began the back-breaking toil of digging down, ever down, before they could track the half-heard sounds – the occasional tell-tale chink of pick on stone – of the incoming mines.

"And when we do find our little moles, we can rip their nasty little snouts off, can't we lads?" grated the Troop Serjeant, Hinde, as he stripped off his buff-coat and breeches to join the dig.

On Gay Hill, five nights earlier, above and beyond the darkened walls, an attentive and respectful group had gathered behind the huge earth-filled gabion baskets of the siege mount. In their midst stood a slim, youthful figure whose natural authority gripped the assembled company like a velvet fist. This was the master of the moles – Prince Rupert of the Rhine, Commanding General of the Royal Horse, favourite nephew of the King and hard-bitten veteran of a score of European sieges.

Tonight, at his personal bidding, fifty Cannock miners – bribed and bullied from their woodland pits in the nearby Chase – were at that moment driving hard towards the northern walls of the huge Close. The springs from Gay Fields and Beacon Hill had been dammed and the deadly quagmire of the northern moat had, for days now, been slowly draining, now low enough for the miners to have embarked upon their stealthy purpose. No man in full command of his senses would have *chosen* to tunnel down into the banks of the age-old morass, but mud-slimed, reeking warrens in constant slip and shifting, moisty, filth were preferable to the fury of a Prince Palatine frustrated in his plans, and so they dug. When Rupert ordered, neither question, nor failure, were options.

In the days to come, three mines would be located and broken into, and snarling, half-human combats fought, slashing and gouging in the foetid, sputtering light of mutton-fat lamps. Miner and counter-miner would thrash in the reeking gloom until two mines were taken and destroyed. Not, though, before Josiah Madden had made the discovery of his life and, unknowingly, stumbled upon the means of his death.

The blackened ruin of the Bishop's Hall served as a backdrop to the countermine excavation that was now wrecking the last tattered vestiges of the Palace garden. The former glories of hammer-beam and linen-fold, and of bleached and weeping murals, lay open to the skies, early fallen prey to the explosive shells of the frightful siege-mortars, dragged from Coventry when Parliament first went against the Close in '42. Along the length of the northern walls, the spoil heaps grew, as sweating gangs dug beneath the shot-battered defenses in search of the incoming tunnels. Furthest to the east, Madden was the first and deepest of his soil-crusted gang. Within the muffling depths of that tunnel, he heard neither the blaring trumpets nor the trembling thunder of drums that brought the garrison lurching to arms. Beyond their labours, on the city side of the embattled Close, an attack in force was sweeping across The Dam causeway towards the South Gate.

In a covering hail of canister-shot, arrows, musketry and wildfire grenadoes, the storming ladders of Gerrard's Regiment of Foot rose above the south walls, whilst their defenders – at first wrong-footed and thinly spread – replied in a rising crescendo of counter-fire. Then, all became an inferno, a formless melee of hacking and scrabbling to gain a foothold on the parapet and the gatehouse itself. Reinforcements from Colonel Russell's 400 strong garrison were by now pouring out along the straggling parapets and down from the shell of the Cathedral Church: a roaring wedge of counter-attack that would shortly break the storm's incoming wave, an assault which, of a sudden eddied in the Gatehouse lee, swirling now with faltering purpose round the pocked and splintered gates. As suddenly as it had risen to smash against the blackened walls, the wave of attackers flowed back in broken disarray across the corpse-strewn Dam, as if sucked back by the tidal force that had dispatched it. A solitary Royalist survivor, abandoned on the wall, was dragged to the beacon-hoist. Noosed and heaved aloft, he jerked and spasmed as his boots kicked in the pitiless void and his bowels emptied onto the stones below.

From the bulwarked safety of the causeway battery, Rupert of the Rhine stared, ashen-faced, across the wicker gabions, enduring the taunts from the embattled walls: "Shoot him down, why don't you? Got no powder for your pistol, Prince?"

His response to the raucous mockery of his legendary marksmanship was nothing more than a slight facial tick, and a hand gripped, white-knuckled, on a gilded pommel. The fury in his eyes the only indication of the silent promise ringing in his head.

When the alarms had sounded, the gang-men had frantically dragged on breeches, boots and breastplates, scrambling off in ragged order to the southern walls.

Madden, sweat-blinded, gasping, and quite unaware of the day-lit drama playing out in the world above, was suddenly, unknowingly, alone. He gouged and levered at the endless black wall ahead, listening, straining, for any tell-tale sounds. Then, without warning, the entire world seemed to fall towards him. As a crushing, searing burn scoured across his left shoulder and side and a blinding shower of earth and rubble deluged down upon his face and head, darkness became oblivion.

A whimpering, wheezing, cry seemed to wake him to pain that flared and blazed all down his side. A choking cough forced a recognition that the mewling cry had been his own. He lay half-buried but still within the tunnel's bore. It had not been the scantily shored excavation that had collapsed but something – *everything* – ahead.

Managing to lift a trembling right hand, he felt around him and found a slimy hardness different from the mud and rubble. His fingers recoiled in involuntary shock from the latent heat of the extinguished lamp, blistering, still, after hours of service. He groped once more, hoping beyond hope for the tinderbox pouched, by lifelong habit, at his hip. There – oh sweet salvation – it was, though half-trapped beneath his twisted form.

With racking pain spasming through his arm and clawed fingers it seemed to take an agonised eternity to first release the pouch, fumble out its contents and then, somehow, to strike, and blow, and coax a tiny flame to life. He willed a numbed and trembling hand to bring the lamp-wick to the box and watched, transfixed, as the oldest miracle brought life to the tallow wick, an eldritch glow that grew and lit the earthen shambles which had engulfed him. He could see now that it had been an enormous, dressed stone that had tumbled first, bringing the black deluge down upon him. Its fall had ripped the flesh from his upper arm and breast. For all the heavy bleeding, movement – agonising as it was – spoke of no broken bones. Gradually he managed to free his legs from the crushing weight of rubble, and with crabbed, floundering, contortion managed to remove what little clothing he wore. He bound the sticky horror of his wounds with torn, earth-stiffened hose which gave no relief, but which might serve to staunch the steady loss of blood already staining the churned soil around him.

Nausea swept over him and he retched over and again, spitting muddy, choking vomit from caked and bleeding lips, until he lay, chest heaving, gasping in the foetid air, against the tunnel wall.

He had stared at the gaping hole ahead of him for maybe minutes, maybe hours, of throbbing pain before he became aware that the fall had revealed a deeper darkness beyond the excavation – a void that seemed, somehow, to radiate a blackness that was absolute in its intensity. He scrambled, first, to his knees with sobbing breaths, and then, lurching into an agonising crouch, lifted the lamp towards it.

In its peep-show flicker, his smarting, mud-encrusted eyes sought to pierce the gloom beyond. A space, a stone lined space – no, *a room* – a chamber, niches glimpsed in the lamp's dim light. A pillar, *pillars*, and an arch. Old, old work, he knew instinctively; more ancient by far than the moulded curves and soaring buttresses above in the lost land of light. This was not the delicate frippery they had heaved down from the West front of the Cathedral, nor the lace-like stonework they had smashed with such relish from the great windows. This was sterner, plainer stuff by far.

As Madden's streaming eyes became a little more accustomed to the ever-shifting twilight, slowly, mistily – like a dissolving film of cataract – a vision beyond comprehension was revealed upon the chamber floor. A flicker of ruby fire, a lucent glimpse of iridescent enamel, an emerald flash, a wink of dull red gold, a jumbled miracle of riches stretched into the darkness. On the edge of the shimmering vision, the dimly recognisable shapes of crozier, candlestick, chalice and cope stood forth from the strewn disarray by virtue of their placing – arrayed around and against what appeared to be a small wooden house. *A house?* Yes, surely that: though its steep, carved gable-ends and pillared, boarded sides spoke more of ancient ships than of any stone-built dwelling in the world he knew. Deep, glowing richness of colour, though dulled by age and gloom, offered half-seen glimpses of stiff and stilted figures painted on its walls; walls, in turn, bossed with metal-set stones that gleamed with pale life in the lamp's tiny, stinking, flame. With the trembling uncertainty of one who fears to ripple the magic calm of a dream-pool, Madden balanced the lamp on the breached sill before him and leaned past it to grasp a niched chalice. His blood-slicked fingers almost lost it, and he kept his hold only by momentarily resting his prize upon a jewelled box-shape below. He brought the cup through and up to his face, feeling the velvet smoothness of the gold against his livid cheek. A blackened tear ran into its bowl as he rolled it to and fro, revelling in its cooling perfection.

Then, reaching down, he found the box-shape was no box at all: its lid, as he strained forward, opened to reveal pages within. A *book*: a great, jewelled, board-bound book, colour dancing in a wild swirl of rainbow-hued beasts and the leaves of Eden. He lifted and held the thick, textured page with trembling fingers, the better to behold it.

At that moment, as if a veil were dropped over his dream-filled eyes, the lamp dipped and died. In the same instant, stygian darkness doused the mesmerising glow, and nightmare flooded back to fill the void. He lost his foothold on the rubble floor and in his lurching, backwards fall the page tore in his grip and he fell, grasping only a ragged scrap. Pain crashed in upon him, and he screamed and buckled from its onslaught. Sweat poured from him as he lay, knowing he was on the verge of losing consciousness once more. He steadied himself with desperate resolution, regaining his knees, drawing deep, shuddering breaths of the foul air. A sudden explosive tremor thudded through the ground as a mortar shell ripped into the turf somewhere in the world above, and he was seized by a frantic urgency. He must somehow hide this lost and secret place.

In total darkness, and with a driven, maniacal strength he would never know again, he felt for the fallen stone, grappling it free from its rubble mound. Weeping, cursing, retching with the effort, the agony, he levered it back into haphazard position, cramming handfuls of bloodied earth and spoil around it. With a shuddering cry, utterly spent, he fell to his knees, knowing he could do no more, just as the muted sounds of calling voices seemed to recall him to a long-forgotten world.

He began to claw towards the sound, stumbling and crawling back along the tunnel's bore as a flicker of lamplight grew ahead.

"Get *back*, get *out*! – *back* if you value your life!" he managed, in a wheezing rasp he scarcely recognised as his own.

"It's all caving in. *Back*, get *back*!" The lamp bearer turned in alarm, colliding with grunting, darkened shapes behind him. "*Out, fast*! Move your bastard bones!"

Calloused hands half-dragged, half-lifted the barely conscious apparition that had collapsed in the tunnel's maw. Bollock-naked, caked with blood and earth, his shockingly white teeth gritted in a rictus of agony. Josiah Madden was, at least, alive.

"'Ow long's 'e bin down thur?" burred a voice among the jostling rescuers.

"Too damned long, judging by the blood he's losing. Careful, or you'll…"

Sound, smell, sight and pain swirled and dimmed. Before final blackness swept in on him, he managed to croak: "…Tunnel, close it…'s a death-trap, don't g…"

The makeshift stretcher was hauled away across the ruined

grass, as the Troop Serjeant turned to the remaining figures.

"Look sharp, lads," he ordered, pointing to a jumble of joists and blackened beams spread amongst the brambles. "Get some of those timbers across that hole, or we'll all find ourselves heading for the Pit before our allotted time!"

Shortly, dragged and dumped, the charred vestiges of the Palace roof lay across an excavation left to the worms.

Ashmole had sat in silence as Madden's dour narrative unfolded, watching the fixed frown and twitching fingers, the facial tic and tensing muscles that strained to bring half-blocked dread back to vivid life. He had succeeded, perhaps more than he knew, thought the watchful man, suppressing a shudder. The dark terror of the countermine had seeped in and filled the firelit room.

"There's more," said Madden, holding out an empty glass, "much more."

20

A Figure of Time, in Brass, gilt, in his right Hand a Scythe; his left points to an enameled Dyal on his Head; nine inches high.

19th April, 1776. "You were well-advised to call me out, my dear," said the Apothecary, quietly, to his wife, as both stood in the gloom of the Hospital entrance hall. Theodosia, having announced that she would be remaining to sit with the invalid, had come downstairs with him, knowing it was the only opportunity for a quiet word.

"I fear that there is a strong likelihood of another incident."

"I felt sure it was more than a case of the vapours," she said, grimly. "Even in our brief acquaintance I have gained the impression of a formidable resolve. She has lost everything at the hands of that vile creature Hawson and yet manages to retain a most engaging and generous nature. For one that has so little left to call her own, she shows no lack of self-regard, where many in her position would simply wilt away."

Only moments earlier, Richard Greene had listened in amazement as the story of old Beasley's ruin had been briefly recounted by his wife, his initial surprise at both the coincidence and the sheer iniquity of her account turning to a quiet anger she recognised in his eyes.

"You have become very fond of the poor lady, I believe," he said, holding her hand in his, "and you are right to be so concerned. She has suffered intolerably, in a manner that must be weighing most injuriously upon her peace of mind. It is not to be underestimated. We know well how pernicious such worry can be." Unspoken memories flashed between them in the dimly lit hall. She moved to take his other hand in hers.

"I simply cannot bear the thought of her being alone, not like this, Richard. If it will help her to talk, to feel that she can unburden herself, well, that can only do good, surely?"

"In every sense, my dear," he affirmed. "I shall make certain that Margery sends over your shawl and a basket – something tasty to see you both through, should the vigil become extended. You'll at least be comfortable in Miss Beasley's big chair, and I know that one of Mistress Ames's girls sees to the fire."

She squeezed his hands and smiled. "How on earth shall you cope without my badgering and hen-pecking, husband? It is a long time since we spent a night apart."

"Oh, I shall find some means of getting by," he replied, grinning. "If you have judged it wiser not to have returned home, I shall be here bright and early tomorrow," adding mischievously, before leaving with some alacrity: "I am sure you won't mind me arriving very first thing!"

Once back at Saddler Street, Greene put the arrangements in hand, forbearing explanation of any kind to a housekeeper wavering between burning curiosity at the Mistress's unexpected absence and annoyance at her interrupted routine. Ignoring snorts and exaggerated sighs, he announced that he would be eating his supper on a tray in the Museum and was not to be interrupted without particularly good cause.

After some time spent winding clocks, wiping finger marks from glass cabinets, and dusting down wall-mounted displays with a large feather duster reserved exclusively for his own use, he bent to retrieve the box from its resting-place and set it on his table. Laying out paper and pens, he was about to open the lid, when he thought he heard a commotion from the street, three floors below. Glancing at his watch, he dismissed any notion that its source could be roisterers from any of the neighbouring taverns and walked to one of the windows to peer down.

The height precluded a view of the street immediately below, and so, in the absence of any further din, he was about to take his seat once more, when the sound of women's voices, raised in obvious altercation, approached from downstairs. Thinking immediately that some crisis must have occurred at Doctor Milley's, he was about to hurry towards the source of the noise when *it* came to *him*. Bursting from the doorway to the Museum, ineffectively pursued by the stout form of Margery, a dishevelled young woman, lank black hair plastered across a tear-stained face, ran towards the astonished Greene.

"Mistress *Crede*? *Agnes?*" he gasped in recognition, before she stumbled, distraught, and collapsed against the table. She, and the box, toppled to the ground, piled papers scattering, pens rolling and ink spilling across the polished floors.

"They took 'im, they took my Joe," she managed, through hiccoughing sobs, her eyes black, furious, as they glared up at him "And the bull, an' all. Knew just where to look, didn't they? When no-one knew but you! Why? Why've you gone an' done the dirty on us now? After all you said 'n' did?"

Aghast at her state and the fury of her accusations, Greene reeled back as though struck.

"You *cannot* – you *must not* – believe that!" he cried "I know nothing of any of this, as the Lord is my witness! How can you believe I would bring such calamity down on you? But *Joe*, what can you mean? Who has taken him, why would..?"

Even before the words were out, he knew the answer with sickening certainty.

Glancing, dismayed, out at the dimming day, he knew immediately that it was too late for any action to be taken until the morn. He turned back, summoning the hovering figure of Margery from where she had taken up sentry duty at the top of the stairs, and with gasping effort together they raised the inert form from the floor, supporting her slack, puppet-like body until he could prop her in his chair. It was as if her outburst had exhausted her last reserves of strength, and she sagged, depleted by her utter exhaustion, as he knelt beside her.

Dispatching the wide-eyed Housekeeper for the brandy decanter, he took a cold, unresisting hand in his and began to speak, urgently, peering into her flat, unseeing stare for some sign of reaction or acknowledgement:

"There is no alternative now but to involve the Constables in this. If Joe has been forcibly removed, then this is abduction, pure and simple, compounded by burglary." He paused, struck by a sudden thought: "Where is the child, your little one?"

The murmured reply was scarcely audible: "Wi' 'er, the old un. What choice did us 'ave?"

"*Us?*" replied Greene, puzzled. "Had you left her with your neighbour before they came for Joe?" She seemed to struggle for a reply, before mumbling:

"It was while I was gone. Came back and they'd 'ad 'im away, the little bull, an' all."

"But why were you putting the little one in care, at all? Were you going somewhere?"

Even before he saw her evasive, downcast eyes, a troubling suspicion was growing in his mind.

"Joe was about to send you into Walhill, was he not, Agnes? He had told you how to go about locating the place of the steps. You must tell me the truth, or face telling the constables. You know that."

She shook her head in abject misery, her lank hair swinging across features that may once have been beautiful. "Joe reckoned as 'ow, whatever 'appened in the selling o' the bull, the secret would be out. Too many folks 'ungry as us, about, not to be puttin' two an' two together, like. Reckoned 'e knew just where to put is 'and on more, afore 'e lost the chance. Couldn't miss the place, 'e said: 'Just 'op over the tumbledown where the frost broke the wall, follow your nose an' look for silver birches, crossed-like, up atop the slope, an' there's the way inside,'idden in the bushes down below.'"

"'E'd seen a big old statue there, broken, fallen-like, lyin' just past where 'e could reach, wi' summat trapped beneath. 'E swears 'e did, an' 'e'd not lie to m…" She burst into helpless tears, her thin shoulders convulsed with grief. "God only knows they'll beat it out of 'im, Mister Greene. God knows they will!"

"But you actually *saw* no-one? Am I correct? You cannot point the finger at Lemman or his crony, you cannot *know* it was them?"

He saw the muddled anger in her face as she tried to understand. "My dear, *I* do not doubt a word of what you say, but how shall the constables – or a court of law – be persuaded? There are no *witnesses*, there are only our suspicions, yours and mine. The hangman deals only in certainties."

She stared at him, speechless, an untouched bumper of brandy clasped in work-grimed hands. Her mouth moved but no words came out, she peered, distracted, from side to side, as if no longer recognising where she was. She was on the verge of complete breakdown, he knew, hysteria scarcely a blink away – and he was to blame. He cursed himself for an unfeeling fool: he had confronted this poor creature with realities harsher than she could possibly bear.

Suddenly he was all brisk efficiency, standing, ordering that a bed be warmed and made ready for Mistress Crede, raising the stiff, twitching woman from her seat, and placing an avuncular arm about her.

"All is far from lost, my dear," he said with a quiet confidence he did not feel. "I shall inform the constables, myself, this very night, and use what standing I have in our city, to convince them that an intervention, in some shape or form, must be made in the morning. Meanwhile, you shall have a draught that will help you to sleep, so that you are best able to relate the background of this business to a Magistrate of my acquaintance. I am not without friends, my dear, and neither shall you and your Joe be. You have my word on that."

Theodosia and Grace Beasley had talked into the small hours, sharing the inconsequential intimacies upon which firm friendships are grown. They had discovered a shared passion for watercolour painting, though Grace favoured *the Picturesque* rather than the flower studies that were Theodosia's chief delight. The Apothecary's wife had enthused the invalid with her suggestion that they would together visit Doctor Darwin's newly established Botanical Garden outside the city, there to pursue their several passions.

"He has built a shell grotto, on the antique model, which is becoming his fern and shade garden, so Richard informs me: a place to satisfy all our requirements. We might even contrive a time there when the Doctor is studying the *sunnier* aspects of his creation!" Had their laughter not been effectively muted by the ancient walls, the Apothecary's wife might have felt at least a frisson of guilt for disturbing the rest of Milley's slumbering residents.

By the time the angular head had begun to show signs of nodding to sleep, Theodosia was settled into the over-stuffed embrace of the apartment's single armchair, a huge, country affair, built, presumably for a farmer's ample haunches. Shawled and well-cushioned, she was asleep even before Grace Beasley's snoring began.

As an habitual early-riser, Theodosia awoke shortly before dawn, though needed several bleary minutes to fully adjust to the why and wherefore of her situation in the tiny, darkened apartment. Drawing a corner of the little parlour's window-curtain back, she peeped out upon a dour, forbidding sky that looked set to win its present contest with first light. In need of stretched limbs and the usual offices, she quietly let herself out, having looked in upon the sleeping Grace. Some moments later, leaving the ancient, somewhat malodorous, privy that looked over the garden below, she retraced her steps past the heavy door of the apartment and along the dim corridor that led, in turn, to a dingy landing. Perhaps it was her memory of the small chapel's role in their providential first meeting that prompted her to cross the landing and, with infinite care, lift the heavy iron latch.

The smell of flowers past their best met her as she ducked to enter the age-old room, a place even less touched by the passage of years than the apartments themselves. Lacking curtaining, the mullions gave back a grey-brown light, which, for all its dullness, drew her to the long sill. Tall shapes defined the outlines of The Close across the still-deserted road, and her eye roamed about the shapes of roofs and spires dimly seen against the leaden sky. Then, though, a light suddenly illumined a high window, off to her left, and her gaze was carried to its source: a narrow rectangle lit against the greater darkness of the tall tower from which it glowed. A figure, dark against the light, stood, unmoving, and though its silhouette gave no clue as to who the silent watcher could be, Theodosia felt the strangest sense that *she* was the focus of the other's gaze, a sense that suddenly, urgently, made her feel she had to turn away, to break a link not of her seeking.

It was as she opened the heavy door and was about to duck under its black lintel that the explosion came. The chapel was consumed by a blinding yellow flash, accompanied by an appalling detonation that shook the building to its foundations. Taken completely unawares, she half-turned and stumbled on the threshold in blinded panic. A smashing impact to her head plunged Theodosia into a skull-splitting second of speechless agony before black oblivion swept over her and she collapsed, unconscious, in the open doorway.

The first feeling was of suffocation, of fighting for breath that would not come, then a salt-tanged wetness all around her on the floor. *Floor?* A numb cheek lifted, a mouth gasping, from a puddle of blood. *What was she doing..?* And then the pain: a spiked wedge that seemed to be levering her skull away from her throbbing face.

A tidal wave of nausea hit her, and she slumped back onto a floor stained red from her grazed and swollen nose.

Outside, other explosions still echoed distantly, no longer shaking the house. She sensed glass still in the window, a window still set in its wall. How had she – how had *anything* – survived? *No, she had not imagined it: there was another, closer detonation*, again, a dazzling slash of razor-sharp light that lit her crumpled body.

Gradually, a vestige of identity and place returned to her and she was able to prop herself in the doorway, gingerly touching her nose and the throbbing lump that now protruded from her temple. She could make sense of none of it, but with painful, swaying effort, regained her feet and stood, breathing raggedly, outside the doorway. Without warning, a door across the landing opened and a wide-eyed, elderly woman stood, gaping, at first with an expression of almost comic disbelief that turned to horror at the sight of the blood-spattered apparition framed in the chapel doorway. Another lightning-flash silhouetted her nightmare vision, and the screaming began.

The Apothecary's promise of an early arrival had been much delayed by the previous night's upset at Saddler Street – an unwelcome demand upon her husband's time and energy of which the suffering and increasingly fretful Theodosia was, naturally, unaware. After making certain that a pair of constables had, in fact, ridden off to Walhill at first light, as promised, Richard Greene had patiently explained the nature of an affidavit to the hollow-eyed Agnes. He had omitted the fact that he had agreed to the swearing of it only with some reluctance the night before, as the sole means of convincing a rarely sober magistrate of his acquaintance of the good character of Joseph Crede and of the threats against the missing man that he had, himself, witnessed. Thus, it had been closer to nine before he arrived at the Hospital door, blithely unaware of what awaited him.

"You say you were unsettled by the figure that you saw, but how on earth could he have known you were there, my dear?" Richard Greene enquired gently, applying the comfrey compress with the lightest of touches to her swollen brow. She winced, despite his care, and replied weakly:

"I just *knew*, that's all. It was as if he'd been waiting for me." She glanced up at him, adding: "If you dare to laugh at me, Richard Greene, you will regret it."

With complete seriousness her husband replied: "I am neither so thoughtless nor so foolish, my dear. The source of this light was in a *tower*, you say? Across the street and to your left? I am a trifle perplexed, that is all."

"Oh, when are you *not*, for pity's sake, Richard. I can bear no more of this cross-examination. Take me home if you have a grain of pity, I've seen enough of terrified old women to last a month of Sundays."

Theodosia sat propped in Mistress Ames's neat lodging, where she had been taken when the uproar had brought the Warden scurrying out. Knowing full well that the lady's brisk solicitude came a poor second to her wanting the object of bloody terror removed from public display with all speed, Theodosia had had little choice but to endure the chilly silence of the Warden's disgruntlement and the notable absence of any form of restorative. As if reading her uninvited guest's mind, that lady had, in fact, commented that she believed strong liquor to be the Devil's tool, offering, instead, a pottinger of thin gruel to her guest.

Before acceding to his wife's request, Greene had excused himself for a time, part of which was spent examining a much-restored Grace Beasley. That lady, having slept the dreamless sleep of the virtuous, (as she said, with a laconic smile, in answer to his enquiries), was looking far better than the Apothecary might have expected. Explaining that Theodosia had suffered a mild concussion from a fall taken at the outset of the remarkable thunderstorm, he reassured the concerned friend that all was well and that he would shortly be taking her home. He did not add that in view of his wife's obvious distress she would be conveyed there by sedan-chair. Nor, on parting with a promise to call again next day, did he mention that the scene of her accident would be his last port of call.

Moments later, he stood at the chapel window, looking across the now-bustling road to The Close beyond. After a while spent gazing at the view, a thought seemed to strike him. He pulled a well-thumbed pocket almanac from his coat and flipped through its leaves.

"Thursday, April 20th," he read aloud, as if confirming something to himself. "How *very* peculiar."

21

A Mahogany Case, covered with Glass. A piece of Gold Lace,
found in a stone coffin in Lichfield Cathedral. In a small Mahogany
Box, in the form of a Coffin, a piece of Flint, in the shape of a
Child's Head, found at Exmouth, in Devonshire; given by Mr Lister.

Thursday 20ᵗʰ April, 1642. Washed, bandaged, and sedated with
enough poppy-juice to pacify a Wildman, no tunnel-sounds
penetrated the billowing clouds of Madden's drugged slumber.
In fact, amongst the oblivious garrison of The Close, no ears at
all caught the tap of hammer, the chink of pick against pebble,
the rasp of timber being dragged unseen, nor the sound of
barrelled powder being stacked – keg upon keg – along the third
mine's undiscovered bore. Beneath the north-west tower at the
corner of the walls, at the end of 120 feet of unsuspected tunnel,
a noisome cave, carved out by Cannock miners, was now finally
packed and ready, its contents every available barrel of black
powder that could be wrested from royalist garrisons the length
of the country.

Beyond the battered walls, across the moat, and, as it would
transpire, far too close to the unsuspected souterrain, stood Doctor
Milley's Hospital, whose unscathed, tall-chimnied survival was
little short of miraculous amongst the blackened, shot-blasted
ruins of every other building within range of the Close artillery.

By strangely tacit consent, its little household struggled to
ignore the dance of death enacted within yards of its porch and –
by equally strange consent – was spared by friend and foe, alike.
The fact that the Hospital's proximity to the walls rendered it

both an unmissable target and an untenable forward-observation post being the only conceivable explanation for its charmed, and continuing, existence. Elsewhere, above and below it, along the length of Beacon Street, the Prebendary Houses, The Vicars Houses, the once-prosperous merchant houses, were burnt-out shells whose enduring brick chimney stacks offered easy sport to gunners numb with boredom.

Shortly before her treasured clock struck seven, Mistress Gentle, Warden of the little institution, fussed around her domain, rekindling the low fire that burned the twelve-month round in the dim hall. She had bent to rearrange an errant firedog, fallen askew during the small hours, when she straightened with a start, in a sudden, dreadful stab of premonition. Somewhere outside, a trumpet sounded and a moment later her world came to its end in a monstrous gale of shattered window-glass and shrapnel.

At a minute past seven – with as much precision as could be ensured by an over-long fuse laid on a tunnel floor most resembling a stream-bed – the first explosive mine to be detonated in war-ravaged Britain, blasted out of its hidden chamber beneath the corner tower. A jarring, bone-shaking tremor rattled and shook every man, beast and building for a mile around, as the colossal eruption slammed through The Close beyond.

Late sleepers crashed from truckle beds, groggy eyes stared in blank, half-wakened terror, cursing figures stumbled into boots and breeches, grabbing for tumbled arms. Plaster dust and rubble rained down on unprotected heads and great shards of flying glass sliced and shattered down from the jagged remains of windows until now beyond the reach of wanton damage.

The entire outer face of the North-West Tower had collapsed onto the palisaded earthen bulwark around its base, consigning its sentries and gun-crew to a rubble tomb. High above, two bloodied survivors, blinded and deafened, flailed in stunned agony amidst the wreckage of a tower-room now laid obscenely bare by the ripping blast. Shockingly breached, the Close walls to left and right haemorrhaged their rubble core in a filthy stream into the moat below.

A cacophony of trumpet calls, muster-drums and the disembodied shouts of impending rout echoed round The Close, as the Royalist storming force poured across the northern moat. With a calculated mix of tact, bluster and cajoling humour, the Regiments of Horse had been persuaded to fight on foot that day; chosen men from Rupert's own Regiment, Anthony Dyott's Lichfield Troop, Colonel James Usher's Regiment of Dragoons and Colonel Digby's Regiment of Horse joined the much-depleted ranks of Gerrard's Regiment to plunge into the breached inferno.

Nothing had been left to chance. With wattle hurdles flung before them, speeding the advance across the deadly marsh, to where – within minutes – a hellish conflict was being fought in the stifling confines of the little courts and alleyways that made a warren of the Vicars' Close. Cracking gunfire and grenadoes hurled down from windows carved hideous swathes in the attack as it boiled through the funnelling passages towards the open Greens around the Cathedral Church itself. A breastwork of the dead and wounded was, by now, heaped across the breach, and the last of the invaders had first to claw their way across this bloodied mound to reach the fight beyond.

Virtually every officer of Rupert's force had fought his way through the breach. Within minutes Colonel Usher was dead from a slashing sabre-cut, Lord Digby was slumped in a porch with a ball-shattered knee, while Rupert, himself, had taken a pistol-shot in his boot which had torn a bloody furrow across his foot. Unseen, somewhere in the carnage beyond, the prince's chaplain, Erskin, was felled by a bludgeoning pike and dragged, captive, into an inner court by a garrison fighting with the ferocity of cornered beasts.

Within the hour, though it had seemed an endless, savage eternity in the choking alleys and dark traps of this medieval village, trumpets and hoarse, powder-burned voices called 'Retreat'. Of several hundred hand-picked men, less than half withdrew from the death-trap they had so spectacularly sprung.

Unconscious on his palliasse, safely removed from the shambles outside, Madden had been troubled neither by the thunderous roar nor the ebb and flow of the unseen battle. A sheen of stinking sweat covered his untended face and neck as his infected body twitched and spasmed with a soaring fever. In the hour, two days later, that his fever broke, so, too, did the faltering resolve of the Garrison Commander. Under a flag of truce an emissary emerged from behind the shattered walls.

In the terse meeting that followed, Rupert's normally implacable vindictiveness was effectively tempered by Colonel Russell's blunt statement that – unless Quarter and Acceptable Terms be granted – all Royalist prisoners held within the fortress Close would starve to death unless, mercifully, they had already had their throats cut in order that their suffering not be prolonged.

Staring bleakly across the swamp wreckage to the scorched sandstone walls, the Prince had no way of knowing that the message had been sent from a garrison possessing but one remaining barrel of powder, with all its match already spent. Equally, the garrison could not know that Rupert was newly in receipt of an urgent summons from his king to ride with all haste to the relief of Oxford. Although the price of its taking would sound only a sourly discordant note his royal master's ears, the Prince Palatine knew that Lichfield was, for now, a spent force: a strategic fortress denied to Parliament.

So it was that, after the rapid appointment of a Negotiator and Broker of the King's Peace, a flamboyant cavalcade of cavalier Horse swept out of the despised siege-lines around the city and disappeared westwards in a cloud of dust and unpaid bills, the Articles of Surrender being agreed within hours of their departure.

With colours flying, drums rattling, and muskets apparently primed, Russell's garrison rode out. For most, the quitting of the pocked and stinking fortress was the source of purest joy, for others an uneasy marriage of survival and bruised honour. For one, though, Josiah Madden, it was an unrelieved disaster.

Jolting painfully along the broken paviors of the old Bishop's Bridge, the carts that bore the wounded carried him ever-further from the darkling vision that still danced and burned behind his exhausted eyes. It would be more than three bitter years before he could finally return.

(22)

In the Center, below the ALTAR Table. In a Glass Case,
a variety of Artificial Flowers, by Mr Coe, of Greek-
street, So-Ho, London, surrounded by Filigree work,
made of Spiral Paper, the Edges of which are gilded.

21st April, 1776. "After being with us for more years than I care to
remember, Tillett is more than capable of doing all that needs to
be done for the next day or so Theodosia. So, do, I beg of you, stop
being difficult." Forestalling his wife's half-hearted objections,
Greene continued: "Frankly, if you feel up to doing anything
whatsoever, you would do me an invaluable service if you could
offer some mite of comfort to poor Agnes Crede. I can hardly
keep her confined to the kitchen, given the state of hostilities
declared by Margery. In the odd moments I have dared to trespass,
it was perfectly obvious that the poor girl is 'in the way' wherever
she sits or stands."

Despite her employer's best attempt to quietly explain the
distressing circumstances of the young woman's enforced stay,
Margery had taken grave – and apparently, irreparable – exception
to being manhandled aside at her own door and being then
powerless to prevent *The Master's* Holy of Holies from invasion.
The fact that *The Master* had subsequently welcomed the intruder
under his roof and been entirely sympathetic to Agnes Crede's
desperate plight was neither here nor there to a Housekeeper at
war.

"But what of the child, Richard?" asked Theodosia in a nasal
croak, "even if the old creature you mentioned could be trusted

with her, that poor girl will not want to be parted from such a little one."

"Precisely the reason to impose upon your good nature, my dear," Greene replied, persuasively. "I mean to ride out towards Walhill as soon as I can. The constables have yet to return and I may well meet them on the way. I shall look in on the crone to satisfy myself that the child is being properly cared for, but that being the case, it is only prudent that Agnes is out of harm's way. She, after all, was the unwitting cause of so much bad blood in the first place."

Having grudgingly acceded to Richard's request, it would only be later, as Theodosia had a chance to observe the distracted, pallid young woman at the close quarters of her sewing-room, that the shrewd gaze assessed Agnes Crede as only one woman can another. Noting the eloquent dark eyes, the angular grace, and the ample figure that not even a homespun kirtle and coarse pinnafore could conceal, the Apothecary's wife pondered on the word *unwitting*, and found she could not quite share her husband's certainty.

For all the gravity of the circumstance that saw Greene sedately trotting through the deep-cut lanes that noontide, the miracle of April could not fail to lift his tiredness and jaded spirits. Already the boles of wayside elms were in tiny leaf, with the mossy banks aglow with primrose and periwinkle now that the brief cold snap of *blackthorn winter* was passed. Beyond the budding hedgerow to his left, he glimpsed the filmy-white bells of wood-sorrel, pale against the dappled shade of a small copse that ran to the lane.

Passing through a shallow ford, he allowed his mare a drink, relishing the sights and sounds all about. He sat, entranced, watching a pair of unseasonally late remaining green sandpipers on the oozy banks, whilst ahead, from the woodlands on the rising ground towards Walhill, came the feverish chatter of some huge, unseen flock of fieldfares, massing for their North Sea flight. As so many times before, he marvelled at the blunt imperative of migrations, as if these Baltic-bound travellers could sense the thawing of the spruce forests and knew they had no choice of destination but there. Scarcely half a mile further on, as horse and rider ambled below a wooded ridge, the exquisite aroma of young larch-sprays seemed to fill the air, where its boughs were home already to the first of the willow-wrens, their soft, dropping song chiming upon the light wind.

He had almost reached the ramshackle cottage when he saw, to his relief, the darting form of a child at play in the lane outside, a kitten scampering away from grabbing hands and the sound of laughter as she renewed her chase. He was about to call out a greeting and dismount when a flicker of movement at the top of the lane caught his eye. Squinting in the sunlight, he recognised one of the city constables by his height and girth, standing beside what was presumably his fellow, both seemingly occupied in some unseen business between their tethered horses. Nudging his mare up past the incurious playing child, he waved to attract their attention. The taller of the two, recognising the mare's rider, beckoned urgently. Greene felt his heart sink as he urged her forward to meet them.

Reining in beside them, he saw, to his astonishment, that what was occupying the men was the inert form of the erstwhile child-minder. He cursed his presumption in assuming that she must have been somewhere near the carefree little girl, the child who now stood, staring up the lane in their direction, her game apparently forgotten.

"She just came a-wobbling out of there," said the one called Hobley, pointing to a broken wall marking the boundary of what looked like an unkempt orchard, "…and passed out, like. Toppled down in the road in front of us, Mr Greene."

The Apothecary dismounted gracelessly, stiff from the saddle, just as a groan sounded from the old woman supported between them. Both relinquished their burden with obvious relief as Greene hurriedly spread a woollen blanket retrieved from a saddle-pannier and bent anxiously over the malodorous form as it began to stir.

Suddenly, as if jolted awake, rheumy eyes snapped open and the beginnings of a thin wail of terror issued from the thin blue lips. Immediately, Greene lifted the head in its grubby bonnet, saying: "You are with friends. You are quite safe. What has befallen you?"

The eyes flickered left to right, as yet no comprehension within them. At his instruction, Hobley fetched a hip flask from the coat rolled across Greene's saddlebow, and the Apothecary held it to her mouth, allowing her no more than one, then a greedy second sip, when the prone figure tasted the brandy.

For a long moment she seemed to gather herself, then with a feeble reaching towards the flask which Greene forestalled, she said: "'E's in there, dead as dead, Master. 'Anged, done awa' wi' 'isself."

Greene sprang to his feet, regretting it instantly as the pain of aching muscles lanced through his legs and back. Ignoring them, he straightened with desperate resolve, already knowing the answer to his urgent question: "Who can you *mean*?" He barely resisted the urge to shake a reply from her, continuing: "*Quickly*, Mistress, who is dead?"

Even before she replied he was gazing, stricken, towards the orchard beyond the wall. "Crede, Aggie's Joe," she whispered. "'Anged 'isself, Master. 'Onest 'e 'as."

Shouting to Hobley's stocky fellow constable, presently gazing hopelessly down at them, to stay with the old woman, Greene grabbed a surprised Hobley by the arm and hurried him towards the gap in the tumbledown wall.

"Run," he gasped, "Find him as fast as ever you can, for pity's sake. He might be still alive."

Panting in the constable's heavy-footed wake, the Apothecary clambered into the run-down enclosure. Beyond them, through the still-ordered ranks of straggling, uncared-for trees, stood the remains of a bothy. "There! Try *there*!" called Greene, watching as the officer veered off towards it. He reached the broken-down gable a moment after Hobley, who was standing, face a bloodless white with horror, staring down at the sight that met them in the ruin's rubble-strewn interior. The body of Joe Crede lay sprawled, his remaining limbs jumbled like a broken toy, the head grotesquely twisted on a broken, rope burned neck. The makeshift noose still bit deep behind an ear ripped half away, the dangling length from which it came, still strung across a beam above.

"It must have broken under his weight," murmured the constable, showing not the slightest inclination to approach the body. Even from where they stood, both men could see the damage the fall had apparently inflicted on the hanged man's face, glistening in red ruin amongst the broken tile-shards and brick rubble where it lay.

The Apothecary spent several, painstaking moments beside the body of the man he had tried so hard to save, sickened by the bestial waste of what they had found, increasingly aware that little in this squalid scene was what it seemed. When he stood, finally, rubbing aching knees, he peered up at the rope-end dangling down, and indicated its end.

"Hobley, you will note the fact, if you please, that this did not break of its own accord. It has been cut."

The constable gaped in bewilderment. "But how could a hanging man..?"

Greene ignored the question, continuing: "You will note also, if you please, that all of these abrasions to the face were inflicted *before* death, not – as it has been made to appear – by the body falling."

"But, with respect, Mr Greene, how can you..?"

"By the simple fact that a human body does not continue to bleed after death, constable. Joe Crede's shirt is soaked in blood from the facial injuries, and here," he stooped to lift the dead man's shirt, revealing welts and bruising around the ribs, "...clear evidence of a vicious beating, delivered, most likely, when the poor soul was strung up here, but before he was hoisted up and hanged. Look at his wrists, and once more note carefully what you observe." Beneath the threadbare cuffs of his shirt, Crede's wrists, too, bore burn-marks from viciously tight bonds.

"You'll be reckoning this is *murder*, then, Mr Greene?" enquired Hobley, dully, as if reluctant to confront the fact. "He didn't do away with hisself after all?"

"Does the evidence of your own eyes suggest otherwise, constable?" responded the Apothecary, with diminishing patience. "Do you see evidence of a crutch? Do you see any means by which a one-legged man might have contrived his own hanging?"

The constable remained silent, though increasingly resentful of Greene's implication.

"It is most important that you fix every salient point of this scene in your memory. You will assuredly be called to give it as evidence when Lemman and his crony are brought to justice."

"*Lemman*, Mr Greene? You are referring to the men Lemman and Pearce, in Mr Hawson's employ?" replied Hobley with a degree of asperity, "I fear you are mistaken, there, on both counts."

"No, I fear I am *not*, constable," the Apothecary replied angrily. "This is the handiwork of that pair of brutes, just as I warned could be the case in this vile abduction. The man was a helpless cripple. *This...*" – he gestured, helplessly – "...no less than what they promised him in my hearing."

"But *what* abduction, Mr Greene?" replied Hobley, carefully, taken aback by the fierceness of the other's conviction. "Not only were there no *witnesses* to any such thing, but Crede's wife said as much herself, and before he left, Mr Hawson explained that none of his men could possibly have had a hand in any wrongdoing, as they had spent all of yesterday – and yester eve – in his constant sight, packing up for his departure this morning. He said we were welcome to talk to them if we wanted to. Most polite and helpful about it all, he was. No point in doing that, though, not after him giving us his word, and all."

Greene, suddenly at a loss to know which question to ask first, pointed down at the brutalised corpse and spoke in cold fury: "So this will be adjudged the work of *person or persons unknown*, in your book, will it, constable?"

"That's for a court of law to d…"

Greene interjected before he could finish: "And why did *you both* decide to take Mr Hawson at his word? His word about the scum he chooses to employ?"

The constable bristled at the accusation in the Apothecary's tone: "Why, because he's a *gentleman*, Mr Greene! Who's to gainsay a gentleman standing in his own parlour?"

The Apothecary was lost for words. He turned and began to walk away. Then he paused, ducking back beneath the sagging lintel to enquire: "And to where has your *gentleman* departed on this fine morning, constable? Did you think to enquire?"

"Of course, we did, Mr Greene. That's our job, isn't it?" came the satisfied reply: "*Foreign parts*, he said."

(23)

Three Chalices of Pewter, much decayed, some Gold
Lace, and a piece of the upper-leather of a pair of Shoes,
found at different periods in making Graves in Lichfield
Cathedral. Most of the above Articles are placed on a lofty
Shelf, or Table, inlayed with Mahogany, and supported
by four clustered columns of the Gothic order.

September, 1646. Time seemed somehow suspended in the little
Breadmarket Street parlour, the muted stirrings of the grate's small
fire the only counterpoint to the soldier's continuing narrative:

"Though saying it might sound like double Dutch, it was
the best and the worst time of my life, rolled into one, Mister
Ashmole," No more the mocking 'master' now, for this grim and
urgent man.

"The hurt I'd taken was more than any man should have to
bear, but what I *saw* down there…" To Ashmole's alarm, a sudden,
racking, sob seemed to shake Madden to the core, but as Elias
rose, instinctively, towards the trembling man, Madden's hand
rose to ward off contact, and – blazing from the scarred face –
fierce eyes blinked back further tears.

"You cannot begin to know what was in that place – gold
and jewels, silver and great candlesticks, but…" – all at once he
looked completely lost, his shoulders sagged, his palms opened
imploringly – "…there was something *more*, besides, something I
can find no words for. It will not leave me, day nor night: dreaming,
not dreaming, oft-times I know not which, I'm off in such a spin.
There's something…" – he fought for the word, screwing eyes

tight in concentration – "...*greater*, *different*, down there, but..." – he stared wildly at Ashmole, spittle hanging from his stubbled chin – "...what more *can* there be than a King's treasures like I've seen. Why am I tormented by this... something *greater*? I do not understand."

As if spent and emptied, all animation fled from him. He slumped, slack-jawed and staring into the dying fire. Ashmole was astounded by the intensity and passion of this strange and secret man and knew, to the marrow of his bones, that some deep, secret thing lay waiting for its time, its call, to come.

Then, as if for the first time, the full implication of what he held in his hand dawned upon Elias. Why was it a *torn* scrap? Why was it stained and ruined? How had Madden come to possess only this?

"Are you saying there was more of the book from whence this came?" he demanded, urgently.

"*More?* It is *all* there, in jewelled covers," responded Madden.

Ashmole looked at him, appalled, unable to keep the dawning horror from his face: "You mean you tore this from its bindings? You chose to..?"

Before he could continue: "*Choice* was no part of it," Madden interposed, angrily. "I was grasping a page when I fell. It tore in my hand. I had forgotten its very existence until I went back to... that place... and found it lying where I must have let it fall. It was not a time of thought, or reason, when I fled that vault. Have you not *understood* that?"

Ignoring the question, Ashmole stared fixedly at what he held, realising with absolute conviction that the mildewed scrap was nothing less than a page of one of the great Anglo-Saxon gospel books. To be more accurate – his pulse raced with the crystal certainty of the realisation – what Madden had touched and torn was the second, the *other* volume whose existence had long been suspected but never recorded.

On that far-off afternoon, Michael East had explained how

St. Chad's Gospels – as Lichfield's great book was known – were incomplete. The volume contained the words of the Evangelists Matthew and Mark, a small part of Luke's text, but none of John. Ashmole vividly recalled how, his eyes twinkling with the mischievous delight of the born storyteller, East had woven a tale of ancient loss or theft, or even treasure trove that hid the vanished words of testimony and witness. Here, now, in an upstairs parlour in Breadmarket Street, he, Elias Ashmole, held the clue, the proof that would unlock an age-old mystery. His head reeled with fantasies of a scholarly reputation made and crowned in one, *The Ashmole Gospels* as centerpiece of a great collection, a grateful nation proffering thanks and...

He landed heavily back in the present as Madden's voice cut through his soaring reverie: "So, Mister Ashmole, I cannot re-enter that place alone. I must have some help – strong and *trusted* help – or all that I have seen must stay and rot in darkness."

Elias, now fully returned to his wits, enquired: "How are we to trust one another, Madden? The lure of riches and rewards has brought naught but disaster since Adam's Fall."

Madden looked shrewdly at the half-lit figure that leant earnestly towards him, before replying: "I think, Mister Ashmole, that in that place lies reward enough for any ten men such as us. For you it may be the book and..." – he gestured around the room's scholarly clutter – "...sundry relics and remains of little interest to one such as me."

He grinned disarmingly, continuing: "Some weighty sacks of gold and jewelled baubles will satisfy my heart's desires for all the years I've left ahead." He stood then and held out a large, calloused hand to Ashmole. "So, shall it be a pact of each man's interests and both men's profit?"

"By God, it shall, Madden. It shall," replied Ashmole rising to his feet. "You make good and simple sense. Together we can accomplish our heart's desire and make our several fortunes." They gripped hands, and then Ashmole refilled Madden's glass, only now taking another drink himself to seal their bargain.

"There is much to plan, in detail, for the endeavour to prosper," said Ashmole, moving to the littered table and starting to pile charts and spread sheets of parchment onto any spare surfaces he could find.

Madden glanced, at first incuriously, at the jumble of sheets, and then bent to retrieve a page from the boarded floor. He peered at the chart, the arcane symbols, the scribbled calculations of Mercury Ascendant and Jupiter's Decay, then looked sharply at Ashmole: "Men have burned for less than this, Mister Ashmole. Have you made a darker pact than ours?" Elias laughed and took the horoscope from Madden's hand.

"Assuredly not, for here's no darker purpose than the movement of celestial spheres and the way that all men's lives may be touched by the time and place of birth. Many believe that there are tides in these affairs of ours, and deep waters to be fished – or crossed – for profit or loss. I and others like me seek only to rescue lore and knowledge from the mire of history, and to preserve much that we believe to be of value from such scraps and relics as survive." He gestured towards the Gospel fragment now set carefully aside: "There is one such clue. Its very age and origin hold a treasure to match all your jewels and coin, though…" he added with a wry smile," both can serve a multitude of needs that I, for one, do not scorn!"

The two parted at first light, having discussed over and again the difficulties of an enterprise whose secrecy was paramount. They had agreed on the means of re-entering the vault and, generally, on how to remove the contents Madden had so vividly described. There was now an easy, tacit understanding that there would be little of conflicting interest in the division of the finds, as it seemed unlikely that more could be removed than could be carried in the brief dark hours at their disposal. They had agreed that only one foray would be possible as even that would pose a multitude of problems for just two men working silently at night.

They proposed to remove all they could to the tumbled shell of the Bishop's Palace, where Madden had contrived a cupboard-like space behind the fallen timbers and overgrown rubble of what had once been the Screens Passage of the Hall. With Madden's prompting, Elias had drawn a ground-plan of the ruin so best to plan access and exit. After the slightest hesitation, Madden had pointed a stubby finger to the approximate location of the covered tunnel, and what he guessed to be its length and direction.

"From your account, this is an ancient vault or cellar long since lost or forgotten. It seems to be no part of what stood above until so recently." The Palace was, he thought, the medieval work of Bishop Langton, but what they sought would seem, mysteriously, to be much older.

Although Elias had made little of it during Madden's description of all that he had seen in the briefly lit vault, Ashmole found himself returning repeatedly to the strange description of *a little wooden house with gabled ends, all painted on its walls.* Something about it stirred a chord of memory, teasing a nagging echo from somewhere in his schooldays, but *what?*

He was still sitting, pondering on this, and dreaming of much else, besides, when the scolding voice of Mistress Joan roused him sufficiently for an early breakfast followed by several hours of stupefied sleep.

(24)

A Pig of Lead, weight near one Hundred and fifty Pounds, on
which, in raised Letters, appear the name of Vespasian, and of Titus
Vespasian, Emperors of Rome. It was discovered in the Year 1772,
in digging for Gravel on Hints Common, about four Miles from
Lichfield, and three Quarters of a Mile from the Roman Road,
called Watling Street, at the depth of four Feet beneath the surface
of the Earth, presented to the Museum by Ralph Floyer, Esq, Hints.

22nd April, 1776. "Well, she has gone, Richard, and that's all there
is to it," said the Apothecary's wife, in a voice hoarse with over-
tiredness and annoyance. "One moment she was there, meek as
a kitten, and butter wouldn't melt, and the next – gone. Bur not
without some small change from the dresser and – Margery swears
to this, too – a carving knife from the box on the breakfast-room
wall. I'll not be blamed for *any* of this, husband, so you can point
that prickly face elsewhere until you accept the fact."

"Oh, my dear, you misread me, I fear," he said coming to
take her hands in his. "You see not annoyance but sorrow – and
downright fury at my own shortsightedness. We found poor Joe
Crede dead, in the most distressing circumstances. It is a foul
business, already being hopelessly bungled by the idiot constables
sent out to do a man's job. They have permitted the creature,
Hawson, to swan off to the Lord knows where, having accepted
his word as a gentleman…" – the unremarkable features registered
their withering contempt – "…that none of his hirelings left his
sight yesterday and were thus blameless."

Theodosia realised she had seldom, if ever, seen her husband in such a fury, as he continued: "The man's sheer mendacity is matched only by his henchmen's brutish cruelty – none of them must be allowed to escape their just desserts. In fact, I've a mind to… a mind to…" He stopped, speechless at his overwhelming sense of impotence.

She came to him and took the small man in her arms: "I know full well how the vileness and the sheer injustice of this must be hurting you, my dear, but you must not permit circumstances beyond your control to send you into a decline. Your selfless actions to help that poor man and his little family do you nothing but credit, Richard, but you must, I beg you, now leave it there. Neither you nor I can be held responsible for that young woman's plight, and I will not permit you – and neither must you allow yourself – to chase after her, now."

At that moment, both knew that the unspoken fact of the stolen knife lay between them like the spectre in a Garrick play, neither of them wanting to dwell upon the use to which it might be put.

"But the *child*, Theodosia…"

She stopped him with a hand to his lips. "…cannot become your responsibility, Richard. From what you have said she is being cared for after a fashion no less typical than you will find in any village the length and breadth of this county."

He looked at her in bleak silence as she continued: "The plight of the rural poor – and their children – has long been an active concern of our Box Club and many others, you know that, but had I permitted myself to rail, hopelessly, against the colossus of inequity to be overcome, you would be married to a madwoman, Richard."

The Apothecary knew that this caring, intelligent woman was unarguably right, but could scarcely cope with the rising tide of guilt within himself. Not only at the squalid tragedy whose next act might well be unfolding even as he sat, inactive, within his comfortable world, but also the fact that Theodosia knew nothing of a white-gold bull nor the extent to which it – and the dark place of its centuries-old concealment – were haunting his thoughts, night and day. He could recall all too well the siren voices that had plagued him on his ride back to the city only hours earlier: *Had Joe talked? Had Joe told them where to look? Had Joe died to protect the secret from his tormentors? Had Joe died in vain, unable to take more pain, unable to protect a secret they had beaten from him before they had left him dead?*

Had his life depended on it, at that moment, Richard Greene could not have given names to the welter of conflicting emotions that raged within him. The sole certainty, though, was that he must try or fail, albeit disastrously, in the attempt. At another, sombre, time in their lives, he had failed to share his fears with her, failed to trust the power of the love that had bound them for so long. Then, he had come within a hairsbreadth of destroying not only their marriage but also their very lives: it was not a mistake he would ever make again. Taking both her hands in his he sat her down, then, trying to find the courage he did not feel, began:

"There is, I fear, more to this than meets the eye, my dear…"

Climbing to his Museum refuge some time later, a chastened but hugely relieved Greene could well have done without the alarming presence that lay in wait for him as he reached the top of the stairs. Margery, face wrinkled in what he read as a mixture of contrition and annoyance, advanced from the shadows, arms folded across her aproned bosom, nodding towards a Museum room only dimly lit from the street below.

"She broke it, you know…" she began, "and that was even before the thieving little hussy took advantage of us all. Cracked all round the edges it is, spoiled for good if you ask me, but then, I wouldn't have let her near it in the first place, but what could I do when you and the Mistress both…"

"She broke *what*, exactly, Margery?" he cut in, not needing to enquire who *she* was, and feeling little inclined to indulge his housekeeper's circumlocutions any longer than necessity demanded.

"Reverend Blomefield's box, that's what!" she exclaimed, triumphantly. "The one he brought you, special-like. The one you said not to touch, nor polish!"

His heart sank. The fact that Margery was forbidden to interfere in any way, with any of the hundreds of exhibits, seemed to have been temporarily overlooked in her righteous indignation, but she was now in full flow – and would have remained so – but Greene raised a peremptory hand:

"You are not only blameless in every aspect of this, Margery, but are doubtlessly required somewhere downstairs *immediately*. As your Mistress is in no mood for company you will permit no-one to set foot across the threshold – or answer to my wife. I think we both understand, do we not?"

With a conspiratorial nod of satisfaction, the alarming presence retreated downstairs and Greene was left to himself.

Looking across the room, he regarded the overturned table, the scattered papers and the upended box with dismay, though not without an inward sigh of relief that nothing had been touched in his absence – not, he knew, from any sense of obedience to his wishes on Margery's part, but rather that the results of the interloper's intrusion should remain in evidence. She was right about the damage, though, as Greene saw, stooping to retrieve the fallen box. The entire base was fractured on all four sides, the superbly patinated wood cracked along... He froze.

After some moments of simply staring at first one side then another, he inserted a fingernail into the fissure in the wood, removing a sliver of... what could it be? Not wood, that much was certain... It was *wax*! Coloured as an exact match to the wood itself! He rolled it between fingers, suddenly clumsy with excitement.

This was not a break, it was a wax-filled joint, impeccably crafted, a joint so perfectly disguised that it had remained invisible, unsuspected, until now. His pulse began to race as he righted the table and replaced the box on it, uncertain, for a moment, how best to proceed. He was distracted by the sound of someone at the foot of the stairs, but before he could react to it, the all too familiar voice boomed:

"It's Reverend Blomefield come to see you, but Mistress is out, so I told him you wouldn't see him even though that little chit broke his box, but he says…"

"Come up, Lionel," called Greene, "Your timing is, to say the least, uncanny."

Within fifteen minutes the tabletop was littered with waxen fragments, and a superbly concealed rim had been revealed some two inches above the base.

"This is a secret drawer to end them all," breathed Blomefield, his eyes gleaming with excitement, "Open it for Heaven's sake, do! The suspense will be the death of me."

Greene raised his head from peering along the join with his magnifying glass, saying: "It must be a pressure-fit, Lionel, there cannot be any sort of hinge. It must be designed simply to press on and pull off." He lifted the box towards the clergyman: "Will you hold the top firmly, and I shall see if I can pull the base evenly, then it should…" The layers came apart with a sigh of air, as the perfectly fitted section slid away from the box above it, a smell of fragrant wood and dry age mingling in the air around them.

Lionel Blomefield placed the box itself back on the table as the Apothecary gazed in rapt silence at the shallow, silk-lined tray revealed in his hands. Within, resting in preformed shapes once again, lay a black-lettered page and several objects.

"*As above, so below,*" he whispered, as if to himself.

"…*'tis perception wherein fortune lies,*" added his companion, completing the gnomic statement from the Ashmole letter, and peering into the tray in Greene's hands.

"What can have been so important to have been hidden with such care?"

"I'm not sure yet," murmured Greene, lifting the substantial sheet of paper from its purple bed. "It is some sort of inscription, by the look of it," he said, after a moment spent peering at the archaic letterforms set within a carefully drawn frame. There was something tantalisingly familiar about it

"…*As above, so*… Of course! Look! The drawn shape – the frame about the text – it corresponds exactly with the empty space in the box above." He grabbed the box and swivelled it towards the still-puzzled Blomefield.

"Whatever it held originally has disappeared – quite probably the result of a casual theft in all the years the box was at St. Mary's – but the coincidence is too great for this drawing not to be a copy of the original, whatever that was." He jabbed a finger at the closely written sheet, exclaiming: "For this to even *exist*, concealed, must mean that it is central to understanding the whole thing!"

He bent to remove one of the two remaining objects from its nest. This, unlike the other pieces had a *newness* – an almost gaudy shine – to it. He turned it over, weighing it in his hand before saying: "It's a button, no more, no less. Tudor giltwork, judging by the rose device embossed upon it. Of passing interest to the antiquarian, perhaps, but of no value." He shrugged, mystified by its inclusion, and set it aside.

In his excitement, the Apothecary had failed to notice his companion reaching into the tray. He now held a small object – the third and last that the tray held – wrapped in the same purple silk as the lining, and virtually indistinguishable from it. With extraordinary restraint the clergyman proffered it to Greene, who said, grinning:

"Your treat, I believe, Lionel."

Laid on the table and carefully freed from its protective cocoon, a torn, discoloured rag of vellum was revealed. Greene bent over it and gasped.

Once again, from a thousand years of dreamless sleep they
seemed to wake: Basilisk and Hippogriffe, the Wyvern and the
Manticore; a bestiary of wonder; a swirling dance of jewelled
hues. A great illuminated letter their focus, fragments of a
perfect uncial hand, their mute observer.

The clergyman watched in silent fascination as his old friend seemed to sway to some internal rhythm, eyes fixed upon the illumination, though seeming to look through it rather than at it. After some moments, he felt moved to reach out and gently take the Apothecary's arm.

"Richard," he said, "*Richard*, come back."

Greene turned a slack, unseeing gaze to his companion, before his eyes began to clear and a puzzled look began to replace the expression of blank wonder.

"There was darkness *everywhere*, Lionel, and this…" – he gestured to the torn page – "…this was at the centre of it, moving, alive, but surrounded by…" he shuddered, suddenly: "…surrounded by a dark that went on forever. A terrible place, Lionel. It was a *terrible* place."

"You, my friend, are clearly overwrought," said Blomefield, not unkindly. "You look a fright. What on earth has been going on, Richard? I know the constables have been involved – but then who does not? The city is abuzz with speculation."

For the second time that day, the Apothecary found himself involved in tortuous explanation, not the least of which being the fact that he had been the natural – though decidedly reluctant – choice of surgeon to carry out the post-mortem examination on the dead man. In this instance, a procedure he had carried out a hundred times but scarcely ever more reluctantly than now. He had ruled adamantly against bringing the corpse to his own premises, and had insisted that a particularly chilly vault beside the Guildhall cells offered both a suitable overnight resting place and a viable theatre for the morrow's task. He awaited, still, confirmation that Erasmus Darwin might assist him, needing authoritative confirmation of the evidence he was certain would damn Joe Crede's killers.

When Greene had finished his account and sat back, spent entirely, Blomefield raised a condescending eyebrow and said: "Can it have been in this very room, no more than weeks ago, that one old friend berated another with words to the effect of 'when we get so much as a sniff, an inkling of something of value squirrelled anciently away, our better judgement turns to putty'?" Greene groaned and announced he was going to bed, though not before, the clergyman noticed with ill-concealed amusement, replacing the contents of box and drawer, and stowing them carefully away. They agreed that circumstances permitting, they would conduct a proper examination, together, the following night.

"I promise not to take so much as a peep until then," said Greene with a wan smile, ushering Lionel Blomefield to the street door.

(25)

A pair of Ear-Rings, composed of Human Teeth. A Syrinx, or
Musical Instrument, composed of ten Reeds of different lengths,
of the kind wherewith the God Pan is usually depicted.

September, 1646. He awoke late in the morning, roused by a
thundering downpour that showed little sign of letting up. When
the rain did finally yield to a cloudy and troubled afternoon, the
streets had become quagmires of backed-up drains and sodden
dung, fouling the feet and bringing howls of complaint in its
trampled passage into shops, through hallways and downstairs
rooms. At times such as this, Lichfield seemed to become one
great, stinking swamp with no beginning and no end to its pools
and moats.

For one glum observer in the city and another in a leaking attic
billet in The Close, the rain spelt even greater woe. Coming at the
end of a largely dry summer, the deluge could hardly have been
worse timed for an enterprise involving an earthen, ill-propped
tunnel, sunk deep in the newly sodden wreckage of the Palace
grounds. Both knew it meant postponement, though both were
equally pressed by the knowledge that time was running short.
How short, Madden had not known until the word had spread
that day: within the week, the rump of garrison would abandon
Lichfield to the owls and scavengers, marching on to join the Scots
Covenanters at Newark. March they might, thought Madden
grimly, but by God they would be doing it without him.

Ashmole relieved his frustration at the untimely rain by
examining – now at his leisure – the purchases from the stable.

The book was everything he had hoped, its damage reparable and its survival a simple blessing. Both the crozier-head and one of the rings identified their source as some nameless Bishop – though perhaps the grubby, dirt-encrusted cartouche might cast some light on both, he thought. Using a paste of vinegar and wood-ash he set to work cleaning the piece, paring a spill to a fine point the better to lift out grime from the engraved letters.

Some thirty minutes of painstaking work left nothing to the imagination, with all but a few stubborn flecks remaining. Beneath his scrying-glass a most curious inscription was now legible. It could be read with even a scant knowledge of epitaph and muniment, but its content seemed to veil as much as it revealed. It was not fine work – this was no guild commission or presentation piece – but seemed written more to convey some heartfelt truth than to impress or eulogise.

He frowned as he scanned the unpunctuated words to be certain he was not misconstruing them, but could still make little sense of what his cleaning had revealed:

he that dyd strive
but later faild
to save y ancient hous
from Hurt
and ruination
did fr hiz soules
owne sake
a heavy burthen take
once from thys place

pilgrim fere not
fr y blessed one
he lyeth still so nere
enow to warm
thys worthie hart
seke him not
he slepes agen
til brazen trump
shal call men
forth to glorie

He read and re-read the words with all the guile and inventiveness of one whose every daily thought and horary could be encoded and deciphered with an ease that had become second nature, all

pilgrim here not
fry blessed our
he hrth still so uer
mon to warm
thys worthie hart
seke him not
he sleeps agen
til brazen trump
shal call men
forth to glorie

he that did serue
but later faild
to saue y ancient hous
from Hurt
and ruination
did for his soules
own sake
a heavy burthen take
once from this place

to little avail. Who was this *he* referred to? – the owner of the rings, the crozier? Madden had said they came from *a bishop's hole*. How could he have failed to ask him where? He returned to another line of the inscription: what *ancient hous*? The Palace, or perhaps somewhere else? Above all else his cryptographer's eye returned over and again to the capital letter *H* – its prominence and form set out to differentiate it from the surrounding text. Was it a key, perhaps? What heavy *burthen* – burden – had been taken? – The burden of sin? Could this all be some Popish concern with confession and absolution? Why, then, should *pilgrim* not fear? More to the point, he told himself, what should any pilgrim fear in the first place? Sin? And this *blessed one* – a soul that had gained absolution?

Ashmole grunted, bad temperedly, and tossed the piece onto the table. He might later seek a clue, some guidance at least, in the motions of celestial sphere and stellar harmonies, but, of this moment, had developed a splitting headache and was sick of the sight of the damned thing; a mood not improved by the message that then arrived.

"A lad of that age shouldn't have ought to be sent out on a day like this," was his notification of its arrival, as a damp fold of paper was thrust at him by his housekeeper. Unfolded, the grubby page read:

canot delay must be toniht. mete at oss pond. darkest.

Darkest must mean midnight, he reasoned, and he knew the Horse Ponds of the Close well. He did not even think to question the stark urgency of the message. He looked up from the scrawl aware, suddenly, of the gusting wind and rising patter of rain against the windows of the sturdy old house. This of all days was not the time for such an enterprise as theirs: everything was sodden, dank and unpredictable, such rain after such drought brought leaks where least expected and floods where least prepared.

The crudely laboured script had allowed for neither argument nor leeway, though: *toniht* it would have to be. He turned to his charts but found no reassurance there.

(26)

A Book, bound in Russia Leather, 25 inches by 20, containing twenty two impressions from Wooden Blocks, in Chiaro Scuro; published at Venice, by J. Baptist Pasquali 1745, this noble work was executed by a J.B. Jackson, an Englishman; and entitled, 'Titiani Vecelli, Pauli Caliarii, Jacobi Robusti et Jacosi de Ponte, Opera Selectiora, a Joanne Baptista Jackson, Anglo, lingo caelata, et coloribus adumbrata'. Presented to the Museum by the Rev. Henry White A.M. Sacrist to the Cathedral Church of Lichfield, and Vicar of Chebsey, in the County of Stafford; a most generous contributor to this Museum.

23rd **April, 1776.** Few would have said that Constable Hobley was an imaginative man, but as the first sounds of the cranial saw pierced the heavy oak door, he had bolted up the dim tunnel to the fresh air beyond, where he stood, now, gasping, whey-faced, trying to regain his normal stolid calm, if not his breakfast. He had managed to remain at his self-appointed sentry post outside the door since the early morning arrival of the Apothecary and his eminent companion. Gentry, such as Doctor Darwin, were rarely to be seen in the netherworld beneath the Guildhall, and the constable had decided that nothing less than a demonstrative devotion to duty would suffice. Earlier that day he had peeped in at the sheet-draped form, stiff on a bier borrowed from St Mary's. Over a warming ale he had confided to the turnkey that the morning's examination was a complete waste of time:

"Only saw the poor bugger with the noose on his neck, didn't I? Rope still over the beam where he'd slung it, face-down where he fell when it broke under his weight. Had nothing to live for, did he? What with his missus pissing off to come here with some cock and bull story, little'un dropped off in care like neither of them could give a toss for her, and him, poor bugger, with one leg and even less of a chance of getting by again. Nothing more to say, mark my words – whatever old clever-clogs Greene reckons. More than a mite too full of himself, that one – s'not like he's even a proper doctor, is it? Not like your big man Darwin. Proper doctor, him, and a gentleman, too.'

He had tapped the side of his nose, knowingly: "Soon be putting old clever-clogs in his place, you'll see."

"D...Damn bad business, Richard, and no mistake. Poor soul took the very d...devil of a beating. Three ribs broken by m... my reckoning," intoned the corpulent figure, peering once more into the bloody ruin of the incised chest cavity. Sometime later, looking back over his shoulder as he washed his hands in a large ewer, adding: "The d...damage to the kidneys alone would have d...done for him. His assailants knew j...just what they were d... doing."

Beyond, in the room's amber light, the Apothecary was bent over the waxen body, busily at work with needle and thread, squinting in the barely adequate illumination of the large lanterns suspended from the vault above.

"Judging by the amount of b...bruising and damage on the torso," Darwin continued, "my f...feeling is that to begin with, at least, his t...tormentors thought to conceal the d...damage they were inflicting?"

"I'm sure you're right, Erasmus," affirmed Greene, trying to suppress his rising guilt at the gaps in the Doctor's knowledge of the circumstances, "although the same cannot be said for the damage to the face. Whoever was responsible for that lost any such inhibition."

He was studiously avoiding the dead man's features, stretched, brutally distorted, trying to put from his mind the humour and the profound gratitude he had seen so recently dancing behind the now-sightless eyes, the voice: *Reckon you can fit me up with a peg-leg like a sailor-man, d'you, Mister Greene? My Aggie'll carve it for me, given half a chance.* With a start he realised that Erasmus Darwin was talking to him.

"B...But they still tried, albeit clumsily, to d...disguise their handiwork. You did well to question what m...many would not have t...troubled to."

Pleased and a mite embarrassed at the compliment from this, the most pedantic of men, Greene replied brusquely, jerking a thumb at the closed door: "Had those buffoons of constables not proceeded to wreck whatever other indications might have remained of the crime, there would have been more to go on. This is why your corroboration of my thoughts has been so valuable." Even with the blessing of the camphor he habitually rubbed below his nose in advance of any dealings with cadavers, his nose wrinkled in distaste as he added: "We must be deprived of even the evidence visible on the husk of this poor soul, shortly. I have arranged for burial later today."

"Do you say that the c...constables failed even to safeguard the cut rope you'd d...discovered?" demanded Darwin, with a shake of his head.

"Indeed, they did," replied Greene, adding: "In the circumstances one should be grateful they didn't simply discard the body, there and then – it being dead already."

He straightened, grimacing at a stiff back, then continued: "Something really *must* be done, Erasmus, if we are to make any pretence of inhabiting an ordered and decent society. Whilst much of our reputation, such as it is," he grinned, ruefully, "is due to the fact of Cousin Johnson's heroic overstatement of us being a 'City of Philosophers', I fear that not all the high culture in the world, nor *improving* pontifications from The Close, can protect us from thieves in the night and the species of pariah that murdered this poor soul. Lord knows, look what the Fieldings accomplished with the Runners – and that more than a score of years back, with no more than eight or ten of them to begin with. I know, mercifully, that we are not London, with all the crimes and terrors of a great metropolis, but even so, are we to be at the mercy of whatever or whomsoever decides to abuse our small society?"

"Mr G...Greene," said Darwin, smiling in some amazement, "if that is not the n...nearest to speechifying I have ever heard f...from you, then I shall eat this w...w...w...!" He gave up and pointed to the untidy assemblage of grey hair mounted on his brow.

The Apothecary simply shrugged, embarrassed at the extent to which he had revealed his feelings. Having dried his huge hands with an almost feminine precision, the Doctor rejoined the Apothecary to stare down at a pallid torso now disfigured quite as much by the brutally invasive surgery as by the crime itself.

Placing a hand on the small man's shoulder, he said, quietly: "If I m...may say, my dear sir, you have taken this d...deeply to heart, have you not?" He indicated the amputee's scars, perfectly stitched around the appalling stump: "You will have been rightly p...proud of that achievement, Richard, and understandably g... gratified by the p...patient's survival, but, unless I am m...much mistaken, your words are expressing a sight m...more than p... professional regret?"

The piercing intelligence of the wide brown eyes seemed to enquire deep within the confounded listener, until Greene replied: "To answer your question, Erasmus, I find myself involved in a degree of remorse and recrimination that is less than comfortable, hence my tardy admission of it. But before I unburden myself, shall we leave this doleful place? As the very least I can do is to offer some refreshment, I had already taken the liberty of booking us a private dining room at The Three Crowns."

"That will do very n...nicely, Richard. I am now b...both hungry *and* intrigued."

(27)

A large extract from a Manuscript Journal of the Committee
of Sequestration, held at Stafford, during the Civil
Wars 1643, which displays the Complection of those
troublesome Times. The Original is in the Possession of
John Floyer Burnes, Esq, of Aldershaw, near Lichfield

September, 1646. It had been agreed that Ashmole need bring
nothing more than his hands and head to the enterprise. Madden
could, with ease, lay his own hands upon the simple tools they
would need. That night, already assembled in the shadow of the
broken Palace walls, were ropes, crowbars, shovels, wicker baskets,
flannel-cloth for wrapping knees and elbows, lamps, tinder, and
more lamps and tinder; the soldier's memory being neither short
nor blunted when it came to the matter of darkness.

Around five minutes after midnight and wrapped in an all-
enveloping cloak, a grinning, empty-handed civilian staggered
nonchalantly past the single, incurious sentry at the Westgate,
headed for some harmless assignation.

*They were leaving the rat-hole on the morrow, so who gave a tinker's
toss anymore? Who might this one be? A Royalist come to recapture the
shit-heap and re-crown the King? He was bloody welcome to it all.*

The trooper returned to the small comfort of his black bottle
and smouldering brazier.

Once within, Ashmole moved with quiet circumspection. Like
Madden before him, he skirted the Cathedral within its dense
shadow and then, crossing the darkened slope, headed obliquely

towards the northeast corner of The Close. He had made certain that the watchful figure, standing near the Horse Ponds, would have seen his arrival and intuited his intention. Best not to meet anywhere in the open, overlooked by eyes in unlit windows.

Sure enough, Madden emerged, soundlessly, from the Palace shadows as Ashmole slipped towards them. They walked carefully into the blackness of the forecourt, where the soldier gestured to the left and onwards. It was only as they entered the jagged silhouette of the walls that the low clouds parted, and both the men and their stark surroundings seemed to spring into focus.

Few words were needed as Madden gestured towards the equipment, which they proceeded to divide between them. Silently, Elias followed him through the tumbled walls and into the moonlit grounds beyond. Suddenly, sinking to his haunches, and beckoning Ashmole to follow suit, he placed a finger to his lips and gestured towards a jumble of nettled ruin. With almost primitive intensity, he seemed to sniff and weigh the night around him – head cocked, eyes darting left then right, and chin poised, gauging the silence. Then he grinned, and said quietly:

"We move the timbers to the left where it is clear and place them down just as we find them, the better to cover up afterwards, so none will note our work."

Ashmole nodded and the work began. The blackened joists with their woven thatch of brambled weed were removed not without difficulty, then carefully placed for recovery as the black pit was shortly revealed. Ashmole, looking down into its unfathomable depths, remembered the day of his father's burial. He had never believed that six feet down could look so deep from up above.

Then, following the soldier's wordless example, Ashmole wound the long, ragged strips of cloth, bandage-like, around his knees and elbows, watching how Madden deftly flexed his limbs to ensure the bindings did not impede their freedom of movement.

"Wait for me!" hissed Madden. "It will be difficult after all the rain."

He lowered basket, rope and tools ahead of him and then, with some awkwardness, dropped noiselessly into the darkness below. Within moments a spark became a blessed light within what was revealed as the tunnel's mouth, and a voice – sounding impossibly distant – called up to him:

"Now, first foot to the left, on the wood. Hold the side and look to me for support."

An iron grip guided his booted feet down the slippery rungs, and shortly he stood in the dim glow of the black, uterine, opening that awaited them. Wistfully, he took one last, lingering look, up at the haloed rim far above him and the night sky framed within it. Light, even pinpricks of starlight, had never seemed so precious. He ducked down and entered the counter-mine's descent as Madden's flickering lamp beckoned him ever deeper.

The choice of movement was either a crippling, crouched shuffle or hands and knees sunk in the almost liquid slime of the sloping tunnel floor. The rain had been the most appalling ill fortune as it removed even a semblance of control from their ever-steepening descent. They part-slid, part-crawled their way through gouged spoil whose continued support seemed to owe more to the intensity of Madden's will than to the sodden props and their gnawing, scuttling denizens. Then, it appeared, they were there: scarcely space for one, but Madden turned awkwardly and beckoned him forward.

Eyes gleaming with feral intensity, he said: "Beyond that is all we seek," his voice sounding dull and flat in the choking confines of the shaft.

Ashmole peered over the crouched man's shoulder at the yellow-lit face of the jumbled obstacle ahead. In the comfort and easy certainties of the world above, a description of this awful place had seemed paltry, almost inarticulate, yet here in the foetid air and flickering half-light the blackened stains, smears, the shockingly graphic handprints congealed upon the crammed stones and the frightful keystone barrier brought the halting words of Madden's agonised fight for survival chillingly to life.

"You shifted *that*?" breathed Ashmole, scarcely able to believe his eyes.

"Needs must, man. The Devil surely drove *that* day!" rasped Madden. "And saving the pleasure of your company..." – the old-accustomed sneer flickered briefly across the scarred face – "...that is why we *two* are here tonight. No man alone could ever think to handle that." He nodded dully at the barrier ahead but seemed little inclined to look at it.

"So, what's to do then?" he enquired, looking to Ashmole under a furrowed brow. They crouched, both gazing intently now at the task that lay ahead, breath coming short, vapoured, in the flickering light.

"Something to support it as it's loosened and brought forth... I think..." Elias gestured at the bundled crowbars by their feet. "Perhaps those two..." – he bent, selecting two stout, short shafts – "...hammered in hard below the stone, *here* and *here*?"

The soldier nodded assent, and each seized a metal rod. Only one at a time could gain the swing and force to strike effectively, but within minutes the two bars were securely embedded in the rubble, well below the blackened stone.

"Now it must be levered out, but *contained*: held from falling," murmured Madden.

Ashmole saw that the eyes above the scarred cheeks had taken on a haunted intensity. Words spoken in the little parlour came back to him as he regarded the driven man: *It was the best and the worst time of my life, rolled into one, Mr Ashmole.* Elias realised that only now was he even beginning to understand what had drawn the soldier back to this tomb-like pit.

Madden's place by the rubble wall and his reluctant knowledge of its nature elected him the lever, with Ashmole's role behind, as the prop – crowbar gripped in white-knuckled anticipation of the keystone's fall.

"Let it roll and we shall both be deadmen. So, be ready, *braced*," said Madden. A look mixing complicity and fierce dependence passed between them, and then Madden set to. As he pried and worked his chiselled bar, both gauged every strain and shift, every falling chunk of loose packing, staring fixedly at that one huge block above. When – shockingly – it fell, it was with such speed and such crushing weight that Ashmole's startled exclamation was somewhere between shout and scream.

Somehow, by the grace of providence, bars beneath and bar beside all held, and the massive, freed weight was – at least momentarily – contained and borne.

"What now?" hissed Madden through teeth clenched in a face drawn with strain, as he struggled with the immense burden.

"If we pull this one free, and let *that* end drop – but still contain its forward fall, we can pull out the other and ground it." Ashmole looked, half in question, to the straining soldier, who managed to shrug, before grinning: "I've no better notion, sir."

28

ITEM:

A portable Barrel Organ, in a neat Mahogany Case, which, by the help of Clock-work, plays sixteen Tunes. Presented by the late Mrs Rider of Barton under Needwood, in the County of Stafford.

26ᵗʰ April, 1776. Theodosia Greene had been surprised and delighted when, summoned from the tiresome and heady chore of overseeing the decanting of a newly made batch of The Apothecary's renowned tonic-wine, she was confronted with a hale Grace Beasley. That lady, with only a moderately well-concealed appraisal of her friend's facial condition, produced a tissue-wrapped bunch of tightly budded tulips and a beaming smile, saying: "These are the smallest token of thanks for your kindness, my dear, as overdue as it is well-intentioned. Belated, as I wanted to be certain I wouldn't fall, face-first, through your famous window, before venturing out."

She gestured behind her to The Apothecary's crowning glory: the wondrous stained-glass window that had attracted business beyond measure since its first installation many years earlier by a headstrong young husband during the absence, in Cheshire, of a parsimonious young wife.

Theodosia, obviously delighted, took the flowers and was about to lead her visitor to the stairs, when the angular woman stopped her, saying: "Forgive me, but I really cannot stay, my dear. The purpose of this flying visit was to invite you on a small but daunting excursion arranged by dear Anna. It is a prospect I find frankly irresistible but not one I would entertain without some robust company."

Unsure quite how to react to being described as 'robust', Theodosia smiled tentatively, and before enquiring into the nature of the outing, pointed to her still-swollen nose, saying: "This is scarcely evidence of a charmed existence, Miss Beasley. Just how robust must this companion be?"

"Well *first*, you must call me Grace, and I shall call you Theodosia, my dear. We are quite sufficiently well-acquainted by now, and *secondly,* you will fit my bill to perfection, I can assure you. We are invited to don sensible apparel, to take our courage in both hands, and to climb The Great Steeple."

"What, *that* one?" replied Theodosia weakly, gesturing in the direction of the Cathedral.

"The very same!" exclaimed her alarming visitor. "Can you *imagine* any greater thrill than the prospect such an eminence will afford?"

Before Theodosia could even embark on the process, the providential return of her husband could be heard from the shop.

"Richard? *Oh, Richard,*" she called, in quiet desperation: "Come through, we have a visitor."

With pleasantries exchanged and the purpose of the visit briefly repeated, Greene beamed with excitement:

"Ladies! What a *splendid* opportunity! It is an excursion that I, myself, have long wished to undertake."

"Then you shall come with us, don't you agree?" replied his wife, grasping at straws, and turning to her visitor for confirmation.

Before Grace Beasley could reply, however, the Apothecary responded with: "Nonsense! I shall not dream of intruding upon Miss Seward's arrangement. It is obviously intended as a ladies' adventure. Husbands are surplus to the day's requirements."

Theodosia turned back to her visitor, exclaiming: "But your *health*, my dear? Surely, in the light of your recent..?"

Before she could complete her final, despairing, gambit, the husband who would shortly be regretting his intervention, cut in: "I can imagine nothing more conducive to your convalescence than healthful exercise of this nature. So long as you take the ascent in easy stages, resting as you feel the need, it can only be beneficial. Don't you agree, Theodosia?" He had obviously failed to detect the venom in his wife's eyes as he continued: "Unless I am mistaken, you will begin your ascent via the small door in the South Transept, ascending to a mural passage that will lead you towards the tower itself, then…"

As the gawky figure made her farewells and left the shop, Richard Greene, blithely unaware of what lay in store for him, exclaimed: "Talking of invitations, my dear, I have had no opportunity of apprising you of yet another – this, to us both – extended only this this morning by Erasmus."

In retrospect he would realise that he should have read the signs, as his wife busied herself with unusual noise and fuss with whatever came most immediately to hand; anything, it seemed, rather than meet her husband's unsuspecting gaze.

"Yes, coincidentally," he continued, "*also* through the good offices of our ever-busy Miss Seward, a theatrical event is to be staged at the Guildhall a week from today, to which we are invited, making up the Darwin party. We are to dine with the family and then…"

"What makes you think I shall still be drawing *breath* by then, Richard?" his wife exploded, with a vehemence that astounded him. "You know I am terrified of heights under *normal* circumstances, but for you to thoughtlessly condemn me to the ascent of The Great Spire indicates a disregard, callous beyond *belief!*"

"But my dear, what could I..?" he began, helplessly.

"*Nothing*, apparently, Richard," she grated. "For that would have required some jot of consideration and concern for my wellbeing which you evidently lack *entirely*."

He was left, standing in the small hall outside his Consulting Room, feeling as if he had recently been at the epicentre of some seismic event, while through the half-open door that led into the rear vestibule of the shop, he could see his staff, eyes averted, bustling about their tasks with unusual absorption. He was about to express his feelings in a rare profanity as the shop door burst open to reveal the red-faced, breathless form of the constable, Hobley. Seeing the figure of Greene through the rear door, he hurried past the puzzled shop staff and arrived, panting, in the doorway.

"Yes? What can I..?" began the Apothecary, annoyed at this graceless intrusion into his place of business.

"There's been a killing, Mr Greene…" – the Apothecary felt his stomach lurch as if struck – "out at the Crede's cottage. He's dead out front of it. Only found by lads up to mischief, what with it being empty since Crede topped hims…"

Ignoring any more of what the fool had to say, Greene attempted to dismiss him with a wave. Pausing only to grab for his bag, he hurried to the stable, with Hobley limping in his wake.

"I'm to go back with you, Mr Greene, Sherriff says, even though my lads will have it all squared away by now." Hearing that, Greene only barely stopped himself from abandoning the call there and then, dumping his bag on the garden path and sharing his thoughts on the treatment of a crime scene with the bumbling oaf now panting in his wake.

"You'll have to wait while I get my horse, Mr Greene. Left it up at Greenhill."

His only response was a stable door slammed in his face.

As the Apothecary had feared throughout his uncomfortably brisk trot out towards Walhill, the constable's words were proving accurate.

Everything had, indeed, been *squared away* by the time of his arrival, and he was confronted with the sight of a pair of constables squatting beside a cursorily draped corpse, sharing ale from an earthen jug with the remains of their bread and cheese sprinkled liberally about them and their immediate surroundings. The disregarded corpse beside them had been carried from the overgrown garden to the roadside verge. Dismounting, the Apothecary surveyed the pair who were only now reluctantly clambering to their feet in acknowledgement of his arrival.

"I see that nothing as trivial as violent death has kept you from your repast," he said, with a withering scorn entirely wasted on the pair.

One, the older, judging by the size of the paunch bursting from an unbuttoned jerkin, replied: "Quite right, Mr Greene. Just passing the time of day while you were fetched, like. Not as if that one'll mind."

A mouthful of brown teeth formed into a grin and he jerked a thumb in the direction of the shrouded figure, saying: "Left him so's you can have a proper look, though. Hobley said as how you'd want to, before he got disturbed, like."

"Oh, he is lying where you found him, is he? Here beside the road?"

They exchanged uneasy looks before the other replied, defensively: "Up to his oxters in nettles, wasn't he? Over on t'other side of the hedge. Thick as thick all round him they were, you'd have not seen him, riding past, like, so, we brung him out to help, like. Best we could do."

"Do you know, constable, I really can believe it was," replied the Apothecary, wearily. "Pray show me where exactly he was found."

"What, before you take a look-see, like? Hobley said as how you'd be all over the poor sod, like a…"

His fellow, at least, saw the look in Greene's eyes and hurriedly led him to a trampled patch on the garden-side of the overgrown hedge.

Greene peered, first, at where the flattened, blood-smeared vegetation indicated the body had lain and then at the hedge. Its inner face – a tangle of greening blackthorn and still-brown beech leaves – was visibly crushed along a man-sized length as though by a heavy weight. He had seen all he needed.

"Pay attention to how this has all been pushed down. I require you to note *precisely* what you see here," he ordered the fidgeting onlooker. Straightening, he called to the constable who had remained with the body: "What do you make of the hedge from your side? Has it been disturbed in any way?" Looking bewildered the thickset figure lumbered over to investigate.

"Looks like a hedge ought to look, Mr Greene. Why shouldn't it?"

Both had to wait for the Apothecary's reply, as he made his way back out of the weed-grown patch, following the well-trampled path made by them.

"Now please uncover this poor wight," he said, with some trepidation, waiting for the coarse canvas to be pulled away.

Had he not previously encountered Lemman on almost this same spot, those weeks earlier, the features that remained intact might have proved unrecognisable, such had been the ferocity of the attack upon him. The once-sneering mouth was a mangled void of smashed teeth and torn lips, one eye and most of an ear had gone, and both cheeks resembled little more than a joint carved to the bone. The sound of retching behind him announced the belated arrival of constable Hobley.

Without turning, Greene said: "His name was Lemman. This is one of the men who should have been questioned for the murder of Joe Crede. Had that occurred there is a very fair chance that he would be enjoying the hospitality of a Guildhall cell now, rather than lying dead in the road." He continued, regardless of the sound of hastily drawn breaths: "He was not killed here, but the body was brought here, almost certainly by more than one man, and heaved from horseback across that hedge and into the Crede's garden plot." He pointed, fiercely, at the younger constable – now busily wiping his jowls with a kerchief: "And you will be able to testify to that fact, *will you not?*"

"Yes, Sir, Mr Greene," he replied, with something approaching alacrity. "Saw it with my own eyes, plain as a pikestaff."

"Just…" Greene added, addressing the other, "as *both* of you will attest to the fact that the grass and nettles about the body were undisturbed from the garden side?"

"Yes, Mr Greene, they were. Lads as spotted him in there were up that tree. Bird-nesting, they reckon."

"That is *one* thing I have no reason to doubt, constable," said the Apothecary. "Now, though, be good enough to return to the hedge side with me, and tell me, once more, that you see nothing."

Wordlessly the constable followed Greene across to the low verge. "Well?" enquired the Apothecary, having scrutinised the immediate area.

"Well what, Mr Greene?" replied the man, genuinely puzzled: "Can't tell you what I don't see, can I?"

Mutely, Greene pointed down to the ground at their feet.

"Oh, *that*, you mean, Sir? Hadn't spotted it afore. *Look at the hedge* you said, so that's what I did."

The single wheel-rut was narrow and, judging by the bruised – rather than withered – state of the grass and primroses it had crushed down, had been made recently.

"Does this suggest to you that the body might not have been brought here on horseback?" he enquired, mildly.

"Well, I wouldn't like to say, Mr Greene," said the older man, suspiciously, scratching his head with a dirty nail, "because weren't you just saying it *was*, like?"

"Indeed, constable, I did say that, before I employed the eyes the Lord gave me – as I should have done before making an incorrect assumption. I believe that this points clearly to the fact of a light coach being used, instead. The height of such a vehicle would have made the disposal of the dead-weight considerably easier."

He could see from their expressions, and the guarded looks that had passed between them, that he had completely lost them now.

"What of the cottage?" he asked, briskly. Both were visibly relieved at the change of topic.

"All shut-up, Mr Greene, no sign of a soul about. First thing we did, wasn't it? And her down the lane is as clueless as they come. Hadn't seen or heard nothing if she's to be believed." He attempted a man-to-man wink, wasted on the Apothecary.

Greene continued: "Was a child still with her?" asking more sharply than he had intended.

"None that we saw, Mr Greene. But then, who'd trust a little'un to that old soak? Didn't know what day it was, did she?"

The Apothecary left the constables as they manhandled the broken body across one of the horses and hurried off down the lane towards a hovel so decrepit and overgrown it appeared to be returning to the soil from which it had sprung in some unguessable past.

The stench of neglect met him as he picked his way carefully down the uneven path, rapping on the half open door partly buried in ancient bramble. A formless croak met him, coming from the stooped, unkempt crone who swayed in the threshold gloom, her bleary eyes devoid of comprehension.

"Good day, Mistress," said Greene, venturing no closer than was necessary.

"Is the little Crede girl still in your care?"

The figure snorted and shook her head: "Tekken away." she croaked, squinting with suspicion at the daylight beyond him. He could smell the sour-sweet reek of gin from where he stood.

"But you were properly paid for your service? By Aggie, no doubt?" the ruined features creased in an expression of disgust.

"Gived us a few pence. Tekken 'er away. Gone off."

"In the coach, was it, Mistress? The one that stopped up the lane last night?"

In response she spat, waving him away, and turned to retreat into her den. Greene, knowing he would get no more from the pathetic creature, let her go. As he walked back up the crazed brick path, he knew, at least, the recipient of the few coins of small change lifted from the kitchen dresser in Aggie's flight. *Drunk for a farthing, dead drunk for a halfpenny.*

Members of his calling were all too familiar with the gin-shop promise. He knew, also, with heartfelt relief, that today he had been spared the sight he had been dreading since Aggie Crede's disappearance: Lemman had not met his end at the hands of a grief- crazed woman wielding a stolen kitchen knife. Today, aching with tiredness, Richard Greene had no intention of thinking past that fact. He rode back to Lichfield in the waning light, thankful for small mercies.

29

ITEM:

In large DRAWERS, marked with Numeral Letters. No.l. A
Miscellaneous collection of Articles from the Island of St.
Vincent, sent by Charles Ashwell, Esq; viz. The Eggs of a Land
Snail, lately discovered at Tobago. Coral from Barbuda. Sea
Weed, or Coral in its first stage. Sulphur gathered from the
Mouth of a Volcano, at St. Lucia. A Sprig of the Cinamon
Tree. Do. of the Garlick Tree. The vegetable Musk.

27th April, 1776. Having seen more than sufficient of the man
Lemman, both dead and alive, the Apothecary – with an easy
conscience – declined the onerous task of conducting yet another
post-mortem. He knew that he could not presume again on
interrupting the protean workload of Erasmus Darwin and had
no intention of sharing already over-spread confidences with yet
another. So, pleading the demands of his numerous patients, he
had recommended that a dull but capable city colleague – not
noted for the demands made on his time – should take it on.

Greene, meanwhile, in the day that followed, had embarked
upon an attempt to restore both his own mental equilibrium and
that of his domestic arrangements. As ill-timing would have it,
the Great Steeple ascent being scheduled for the following day
meant that his wife was in no mood to forgive and forget. So, still
bone-weary though he was, he gladly accepted the newly delivered
invitation to join Lionel Blomefield for what his friend enticingly
described as *a bachelor supper* at Breadmarket Street.

At around seven o'clock, with a thoroughly swaddled box
carried ahead of him by Grice, the youngest of their shop-boys,

the Apothecary left the prevailing sub-zero atmosphere of hearth and home with a small sigh of relief.

On arrival, and having been shown up the dogleg stairs to the small parlour favoured by his host, he was surprised, and not a little put out, to realise that he and Blomefield would not be dining alone. Too late, Greene realised that his discomfiture must have been apparent on his face, when the elderly cleric turned to the tall figure standing, expectantly, beside him and said: "I've kept your arrival a surprise, Charles, knowing this curmudgeonly old dog would not be persuaded out if he'd known there'd be company."

Greene was torn between an urge to turn on his heel and leave, or to laugh at the blunt perception of his old friend. The decision was made for him when the newcomer stepped forward, a hand extended in introduction and a somewhat sardonic smile lighting sharp, clever, features.

"You will appreciate that the role of *ambuscader* has been thrust upon me, Mr Greene, though I should have been mortified to miss you."

"*Mm*, Lionel has always been something of a thruster," replied the Apothecary, shaking hands and returning the smile, "though I fear you have me at exactly the disadvantage he planned..."

"Richard, allow me to introduce a fellow alumnus, my dear friend Charles Caisley, Knight of somewhere or other perilously close to the Outer Hebrides, is it not, Charles? I never can remember."

"Sir Charles," Greene nodded, politely, in acknowledgement.

"Lord, none of that between friends, for pity's sake!" the other, exclaimed, "Whilst *you*, Mr Greene, need no introduction. Your reputation precedes you."

Caught unawares, the Apothecary blushed, artlessly, with pleasure, but managed: "Exaggeration is one of Lionel's lesser vices, but then you will, no doubt, be familiar with his entire gamut?"

Unusually for Richard Greene, he felt immediately comfortable in the newcomer's company and, within moments, glasses now in hand, the three men were in animated conversation, seated around the small room's fire. Caisley, it transpired, was breaking his journey through to Chester, having left Oxford two days earlier and spent the previous night in purgatorial accommodation near Warwick.

"I swear you could *hear* the fleas. They were such a size!" he exclaimed, scratching ruefully at a bite. "One could have harnessed a Calash to the damn things!"

"I shall send around a cream in the morning," Greene volunteered: "The bites can be most vexatious if they become infected."

Caisley laughed, easily, "Which is of course, telling me, with *courtoisie parfaite*, to stop scratching! Forgive me, gentlemen, I have become a boor: I spend too much time with dust and books."

"Hence your invitation," declared their host, delightedly, his face already flushed from the wine, his spread arms open to embrace the company: "Hence, in the brief but perfectly timed absence of my dear wife, our bachelor supper! This, Richard, in the shape of the Knight of *Kirkuddy* or somewhere thereabouts, is my *man in Oxford* – the source of all the Ashmole-related nuggets I have been so assiduously gathering to assist you!"

"Then I am doubly pleased to make your acquaintance," said the Apothecary: "As I must admit that, for anyone other than the intended recipient of the wretched box, the decipherment of its contents is proving every bit as difficult as the late Mr Ashmole obviously intended."

"Oh, they *will* be," said Caisley with some relish, "You are dealing here with one of that century's most ambiguous and elusive characters. To many he was an enigma while he lived and a source of endless disagreement since he died. You have not embarked upon an easy task, my friends, of that I can assure you."

"Supper first!" Blomefield insisted, nodding towards the Apothecary: "I know that if Richard is given his head we shall not dine before dawn."

Several hours later, as the sated trio sat around the noisily cleared table of the dining room downstairs, the sleepy housemaid was ordered to bring the box in from the hall, before being sent off to her bed. When she was safely out of earshot, their host, gesturing to the unwrapped box, confided:

"This and everything within would be in the midden by the morn, if that girl were left to her own devices. I sometimes think that if her head were to be opened it would be found to contain nothing but porridge. Being our housekeeper's niece though – more's the pity – she cannot be quietly sent packing without causing a palace revolution."

Greene decided not to expound on the vexed subject of domestic staff and, seeing Caisley's eyes drawn to the object on the table, said, instead: "I imagine Lionel has not had time to apprise you of our discovery, such as it is? We may finally be onto something. Though, until now, I have had no opportunity of pursuing matters further."

"*And* had given your promise not to proceed until both of us were present, if you recall, Richard?" added Blomefield in mock admonition. "So, reveal all to our guest, Mr Greene: I believe you will not be disappointed."

Although curious at whom the last statement was directed, the Apothecary obliged and, assisted by Lionel, reopened the concealed layer, and laid out its contents to join the rest on the surface.

"I have been studying my own copy of Elias's original letter," said Caisley, pulling a folded sheet from a waistcoat pocket. He paused then, seeing the look that passed between the Apothecary and their host: "...as supplied by Lionel, along with strict admonitions as to its confidentiality." He smiled at Greene's nod of approval, before continuing: "...and can, I believe, shed some light on at least a part of it." Greene intrigued – not least by Caisley's easy familiarity with their subject and the small fact that Lionel had omitted to mention the copied letter – gestured for him to continue.

"Well," he began, with obvious relish: "We have mention of *the key* to our secret being *wrought by Old Row. Lee*. The answer to that, my friends, is simpler than one might imagine. This is *not* a reference to the nickname bestowed upon Charles the Second, 'Old Rowley', but to a Bishop of the previous century. *This* century, in fact…" he said, picking up the gilt button with its Tudor rose and examining it thoughtfully before continuing:

"During that tumultuous time, Rowland Lee played a role that could scarcely have been more pivotal. It was he, as Royal Chaplain, who discreetly married Henry the Eighth to 'The Hoor Bollin' – as that poor lady became popularly known."

"Boleyn, Anne Boleyn," said Blomefield to himself. "Well, I never. But how..?"

Caisley stopped him with a smile, continuing: "So here we have a singularly well-placed, highly favoured cleric moving rapidly on to become, first, Bishop of Coventry, and finally – at the behest of a grateful monarch – Bishop of..?" Teasingly, he left the sentence unfinished, inviting his rapt listeners to complete it.

"Lichfield?" both chorused, obediently.

"Correct," said Caisley, adding: "He retired in 1543 and later died and was buried in Shrewsbury – I'm not sure when, exactly."

The sharp face creased in a grin: "So my friends, over to you. We should proceed, perhaps, by enquiring how the secreted contents of the tray relate to one another, and to our 'key-holder', Rowland Lee, for knowing something of Elias's mind, I believe they surely do."

"My thoughts entirely," said Greene hurriedly, not a little put out to be playing second fiddle here.

"So…" Before he could continue, Lionel Blomefield played the masterstroke he had been conserving – with fraying patience – for the past two days: "I believe I can identify, with some authority, a possible – even, if I dare say, *probable* – source for this…" He carefully lifted the torn vellum from its wrapping, before adding: "It is a find of extraordinary moment, if I am proved correct."

Seeing the look on the Apothecary's face, he hurried on: "As might be expected, a lifetime spent around and about our Cathedral has provided one with a more than passing familiarity with its treasures, or rather, those that a particularly malign history has left us. Chiefest among them is of course our magnificent Anglo-Saxon Gospel Book – St Chad's Gospels, as it is popularly known."

"Are you saying that..? Greene began, but Blomefield was not about to surrender his moment of triumph, continuing:

"Being incomplete, however, in its lack of the Gospel of St. John in particular, there has long been a belief – a forlorn hope, one might say – that there was once *another* book, a second book, long-since vanished from history. If, in fact, it ever existed."

He paused, with solemn theatricality, then, holding the scrap for their gaze, said: "This, I believe, is proof-positive that it did. I have taken the time to renew my long acquaintance with our Gospels and can state that this is most certainly the work of the same illuminator, whilst the uncial text is identical to one of the several scribes' hands identified in our own." He spread his hands, saying: "I believe Ashmole was telling Harrison, covertly, that he had found the other volume."

All impatience forgotten, Greene nodded, thoughtfully, then said: "Yes, but could that be only *part* of his intention? Howsoever history might judge him, Ashmole was no vandal. He would never have torn a page from such a find, so, surely, we should presume he was only ever in possession of this ruined vestige. Is this, *all* this, though…" – he indicated the objects before them – "…pointing out where the whole book might yet be found? Ashmole is evidently entrusting Harrison with *some* task which he himself, for some odd reason, could never complete? My growing conviction, though, is that more than the book is at stake here."

"I agree entirely," said Caisley. "Lionel, why do we not retire to that cosy parlour of yours and examine this…" – he lifted the closely lettered sheet – "…over the cognac I am sure you were about to offer your guests."

It was some time before Caisley returned the sheet to the table beside them, saying: "Forgive my absorption, I have not had your opportunity for mulling this over. Several thoughts have occurred to me, thanks to your patience."

Greene and their host had sat at ease in the amber firelight, content to watch its play on the fine old tiles around the grate, whilst the other read and read again, squinting at the archaic letterforms of the drawing.

"Returning to our consideration of Henry's England, we should, perhaps, remind ourselves of the nature and the timing of its single most devastating event," Caisley prompted.

"The Dissolution of the Monasteries, of course," murmured Greene.

"Absolutely!" exclaimed the other, "But more, far more than that: the systematic pillaging and destruction of the great Shrines brought in as much – if not *more* – revenue to the Crown, than the seizure of dozens of the smaller houses combined."

"Becket's Shrine at Canterbury, that of Our Lady of Walsingham," agreed the Apothecary. "They attracted generations of pilgrims from across Europe, on a par with Compostella, certainly." He paused, only now seeming to become aware of the train of thought upon which they had embarked. "Oh, my Lord, and of course not omitting…"

"…*St. Chad's Shrine*, right here in Lichfield!" Lionel exclaimed, beaming with excitement.

"Exactly so," said Caisley, "though in terms of that, my research into Lee turned up something really rather peculiar. Apparently, our Bishop had sufficient influence with Henry for Lichfield's shrine to be exempted from the general forfeiture and destruction."

"But no trace remains…" began Greene, simultaneously amazed and confused by the revelation.

"Due, sadly, to the fact of Henry being the most inconstant and rapacious of monarchs," continued Caisley, "Lee's efforts soon came largely to nought, with Henry reneging on his promise and the great stone-built shrine being reduced to rubble along with the others."

"You said *largely*," said Greene, perceptively.

"I did, indeed," smiled Caisley, "because Lee, somehow, managed to wring a concession from the King that the shrine's fixtures and fittings, its various adornments, could remain the property of the Cathedral and be used for the benefit of the diocese."

"Not the sort of concession, though," said Greene, "that Henry would *ever* have agreed to unless the value of said items was too trivial to be of account. It would have been completely out of character with everything we know of the appalling man."

And then a thought struck him: "The capital letter 'H', of course!" – he grabbed up the sheet – "*That* is what the emphasised letter is referring to: *Hurt and ruination*, by courtesy of Henry Tudor! It *must* be that, and here is the button to make the point! Somehow, this all concerns what happened *then*, with Lee. I know it does."

"Are we omitting to ask a most important question, then?" said Caisley, in implicit agreement. Both turned to him, expectantly.

"What was the single most important thing about the shrine? What attracted pilgrims to it for the best part of eight centuries?"

"The relics *themselves*," replied Greene, beginning to understand where this might be leading: "The bones of St. Chad."

Nodding, Caisley continued: "So here, in Lichfield, you have the erstwhile Bishop of Coventry, who had been unable to halt the pillaging and destruction of that Cathedral's reliquaries. Given his first-hand knowledge of the nature of his royal master, would he ever, in truth, have trusted the King's intentions again?"

"Or," breathed Greene, tense with possibilities, "might he have embarked upon some form of pre-emptive rescue of all that he held most sacred?"

"Indeed, he might, and – in the circumstances – how could he *not* have gone all-out to save something of such inestimable value to his Cathedral? Such a major medieval pilgrim shrine would have been immensely wealthy, with century upon century of endowments behind it. Here, in one, surely, is the *heavy burthen* that Lee assumed?"

"But if he was unable to save the actual shrine itself – various bits and pieces of that were still lying about for years, as I remember – then what is all this business about saving '*y ancient hous*'?"

"But Lionel," blurted Greene, trembling with excitement, "was not the original casket, the original reliquary, referred to as resembling a little house? I'm *certain* I've come across reference to that, somewhere, haven't *you*?"

"I do believe you're correct, Richard," replied Blomefield, catching his excitement. "In fact, *yes*, I'm certain of it."

"So now, we appear to have a context within which so much else can slot into place," said Caisley, returning to the text with animation.

"Look here, this is a reassurance to the 'pilgrym' who can no longer find what he sought: 'fere not for y blessed one...' which must surely refer to Chad: 'he lyeth still so nere'."

"But I regret to say," interjected Blomefield, "does the next line not confound our idea of Lee's involvement, if his is 'thys worthie hart', to which allusion is being made? He was no longer lying *nere* anything within our ambit, if he was buried – as Charles says – in Shrewsbury?"

They digested the implication in silence for some moments before Caisley to the alarm of his companions jumped, excitedly, to his feet, smacking a hand against his forehead in exasperation:

"I call myself a Scot? I should be ashamed!"

"Surely, it's not *that* bad..." began Lionel, in bewilderment at the outburst. "It's the *heart*, man, the *heart*! Do you not see?"

Both members of his audience were now equally perplexed, as he continued: "Even dyed-in-the-wool *Sassenachs* such as yourselves will have heard of one of the great names in Scottish history: *Wallace*, William Wallace?" Both nodded, tentatively.

"Well, my friends, legend has it that his dying wish – before being hanged, drawn and quartered for the satisfaction of an English King – was that his heart, *heart*, mind you, be buried at Melrose Abbey, knowing, presumably that the rest of his body was destined for the crows."

"So, if I understand what you are saying, most, if not all, of what Ashmole somehow assembled here, must have come from some cache, a hiding place if not a tomb proper. This is what you are suggesting? The place wherein Lee's *heart* had been buried – at his particular behest?" exclaimed Greene, continuing: "and one *nere enow* for *thys worthie hart* to be warmed by the presence of the saint whose relics he had preserved?"

Caisley agreed with an eloquent shrug: "I think it makes as much sense as may ever be revealed, here. The problem, gentlemen, is that, for all its fascination, it gets us not one inch nearer to finding the source of this." He indicated the vellum scrap: "We do not, more's the pity, have a single clue as to where, even, *the cache* might have been unearthed, let alone that to which it might be close."

"But you *are* saying that where one finds the book, one will find the shrine?" yawned Blomefield.

"Assuredly," Caisley replied. "Where more perfect a resting place for one of St. Chad's Gospel books than with the saint himself?"

"The celestial equivalent of bedtime reading, perhaps," said the Apothecary. "A suitable note on which to wish you both a good night, I believe."

He stood, shaking Caisley's hand in both of his. "To say it has been a remarkable evening smacks of understatement, Sir Charles. In the morning I shall bring you your witchhazel cream in person, so that we may make a proper farewell. The quality of Lionel's judgement has soared in my estimation. It has been my pleasure to make your acquaintance."

They parted at the front door, a somewhat unsteady Greene

having agreed – after a moment's reluctance – to leave collection of the box until the morning. He was already regretting his decision as he walked the length of the sleeping street. He would be there bright and early, he promised himself.

30

ITEM:

Within the Table, in the middle of the ROOM. A
Gentleman's Cap, very ancient, neatly worked with Silk, in
Flowers; and ornamented with Gold and Silver Spangles.
Another, worked with Gold Thread, laced and spangled, worn
by Burleigh, Lord Treasurer; Presented by Miss Astley of
Tamhorn, now Mrs Dyott, of Freeford, near Lichfield.

28th April, 1776. By prior arrangement, the small group had
assembled inside the South Transept of the Cathedral Church.
Having left a balmy spring morning outside, Theodosia Greene
was shivering in the gothic chill of the gaunt interior and
wondering, glumly, if she was alone in wishing for nothing more
than a speedy return to it.

Her companions, though, all seemed fired by the same breezy
anticipation of the adventure ahead.

With the exceptions of Anna Seward and Grace Beasley, the
four other ladies making up their party were scarcely known to the
Apothecary's wife; she knew them all to be the wives or – in one
case – the daughter, of various prominent figures in city society,
but had done no more than nod the odd acknowledgement to
them at various functions. Introductions once made and a number
of inconsequential conversations begun, they awaited the arrival
of the Verger who would lead them on the ascent.

Noting the deathly pallor of the youngest member of the group,
an adolescent girl who was the daughter of a prosperous city
lawyer, Theodosia gravitated towards her in the hope that this was
a fellow sufferer. However, what she had misread as shared dread

was rapidly revealed as vapid inertia on the part of a young woman so languid as to appear scarcely capable of making the effort to remain upright. One only in attendance because *Papa says I must get out more.* Theodosia leapt at the opportunity presented by the arrival of their tardy guide to rejoin the company of Grace Beasley, just as the perspiring and obviously embarrassed young man made his apologies and embarked upon his preamble to the climb.

"As you will doubtless be aware, ladies, a large amount of what you see about you, and what we shall be encountering up above, is restoration work, and in the case of the Great Steeple itself, complete rebuilding made necessary by the scale of destruction during the Civil War of the last century. For the best part of twenty years, the nave was largely unroofed and derelict following the collapse of the original steeple, with the only part of the fabric that remained habitable being the Chapter House, over on the north side from us here.

"Whilst I can assure you that everywhere I lead you today has been restored to a safe and stable condition, I do urge you, Ladies, to stay within the roped ways as we traverse the roofs and not to leave the party. There are still areas of rubble and unrestored damage, well beyond public gaze, of course, but for your safety and comfort I must ask you not to venture near them. I shall be taking the lead with my lantern, whilst the rear will be lit by our Mr Field." He indicated a small, scruffy man presently lighting the candle-lamps. "Now, if you have no initial questions, shall we begin our ascent?"

Fighting the urge to enquire how soon they would be regaining *terra firma*, the Apothecary's wife allowed herself to be ushered through the low doorway by the portly form of Anna Seward.

"Isn't this just the *jolliest* jaunt, Mrs Greene?" she beamed. With a sickly smile of assent, Theodosia edged past her.

The sheer immensity of the hidden world which they were entering was finally revealed as they clambered up into the roof void above the vault of the South Transept. The smell particular to ancient lofts – centuries of bat droppings, dust and invisible lumber – filled their nostrils as they crossed a wooden gangway and looked down upon the lime-mortared vault below their feet. They were already at a height Theodosia had no wish to dwell upon. Passing through a small doorway, the enormous roof space of the nave became dimly discernible in light from their guide's raised lantern, though past thirty feet or so it tailed off into impenetrable gloom. Within the pool of light, they were shown the huge scale of rebuilding that had been undertaken in the past century. They continued upwards, now ascending the anciently worn treads of a spiral staircase, corkscrewing up through the immense walls of the central tower, emerging, at last, into the huge chamber beneath the Great Steeple.

Their guide's first act was to light lanterns found already in place, and in their rising glow a stone wonderland was revealed. Great portcullis-like lattices of stonework rose behind the external windows of the tower, designed to support the giant oak timbers which, in turn, bore the vast, unseen, weight of the Spire above.

"This is absolutely untouched medieval work, ladies," intoned the Verger. "One can almost imagine the moment when the last chisel was packed away and the last mason gave his creation a final glance before descending to the church below."

Despite the poetic evocation, Theodosia's imagination was elsewhere, though nowhere comfortable. She felt utterly oppressed by the gigantic structure, dwarfed by a scale beyond her ken. Here within it, at its very core, the sheer physicality of this vast edifice bore no relation to the familiar, comforting skyline that had shadowed her daily life for so many years. There seemed to be a stark, unremitting brutality in the sheer size, the volume, of its beams and joists, its vast dressed stones. Her chilled reverie was interrupted by a voice saying brightly: "…And now, ladies, if constitutions permit? The most spectacular aspect of our climb awaits!" With numb resignation, Theodosia joined the shuffle towards her worst fears.

The pinchback staircase was so narrow that the climber ahead seemed to completely fill the airless space, as they laboured awkwardly up the final steps, to finally squeeze out through a miniature doorway that opened onto the parapet of the tower. Emerging, the view swept over her like a breaking wave. Lurching backwards with a petrified gasp, Theodosia thought she would be sick, grasping frantically for something on which to cling.

When, at last, the deafening pounding of her heart began to recede from her ears, she managed to open her eyes sufficiently to see her companions clustered at the parapet, busily enthusing over the panorama that lay beyond them. Paralysed with vertigo, she could do more than take deep, shuddering breaths, in a vain attempt to calm the terror within her. It was as if some malign, irresistible force was building behind her, willing her, impelling her, away from the support at her back and towards the unspeakable abyss beyond the parapet. It was then she glanced upwards, tearing her eyes away from the half-glimpsed rooftops and distant countryside, to scan the sky above – anywhere that would remove the dizzying threat of height. She took one look, vertically, at the vast needle of stone looming above, and shrieked.

Suddenly, she was surrounded by concerned faces – faces whose chief comfort lay in their blocking out the appalling sight that lay beyond them. "I must go down," she gulped to Anna Seward, just as their guide – unaware of the drama being played out along the parapet – announced that they would all now scale the final obstacle, saying: "It will mean negotiating the void beneath the Steeple, ladies, though I do assure you the planks are quite stable."

That was all Theodosia needed to hear. Somehow, she regrouped her tattered defences and stood, decisively, eyes avoiding what lay behind the plump shoulders. "You must go on my dear. I shall be as right as rain once back down those stairs," she said, with a heroic air of confidence. "I refuse to spoil the fun, so off you go, and we can all rejoin forces down below."

A mixture of doubt and relief met in the round face as Anna

said: "Well, only if you are quite certain, my dear?"

"I am, I am," replied Theodosia attempting to inject a note of humour, "So off you go. Everyone has come too far to miss the highspot now!"

With overwhelming relief, she watched the others clamber through the large stone lancets at the base of the spire and waving, disappear within. Crab-like she felt her way back to the tiny door and virtually crawled into the womblike security of the spiralling walls beyond it.

Moments later she reemerged into the ringing chamber below, lit still by its lanterns. She sat, panting with relief on some large stone fragments stacked against one of the walls, fighting to restore some degree of normality, to no avail. In spite of her initial gratitude at regaining this level of the huge tower, her earlier sense of the oppressiveness of the great stone cube began to return with a vengeance, and she knew that if her life depended on it she could not possibly remain there, awaiting the party's eventual descent. Confident that the climb down would be as nothing to the horrors she had just undergone, she moved to the small doorway to the stairs. Gathering her skirts and her resolve firmly about her, she began the descent.

Although at a loss to explain it to herself, the lower she went the greater became her sense that these were not the same stairs she had climbed so recently. The dank air became closer, mustier, her lantern revealed dust and rubble on the treads beneath her cautious feet – *she was on the wrong staircase* – there had to be more than one from the Ringing Chamber down to the roofs below.

Before she could either turn or give in to the panic that welled in her breast, an obstacle suddenly presented itself in her path: a door – a locked door. She could have wept.

Breathing with difficulty in the dust-laden air, she realised that she was perspiring heavily in the confined space, suddenly weak, dizzied by the corkscrew descent. As she began to manoeuvre herself awkwardly in the cramped confines of the dead-end, she saw now – through a wide chink at the side of the ill-fitting door – that she had descended on the wrong side of the transept visible below. The level at which they had earlier crossed above the vaulted roof lay ahead of her across the void, but before she could utter the unlady-like profanity that was forming on her parched lips, something below her grabbed her attention with jolting impact.

Staring directly up at her vantage point, a squat, foreshortened figure stood stock-still. It was helmeted in an archaic, lobster-tailed style she recognised from the Museum collection, and appeared to be clad in breastplate, buff-coat and baldric. The day must have clouded rapidly, as the light below was barely sufficient to give the impression of a blank, hard face staring with total fixity towards her place of concealment. The helmet's barred visor seemed to cast shadows like long raked scars across a rawboned cheek. Then, in a movement that she would never forget, it lifted one gauntleted hand, pointing, in utter silence, firstly at her concealing doorway, and then, with absolute deliberation, off towards the Chapter House.

Transfixed with emotions beyond her understanding, she blinked sweat away from her stinging eyes, and when she looked again there was no figure, but simply an empty flag-hung Transept below and the drumming of blood in her ears.

For just an instant she was back at Milley's Hospital, standing in the dawning light, across from where a watching figure stood, waiting, in a half-seen tower. Then she was back, sobbing, shaking in the grip of a nameless terror, her sweat seeming to freeze around her in the dank claustrophobia of the blocked passageway. She turned, desperately, to fight her way back up the staircase in the ancient walls.

31

ITEM:

A Mahogany Case, covered with Glass. A Chalice of Nottingham Ware, supposed to have been used for religious purposes, mounted with Silver, curiously carved and gilded. An antique Candlestick of Brass enameled, in which a Wax Candle, painted with the Image of the Virgin Mary, holding the Infant Jesus: This candle was brought from Loretto, by Mr Bruiton of Birmingham.

September, 1646. There it lay, beyond the tumbled stone: a deeper darkness, absolute in its profundity. Both men were, for the moment, slumped in exhaustion, drained by their battle with the dreadful obstacle now sinking under its own weight into the tunnel's muddy floor. Madden leant back, still gasping with effort and emotion.

"Now all is open. Now all is possible," he whispered, speaking to himself though he stared straight at his companion. Gradually, he seemed to recover himself, and said: "I know what lies beyond. I *know*." His breathing seemed to ease and his tension with it. A smile of almost beatific contentment came to his blackened lips: "Now you shall see for yourself that every word I spoke was the truth: look through, Mr Ashmole, look through…"

Elias scrambled stiffly to his feet and clambered across Madden's bent legs towards the exposed sill. The soldier reached up and passed him the nearest of their lamps, with a smile that was both intimate and proprietorial. "*Now* you'll see. Reach through and hold this high…"

Since the far-off day when an apple-cheeked Piper had promised to reveal the Land of Faerie, Elias had longed for such a moment. Suddenly, though, he felt nothing but fear at the prospect of peering beyond the veil; of entering the beckoning darkness.

"I cannot... I..." he began, turning imploringly to the watchful man. Madden, seeming perfectly to understand, simply waved him forward with a knowing smile.

He knelt upon the massive stone of their labours and, leaning forward, rested lamp and elbows on its erstwhile foundation. Here the light seemed slow to pierce the depths beyond, as if reluctant to take on such absolute darkness.

Slowly, gradually though, Ashmole's incredulous eyes began to make out how the chamber was revealed. With gasping breaths, he gazed in dumbstruck wonder at what lay below and beyond him, by the second becoming more transported, more transfixed, by the ever-shifting sea of gleam and flicker that his lamp drew forth from the jumbled array. This was no *tomb*. This was a *storehouse*, a treasury crammed beyond belief. He began to pick out objects from the shifting dazzle of the hoard: censers, pattens, pyxes, plates, great candlesticks like leafless trees – all could be discerned across the shifting dance of silver, gold and stones that seemed to shoot back fire and starshine to his aching eyes.

And then, in the darker distance, where the shadows fought against the prying light, he saw the little house, and knew, deep-down, this was the fulcrum, the *focus*, of this realm of dreams. To his eye, both it and the chamber seemed of extraordinary antiquity, speaking of an England before The Conqueror came. Here were none of the Romanised arches and barrel-vaulting of a Norman mason's making, but something older, cruder by far. And yet, as his eye roved voraciously across the strewn hoard he picked out things he thought he knew. *There*, surely, was the enamelwork of Limoges, *there*, the narrow, arching forms of Plantagenet work, and across..."

"Did I not speak the simple truth, Mr Ashmole?" said a voice at his shoulder that wrenched him away from the dazzling vision beyond the broken wall.

"It's…" he croaked, and had noisily to hawk to clear his throat and tongue-tied mouth. "It is a place beyond belief, Madden – but *why*? What can all this be *doing* here? No-one simply walks away and forgets something like this."

Then, as if only now remembering, he exclaimed: "The *book*, Madden – the one you tore? Where..?"

"Below you and to your left," the soldier grinned, his teeth white against his mud-caked features, "though it will not be an easy stretch from this side."

Elias brought the lamp below the sill and there, indeed, it was. For all the world resembling a jewelled box, its lid a gem-encrusted board. As he strained forward to reach it, he glimpsed, in passing, a small bright object well within his grasp. Not a coin, a brooch, perhaps. He slipped it into a jerkin pocket with no further thought, then made to reach out again, only to be forestalled by Madden's gruff admonition:

"There'll be time for all that and more. The book is yours and no debate. We must enter and begin, though the time is short and I hate this bloody hole."

"Much of what lies within will be too cumbersome for us to hope to shift through. The small pieces must be our goal," replied Ashmole, not turning, unwilling to tear away a gaze still fixed upon the jewelled shape.

"I'll not argue on that score," replied Madden. "It will be best if one's within and t'other's here, without, and all stacked there, behind, before we carry up. I'll first go through with lamps."

With no room for more than one at the gaping hole, Elias moved awkwardly back once again whilst Madden spread his gear carefully about him. As he waited for the soldier to complete his preparations, little, if anything, could be seen past the busy, crouched form, but for Ashmole what remained, glowing, in his mind's eye more than sufficed. Nothing in his life had prepared him for the priceless vision beyond the broken wall, though something nagged at him, tugging at the sleeve of memory to gain attention:

the dimly seen shape that somehow dominated all around it – the small, kennel-like shape, Madden's 'little house' – and, in an instant, it came to him: the memory of a long-distant schoolroom, of Michael East leaning at ease against a Song School lectern.

That day, his story had been of past tribulations and ancient glories, of centuries when the faithful flocked to Lichfield's shrine, when Chad had rivalled even Becket in the pilgrim heart. His story darkened then, as he had told them how the smashed and violated shrines, the desecrated statues and the roofless choirs became the black epitaph for old Hal Tudor. And then an echo of the well-loved voice returned: *Though in early times the saint's relics lay in no more than a little house of painted wood, its fame and sanctity brought such wealth to our Cathedral that a great and beauteous shrine of stone was built about it to praise the saint's blessed memory and to the glory of the Lord Almighty…*

Ashmole, squatting in the ankle-deep mud, could scarcely credit where his thoughts were leading: *Blessed memory? …y blessed one…y ancient hous…Madden's little house…* Sweet Jesu, how could this be happening? The dawning truth was simply too big to grasp: *…saved from Hurt and ruination…* But how? By whom?

Pure intuition sent a hand plunging into his jerkin pocket to retrieve what he had found. Then, as if swimming up from the depths of a dream, he gazed at the object in his hand, an awesome revelation dawning as he read the emblem, the unmistakable emblem, raised upon its face. He gasped aloud at the sheer force of clarity that blazed into his muddled head: the full realisation of what lay beyond the wall, the certain knowledge of who had placed it there. His head and heart seemed fit to burst with the knowledge as he slithered to his feet. With a wild croak he lurched towards the disappearing form of the soldier. In that occult moment their universe was transformed.

For one crystal instant all beyond was in his eye – all he had glimpsed, all he had come to understand – in the ragged frame made up of mud, of broken stone and, suddenly, of Madden's turning head and shrieking mouth. Then, as if a great black blade slashed down, a crow-black wing beating against the light – a stroke so absolute it cancelled life itself – the weight of the world and all its sins collapsed upon Josiah Madden.

His head and shoulders, chest and ribs, had been across the rubble sill, a wriggling fulcrum when the fall came down, as rock and roof and earth and stone were all sucked down, as if to fill the vacuum that he'd straddled with such hapless joy. Everything about them shook and yawed as Madden was engulfed before the other's fear-crazed eyes.

Shrieking, Ashmole hurled himself back from the twitching, kicking, dance of death that was enacted in the choking gloom, until the soldier's legs were still.

Then, though, as if a dowel-pin had been pulled or a kingpost knocked aside, he sensed the entire length of the mine begin to shift and slide, as props began to come away and groaning timbers splintered in the dying light. He turned, slithering, flailing, gibbering with terror, scrambling back up the mudslide of the tunnel floor, his ears filled with the dull thunder of collapse.

When, moments later, the blood-stained, filth-encrusted spectre emerged, sobbing for breath, into the open pit beneath a starlit sky, it was as if an alien being had returned to some half-forgotten land, survivor of an odyssey beyond this place and time. He stood, quivering, new-born to stark horror – to a retching, solitary nativity with none to celebrate his coming.

32

ITEM:

Returning from the Inner Museum; on the right hand, a large medal
in Copper, gilded, of Dr Stukeley; Reverse, a representation of
Stone Henge on Salisbury Plain. Linneus, and Thomas Pennant,
Esq; of Dowming in Flintshire, in Plaister of Paris coloured

28ᵗʰ April, 1776. The Apothecary had returned from a more
protracted morning interlude at Breadmarket Street than he
had intended, to be met with the singularly unwelcome news
that his wife had been taken ill during her Cathedral visit. "Miss
Beasley is upstairs with her now, Mr Greene," explained a clearly
distressed Tillett. "Miss Seward sent her and the Mistress back in
the Canon's coach. Taken poorly up the tower so I…" Greene was
already hurrying to the stairs.

Only now, a good hour later, was he able to speak to her, as
she lay, pale and drawn, propped against a bolster. So great had
been her distress, Grace Beasley recounted, that the Seward's
housekeeper had forced a large bumper of neat brandy upon her,
resulting in the near stupor from which she was only just emerging.
Mindful of how roles had become reversed, but deeply grateful for
the woman's quiet, no-nonsense support, he asked her to remain
with his wife while he mixed a potent restorative downstairs.

When he reseated himself beside their bed, and embarked upon
spoon-feeding the unusually passive Theodosia, Grace Beasley
insisted that she leave husband and wife to their privacy; he
though, requested she wait for him downstairs in the comfort of
the parlour. Ringing down, he arranged for a cordial to be served,
by a housekeeper on the verge of exploding with unsatisfied

curiosity and unresolved alarm. "You might be good enough to briefly reassure Margery of her mistress's imminent recovery, Miss Beasley; I fear she invariably seeks a second opinion."

He held the soft, white hand, marvelling, not for the first time, how a woman of such industry and vigour could have retained the delicacy of a little maid in school. He sat, aching for her distress, willing himself somehow to understand the source of her anguish. Once restored she described her ordeal.

"You felt you *knew* him, my dear, that somehow *he* knew you? – am I understanding this correctly?"

She nodded, weakly, replying in an alarmingly small voice: "I do not begin to understand what occurred, Richard, but I must know that you believe me. Others would take me for a madwoman – you must tell me I am not."

"It is a refutation I shall never make, my dear, for even to consider it would mean that such a possibility could be entertained. You have, now, on two separate occasions, seen sights that can not be easily explained, and, on each occasion suffered considerable pain. Whether it was physical or – in the case of this vertigo whose likely effects I so shamefully underestimated – pain of a mental nature, the effect upon us that such distress can have, cannot be underestimated."

"Husband, are you suggesting..?"

"Hear me out, I beg you, Theodosia... I am in no way demeaning or denying the cruel intensity of either occasion, I am simply trying to explain – to myself, I suppose, as much as to you – where one explanation of your experiences might lie. In times of travail and adversity our minds can play the strangest tricks upon us."

"*One* explanation, you say? You admit to the possibility of others then?" she replied. He noticed with relief that her accustomed colour was beginning its return to pallid cheeks.

"How could I not, my dear?" he shrugged. "As your husband I am convinced that you would never knowingly lie to me. So.." He hesitated.

"*So..?*" she echoed.

"Before I answer that, I must confide a matter that I have avoided until now. It is not something that I have purposefully kept from you but, frankly, it perplexes me to such an extent I am uncertain how to begin."

Before she could form the words that could be discerned in a hardening of her eyes, he rapidly continued: "You have, once again, recounted what occurred that morning at Milleys: the figure in the tower, the sense you had been *awaited*, were being watched." He squeezed her hand, then, saying: "Dearest, I know that you do not share my familiarity with all the ancient piles that dot our small city, but be assured that no tower has stood on that spot for more than a century; one hundred and thirty-four years, to be precise."

He saw incomprehension, bewilderment, and the beginnings of real anger meeting in the face he loved so well, but refusing to relinquish his grip, continued: "The mystery, my dear, lies not just in what you saw that morning, but that you saw what you did at *exactly* the time and on *precisely* the same date that marks its destruction: around seven in the morning of April the twentieth, 1642. Which is to say one hundred and thirty-four years ago."

Theodosia gaped at him, lost for words.

"The reason we can be so exact in this is that the explosive demolition of the tower – and Prince Rupert's subsequent storming of The Close that morning – have gone down in the annals of history, a history – of Lichfield, at least – with which I have a more than passing familiarity."

"And the man I saw..?"

"He would appear to have been one of those self-same combatants, down to the last detail of your description, my dear: hence my absolute perplexity."

"Oh, Richard, I am more than *puzzled*," she said, increasingly infuriated by his apparent detachment "I am so very frightened. He *knew* I was there, behind that door!"

"And he pointed *where* did you say? Towards the Chapter House?"

She burst into tears and would have heaved a bolster at him, had she but the strength to lift it. Abandoning even the thought, she sank, sobbing under the counterpane, pulling it up over her head.

Retreating wisely, he said: "Try to sleep, my dear. I am sure the preparation will assist you in that." It was only then that he remembered Grace Beasley.

The bright, intelligent eyes smiled up at him as he hurried into the room where their visitor was seated, very much at her ease, a small periodical open on her knees. Before he could apologise for the wait she had endured, Grace Beasley said: "I took the liberty of looking through several of these," she indicated the slim publications neatly racked on a low stool, "I had no idea you were such a regular contributor to *The Gentleman's Magazine* – it was my poor, dear brother's constant companion. The scope of your erudition leaves me feeling quite the hoyden, Mr Greene."

"No, no, Miss Beasley. You do yourself a grave injustice. These scribblings are no more than the rambles of one crusty old man's fancies for the benefit of other such old bores," he said, grinning in modest disclaimer. "It is simply that if we limit our bookish effusions to the pages of our magazine, it makes life a deal more tolerable for those that must suffer us on a daily basis."

"But if that be the case, your Museum..?" she added, with every appearance of a mischievous glint of amusement in her eyes.

"Ah, there you have me," he admitted, smilingly, raising both hands in mock surrender. "There are those of us conspicuously less successful in limiting our passions. Theodosia has, I fear, long been a forgiving victim of mine."

"We were all very worried about her today, you know," she replied, in all seriousness. "She was more distressed than I ever hope to witness again in such a friend."

"I know," he said, simply. "For all my heavyhandedness in

dealing both with her earlier misgivings and her subsequent distress, I remain in no doubt now of their effect and will take all steps necessary to remedy my shortcomings. Theodosia is not, though, my sole concern today, Miss Beasley," he said, staring into her face with what she supposed was a professional squint: "If I am any judge, you, yourself, are far from recovered from your own *incident*?"

Clearly taken aback, she took a moment to reply, but then said: "I had no idea that one's headaches could be so plainly read, Mr Greene, but, yes, you are not mistaken. They have been plaguing me these four, or five, days past."

"This may sound the unlikeliest of enquiries, Miss Beasley, but please indulge me: are you experiencing any unexplained odours?" he enquired. Her eyebrows, arching in her sudden surprise, answered his question.

"How on *earth* could you know that Mr Greene? I am, indeed. A smell of burning, *singeing*, seems to have become a most unwelcome companion, though having no apparent source," she admitted. Then, in an attempt at levity, continuing: "Is my nose wrinkling visibly in its pursuit?"

"Certainly not," he responded, gently. "I do feel obliged to tell you, however, that what you have described may indicate the existence of something akin to a cyst within the cranium whose growth exerts pressure upon that part of the cerebrum closest to it, hence the severity of your headaches."

"I see," she replied, eyes downcast. "And is this… *cyst*, treatable, at all? Or must I continue to endure headaches?"

"I shall prescribe a liquid tonic that will certainly relieve the discomfort, and a course of tablets that will seek to reduce the inflammation within, Miss Beasley. In extreme cases, cranial surgery is an option, though not one I should wish to pursue before we have exhausted less drastic measures."

"It could, then, prove to be..?" she seemed unable to finish the question.

"Let us not dwell upon *might be's* and *what if's*, dear lady," replied the Apothecary. "Not until we judge the efficacy of the prescription. It may well prove to be all that is required."

"Thank you for your frankness, and, not least, your kindness, Mr Greene. It comes as no surprise that you found such a match in your dear wife. You are perfectly suited and blessed for being so." There was such a note of sadness, of regret, in the gracious words, that the Apothecary – to his own amazement – heard himself asking: "And has there been no such comfort in your life, Miss Beasley? In the years since you left us?"

"After all too many spinsterish years I came to believe there was about to be, Mr Greene, or so I foolishly thought." She replied with an expression of such anger, such *loathing*, invading the severe planes of her face that Greene found himself regretting he had ever embarked upon such unpardonably intrusive questioning. Before he could make amends, she continued: "It is not without a certain vile irony that I should perhaps be thanking the creature Hawson for revealing the true nature of my suitor, for had he not deprived me of my inheritance at a stroke then *my beau* might never have been revealed for the fortune-hunter he was. The day I confessed my penury to that gentleman was the day he discovered a pressing reason to be elsewhere. A reason so pressing, in fact, that it apparently required the contents of my jewel box to finance his rapid retreat."

"Surely you must have had him pursued, not allowed to get away with such..?" Greene began, appalled by the agonised admission from this remarkable woman.

"And reveal myself as some pitiable, aging creature able only to belatedly find a lover, a helpmate, by means of her purse? No, I think not, Mr Greene. The small satisfaction of his apprehension – even if ever the theft could have been proven – would have been paltry recompense for the scale of his betrayal."

She rose to leave. "You, however, have shared quite enough of my woes for one day, Mr Greene. I will though, ask one last favour of you before allowing you to return to your wife? You will please call me Grace if I may call you Richard? Do you not feel that formality tends to sit uncomfortably between folks such as?"

"I do, indeed, my dear," the Apothecary replied, "Theodosia has said much the same."

"Well, of course she has, Richard. Did you not pay mind to what I said earlier? Now, when should I call for my medicaments?"

"I shall send them by the boy, later this afternoon," Greene replied, taking her hand. "Then, we shall see what we shall see over the next week or so, and act accordingly. I have every confidence of a satisfactory outcome."

"As I have every confidence in you, Richard. I shall see myself out."

Insisting, he accompanied her downstairs and out through the busy shop. Turning in the doorway, the dappled colours of the stained glass somehow softening her gaunt form, she seemed, momentarily, to be sniffing the air of the street outside.

"Will you show me your Museum, someday soon, perhaps?" she asked.

"Nothing would give me greater pleasure," he replied, realising he meant every word of it. He waved her out, and through the coloured panes watched the bony figure stride away.

"It should be soon," he thought.

(33)

ITEM:

A neat representation in Paper (cut with a pair Scissers)
of Mr Garrick and Miss Younge, in the character of
Tancred and Sigismunda, by Miss Selina de Chair. A
Peacock, cut in like manner, by Mrs Greaves of Culcheth,
Lancashire. General Wolfe, cut in Writing Paper, with a
Penknife, by Thomas Hunter of Edinburgh, 1769.

28ᵗʰ April, 1776. That evening, as he sat, at peace for what seemed the first time in many days, relishing the ordered calm of the Museum rooms, his thoughts returned to the morning's conversation at Breadmarket Street. Arriving shortly after Lionel Blomefield and his guest had come down to an unusually late breakfast, he joined them at table, gratefully sharing the strong coffee which appeared to be the major component of the meal; none at the table seeming the least inclined to embark upon the contents of the sideboard chafing dishes.

The witchhazel cream had been more than gratefully accepted by Charles Caisley, to the extent that he had absented himself for several moments to apply the soothing remedy, grinning with obvious relief when he returned.

"I declare that given the chance, I shall dispatch fire-raisers to burn that wretched hovel of an inn to perdition," he said, regaining his seat. "Such places are an affront to our century and should be obliterated without compunction."

"Talking less of our own, but rather of another century, Sir Charles," replied Greene, seizing his opportunity. "Last night you mentioned *en passant* that Ashmole's reputation has been parlous both in life and death. May I impose upon you to expand upon that? I feel I need to gain whatever knowledge is to be gained in that direction, if ever a solution to our conundrum is to be found."

"I shall do my best, Richard," the other replied, toying briefly with a congealing lamb chop before thinking better of it: "You may well find, though, that my account is as partial as any other, his being a life at considerable variance with the sum of its parts. Where to begin..?" They sat for several moments as Caisley marshalled his thoughts with help from the coffee pot.

"Almost certainly," he began, "the abiding foundation, the very root, of Ashmole's subsequent celebrity was his passionate and consistent royalism. This was a loyalty stretched to the limits in the last, dark days of the Great Rebellion, though one with which he steadfastly kept faith throughout the years of Cromwell's commonwealth, when, as you can well imagine, it became a less than comfortable persuasion." Greene and Blomefield sat, listening in rapt attention.

"Obviously, many details remain obscure after all this time," continued Caisley, "though it seems that Elias's abiding passion for the study of Heraldry, and the rituals and trappings of the ancient institutions such as The Order of the Garter – studies assiduously cultivated by him during the long years of *interregnum* – were to stand him in the very best of steads with the restoration of Monarchy Triumphant in the early 1660s He appears to have become rapidly and uniquely well-placed to advise and consult on the remaking of all the panoply of state required to launch the reign of Charles the Second in appropriate fashion.

"To cut a long, and I suspect, *contriving* story shorter, over the following twenty years his star rose ever higher in the national firmament, with his successive appointments to such exceedingly lucrative posts as Commissioner – then Comptroller – for Excise of London, eventually reaching the dizzily well-imbursed post of Accountant General, controlling, thus, one of the major sources of crown revenue. These preferments in addition to a talent for marrying well on, as I recall, three occasions, provided him with the wherewithal to indulge his personal passions. We know him to have been a Freemason, in fact the first of that shadowy brethren to be recorded in England, and one initiated at much the same time as his brief return here, to Lichfield."

"Here, to *this* very house," interpolated Blomefield, proudly.

"To this very house, perhaps this *very* room, Lionel," agreed Caisley, smiling, before continuing: "That profound attraction to the hermetic, the *hidden*, would be one of Elias's guiding passions through the rest of his life. That, and, of course, his astonishing energy and virtuosity as one of the great collectors of our history. More, though, of that in a moment. His fascination with all things Occult led him into scholarly study of the Elizabethan Magus, Doctor Dee, and, subsequently, what appears to have been an unsatisfactory correspondence with Dee's son, who – in spite of poo-pooing his late parent's most cherished beliefs – failed to diminish Elias's fascination for the old man by one whit. In tandem with that, though, he seems to have developed a most unhealthy interest in the supposed writings of one of Dee's more unsavoury cronies, a creature by the name of Kelly – a necromancer and diabolist who, apparently, only narrowly missed the judicial fate he richly deserved. Oft-repeated suspicions of Elias's own involvement in such parlous activities, can, however, be neither confirmed nor denied."

"Ashmole published with some degree of success, did he not, Sir Charles? Early on in my career I often made reference to his excellent work *The Way to Bliss.*"

The Apothecary then turned to Blomefield by way of explanation, continuing: "He brilliantly combined the writings of Galen and Paracelsus, promoting therapeutic remedies and recommending…"

"Yes, *yes*, Richard, now let Charles continue. I can listen to you any time!" said Blomefield, tetchily. Greene acceded with an embarrassed grin.

"You are right, of course, Richard," agreed Caisley, courteously. "His *Theatrum Chemicum Britanicum* is still held by many scholars to be the apogee of alchemical compendia."

"He was an alchemist, too?" The Apothecary failed to control his curiosity despite his companion's glare.

"More the student, the *collector* of all such writings, it is now felt. Though I believe it was this belief in a hidden *corpus* of divine knowledge, his search for the Universal – whether in ritual magic, astrology, alchemy – or wherever his fancies took him – that drove his frenzy for acquisition and investigation. Here, on the one hand, we have the New Man of his age, a founding member of The Royal Society, whilst on the other, the magician, the mystic, the dabbler in many of the dankest pools and backwaters of the human condition."

"Does there not remain a great deal of suspicion surrounding his acquisition of the very collection that is the backbone of the Ashmolean – his greatest monument?" enquired Blomefield, regarding the nearby box with a suspicious squint.

"Alas, in this case at least, the poor man would appear to be the victim of a history quite beyond his control," explained Caisley. "You are referring, of course, to the undisputable fact that by far the major part of his gift to the University of Oxford is composed of the vast collection built up by the remarkable Tradescants – father and son – and bequeathed by son to Ashmole, after more than a decade of friendship and scholarly partnership."

"A fact, if I recall, hotly disputed by Hester Tradescant," Greene interposed, wryly, "Did she not swear until her dying day that her late husband's gift was made whilst in his cups?"

"She did, Richard, until the day that Chancery found in Elias's favour after a two-year wrangle, and she, poor lady, was found drowned in her own garden pond..."

They exchanged glances, as Caisley blandly continued: "It must be said, though, that our man did his subsequent reputation scant service by the sheer aggressiveness with which he pursued his claim. It has done little to recommend the sweetness of his nature to posterity. No, the unfortunate historical circumstance to which I alluded is the simple, if tragic, fact that by far the greater proportion of Elias's own collection – manuscripts, thousands of coins, curiosities reputedly beyond compare – was destroyed by a fire whilst in storage at the Middle Temple in the late 1670s."

"So, he remained resident in London for all the years after leaving here? Never returning?" asked Blomefield, attempting to keep the disappointment from showing.

"We know that in later years he gifted various fine prayer books to the Cathedral, apart, of course, from his being instrumental in the saving and restoration of the very fabric itself. He obviously held the Cathedral in the highest regard – though not a regard whose memory was ever preserved with any great enthusiasm, due – one must suspect – to the *breadth* of his other interests. History, *Lichfield's* history," he added, "may well have taken a slightly different course, however, had his later wish to become the city's member of Parliament ever been permitted to come to fruition."

"*Permitted*? By whom?" enquired Greene.

"By no less than the King himself," Caisley replied, "though now, by the regrettable James the Second rather than his late lamented brother, Charles. No, for all the likelihood of Elias's election – being known as the favoured candidate of local electors – he stood down at his monarch's express command, and some royal favourite was duly elected in his stead. Though," he concluded, wryly, "one suspects that Elias would yet again have prospered from some *quid pro quo* from an appreciative monarch. His was a life built upon such *accommodations*."

Reaching for the long-cold coffee pot, Caisley tilted it with a show of optimism missed entirely by their host. Replacing it with a sad shake of his head, he spread his hands, saying: "There you have it, gentlemen: the sum – in total – of my own small knowledge of our enigmatic Elias. Whither, one wonders, does it lead?"

"Oh, my Lord!" exclaimed Greene, glancing at his watch: "In *my* case it must be back to the shop. I do not know where the morning has gone."

"Nor I, the coffee," added Caisley, looking pointedly at the oblivious cleric.

ITEM:

In a lofty Glass Case, the left hand the entrance to the Inner
Museum, are the following articles brought from Otaheita,
O-why-ye, New Caledonia, Easter Island, Sandwich, Friendly,
King George's, New Amsterdam, and other Islands in the South
Seas, viz. A Formee or Military Gorget, worn by the Warriors,
composed of Feathers of the Tropic Bird, Teeth of the Shark,
and fringed with Hair of White Dog, in a curious manner. An
ornament for the Forehead, of Cock's Feathers, and the Shell of
the Pearl Oyster. The weapon called Pattow Pattow, in Wood.

2nd May, 1776. The soothing passage of time, in the form of several
days of enforced rest, had restored not only Theodosia to her usual
spirits, but also those of the larger Greene household, inextricably
bound up, as it was, with both shop below and museum above.
Relief at the Mistress's recovery, not less than her own marked
sweetening of temper, had found its foil in perfect spring weather,
a fact not missed by a newly attentive husband.

"I propose a small excursion, my dear. It is an age since we have
enjoyed the pleasure of a day at the races, so tomorrow why do we
not leave the shop in Tillett's hands for the afternoon and take
advantage of what promises to be a most clement day?"

Although delighted, and not a little surprised, by the spontaneity
of the invitation, Theodosia looked up from her accounts, frowned,
and consulted the desk almanac open in front of her.

"There is but one small fly in your ointment, Richard: we
have, as usual, missed the March meetings and must now await
September's, which is rather longer than you intended, I imagine?"

"Ah, there I must correct you, my dear. It was not Whittington Heath I had in mind – nothing so grand – but rather the simpler pleasures to be enjoyed at The Shoulder of Mutton Steeplechase meeting, tomorrow afternoon, out on the London Road. There will be all the fun of the fair, so to speak, but without that intolerable press of coaches and crowds that I do so hate on the Heath."

"Oh, husband, is there no *end* to your extravagance?" she enquired with a smile, adding: "Yes, I think it would be a capital idea. In fact, if you are agreeable, I propose we invite a few friends and make up a small party?" She studied the almanac once more, before exclaiming: "Heavens above, Richard! Mid-week diversions at The Shoulder of Mutton *and* a theatrical outing on Saturday? Can a girl *contemplate* so much excitement in the space of a single week? And all in this little city so unkindly slighted by Cousin Johnson – or so Miss Seward would have me believe."

"Slighted? By Samuel? I find that hard to…"

"Oh Richard, talking of the family Bear," said Theodosia: "It quite slipped my mind that the London carrier delivered a long and dangerously pointed package some days back. Might it be your promised exhibits from that quarter? I had Margery put it in the woodshed."

Biting his tongue, and well remembering the storm conditions prevailing at the time of the carrier's delivery, he nodded his thanks with masterly restraint. Having fetched the package, he carried it carefully upstairs where he unwrapped it in the Museum. As already identified by his astute wife, the contents proved to be the promised lance and dagger.

"*Abyssinian*? Hmm, I think not," murmured the Apothecary to himself, turning the unsheathed dagger over in his hands, its hooked, heavily ribbed blade dull with grease: "Arabian, more-like, though this…" – he hefted the painted and tufted shaft of the heavy spear, admiring its balance and obvious lethality – "this I can *well* imagine being from the land of Prester John."

Making a mental note to send prompt thanks, he was already

sizing up the precise area for their display and deciding that in the interests of familial harmony – if not in strictest accordance with academic niceties – that both objects comprising 'The Doctor Samuel Johnson Rasselas Loan' would be labelled 'Abyssinian'. One never could tell when another visitation might occur.

After a light sprinkling of rain before seven, the proverbial promise of an improved day had materialised by mid-morning, the earlier shower lending a lucent sparkle to the hedgerows and fields along the London road.

They had trundled by the Grammar School, only barely negotiated the scaffolded arch of the much-decayed South Gate and passed along the sentinel rank of red-brick chimneys that distinguished the ancient pilgrim hospice of St John's Without The Barrs, and were now ambling below the wooded eminence of Borrowcop, all feeling they had left the confines of the city well behind.

As the heavy horses pulling the well-sprung wain bore the Greene party and a dozen other racegoers at a leisurely plod towards their destination, a blue-liveried coach and six, driven with little regard for the jovial throng upon the London Road, plunged past at breakneck speed. Scattering all in its path, its passage was followed by angry shouts and shaken fists. A momentary glimpse of flushed, laughing faces within and a coachman, guard and postillions stiff and unresponsive, above, was all they received as the large vehicle and its carefree occupants careered along the road.

"If I'm called to mend any broken necks in that direction, they can all go whistle as they look elsewhere," said Greene, angrily, dusting himself down from where he and the wain's other occupants had been jostled from their benches by horses rearing in alarm at the others' passage.

Gradually, order was restored, horses soothed, and their destination could be seen at the centre of the crowds gathering in the road outside the substantial inn to their right. A boy, bearing a satchelful of handbills, ran up alongside the lumbering wain, handing his wares up to reaching hands. Greene removed spectacles from a waistcoat pocket, the better to read:

Shoulder of Mutton Meeting, 1776. To be run for, on Wednesday the 3rd May, across the fields near The Shoulder of Mutton, Lichfield, for a NEW SADDLE complete: by mounts under fifteen Hands.
Same day one clear heat for a NEW BRIDLE, though the winner of the saddle not allowed to start.

The Apothecary decided he was going to enjoy every moment of the afternoon ahead and found himself grinning around the members of their small party: Lionel Blomefield grimaced back, looking uncomfortable in a broadcloth suit whose best days were long since gone, its once black pelt now turning a distinctly greenish tinge.

"He will neither shop with me, nor I suspect, settle his tailor's bill," Elspeth had informed Theodosia, "so from now on I have informed him he will bear the consequences of a wife dubbed Mrs Scarecrow."

The prospect seemed to have had little effect on the elderly cleric now busily attempting to brush spilt snuff from his lapels. As they were deposited in the teeming coach-yard behind the inn, Greene, in the act of handing the ladies down, glanced up to see the first-floor gallery that ran the length of the building was already packed with the more well-heeled customers staking out the optimum vantage point for the finish-line. As he led the party towards the small Stewards' Enclosure where he had arranged seating and refreshment, their senses reeled from the competing allures of frying onions, pie-stalls, hog-roast, spitted mutton and beef. All this was noisily complemented by the sideshow barkers, the tinny skirl of a barrel-organ and the competing cries of the dozens of vendors invariably drawn to the city race-days, bear-baitings and – less frequently – the hangings on Gallows Wharf.

Unlike the huge biennial meetings out on the Heath, where all the city hostelries of note set up their booths to compete for the purses of the thirsty hordes, here, the landlord of the Shoulder made certain that he, and he alone, controlled the commerce of food and drink. It was always said that as his cookhouse baked day and night for a week before a Wednesday race-meet, the wary diner should keep an eye well-peeled for *Thursday pies*.

Intending to gain some higher vantage of the far-flung course, Greene passed through the densest of the crowd, moving off towards the side where a variety of vehicles, including their own, were haphazardly drawn up against the straggling treelined hedgerow that marked the showground's boundary. There, amongst a smaller cluster of the finer conveyances stood the blue-liveried coach, its magnificent team now unhitched, four tethered and grazing, the lead pair, superb roan stallions, being walked by a powerfully built young groom obviously well-practised in the control of his mettlesome charges. Searching in vain to spot the coachman who had driven through them with such disdain, Greene stiffened, abruptly, at the sight of another figure, climbing down from his perch atop the gleaming vehicle: Pearce, the sheep-like bully-boy, player of second fiddle to the unlamented Lemman, late of Walhill. Determined this unwelcome presence should not blight their day, Greene turned and walked away.

The afternoon passed agreeably, with its single greatest surprise being the revelation of Grace Beasley's knowledge of horseflesh. "I was something of a disappointment to my dear, late Mama," she confessed to the party at large, having only just finished counting her substantial winnings into her purse with obvious relish. "She always maintained that had I not misspent my girlish years in tree-climbing, target-shooting and, worst of all, bareback riding in my brother's company, devoting them instead, to proper, lady-like pursuits, then I would indubitably have snared a baronet by the time I was twenty!"

General laughter met her admission, as she was proving to be the most animated companion any could have wished for, particularly when she added: "If nothing else, her dashed hopes in that direction *did* illustrate the particular shortsightedness demonstrated by doting parents the world over: a comprehensive inability to see their own offspring as others do."

Waving away gallant protestations to the contrary, she rose and, linking arms with the Apothecary, requested he accompany her for a look at the remaining competitors, being shown for the afternoon's final heat.

As Greene escorted her through the jovial crowds, back towards the inn and the enclosure, a burst of raucous laughter from the balcony drew their attention up to the crowd at its rail.

"It's *him*, Richard," she murmured, eyes never leaving the garrulous figure, who by some accident or design looked down towards them as she spoke. For just a moment he seemed taken aback by the sight of the staring woman below. Then, though, with the most deliberate pantomime of courtesy, he doffed his hat and acknowledged her presence with a humourless smile. She flinched as if struck, and turned away, swaying, as if about to tumble. It was only as he moved to hurriedly grasp Grace's shoulder, that the Apothecary glimpsed another face in the crowded yard: pale, haggard features beneath lank black hair scarcely contained by a coarse bonnet, another face apparently transfixed by a large man who had now turned back, laughing, to the cronies that surrounded him.

As if somehow sensing Greene's shock of recognition, Aggie Crede's head jerked round, her mouth opening in an 'O' of discomfited surprise before she ducked away, losing herself amongst milling ostlers and the early leavers of the day. Unable to do more than help Grace Beasley to a newly vacated bench against the inn wall, the Apothecary scanned the ever-shifting crowd to no avail: the gaunt young widow had disappeared as if she had been no more than a figment of his imagination. He knelt in concern beside his distressed companion, noting the sheen of sweat on her high brow and the pain he sensed behind the screwed-shut eyes.

"The headache?" he enquired gently.

"Worse than ever," she whispered. "Forgive me, Richard, it was the shock of seeing that... that..."

The distraught woman begged to be taken home and was obviously in such terrible distress that Greene had little option but to accompany her. Comforting as best he could, he led her back to where he could wave and summon Theodosia from the enclosure. Together they hurried her to where the chairmen waited, out beyond the inn. The Apothecary, though mindful of their other guests, elected to accompany the distraught woman.

From the wreckage of the outing he would take away one bitter consolation: he could now put a face to the name he had come to loathe: a face – he silently swore – that he would see one day at Gallows Wharf.

(35)

Above the Alcove. The artful carving, in gilded limewood, of a
winged cherubic head, personifying a Zephyr. A Weathervane,
much decayed and of great antiquity, of a bird of prey

The Ashmole House. Lambeth. May, 1692. Again, the dance, the
damnable dance: disembodied legs *bent...legs straightened...legs
stretched...and parted...and together ...feet joined. Then, kicks to the
left, kicks to the right...Point and heel...twitch and kick...and still...
and kick...and still...and...still.*

The Dancing Master bends low, in the courtliest of bows:
plumed hat, ringleted periwig and face all removed with one
scything sweep of a lace-cuffed arm. Yellow corpse-teeth click and
rattle in the oldest grin and empty sockets leach the light to fuel
their utter darkness. Cuffs fall back as up he stands, a raw-boned
finger lifts a lower jaw in studious appraisal, a skull tilts back as if
to view, though neither cartilage nor nostril yet remain to flare or
wrinkle up in rapt consideration. Then arms flail together, bones of
hands and fingers thwack and rattle in percussive glee, applauding
for the dancer, slumped, askew forever in the tunnel's maw.

The watcher kicked out in terror to free himself from the
crushing weight of night, the grinning horror that bore down
upon him, skeletal arms raised in obscene invitation: *Now ye'll
dance; not will ye dance? There is no other choice.*

"No, for Christ's sake, no!" a voice was shrieking, as his legs, his
leaden legs, seemed weighed, dragged ever further down, into the
dark that pulsed about him like a living thing. Then he was awake,
stinking with rank sweat, bandaged legs and gouty feet tangled

in an agonising knot of sheet and quilted counterpane. A blessed glow, an angel from the world of light, moved rapidly towards him, fighting through the endless night.

Propped against mountainous bolsters, the old man lay twitching, gasping for breath and staring, still wide-eyed, as if to catch the final wraiths of nightmare as they slipped, sniggering, away. The seventy-five-year-old Elias Ashmole was awake now, utterly spent by the appalling nightmare that has plagued his sleep for so many years. Tonight, had been the worst ever, its horror seeming to cling to him, a miasmic shroud.

Within minutes, a terrified maidservant had been summoned with cloths and hot water, followed by a large bumper of strong spirits, placed now in his quietening hands. He was helped down from his bed as it was remade, and he sat, feet propped on stools, beside the re-stoked embers of the chamber's fire.

Nothing had dimmed the terror of that eldritch dance of death. Not one of the forty-six years since that ghastly night had softened or mitigated the stark memory that slithered back to haunt his nights and waking dreams. Exalted old age might have played its part to keep at bay the gnawing rodents of recollection and unending guilt, but no coat of arms, no honours, nor favours from a grateful king, could arm him against the phantasm of the small hours when the soul must somehow find its way to dawn.

Suddenly, it came to him: he must be done with this before it did for him. He was only too familiar with his aged body's dissolution and dysfunction not to recognise the lancing pains to which he had woken. He would be done with the *substance* of his damnable memories. That was it. It was a cup that must be passed, that *could* – for some reason – now be passed, though he had neither the energy nor the will to understand quite why. The box and the papers must go to where they would be safe, to one who would know best how to act upon the message they contained.

Furiously resisting attempts to get him back to bed, he gave terse instructions that a secret cupboard in the wainscoting be opened and the box it contained brought to him with pen and paper.

The manservant had known better than to equivocate and had slipped the small key into the artfully disguised keyhole in the room's dark panelling, revealing a sizeable cupboard as the perfectly fitted door swung open. Bundled papers, the box in question and... *no*! Best not to even *glance* too long at anything Old Ashmole wished concealed. Twenty-three years in the employ of a man whispered to be a Magus among magicians had taught him that his master's little ways were best accommodated without question or comment.

Elias Ashmole was left alone in the flickering twilight, casting a misty gaze at the long-familiar chamber around him. He remembered so many other firelit rooms, soft, pale flesh warmed and mellowed by the dance of flames, memories of schemes hatched and assignations planned, of rituals and conjurations, of casting horoscopes, of sigils and 'the antient art', of food, good wine, and conversations spun out through sleepless nights.

Now, though, the time was long overdue: a time to act and then at last to sleep in guileless peace once more before the dancing master came again. His hand trembled badly as he inked the quill, black stains blooming on his swaddled knees.

Brother Harrison..., he began.

(36)

In a neat gilded FRAME next the Fire-place. Two pilgrim ampullae
in leadwork bearing the seal of the antient Priory of Our Lady
of Walsingham and a fragment of a Palmer's badge in the form
of the Holy House of Nazareth, from that celebrated Shrine

4ᵗʰ May, 1776. When Greene came across an unannounced letter,
propped on his mantelpiece, it simply provided further evidence
– if any were needed – of Margery's unspoken fury at being
prevented from placing her usual Shoulder of Mutton wager
by her employers' thoughtless decision to go to the steeplechase
themselves. Whilst the Apothecary had resigned himself to days
of frigid resentment to come, he had little way of guessing just
how much worse today was about to become.

My dear Greene…, the letter began:

*Whilst being most grateful for your kind consideration in the
matter of the Tauroctony, I feel I should apprise you of the
strangest coincidence. I shall, though, with your forbearance,
preface that explication with a word of preliminary
clarification:*

*I am particularly well-served, as you know, by a number of
agents who seek out Curiosities and Objets de Vertu for my
various collections, and it was from one of these, a trusted and
decent fellow in Chester, that the coincidence, if such it can be
called, now stems.*

Scarcely a week after the arrival of your intriguing description
– my response to which is shamefully tardy due to my absence
on parliamentary business – he appraised me of a piece whose
description tallies in every respect with your own, the piece
being cast in white gold and of identical dimensions.

He was, in truth, somewhat coy when pressed on its
provenance, prepared to say only that it was the property of
a gentleman who, in turn, deals only through a man of his
own. I was left with the strong impression, however, that the
possibility of further antiquities was being hinted at, from the
same source. Whilst remaining non-committal, as you will well
appreciate, I have requested that the object in question be made
available for my inspection next week, when a matter concerned
with the Assizes calls me to Chester. Whilst, of course, satisfying
my own curiosity, a close inspection will permit me to ascertain
whether the piece bears the same marks of mutilation you so ably
described.

Might it be possible that you are being played false in this,
Richard? Coincidence surely has its bounds. I ask only out of
concern for an old and valued friend,

as, Sir, I remain truly yours,

Ashton Lever. Alkrington.

Shocked though he was by the letter, it confirmed Greene's
grimmest suspicions: the helpless Joe Crede, tortured into
revealing the whereabouts of the goose which laid the golden
eggs; also of an incredible relic now for sale at sufficient distance
for, supposedly, no connection to be made of its acquisition. It was
only now that an awful suspicion dawned on the Apothecary: had
they been overheard at Crede's squalid bedside when the little

wonder was revealed? Had there been a hidden eavesdropper outside the tumbledown hovel?

Then, though, came another, unwelcome, realisation. Apart from a barely literate widow flown, one to whose testimony society would pay little heed, he alone remained to make the connection of kidnap, torture and murder, to point the finger at Hawson and his remaining thug.

An afternoon of blessed normality, of the minor surgical procedures that occupied much of his time each week, gave Greene the opportunity to consider their ailing friend.

The rate at which Grace Beasley's condition was deteriorating filled him with a mixture of impotent rage and professional despair. For all his reassurances to her that surgery remained an option, he had, once before, lived with the tragic result of just such a well-intentioned course of action.

Admittedly, the severity and location of that patient's tumour had stretched both his surgical dexterity and knowledge of the cranium past their limits, but – for all the family's gratitude and understanding – the resulting debilitation of the man had been a constant reproach to the Apothecary for the few remaining months of his patient's life. The thought of leaving Grace Beasley as a blind, drooling shell of her former self was not something he could contemplate, though the inevitable, plummeting decline that had now begun, was scarcely better.

Theodosia had insisted that she would sit with Grace for the evening, so after a solitary supper, he took the opportunity of a stroll into the bright evening, relishing the still air and the medley of birdsong across the Minster Pool as his footsteps took him through the ivied ruin of the South Gate and into the other-worldly calm of The Close.

So absorbed was he in his own thoughts, that he failed at first to see the hobbling figure leaving the Palace and walking slowly down the sloping path towards the door of the north transept.

It was the stooped, elderly man himself who paused upon his stick, breathing heavily, before calling out a greeting to the oblivious Apothecary.

Roused from his reverie, Greene saw Canon Residentiary Seward and returned his wave. Hurrying down the gentle incline of the short-cropped grass, he approached the bent figure with genuine pleasure: "Canon Seward! What a pleasure to see you out and about; Theodosia had told me you were somewhat recovered, though I see now she underestimated the extent of your convalescence."

The elderly man smiled wryly and replied: "I have been persuaded to recover to at least the extent that I need not call upon poor, dear Anna at all hours of the day and night. Though the longer-term prospects for a dotard of such parlous health are, I fear, in hands other than mine. I can at least give thanks for the renewed ability to shuffle to and fro, if it keeps me from under the family's feet."

The Apothecary, wearily familiar with the distressing effects of such nervous and muscular deterioration as had kept Canon Seward to his bed for several months, marvelled at the sheer strength of character that had brought Anna's dearly loved parent back to even this degree of mobility.

"Your recovery must be due in no small part to the devoted attention you have received. It is, in my experience, the sovereign remedy for those fortunate enough to enjoy it."

"Talking of which, Richard, I am aware of how much Anna has enjoyed the company of your own dear wife. I trust she is recovered? Anna was most concerned at the turn she took."

"She is quite recovered, Canon Seward, though I still cannot put my own culpability behind me. Knowing – even though underestimating – the scale of her vertigo as I did, it was thoughtless in the extreme to permit her to place herself in such jeopardy."

"Ah, well: *least said soonest mended* – as the old saw would have us believe, dear fellow. You must stop blaming yourself, as I feel certain the good lady will have done. Now, might one impose upon your *own* good nature to request a small kindness?"

"Of course," replied the Apothecary, "How may I be of assistance?"

Canon Seward indicated the bulk of the Chapter House rising below them: "I shall not be so uncharitable as to say *badgered*, Richard, but one has been repeatedly *requested* by certain parties to examine the state of our Chapter House."

"Is that not the role of the Clerk of the Works?" enquired the Apothecary, puzzled as to where this was leading.

"*Yes* and *no*, one might say, though 'no' when it comes to the vexed question of our library. The upper rooms – the old Treasury in particular – are perceived, in certain quarters, as the prime location for its re-establishment, though, frankly, one has grave misgivings, not least for its stability. I have capitulated at least to the extent of agreeing to examine it for myself, though the stairs are not a prospect I relish. In truth, the thought of that particular ascent has lent no wings to my visit. It must be twenty years since I ventured there, as a far sprightlier man, one must confess."

"I shall be delighted to accompany you, Canon Seward, particularly as I have never visited the upper chambers myself." Even as he replied he heard the echo of himself asking: *And he pointed where did you say? Towards the Chapter House?*

Both men were out of breath by the time the small landing had been reached, though the Canon needed several moments before he could proceed. Drawing a large, blackened key from his pocket, he wheezed: "Would you be so kind? I find I scarcely have the strength to lift the blessed thing, let alone negotiate one of our more ancient locks."

The key did, indeed, take all Greene's strength to turn, though finally, with a shriek of complaint, the lock capitulated, and rusty hinges gave up their struggle against the small man's shoulder.

They stepped through into a musty, green twilight, the pale

radiance of a spring evening leached by the cloudy glass and revealing a sprawl of lumber, scaffolding and the unloved detritus of a forgotten loft. The cobwebbed vaulting sprung like great stone wings from a central pillar, as in the Chapter, below, meeting corbelled supports spaced around the octagonal chamber's walls. Those, Greene saw, were scarred by all the marks of a violent past, pocked by shrapnel and crazed with clumsily rendered cracks.

Seward followed his gaze, muttering dolefully: "This bore more than its share of the Great Steeple's collapse, it would seem. It appears to be a classic case of 'out of sight, out of mind', does it not, Richard? The tokens of that hellish destruction persist in all our nooks and crannies, as you will have noticed. I am ashamed to admit that they have lost none of their ability to move me to most unchristian sentiments towards their perpetrators."

Greene nodded in mute agreement, clambering, with some difficulty, across the littered floor to stare out across the Palace grounds beyond. As he turned to renegotiate the jumbled obstacles, he barked a shin against a large stone fragment. With a sharp intake of breath, he managed to suppress the profanity that rose to his lips, conscious both of the company and the place in which he found himself. Noticing his obvious discomfort, the Canon called across to him: "You have stumbled upon the remains of the shrine, I see."

It took a moment to realise that his aged companion had made a joke, though Greene – after managing a strained smile in response – now peered about him with a new, sharp-eyed interest to where a dozen formless fragments of stone were roughly grouped.

"One should, I suppose, provide even those sad remnants with a decent home," the Canon said, "though what interest they would hold for our increasingly secular times, I can scarcely imagine. Perhaps some things are best left undisturbed."

Something in his tone caused the Apothecary to look across at the preoccupied elderly man with new attention, though the Canon appeared, already, to have shifted his interest towards the low doorway that led through into a small chamber above the vestibule below.

"As I recall, it is in there that the most apparent evidence of destruction remains." He disappeared through the low arch, to be joined a moment later by the Apothecary.

"The west wall here will need complete rebuilding, d'you see, Richard? Opposite where, once, the altar must have stood." He pointed to the jagged crack, running a hand's breadth from floor to ceiling, though Greene's attention was elsewhere.

"*The altar*? Forgive me, Canon Seward, you have lost me."

"Oh, did I not say?" the old man replied, "This was once a chapel, though many years ago. One of two dedicated to St. Peter. Really quite unusual, I have to say, finding one upstairs so to speak, but here it was. Have you never come across Stukeley's description of its mural? Scarcely a trace remains…" He squinted towards the dim, stained wall in the fading light: "Look, just there, and to one side there: the outline, in part, of Peter's inverted crucifixion, with – one presumes – a last vestige of a standing figure to the right."

The Apothecary became suddenly, acutely, aware of a strange sensation in his head, as if a small, seldom-used cog was being nudged, coaxed, into movement before it could engage another; a mechanism stirring, tensing, with the sense of impending activation.

"Soon, even that sad trace will have gone," the Canon continued, "like so much else in the poor old place, and one will just have to imagine him, head down, staring at the pavement."

No, it would not come. He shook his head in sheer frustration: there was something either about the Canon's words, or the place, *this place,* itself, that he was missing. He *knew* it, his every instinct itched, prickled, with its nearness, and yet, like a movement sensed just past the edge of vision, it danced away, mocking his dullness as it went.

"Well, it is much as I feared," – Canon Seward's words broke his frowning concentration, and the moment passed – "and not improved by the negligence of our own times. If we are to have a Chapter House at all, monies will have to be found. Without a doubt, those cracks will be growing wider by the year."

The elderly cleric lent confidingly towards his companion, before adding: "Though not a sentiment I would normally voice aloud, Richard, I must confess to growing doubt about the ultimate fate of these ancient piles. Magnificent as they were in their intention, and in their day, are we, the faithful, to be burdened to an ever-greater degree by the voracious demands of their maintenance, their very survival when all about us we see the needy, the poor, the wrongs which cry out for righting?"

Shocked, to his own surprise, the Apothecary replied: "Whilst I can applaud and admire the essential goodness of such sentiments, Canon Seward, I am committed to my own belief that it is only through our connection with, our understanding of, the past, that we can make any true sense of our present – let alone our future. I believe that in the case of this, our own Cathedral, it is the very miracle of its renaissance, its rescue from utter ruin, wherein the true value of its spiritual message lies. Can we not see in its resurrection the perfect metaphor for that of our Saviour? The promise of hope eternal, of renewal without end? Given the paucity of man's imagination, I believe that the craving for a *tangible* grace, for the *visible* majesty and beauty of such places, surely goes to the very roots of our being: they *feed* us, as we, in turn, must nurture them."

The stooped man regarded the quiet sincerity in the Apothecary's eyes for a long moment before saying: "I do believe I have been put in my place, dear fellow."

Before Greene could demur, he continued: "Perhaps in living where the spirit calls, it is one's constant *proximity*, one's over-familiarity, with the church, that can blind one – or at least dull one – to those very qualities you so eloquently defend."

He smiled, sadly, placing a hand on Greene's arm, before saying: "The fact that you should be placed in the position of defending such simple truths reveals the measure of my own shortcomings to a degree I could not have imagined, Richard. Who is to say that our meeting tonight was not ordained to serve that very purpose, when I could see no further than my own preconceptions and convenience? I am in your debt, my friend."

Embarrassed and moved in equal measure, Greene could do no more than nod, staring once more around the dank walls of the unloved space, saying finally: "It would, I think, make a capital library, for might it not be entirely fitting that a collection rebuilt so laboriously, so lovingly, from the fragments of its original glory, should be displayed in what became the sole viable remnant of its original home?"

"Ah, 'The *genius loci*', indeed," smiled Seward, in agreement: "though it has taken our conversation to remind me that it was that very *spirit of place* that drew me here from Eyam, so many years ago. I trust I shall never again take it for granted. If you can spare a short time more, to hand a tottering oldster home, perhaps you will do me the honour of taking a cordial at the Palace? I know Anna will enjoy your company as much as have I."

"Whilst I am, of course, overjoyed to hear of Mrs Greene's complete recovery, my concern for poor Grace grows by the day, Mr Greene." Though burdened by the habitual limp from a fall in adolescence, the plump figure of Anna Seward moved with a singular grace as she came across the elegant room to refill his glass

"Although I do not presume to trespass upon your professional confidence, is there nothing I can do? She seems to fade before our very eyes."

The Apothecary hesitated, torn between his own personal concerns and those of a sacrosanct confidentiality.

"Your friendship, by way of company and visits, can only be efficacious, though it should perhaps be judged by your own perception of the lady's preparedness to receive you, Miss Seward.

Some of the time she will doubtless be delighted, though at others, however much she may wish for company, the unpredictable nature of her... condition... will preclude it." Anna Seward recognised courteous equivocation when she heard it and enquired no further.

"I am reliably informed that the creature Hawson has returned and was seen at Wednesday's race-meeting, Mr Greene. I am not unaware that poor, dear Grace will have been confronted by that unwelcome and untimely presence. I regret that my own enquiries in that direction have borne little fruit, other than to reveal that his mercantile activities extend to anything on which a quick profit can be turned. I have learned of land transactions on the Wirral, speculation on wheat and barley futures at the Chester Exchange and, of course, continuing involvement in that other trade we so abhor.

"My correspondent has ascertained he owns one large vessel, the *Medusa*, outright, and has a major stake in another, both sailing out of Liverpool. Other than those scrappits of intelligence, he would appear to be one of those men sufficiently insulated by his wealth to make any form of investigation into his affairs difficult."

The Apothecary regarded his hostess with renewed admiration, then, said: "Whilst not at liberty to discuss the matter at present, I, too, have gained a *scrappit* which I intend to pursue, though to what end, I cannot predict. I shall be happy to keep you informed should the matter prosper. I am intrigued to hear of these other *mercantile* activities of his, as I live in hope that one such might, just *might*, prove to be his undoing."

She nodded with satisfaction: "I shall add my fervent hope to your own."

As she saw him to the door, she paused on the threshold and said: "I gather from dear Doctor Darwin that you shall all be coming to my small theatrical event at the Guildhall, Mr Greene?"

"We anticipate it with relish," responded the Apothecary. "Am I correct in thinking that the lady in question is a friend of yours?"

"Mrs Siddons is, indeed, an old and valued friend, which is

how I prevailed upon her to include our sorry old Guildhall in her provincial tour. And though I say *old* of our friendship, she – most fortunate of creatures – is the possessor not only of great beauty but of all the vigour of youth, to boot!"

"I have no doubt it will be a most memorable occasion," said Richard Greene, taking his leave.

37

A curious deception in a neat gilt Frame; being a Metzotint
of his Majesty King George III. which, by a touch, is
instantly changed into a resemblance of the Queen. The
work of Mr Obadiah Westwood of Birmingham.

4ᵗʰ April, 1776. The Apothecary had returned home to an empty
house, and, feeling still inexplicably disturbed by the experience
with Canon Seward, had taken a glass of brandy up to the
Museum, where he sat now, in the still twilight of a large room
lit only by the few lights from the street below. What was it that
had eluded him? What insight, what revelation had flickered just
beyond his grasp? He could sense something there, still, like a
maddening itch that could not be located, let alone scratched. He
sighed and took an absent-minded sip from his glass, knowing
that no amount of straining, no furrowed brow nor anxious pacing
would bring it any closer. These things, these nameless, formless,
promptings that he had come to know so well, came and went
in their time and their time only. Still, he might just try to help
things along.

He lit several large candles, procured for their inordinate size
and longevity from the small shop on The Dam that had provided
the innumerable accoutrements of cathedral and diocesan ritual for
as long as anyone could remember. On their tall, gilded sticks, they
lit the rooms with an amber glow whose warmth at once caressed
and soothed Greene's racing mind, so that within a few more sips
and sleepy glances at the dancing flames, his head fell forward on
his chest and the sound of breathing turned to steady snores.

As first one, then two, and finally a trio of the Museum's collection of clocks chimed to mark the hour, the sleeping figure stirred with a grunt, then sat bolt upright, suddenly wide-eyed, in a startling metamorphosis:

"Peter! *Thou art Peter!*" he exclaimed to the empty rooms, jumping a mite unsteadily to his feet.

He hurried across to where the box lay beneath the cloth-draped table and hauled it up. Throwing back the lid he located the sheet he sought: the line drawing of a cruciform object whose inscription and oddly matched text had so perplexed him. Laying it on the tabletop he pulled one of the tall candlesticks closer, and as he bent to scrutinise the sheet once more, heard the canon's words:

> *…the outline, in part, of Peter's inverted crucifixion…one will just have to imagine him, head down, staring at the pavement.*

"Oh, Elias! your wily man," he breathed, eyes fixed to the sheet as if its contents might fade in a blink. Now, he could read the archaic inscription with perfect ease, for it was not the *INRI* that spelled out the title of Jesus on an infinity of crucifixes – why *should* it be? He heard himself laugh aloud – *for this was no crucifix*: 'AASB', this read, instead. That last character was an Anglo-Saxon form of 'B'. He said the words out loud, then, repeating them in the childlike singsong of the nursery rhyme: 'As above, so below, as above, so…'

> *…Peter, inverted…head-down…*

He turned the sheet upside down and smacked an open palm against his brow. There it was! – for even the simplest soul to see: the ground plan of the Cathedral, set within the outline of a meaninglessly decorative cross. *Here* were the four great pillars of the central crossing beneath the spire, *here* the slender pillars

of Nave and Choir, *here* the buttressed apse of the east end – the Lady Chapel, and – best of all – *here* the exact position of the Great Shrine when it had stood in all its glory. He thought he might explode with the excitement of the revelation, though how he could have missed it until now..? How could..?

Theodosia's voice cut through his racing thoughts: "*Richard? Richard!* Will you come down? I am too weary to face more stairs."

She had left Milley's only when she was certain that Grace

was sleeping restfully, rather than waking fretfully from the dozes which had occupied much of the evening.

"It is the strangest and, in some respects, the most distressing thing, Richard. For much of the time she is the very soul of lucidity and good humour, until she is overtaken – overwhelmed might be a better word – by the pain of her aching head.

"Could you not do her the kindness of increasing the potency of the doses? Even to *witness* the agony she is enduring is almost more than I can bear. I simply cannot comprehend how she can retain her sanity in the face of such assaults, Richard."

He saw the unshed tears glistening in his wife's eyes and went to take her hands in his, as she continued: "I am certain that she could see nothing, in her extremity earlier tonight. And I could *do* nothing more than hold her as if she were a babe in arms."

"I regret that from the very outset I have prescribed to the fullest extent, my dear, so rapidly advanced did her condition already appear to be. To increase her dosage would be to render her insensible, incapable of independent movement at the very least. In truth, I have been amazed at her ability to function as she does under the present regime: it would incapacitate stronger constitutions than that of poor, dear Grace."

She sat back, brow furrowed, eyes closed with tiredness: "She spoke so wistfully of her childhood, of all the happy years spent up at Walhill. You know that she is determined, *desperate* one could even say, to see it once again? The Lord only knows how that might ever be possible, though."

She paused, leaning forward to warm her hands at the low fire. "It is as if in being denied return to the happiest place of her life she has lost some integral part of herself, her very heart. Walhill's loss and most particularly the *circumstances* of its loss seem to be consuming her."

He wished he had words of comfort but could find none. For some moments they sat in a morose silence broken only by the chiming of the half-hour from the tower of St. Mary's and the indecipherable sounds of the small city beyond their windows. Finally, the Apothecary turned to his silent wife and said: "I believe I may finally be on the way to breaking old Ashmole's code and all that it conceals, my dear – you know, the matter of the box that has had Lionel and I so foxed?"

She stood, abruptly, speaking as she looked down at him, the desperate weariness of her tone infinitely more disturbing than any flare of anger: "There are times when *I* believe your single-mindedness may one day break my heart, Richard Greene. I cannot bear to hear another word. I am going to bed."

He had the heart for nothing after that, and waited only long enough until he could slip into their darkened chamber and clamber, carefully, into bed. He lay, listening to the settling rhythms of his wife's breathing, his head a whirl of conflicting emotions and vagrant thoughts. One though, pushed and prodded to the forefront of his tired mind: *I'm here now, as I've always been; not hidden, just concealed; you'll find me only when you have the eyes to see.*

38

ITEM:

A Miscellaneous collection of Coins and Medals in Silver and
Copper, viz: Innocent 8th. P.M. Paulus Venetus. P.M. Anno
Christi MCCCLXV, (Copper). Late Lord Anson, by Pingo;
Reverse, Saunders, Brett, Denis, Campbel, Keppel, Saumarez;
the Officers, who accompanied him in his Voyage round the
World, (Silver). Alexander Pope, 1741, (Copper). Augustus
Keppel, (Metal, gilt). General Washington, (Copper).

6th May, 1776. Neither the softening grace of candlelight nor
the excited, well-dressed audience for the evening's performance
could disguise the fact that Lichfield's crumbling Guildhall was
more suited to an auction of livestock than to the thespian treat so
eagerly anticipated. Even the tireless energies of Miss Seward at
her most formidable had failed to solve the problem of the birds.

The nests in the cobwebbed rafters had, for the most part,
been raked and prodded down, but their dispossessed occupants
still defied all attempts to remove them. Two cats – protesting
with tooth and claw – had been bundled up into the gloomy
stratosphere of the roof-joists, until prodded out along the dusty
beams towards the offenders. Their intended prey promptly
swooped and fluttered away across the bare boarded expanse
below, leaving the erstwhile hunters to be rescued from unsafe
ladders by cursing men with badly mauled hands.

Birdshot had been tried once and once only, when, in addition
to the single swallow being brought down, a deluge of rotten lath,
plaster and the accumulated muck of centuries had fallen upon the
marksman and his supporters, below. The final, inspired, expedient

of a hawk was decided upon, though neither the promised bird nor its handler had materialised by the time that the seats were being set out for the show.

Then there was the matter of the smell. The poison scattered liberally about the premises for some weeks in advance had been considerably more successful in its lethal intentions, with several dozen prime examples of *rattus rattus* being removed prior to the day. The problem, however, was those uncounted victims that had simply crawled away to die in runs, crevices, nooks and crannies that were beyond the scope of ingenuity to reach. The result was appalling, and in spite of opened doors, the burning of fragrant herbs in the room's single fireplace – itself largely blocked by birdnests – and the liberal spreading of rosewater and scented soaps, the overriding odour remained that of decomposing rodent, albeit with floral notes. A single tentative attempt to open one of the windows had resulted in the collapse of the entire frame into a mercifully unfrequented yard below, the remaining hole in the wall being now more or less blocked with a cannibalised tabletop nailed into the remnants of the mullion.

Tonight, however, once past the business of the universal wrinkling of noses on first entering the narrow, barn-like hall, the avoidance of scything draughts, and the brisk removal of birdlime from seats and the odd, unfortunate, hat and shoulder, here was an audience abuzz with expectation.

The more knowledgeable voices amongst the capacity crowd were holding forth to friends and families on the merits and demerits of previous performances and the most particular distinction of tonight's star turn:

He was here, of course, performing 'The Recruiting Sergeant' in this very hall; the good lady's father, John Kemble. Though that was around '70, long before she became Mrs Siddons.

They say that Drury Lane was simply not enough to keep her in

London. Garrick is said to be mortified by her flight.

One gathers her Portia was met with less than rapture; but we shall just have to see…

She is performing only in Lichfield, York and Bath, unable to find other venues of a stature to match her genius…

And then it began. The small, plump figure of Anna Seward, demure and composed, rose to her feet from her place in the front row, to stand in front of the low stage. She turned with a smile, to await the full attention of the audience whilst the hall's subsidiary candles were extinguished, leaving only the large chandelier burning above the stage.

"My Lord," she began, nodding graciously towards the tall man at the centre of the Marquis of Donegal's party, "Ladies and Gentlemen, this evening it is both my honour and my great personal pleasure, to present for your edification and delight, one of the greatest actresses of our age. The lady will be giving us a number of dramatic renditions from plays which she has made her own, each of which, at her request, I shall briefly – and I do *assure* you of brevity…" – a remark met with a murmur of laughter – "…announce. To open, in the role of Belvidera in Otway's *Venice Preserved*, may I present Mrs Sarah Siddons."

From the first moment the tall, striking figure strode onto the small stage, the room was captivated. Pausing as if to survey the sea of expectant faces, her darkly expressive eyes seemed, somehow, to engage with each and every person there, whilst the solemn, statuesque dignity of her demeanour sent a thrill of anticipation down every spine even before she spoke. When at last she did, her deeply sonorous voice carrying to the furthest reaches of the packed hall, she had them all in thrall. That night it was as if time dissolved for the astonished crowd, so complete was the attention her performances demanded and received. Following a trio of recitations and a rapturously received Calista, from *The fair Penitent*, an interlude was called, though nothing could diminish the mounting waves of adulation Sarah Siddons was conjuring forth.

Greene, with Theodosia on his arm, was in animated conversation with friends, leaving Darwin to be lionised by the gorgeously attired ladies of the Donegal party. Anna Seward, radiant with the runaway success of the evening, waved to them in passing, only to halt – in obvious dismay – at a sight of the Apothecary, a smile freezing on his round face, stopping in mid-flow to glare, furiously, towards the rear of the bustling hall. Following his gaze, the sight that met her eyes was a large, florid-faced man holding forth amidst another opulently dressed party. With a sinking heart, she knew instantly that this must be the Master of Walhill, oblivious to the effect his presence was having on the irate figure of Richard Greene. He though, becoming suddenly aware that she had joined her attention to his own, hurried to her side, seeing the flush of an anger she was making no attempt to conceal.

"My dear Miss Seward, whilst no-one could have foreseen that loathsome presence here tonight, may I suggest this is neither time nor place to make our feelings felt. I must beg your forgiveness for permitting mine to become apparent, even momentarily. You have created a memorable occasion. The likes of Hawson must not be permitted to spoil it."

She turned gratefully to the earnest presence at her side and said, brightly: "You are, of course, correct, my dear Mr Greene. He shall be ignored much as we are ignoring several of the evening's other calamities, though in truth, I should prefer the rats."

With that she was gone, a sparkling, effervescent presence as she moved among her friends and admirers. A gong introduced the final performance of the evening.

"For the very first time on any stage, Mrs Siddons will now present her interpretation of one of the greatest roles in our

English canon – that of Lady Macbeth, in what I am told I must only refer to as 'The Scottish Play' from the sublime pen of William Shakespeare. We come upon that Lady with her husband in a court within the Castle of Inverness, plotting the awful fate that lies in store for their guests: the unfortunate Banquo and his servants. The role of the Lady's husband is played by Mr Tompion, who will subsequently be joined by Mr Willis."

Although no longer alone beneath the guttering flames of the candelabra, the imposing figure, now appearing gaunt, black-eyed with wickedness, commanded the rapt attention of every person in the spellbound crowd as she began to pronounce her immemorial sentence of death: *That which hath made them drunk, hath made me bold. What hath quenched them hath given me fire…*

Time was suspended in the decrepit Hall, as the serpent voice of ambition wove its pitiless spell, as ever-fouler murder stained the Scottish throne and finally a nemesis, not born of woman, brought the wood of Dunsinane to the castle walls.

Transported witnesses to the final words of haunted dementia, they craned towards the dreadful scene, towards the solitary horror of the sleep-walking automaton, unwilling to miss a word, a single nuanced flicker from her baleful, unseeing eyes: *To bed, to bed; there's knocking at the gate. Come, come, come, come, give me your hand. What has done cannot be undone. To bed, to bed, to bed.*

Then it was over. For a moment that seemed to stretch beyond any possibility of silence, they sat, mute, immobile, dwarfed by the immensity of tragedy and madness that had been laid bare before them. At last, one, then another and another sprang to their feet, movements that crazed the moment, broke the spell, that had bound them all. As one voice their roar of adulation soaring to the rafters of the ancient hall, birds scattering as if blown upon a gale, as the thunderous applause and wild cheers threatened to lift the roof itself. Their adulation not one whit diminished by her disappearance from the stage, the applause persisted. Then, *en masse*, they seemed to surge forward as the solitary figure re-entered from the small side door, the ovation swelling to even greater heights as Sarah Siddons, suddenly smaller than she had seemed just moments before, took her final bow, arms full of flowers, a trance-like smile upon her face.

As candles were relit to facilitate the departure of the enraptured crowd, Greene saw that Hawson's party was already making moves to head the queue for the single, narrow door at the head of the stairs, and turned back to greet a variety of acquaintances. Erasmus Darwin, beaming proprietorially as he began the long-winded business of shepherding his own party towards the congested stairs, was calling greetings to all and sundry, appearing to know most of the departing grandees clustered around the Donegal party. They, the Apothecary sensed, were unused to queuing in any shape or form, and from the looks of strained *politesse* they were giving out, had obviously expected to leave the hall borne effortlessly upon the accustomed wave of entitlement and natural priority.

The Marquis was giving a small reception for Mrs Siddons and the Sewards' invited guests at his palatial townhouse beside the Guildhall, and milord was obviously chafing at the delay.

Having no distance to travel, the Greenes were content to bide their time and wait for the main crush to disperse, comparing enthusiastic notes with the familiar faces in the patiently shuffling crowd. When, finally, they gained the paving outside, it was only to discover that the majority of the night's audience seemed in no hurry to disperse, standing in convivial groups beneath the flambeaux's gusting light and watching others depart as the coaches and chairmen formed yet more queues along the road leading up to Greenhill, awaiting their turn to collect.

Seeing the large, blue-liveried coach still some vehicles back, the Apothecary realised that the Hawson party – for all their pushy bid to beat the crowds – must still be in the waiting throng. It was as he scanned the sea of animated faces that the first scream rang out.

As a sudden commotion rippled out from a knot of bystanders in the shadow of St Mary's church, it was closely followed by hoarse shouts of alarm, more screams, and the sudden flat report of a pistol shot. In consternation, the crowd flinched back from its source, though others – not least the Apothecary – ran towards the melee that had erupted in their midst. He was met by the sight of a wigless, wild-eyed, Bartholomew Hawson, blood streaming from a wound in his neck, bellowing with shock and pain. As Greene pushed forward, he saw the badly injured man stagger back, as if seeking the support of the church wall behind him, a small pocket pistol in his hand clattering to the ground as he stumbled and fell. Whilst some rushed to his assistance, those immediately in front edged back, horror and shocked disbelief written across every face. Greene looked down and cried aloud.

There, on the broken cobbles, lay the sprawled, twitching, form of a woman, Agnes Crede, her blood a black stain blossoming across her powder-burned breast. She had been shot at close range and was close to death. Heaving a way clear, Greene dropped to his knees beside her, reaching for her hand.

She knew him for a moment, he could see that, and the chapped lips in the ashen face made to form a word. He strained forward, seeing the pale blue of a vein pulsing in her neck as she tried to speak: "…auntie… she's wi''er…" Then she was gone.

He knelt, head bowed above her, oblivious to the consternation surrounding them, her fallen weapon still lying by a nerveless hand. He made to retrieve their kitchen knife then thought better of it.

(39)

In the lower part of the CASE. A great variety of Fish-hooks,
mostly of Pearl Shell and Tortoise Shell; some of Fish Bones
tied to pieces of Wood. A Basket neatly Woven, ornamented with
small white Shells; it contains a curious Fishing Net, the Floats
of light pieces of Wood, the Plummets Bits of Coral Rock. A
Shield of twisted Cordage, coiled up in an artful manner. All the
before-mentioned Articles were brought over by Captain Cook
and other Circumnavigators, and presented to the Museum by
the Right Honourable the Earls of Uxbridge and Donegall

6th May, 1776. "...nearest by far... Greene, Mr *Greene*... must be
attended to before he bleeds to..." The cacophony of voices and the
press of jostling limbs summoned him back to the scene around
him, to the wetness of his cheeks, to the fact that he was still
fiercely clasping the dead woman's bloodstained hand. Looking
up, owlishly, into the blur of faces, he realised he was being spoken
to by the towering figure of Erasmus Darwin: "The b...bleeding
won't be s...staunched, Richard, we must get him to Saddler S...
Street. You are the c...closest by far."

As if in a dream, he somehow found his feet, to be propelled
forward through the gaping throng, many hands clearing a
passage, a two-wheeled bier – produced from God knew where –
bearing the victim of the murderous ambush ahead of them. Half-
heard words, broken phrases, seemed to travel with the headlong
surge along Breadmarket Street and down the length of Saddler
Street towards the cheerful glow of the Apothecary window: ...

out of nowhere...rabid...self-defence...no choice...madwoman...ran out and stabbed him with a foot-long blade...would have struck again if he'd not...

Before he could order his thoughts, shout out the words of protest that seemed lodged in his bone-dry throat, his furious refusal to lift a finger for this foul creature, he found himself fumbling for his keys amongst the shouting mob around his door. Then, as if possessed, impelled by some occupying power that would not be denied, he led the surge in towards his Consulting Room, many hands bearing the unconscious Hawson through the dimly lit shop.

As the limp figure was laid upon his operating table, Theodosia's imperiously raised voice could be heard from the shop, shooing out the concerned, the prurient and the downright curious that were attempting to follow the wounded man in. Moments later, flushed and flustered, she appeared in the doorway as her husband, assisted by Harry Franklyn, was busily engaged in cutting away the blood-drenched shirt and waistcoat.

"Doctor Darwin has returned to collect his own instruments, Richard. In case you should need his assistance, he said."

The Apothecary simply nodded, staring intently at the wound they were cleaning: "I believe the force of the downward stab has sheared a sliver of bone, Harry. It must be that, driven into the jugular, which is responsible in part for the continuing blood loss."

The younger man squinted to follow Greene's pointing finger, and nodded his agreement as he saw, momentarily, the inch-long nick in the exposed clavicle, before the blood welled back.

"I must remove it and attempt to mend the lesion, before we can address the larger wound. Once I have extracted it, you will need to act with the utmost dispatch. You will kindly clamp after me with the smallest instrument, *there*," he nodded towards the gleaming array of surgical kit spread beside them, "but pass it to me first, if you will. I shall sear it first, as it must be without taint of any kind. I shall then endeavour to stitch close beside you as you move your grip by a hairsbreadth at my instruction. Do you understand?"

"Perfectly, Mr Greene. It shall be just as you say."

He watched, intrigued, as Greene ignited a small spirit lamp, and having adjusted the flame beneath its wire-gauze mantle, proceeded to bathe the small clamp and his miniature forceps in its focused heat.

Erasmus Darwin returned, and pushed his way through the milling crowd around the Apothecary shop to its closed door. Theodosia had seen his approach and opened it to let him in.

"I swear there are folk in that street who would be sitting on Richard's shoulders for a better view, if they could," she declared with exasperation.

"T'was ever thus, d...dear lady," replied the Doctor, grimly, removing his cloak before going through. "There would be t...ten times the throng if a hanged man were on d...display."

"I live in hope of just that," came a voice from the passageway. Richard Greene emerged, drying his hands on a linen towel.

"He remains unconscious, and perilously weakened by the amount of blood he has lost, but the bleeding is now staunched and the wound sutured to the best of my ability. Though I apparently had no choice in the matter of treating him, I will not have Hawson on these premises a moment longer than I must, Erasmus. My best hope is that I might have saved him for the hangman."

"*Richard!*" Theodosia interjected, "How could you..?"

Darwin, too, seemed shocked by his vehemence, exclaiming: "But it was m...manifestly self-defence, Richard. The m... madwoman came from nowhere! She would most certainly have f...f...finished the job had she been permitted to strike a second t...time."

"If *mad* poor Aggie was, then she was driven to that state by grief and loss – both visited upon her by that vicious excuse for a *gentleman* in there," retorted Greene, jerking a thumb over his shoulder. "Believe me when I say that I have seen a sight too much of his handiwork to shed a tear on his account. Whilst the choice of whether he lives or dies is not in my hands, the choice of *where* he lives or dies is. It shall not be here."

Seeing the furious resolution in the Apothecary's eyes, Darwin nodded in tacit agreement.

"I have no idea of the w…whereabouts of his party, do you, Mrs G…Greene?" he enquired, attempting to peer out through the kaleidoscopic glass at the sea of faces attempting to see in.

As if on perfect cue, a peremptory rapping sounded on the still firmly closed door. Before making any move to open it, Theodosia looked closely through it and said: "One at least may be attempting to announce himself. I do believe he has one of your colleagues in tow, Doctor Darwin: *Gough*, is it? That fussy little man from Brownhills?"

Darwin stooped to check: "Mmm, you are correct, Mrs Greene. No friend of m…mine, but best let 'em in."

Puffing self-importantly, the first through the door surveyed the shop and its occupants with undisguised disdain: "How long did you intend to keep this Doctor waiting in the street, my good woman?" the man exclaimed. "Take us to Mr Hawson. He must be attended to without further delay! His coach will be here momentarily, when a way can be cleared through this city-full of gawpers."

Theodosia, stiffening visibly, looked the newcomer up and down with unhurried attention before replying: "I intended to keep both him and you out in the street for as long as it took to establish you were not *gawpers* yourself, Mr *whomsoever-you-might-be*. So far, you have failed to establish that you are not."

Before the taken-aback figure could frame a response she continued: "Furthermore, had the treatment of your Mr Hawson depended upon this gentleman's arrival…" – she nodded towards Gough – "…your Mr Hawson would, by now, be dead." She indicated her husband, who had now been joined by young Harry Franklyn. "So, perhaps, you would *first* care to introduce yourself, then to apologise for your tone, and finally, thank the providential intervention of my husband and Doctor Franklyn. You might then care to ascribe the *additional* presence of Doctor Darwin to the fact that not all our citizens are *gawpers*."

She raised her eyebrows in anticipation of his reply, but before the newly dumbstruck man could respond, his companion pushed past with an ingratiating smile, exclaiming: "Doctor Darwin! No offence meant, none taken I'm sure. We are all upset at the evening's turn of events, to be sure. All a touch overwrought, are we not?"

He made the mistake of winking in the direction of the impassive Darwin, who responded coolly: "Overwrought we might be, Gough, but not to the extent that d-d-due apologies will be foregone." He turned to Riddick's companion, now fidgeting with unease beside him. "Well, Sir? What d'you have to say for yourself? We are waiting."

"My only concern was for Tolly," the other began, scowling with discomfiture, "I intended no rudeness, madam. Accept my apologies. If you have already treated Mr Hawson, then there's no more to be said. He will, no doubt, settle your account when he is fully recovered."

As if sent to cover his embarrassment, a sound was heard of a large vehicle pulling up, outside. They could see postillions jumping down and approaching through the opening crowd.

"He really should not be…" began Franklyn, only to be hushed by a fierce glint in the Apothecary's eyes.

"We have done what could be done, but your Mr Hawson remains gravely ill. In choosing to move him now, upon his and your head be it," Greene said, with a note of callous finality to his voice that his wife had never expected to hear, continuing: "As to thanks and payment, I require neither. The cost of a needle and thread counts for little when weighed against the life of a brutalised young woman lying dead on our street."

As the two heavily built postillions ducked into the shop, Greene, seeing them at close quarters for the first time, knew them instinctively for what they were: a pair of bare-knuckle pugilists decked out in braid. Then, though, his attention was drawn away from the hard, scarred faces to the thin, foxy, features of another man: Pearce, in the doorway, standing behind the bruisers, his pale eyes opened wide in obvious recognition of the Apothecary. Gough appeared to be about to speak. Greene cut him dead:

"I am already weary of hearing that it was an act of self-defence, Doctor Riddick. Just be good enough to remove your patient from my premises."

As the trio in the doorway made to move through to the rear, Greene raised a peremptory hand, pointing at Pearce: "He does not enter my shop. Get him out."

Without further explanation, and paying no attention to the venomous glare from the dismissed Pearce, the Apothecary said to Franklyn and Darwin: "Gentlemen, will you join us for some refreshment?" He turned for the stairs without waiting for a reply.

"Your patient awaits, Doctor Gough," added Theodosia Greene, ignoring his companion as if he had simply ceased to exist and gesturing to the passageway through to the Consulting Room: "Two of these men should suffice to remove him."

ITEM:

On the Wall, the left hand the ALTAR PIECE, in Glass
Cases. The Tail and Claws of the Bever. A Camelion,
Lizard, Leghorn Lobster, a Crocodile, as just taken from
the Egg, Shells of the Land Tortoise, Ostracion, or
Triangular Fish, Rhinocerous Beetle, very large, Sea Bat,
Scarabeus Cervus, or Stag Beetle, Flies from Virginia.

7ᵗʰ May, 1776. "No, Theodosia, I will *not* have it!" He spoke with
a vehemence that surprised them both. Carefully modulating
his voice, he continued: "It is neither a matter of ignoring your
well-meant and, indeed, well-founded advice, nor is it a matter
of taking the law into my own hands, but that poor ravaged soul
spoke her last words on this earth to me, and I shall not – cannot
– ignore them. Do you honestly believe I could stand at her
graveside, as I must in but a few hours, knowing her last plea was
to go unanswered?"

They had both spent a wretched night, tossing in anguished
sleeplessness, and now – in the first light of an overcast dawn – sat,
red-eyed and fractious, across their untouched breakfast.

"Dear Lord, Richard, are we *never* to be free from this wretched
business? You tell me you cannot ignore that poor woman's words,
but – though it pains me to say so – I tell you that you simply
cannot afford to *heed* them. The idea you can even contemplate
the search for a nameless child *somewhere in Walsall* is worrisome
enough, but your belief that there is still a way in which you can
lay her father's murder at Hawson's door verges on the fantastic!
How in the name of goodness do you suppose that it can ever

be proven in a court of law, after such time has elapsed and – by your own account – when all meaningful traces have been lost or destroyed by those fools of constables? See reason, husband, I beg you."

"At the risk of sounding pompous in the extreme, my dear, what I *have* seen is the very face of evil, and the loathsome mark it has left upon lives already crippled by adversity. I will not turn my back on what I know to be a foulness that will come to taint all it looks upon. In their power to corrupt, to exploit and destroy, the Hawsons of this world forfeit every claim they might have upon the consideration of decent people. I could not live with myself if I did not do what little I can to expose him."

"And shall you be more able to live with yourself as self-appointed righter of wrongs when that rectitude could cost you – cost *us* – so dearly, husband? You are no longer a young man, and Hawson is known to be a violent and vengeful enemy. Has Grace ever told you *why* he embarked so single-mindedly upon the ruination of her brother?"

Seeing the question in her husband's eyes, she nodded, continuing: "No, I thought perhaps not. It was because, early on in their gaming acquaintance, poor, foolish Beasley made some disparaging jest – a rather too *public* jest – concerning Hawson's less-than-genteel manners at table."

"And he brought Beasley to ruin for that?" breathed Greene. "I had supposed it to have been a simple matter of avarice."

"He drove him to the *grave* for that, Richard. This is the creature on whom you would set your sights, is it? All for some obscure sense that justice must somehow be done? I had believed you to be wiser in the ways of our world. Avoid him for the plague he undoubtedly is."

Shaking his head in sheer perplexity, the Apothecary mumbled something about a walk to clear his head, and went downstairs, out into the drab day. Once out in the street, he pulled up the collar of his coat against the unseasonal chill of the early morning air and stumped off he knew not where. On their several ways to work, Tillett and one of the shop boys passed him as he crossed the marketplace, but received no acknowledgement to their greeting from the preoccupied figure.

It was only as he retraced his steps, an hour or more later, returning from a walk that had taken him over Greenhill and out towards the hamlet of Streethay on the Burton road, that he had regained sufficient composure to respond to a greeting called from the bakery near St Mary's.

Emerging from the enticing aromas of fresh-baked loaves, Lionel Blomefield had spotted the hunched, striding form of the Apothecary about to cross the road into the Marketplace. Waving a newly purchased loaf aloft, he finally gained his absorbed friend's attention. Greene stopped, eying the elderly cleric's purchases with a small smile.

"Let me guess," he said: "If you want fresh bread then make yourself useful and go and get it yourself, Lionel. Can't you see that the staff have their hands full already?"

Blomefield winced at his friend's acuity and said, ruefully: "I swear, I'll be blacking the range next if it makes work for what my dear wife will insist on calling my *idle hands*. Just what is a man supposed to do with his retirement? Become a mountebank and take up juggling?"

For all his bantering tone, Blomefield took the opportunity of peering closely at his old friend: "Are you at all recovered from your ordeal of last night, Richard? What an unspeakable affair this has become."

"As recovered as one might hope to be, faced with the morning's most immediate prospect, Lionel. I envisage precious few mourners at this pauper's grave."

"I fear you will be proved right, so, shall accompany you, if I may, Richard. This is not a burden you should bear alone."

Greene nodded his gratitude, then shrugged, saying: "It is less a burden than some last, small service to one broken by an extremity beyond endurance. Every fibre of my being aches on her account, Lionel. Am I no more than a sentimental old fool?"

In response, and having no words to cope with his old friend's most uncharacteristic admission, Blomefield rapidly changed the subject: "News, of a sort, from the Knight of Kircuddy! Yesterday I received a package from Oxford, in which he enclosed a map for our perusal. I can discern nothing of substance in it, but perhaps you will join me later so that we may put our heads together, so to speak?"

"Yes, indeed," replied Greene, with a lack of enthusiasm that Blomefield found even more worrying than his introspection.

"Until later, at Greenhill, then Lionel." he murmured and walked away. "We might walk up together. Around what o'clock?" called the cleric, to be answered only by an absently waved hand from the departing figure.

(41)

The DRAWER B. A Magical Crystal, by which the adepts
in Astrology pretended to look into futurity; presented
by Mr John White of Newgate-street, London.

The Ashmole house. Lambeth. 11ᵗʰ May, 1692. His head swam
and fogged. He had intended to say so much more: *The tunnel,
the haunting glimpse of all that lay at its heart, the numbing, heart-
stopping realisation of who and what slumbered on in that velvet,
crushing, darkness with its dancing…*

The door opened abruptly, and a severe, middle-aged woman
swept into the bedchamber, a manservant and a maid close on
her heels.

"Well, Elias. Not content with scarifying your entire household
once again, you are now, it would appear, intent on catching
your death of cold. I know well enough that you are devoid of
common sense, but could you not show some grain of concern for
those who must cope with your vexed humours and your habitual
contrariness?"

The time for parry, riposte, or even half-hearted resistance, was
long past, and the trembling man was led, unprotesting, back to
his remade bed. His wife attended briefly to the servants as they
tucked and smoothed him into starched confinement, and then
turned for the door. "I am to be kept informed of your master's
condition. You, girl, will sit with him until morning." Then,
nodding curtly as if to confirm the newly ordered scene to herself,
she stalked out.

Exhaustion could not prevent Elias Ashmole's final resolve and, having freed an arm with some difficulty, he beckoned, weakly, to his man: "The box and that letter…" – a wavering finger pointed to the pages that lay nearby – "…they are to be dispatched to the Reverend Harrison of Lichfield, you understand? St Mary's, Lichfield? Let me see you seal it and place it as I have instructed. Do you understand, *Harrison*? He must…"

He was already asleep as the sealed letter and the box were removed from the chamber.

The following morning, old Mr Ashmole was clearly still unwell and knew nothing of the carrier's arrival and the box's removal as per instructions. Acting punctiliously to fulfil his remit – and in the conspicuous absence of his master's wife – the manservant had no way of knowing that its intended recipient had died some dozen years earlier. Neither was he to know that the final stage of old Mr Ashmole's mental and physical decline would be quietly and painlessly reached at twilight that same day.

In fact, the historian of the Order of the Garter, the Herald and genealogist, Magus, connoisseur and collector, slipped imperceptibly from this life at much the same time as the fairies were said to dance for those who had the eyes to see and the heart to feel.

(42)

A List of the Names of the Inhabitants of the City of Lichfield, who also were voluntary Soldiers, under the command of Captain Richard Dyott, with the several and respective Sums each of them subscribed, for the use of his Majesty King Charles the 1ˢᵗ. In the proper hand writing of Sir William Dugdale Receiver for the City of Lichfield. Dated 30ᵗʰ October 1661.

Saddler Street. 10ᵗʰ May, 1776. The faintly drawn plan lay spread between them, its folds brittle with age, the must of its yellowed parchment scenting the air around the table: *With all our talk of Bishops, I had forgotten we hold this curiosity...* Caisley's accompanying note read, before continuing:

> *I have no idea whether it may prove of the slightest relevance, though it does now exhaust my small repository of Lichfeldiana. Failing all else, it may well intrigue the Sewards who, I gather, reign so high in your civic regard, it being the sole remaining record of which I am aware, pertaining to the original state of their home. The fact that it might also go some small way to mitigating the righteous wrath of that most particular Canon Residentiary towards our library plays no part whatsoever in this generous and selfless loan. For, dear Lionel, loan it must be, as I cannot be seen to be disbursing our collection willy-nilly, however deserving might be the cause.*

> *I remain, Sir, your generous and selfless friend, Caisley. Oxford.*

"What *library*, Lionel? What *collection*?" asked Greene, looking up from the note, bewildered: "And why on earth might Canon Seward have an axe to grind concerning it?"

"Oh, did I not mention it earlier," murmured Blomefield, "Charles looks after all the Bodley business for the University – when he has the time, that is. He has fingers in many pies, does Charles. As for the *axe* you mention so colourfully, the Bodley collection contains more than a few volumes once owned by the Cathedral Library. Looted? Sold-off by the Parliament? Who knows? Won't give 'em back is the problem. I stay well clear of the whole thing. You should, too."

"You forgot to mention that the man with whom I dined at this very table *looks after* the greatest library in the kingdom, Lionel? What shall you forget *next*, your head?"

He looked in mock despair at the oblivious figure now fiddling with his snuffbox, before returning with renewed interest to the plan before them. After some moments, he looked up, glancing at the clock on the mantelpiece.

"Look, might I borrow this, Lionel?" he said, indicating the plan. "I'm making little sense of it as it stands, but would like to take a proper look later, when I've more time. Theodosia has become a trifle sensitive to my absences, of late, so I should better..."

"Oh, by all means," replied Blomefield, airily. "It is obviously of more import to the Sewards than to us. Charles is, I suspect, simply using us to make good some unmended fences. Being a Scot to the bone, he rarely acts without some motive or other."

As he entered the street door to the kitchen, Margery bore down upon the Apothecary waving something in a large, flour-dusted hand: "Letter came for you when you were at the funeral, earlier, so you missed it when it came, being out. Though why you wanted to pay any respects to that..."

Greene seized the letter, placing an admonitory finger to his lips: "We shall have no speaking ill of the dead in this house,

Margery, whatever our feelings in the matter might be. Do you understand?"

"Just didn't want you just leaving that unread, upstairs, not like you do. No point in leaving things for your attention half the time, Mistress says."

With a snort she turned away, about to return to her pastry-making on the kitchen table.

Retreating with his prize as fast as he could manage, hearing, as he gained the stairs: "…though why you wanted to pay any respects to that…"

He returned to find his wife absorbed in her needlework. She greeted him with an absent-minded smile: "Marjorie said that a letter came for you earlier. She had to hand it to you personally, though, she said. *Didn't want it going astray.*" She raised her eyebrows, and they exchanged a brief smile of wordless complicity.

"Margery is so unfailingly caring," murmured Greene, signalling his intention of continuing upstairs.

"Don't be too late, Richard. It's been too long a day."

He had immediately recognised Ashton Lever's distinctive flourishes on the envelope, and, once at his desk, opened it with a degree of anticipation. He was not to be disappointed:

My dear Greene,

Your most recent correspondence forewarned and forearmed me for my meeting at Chester. The object, now safely in my possession, is, without doubt, the piece which you so ably described, lacking as it does all the subsidiary elements of what must once have been a truly momentous work of art. I played the caution card with the vendor's agent, insisting that I could not contemplate a purchase of such magnitude without the fullest provenance, and stating that I had no intention of ignoring the dictum: caveat emptor.

The upshot was that, rather than place the sale in jeopardy, the vendor's identity was at least partially revealed as being: 'a gentleman, of mercantile interests, resident of the County of Staffordshire, on whose estate the piece was recently discovered'. The agent claimed to have been specifically forbidden from disclosing the vendor's name, and judging from the fellow's demeanour I could see that this was not a prohibition taken lightly. If I am any judge of character whatsoever, my sense is that more than legalistic penalties are at stake should he disobey his instructions. This was not a man at ease with his principal. Appearing to settle for what he was prepared to offer, I did, however, insist that it be put in writing and notarised for my protection. That is now safely lodged with the object and will be made available to you as required.

Having by now firmly established my credentials, so to speak, I was treated to the strict confidence that three further pieces of significance might shortly be available. These he described as a 'another white gold piece – an image of the sun in splendour, a hand's-breadth across – and two marble figures, half of life-size'. These, he added, would be offered in tandem with fragmentary sections of a tessellated pavement bearing various images. On requesting whether they derived from the same source, he intimated – by way of verification, I suspect – that this was the case. When, though, I requested that the description of the remaining artefacts be committed to paper, he demurred, and I did not press the matter. Our conversation was, however, noted verbatim by my secretary who, on my instruction, was secreted within earshot for that very purpose.

Knowing your fervent hope in this matter, is there no way – other than by your given word – in which the object in question might still be tangibly linked to its source? Are none of the sundered fragments still to be found? Unless that might be the

*case, then though it pains me to say this: I cannot see how the
desired connection, the trail of guilt, of consequence, can ever
be established in anything other than a circumstantial manner.
With regard to the newly promised items, however, if I am not
mistaken, these may still reside at their source and, if so, would
surely provide a most persuasive argument to your thesis.
You will know how best to proceed with this, Richard, but I do
urge caution. In the light of my dealings – albeit by proxy – I
become increasingly convinced that the fount of this mischief is
one who will go to some lengths to dissuade investigation into
his affairs.*

*Kindly advise me at your earliest convenience of how you wish
to proceed with this matter as, circumstances permitting, I
intend to install the Taurocthony as a centerpiece to one of the
new rooms of my Holophusikon in Leicester Square. Having
grown so weary of the insolence of the common people indulging
the sight of my collections here at Alkrington, I am delighted
to say that both the aesthetic and remunerative aspects of the
London venture are exceeding my expectations. I trust that your
own most admirable venture flourishes in equal measure.*

*You shall, of course, have every assistance I can provide, as I
remain, Sir, your friend and servant.*

Lever. Alkrington.

The Apothecary took some time to fully digest the implications of
the letter, sitting in the light of a single candle-lamp. Allowing his
tired eyes to fix upon the flicker of the flame, he felt a cooling sense
of calmness spread, a blessed soothing of a head aching from a day
of jumbled thoughts and tangled, raw, emotions. It was then he
felt the stirring that he knew so well, an inkling – he had no better
word for it – that prompted him to read the letter once more,

searching for the thing his waking mind had missed. He knew it, then, as he reread the words: 'Are none of the sundered fragments still to be found?' Unbidden, his thought sped back to the last conversation he had had with Joe Crede, the anguished admission wrung from him, the question left unasked, unanswered: *Us 'ad no choice, Mr Greene. I cut off all they bits you've said, melted all but one of 'em in an old shot-mould, bit by bit…*

All but one… how could he have failed to follow that thread, there and then? No, with a shake of his head he knew why: the sheer momentum of their conversation, the admissions, the recriminations, had impelled them with a force all its own. The moment had passed, soon to be forgotten until now, until Ashton Lever's words had teased out a memory so easily overlooked. He saw, again, the woman's arm reaching, feeling, inside the bread oven by the empty hearth, removing a cloth-wrapped bundle from somewhere deep within. The Apothecary knew in that instant that he would have to return to the locked and loveless hovel where it had all begun.

ITEM:

A CABINET on the right Hand the Fire-place. On the top,
a Grotto form'd of Ores, Spars, and other Minerals, mostly
found in Derbyshire, covered with a large Glass Bell

Saddler Street. 12ᵗʰ May, 1776. Had any doubt remained as to
his course of action, Theodosia's announcement dispelled them in
a trice. It transpired that she, too, had received mail. Hers, though,
being of the obviously domestic variety, had passed by both the
Apothecary and the eagle-eyed scrutiny of their housekeeper,
until now.

"That's all very well," Margery opined, "Mistress upping and
saying as how she'll be away for a week or so, but how's a soul to
make proper arrangements when all the world goes topsy-turvy?
A week's a proper week, and no mistaking that, Mr Greene, but
what's the rest? Is this *orso* a day or more? Even three or four?
How's the baking to be done aright when no-one's got a clue
what's going on? It grieves me, Mr Greene, it truly does. I do my
best, God knows I do, and this is all the thanks I get."

Later, the Apothecary would marvel at the transformation he
witnessed in the moment, just then, that his wife, bustling with
purpose, unexpectedly entered the kitchen. From the doleful,
red-faced grump of only seconds before, beetroot-stained hands
flapping an apron to cool her fevered brow, Margery became the
very embodiment of brisk efficiency, announcing, unprompted,
that all was agreed with the Master for the smooth running of the
household in Mistress's brief absence, and that she need concern

herself with nothing other than enjoying a well-deserved break in Knutsford.

Puzzled but evidently pleased with her housekeeper's unusual, if not *unique*, compliance, Theodosia said: "I do regret springing this on you at such short notice, Margery, but needs must. My dear friend Helena is getting no younger and sciatica is not to be endured alone, particularly now that her young have flown the nest."

"Well, if a soul can't lend a helping hand what's the world come to? That's what I always say. And it's not as if you'll be gone for more than a week orso," she replied, glaring at the Apothecary for confirmation.

"Unfailingly caring, as ever," he said, with perfect composure. "You see, my dear, everything is arranged. When shall you be leaving?"

It was not without a twinge of guilt that the Apothecary waved off his wife from the coach-yard of the George, next day, though he later went to some trouble consoling himself that undue worry on his behalf would have been a burden too many for an already concerned wife.

"In the light of your insistence that I could not so much as even *guess* where to begin a search, you have my promise that I shall not be venturing anywhere near Walsall, Theodosia," he had assured her, in the face of a probing cross-examination of his planned activities for the coming week.

Though sensing a certain *economy* in her husband's bland assurances, she had resigned herself to a situation that would be beyond her control for the duration of her absence and busied herself with last-minute preparations.

When, for the first time, Grace Beasley had learned of the tragedy outside the Guildhall, her overwhelming sense had been one of pity for the poor, deranged girl left dead in the street, followed by a numbing depression at the news of Bartholomew Hawson's survival. By what seemed to her to be the twentieth time of its increasingly garbled retelling, a strange, dream-like composure had replaced her earlier emotions: a sense where quiet, orderly meditation upon events replaced the vortex of emotions that had been her constant companion for as long as she now cared to remember. In the enforced absence of Theodosia, and in between the irregular visits from Anna Seward and the only sporadic company of a couple of other acquaintances, she spent what time she was able, in sitting, placidly, at her open window.

She listened intently as the nest-builders foraged for moss and wind-blown twigs from the guttering above her, then watched, entranced, as wrens wove their elusive nest, hung among dead bracken fronds in the little-frequented garden down below, its weight borne up by brambles, its sides built up and camouflaged by other ferny fragments carried in with tireless zeal. The greening of the tired plot beyond their walls seemed to drive back the drabness that a town imposes on its environs. It was, she thought, as if a foray from the open lands beyond had claimed the shabby fringes back and raised the flag of spring triumphant. Then she remembered what was lost and the headaches crashed down upon her once more, sending her tottering to her bed, incapable of thought or prayer.

When next she was able, she sat again and stared out at the scudding clouds, listening to the whitethroats' chit-chat and the double murmur of the turtle-doves from somewhere deep within the hawthorn clumps, and made a simple plan. When its lineaments were clear, she stood, carefully, and rang the small bell by her door. Moments later when the housemaid shuffled up, she asked for her small travelling trunk to be brought out from its place of storage. She smiled, faintly, at the question in the girl's eyes: "No, my dear, I am going nowhere in particular, I simply require something from it. You may return it to store immediately I am done."

Once delivered, she waited, pointedly, for the staring girl to depart, before unlocking the small hasp with a key from her writing box. Lifting the lid, she breathed in its scent – its infinity of memories – re-read its stains and scuffmarks: tokens of a time gone by, a life long lost. She knew exactly what she sought and found it straight away. Lifting out the cloth-wrapped bundle she transferred it with care to her linen drawer, then, called the girl and gave her tuppence for her pains. When the trunk had been removed, she resettled herself at the window, feeling an obscure sense of satisfaction. She would pen the note to dear Anna while she could, requesting that especial favour from her dearest friend.

(44)

In front of the ALTAR. A model of a double Pump, worked
by rarefaction and gravitation. A Book containing the life and
sufferings of our blessed Saviour Jesus Christ, exemplified, in
thirty two Copper Plates, 21 inches by 14; to which are added, the
Martyrdom of St. Stephen, and the conversion of St. Paul; designed
and engraved by Gregory Huret of Leyden. A. Domini, 1664.

Walhill. May 13th, 1776. "*No*, and no *again!*" exclaimed Lionel
Blomefield, aghast. "I am not about to entertain thoughts of
burglary for you or anyone else, Richard. Have you taken leave
of your senses?" He peered nervously about him as if even his
vehement refusal might be construed as conspiracy. "How can you
even *contemplate* such a madcap adventure?"

"I can contemplate it quite simply as being the sole means
that might remain to tie Hawson and his bully-boys into murder,
Lionel. All I am asking is your presence as a witness to anything
I might find. Put simply, without corroboration any evidence I
might come across will be worthless."

"Stop saying *simply*," replied Blomefield, tetchily. "There
is nothing *simple* about this lunacy, apart from the simple-
mindedness that appears to be its driving force."

"Look, let me go through it once more: all I propose is that
after forcing the door of an isolated, abandoned cottage…"

They had left the horses tethered in the overgrown orchard further
up the lane, having ridden at a leisurely pace past the blank
windows now mostly obscured by rampant brambles. Hobbling

beside the Apothecary, aching from the unaccustomed rigours of a three-mile ride, the elderly cleric shot worried glances to left and right as if the blooming hedgerows might contain a lurking ambush.

"Lionel, you could scarcely look more furtive if you tried," said Greene, with a nervous smile. "This is not what could be described as a thoroughfare by any stretch of the imagination. We shall have the place entirely to ourselves, never fear."

"The only thing being stretched is my fool-headed credulity in permitting you to cajole me into this," grumbled Blomefield. "Let us get it over and done with, for pity's sake."

Led by the Apothecary they pushed through the weeded path to the front door, bypassing that to skirt the lichened walls and reach the backshoot, where beneath the sagging wreckage of the mildewed thatch, a low, boarded door led into the scullery kitchen. A single wrench of Greene's short crowbar had it open, and they stooped into the musty twilight, pushing the door closed behind them. Both started, nervously, at a sound from the room ahead, but relaxed as they saw the long grey tail disappearing behind a broken lath.

"It will be there if it is anywhere," said Greene quietly, pointing across to where the cast door of the small oven hung askew.

"Then look and let us be gone, for heaven's sake," hissed Blomefield, "I hate rats only slightly less than I hate myself for being here."

Looking over to the threshold, Greene could still dimly see the blackened stain the blood had left but made no mention of it as together they crossed the bare, earthen floor.

"Here goes," breathed Greene, steeling himself to thrust his arm into the unlit recess. Blomefield glared around the squalor of the empty room, silently appalled by the tragedy he knew had unfolded here. For what seemed like an eternity he strove to ignore the Apothecary's laboured breathing as Greene strained up on short legs to reach the furthest depths of the oven. Just as he was about to admit failure his groping fingers met something small, mobile, that rolled away from his grasp.

"There's something!" he gasped, "but I can't quite…"

With a snort of exasperation, Blomefield came to his side and said: "Where, for God's sake?" stooping to reach past Greene's extended arm. After a moment, he straightened and opened an ash-blackened hand: "Is this what you've dragged me here for?"

The Apothecary grabbed a small, cloth-wrapped object – the size of a conker – from the outstretched palm. Eyes wide with excitement, he peeled back the filthy covering to reveal its contents: "Oh yes, Lionel, this is what we came for."

Both gazed down on the pale gleam of white gold, a superbly sculpted head wearing a Phrygian cap, its eyes wide, its mouth contorted with the act of driving a blade into the throat of a great white bull.

"This is Mithras," said the Apothecary, his voice husky with emotion, "and with his help we shall see Hawson hanged."

(45)

In the Center, below the ALTAR Table. *On one side hangs a Model of a Labradore Indian in his Canoe, covered with Seal Skin. Over this Canoe is a feathered Necklace, called Erei, worn by the Females of Sandwich Island, it is composed of Scarlet Feathers picked from the Neck of a small Bird of that Country. Presented by Miss Seward of Lichfield, whose works have rendered her Immortal.*

16th May, 1776. To his own surprise, Richard Greene found himself chafing with frustration and an inexplicable unease at Theodosia's absence, there being no-one to share in his discovery, and, most particularly, no-one to counsel – or simply prohibit him from the unwise course of action upon which he was about to embark.

To compound the Apothecary's feelings of isolation, he knew that Lionel Blomefield – still out of sorts from what he claimed to be the nervous exhaustion occasioned by their trespass– would be of little use for what he now had in mind. To that end, he fortified himself with the formidable combination of a hearty breakfast, a judiciously chosen stick from the Museum and a small, easily concealed, pepper-pot pistol whose four barrels he pulled through and loaded with care. He was as prepared as he was ever going to be.

Resolutely banishing all thoughts of what his wife would have to say about his decision, he sat at his desk and, after several moments of thought, wrote a letter in his small, neat hand. Descending to the shop, he first collected his bag from the Consulting Room and then spent several minutes consulting his notes and filling a number of vials and jars from the cornucopia of the laden shelves. So far, so good, he thought. He would be seen by his staff to be leaving in his normal, unhurried fashion, for all the world to see, fully prepared for his rounds.

As he was about to leave, he called Tillett aside and handed him a sealed letter. As if nothing could be more normal, he instructed the shopman to deliver it to the Guildhall office by two o'clock that afternoon, if he had not returned by then. Seeing the guileless face crinkle with an unspoken question as he read the title of the addressee, Greene said, as casually as he was able: "The City Sheriff awaits my account for that last post-mortem business. I shall deliver it myself if I return in time, though I have kept forgetting to draw it up these weeks past and want it done with."

Satisfied, now, the shopman stowed it away in the counting-desk, assuring the Apothecary of its timely delivery if so required. Tillett, the least imaginative of men, was, Greene knew, the most punctilious in carrying out his employers' instructions to the letter.

Greene had decided against his accustomed route, having no wish to pass even close to the forlorn Crede house, and so took some time to reach the rambling boundary of the Walhill estate, content that not even the few souls who might have remarked upon his earlier visits to the neighbourhood should have cause to notice him today.

An early shower had brought a dense lustre to the colours of the hedgerows and the infinity of spring-greened leaves that overhung the narrow lane, its high-banked meander marking the outer perimeter of the sprawling estate. Today the Apothecary had eyes for only one part of the seemingly endless ribbon of brick and coping stones: *the tumbledown* – in the words of poor, dead, Aggie, that was where he would begin to follow his nose, just as she had been instructed. He had to find the place for himself. That was all he knew.

When he came upon the frost-damaged wall, he realised how easy it would have been to pass it by, unremarked, wholly unremarkable as it was: a narrow cleft in dappled shade, behind a stand of self-sown elder rising from the bank. He might, in fact, have passed it by, himself, had he not started a lanky hare that sprang from concealment only to stop, staring at the mounted intruder for a moment, before loping unhurriedly away.

The Apothecary rode on to the field-gate he could see ahead, dismounted, and tethered his ever-patient mare behind the hedge; not concealed from any purposeful search, but neither tied up, for any passer-by to see, beside the broken wall through which he now clambered. As he made his cautious way across the scree of scattered brick and spilled-out rubble core, he missed his footing amidst the damp jumble, falling heavily, painfully, against the broken rubble. Wincing, he picked himself up, but within only a few, halting, paces, realised his ankle had been badly jarred. Cursing beneath his breath he limped on, though now relying heavily upon the stout cane he had been carrying, and banishing phrases such as *ill-omen* and *bad beginnings* from his mind.

Avoiding the dense, ferny thickets where all-concealing groundcover could hide a multitude of pitfalls, he kept to the game-tracks that snaked ahead: *follow your nose until you see the pair of silver birches ahead, up on their bank.*

And suddenly, there they were, visible straight ahead. Two unmistakable, peeling trunks, stark against the broken cloud and patchy blue above. It was only as he pushed towards them, breasting bushes and the shoulder-high saplings in his path, that he saw what lay ahead. The sight hit him like a physical blow to the diaphragm. He thought he might be sick.

Huge soil-heaps, their surfaces littered with broken tile, brick shards and shapeless fragments of stone, were piled to left and right of a gaping hole, with ladders protruding from its depths and up-ended barrows propped against the bole of a large fallen tree to one side. Leathern buckets, discarded tools and coarse-woven panniers were scattered randomly around the excavation – as if simply abandoned – completed a picture of brutal desolation.

Unable to contain himself, he hobbled from the cover of the thicket and picked his way across the rubble-strewn ground towards the ladder-head, seeing to his dismay, recognisable fragments of painted plaster and a scattering of tesserae around his feet. The view into the pit confirmed his worst fears. The diggers had hacked their way through the painted ceiling of what had almost certainly been a barrel-vaulted chamber, ripping it out almost in its entirety to lay bare the ground-plan of what it had covered. Even from where he stood, the Apothecary could discern the broken walls of a central chamber surrounded by the vestiges of what he quickly tallied to be seven small apse-like spaces, just as he might have expected. One 'chapel' for each of the seven stages of Mithraic initiation. Looking down to where whole sections of superbly decorated tessellated flooring had been clumsily levered up, broken, then obviously discarded, he could have wept. Attempting to ignore the throbbing reminder of his wrenched ankle, he knew he had to take a closer look, and, tucking his stick beneath an arm, clambered awkwardly astride the nearest ladder and eased himself down the mud-caked rungs to the ruined floor below.

Even laid obscenely bare to the open sky, the temperature in the desecrated Mithraeum was degrees colder than the ground above, and the Apothecary pulled his coat tightly about him as he picked his way across the wreckage.

Ahead of him, visible through a hacked, membranous, curtain of tree roots, the smashed remnants of what he presumed to be the principal altar stood. Gouged spaces to the left and right of its mutilated reredos were where guardian figures had been cut and levered out, above and between them an empty circular bas-relief – *a hand's-breadth across* from whence an emblem of *a sun in splendour* had doubtlessly been prised away. Beneath them lay the table-slab itself, split and crushed by some ancient collapse of the ground above. This would have been where the image of a dying white-gold bull once stood, focus of lost centuries of sacrifice and lamp-lit ritual.

Greene shivered, profoundly ill-at-ease, the dank, violated walls seeming to close around him. He hurried back to the ladder and wincing at the strain upon his ankle, began to climb back to the world above.

As his head lifted above the unshored edge of the dig, a shadow fell across him as a black form loomed against the sky. He realised he was looking into the barrel of a fowling-piece, held only inches from his face.

"Well, if it ain't Mr High-and-Mighty Greene!" crowed a voice from above: "Caught a-poking 'is little snout about and a-crawling from the shite 'ole 'e belongs in."

A booted foot stamped brutally down on the left hand gripping the ladder-rung. The Apothecary shouted with pain, all but losing his precarious grip on the ladder, entirely, but just managing to steady himself with the other.

Pearce leaned forward, his grin revealing a mouthful of yellowed teeth, spittle at the corners of thin, cruel lips: "Kick you down to rot, shall us? Pull up the ladder and watch you piss your pants, down there with a belly-full of shot and just the rats to watch you die?" He leant closer still, hissing: "Cos that's just what I'd do, you little cunt, but Master won't want to miss the chance 'isself. Not after finding you poking about in 'is business again. Reckon you can treat Mr 'awson like tuppence-worth of tripe, do you? We'll see what Master 'as to say about that! Make you wish you'd never been born. 'E knows all the ways!" The barrel jerked. "Get up 'ere, sharpish, or I'll 'aul you out by your sodding ears!"

Still, somehow, managing to grip his cane beneath his arm, the Apothecary laboured up the remaining rungs, to stand, trembling, panting with the effort, leaning heavily on the cane for support and attempting to nurse his swelling, bleeding knuckles beneath his arm. Pearce, all-but dancing with pleasure, looked him up and down, sneering: "*Get 'im out! Get 'im out!*" in delighted mockery.

"Not so High and sodding Mighty now, though, eh? Not now!" He lunged forward, knocking the cane away with his gun, laughing as the small man swayed and almost tumbled: "Not a leg to stand on, eh?" Levelling the gun, he said: "Let's see 'ow tall you stand up at the 'ouse, eh? *Move!*"

Greene gestured, helplessly, saying: "I can't walk up there without my stick. I turned my ankle. It is as much as I can do just to stand."

He watched indecision work across the feral features, until Pearce said: "Try anything on and I'll stick 'im right up your arse 'ole. Pick 'im up and get walking."

The Apothecary said a silent prayer of gratitude and bent, painfully, to retrieve the cane. He knew he would have only one chance. Straightening, and as casually as he could manage, he brushed a tentative hand across the right-hand pocket of his coat. As if he had been expecting it, Pearce's thin face cracked into a grin of malevolent joy as he caught the movement:

"Thinking on 'ow much you'd like to put a bullet in me, are you?"

He pulled Greene's pistol from his own jerkin and dangled it, derisively, a crooked finger through its trigger-guard. The Apothecary barely suppressed a gasp of dismay.

Pearce looked at it, appraisingly, mockingly: "Dropped it when 'e tripped over and hurt 'is ankle, did 'e? Ain't that just too sodding bad?" He slipped it back into a pocket, sneering: "Tipped me off a treat when I saw it, didn't it? Knew some nosey cunt was a-creepin' and a-pokin', then, didn't I? Always keeps a watch on that old tumbledown, just like Mr 'awson says."

"Ever since you and your late pal, Lemman, missed your first chance to kill Joe Crede, was that?" asked Greene, evenly, as if in conversation with an acquaintance.

"You leave Lemman out of this, you little piece of shit," he snarled, lifting the gun menacingly. Greene knew he had touched a raw nerve.

"You thought you were going to keep the bull all for yourselves, did you?" he enquired, quietly, intuitively. "I wonder what happened when you realised that your greedy gaffer had no intention of sharing it with you or anyone? I would wager you saw your chance then…"

"Shut your sodding mouth or I'm going to…"

Greene plunged on, regardless, impelled by a growing fury in the face of this verminous bully: "…saw your chance to be your own man at Lemman's expense, to replace him in Hawson's favour."

He watched the wince of disclosure in the thin face, the dark smudge of guilt behind the glittering eyes: "So you told him that Lemman had the bull. You told him how you and Lemman had beaten the secret of its finding out of poor…"

Though the Apothecary saw it coming and managed to raise his left arm to deflect some of its vicious force, Pearce struck him a single, up-swinging blow with the gun-butt that knocked him sprawling amongst the bluebells by the path.

"Think you know it all, you little cunt?" he shouted: "Think I don't know you'd 'ave 'ad the bull, given 'alf a chance? Watched you dribbling over it, almost fetchin' in your pants."

"So, it was *you* spying on us that day, was it? I might have guessed as much," Greene gasped: "Your pal Lemman didn't know what you were about to let him in for, did he?"

"I didn't know 'awson was going to do 'im in, did I? Beat 'im til 'e couldn't raise 'is arm no more, just went raving mad." Then, as if realising he had given away more than he should, added: "Reckon 'e'll 'ave some o' that for you, too. Almost bust a gut when 'e got told as 'ow you'd turfed 'im out of your poxin' shop, didn't 'e? So best shut that gabby mouth of yourn and *walk*," rasped Pearce, raising the gun-butt, afore I give you more o' this."

Greene fought through a haze of pain to struggle back to his feet, only the support of the cane enabling him to stand at all. Pearce jerked the gun and began pushing him ahead, up the sloping path through dense undergrowth towards the house. Greene knew, quite simply, that he would be a deadman if they reached its walls.

As they breasted a shallow rise he paused, head-down, gasping for breath, raising his ankle from the ground and wheezing: "Give me just a moment to..."

Just as he expected, Pearce strode forward, gun-butt raised to force him on. In that instant, Greene pulled the two-foot length of blade free of its cane scabbard in a single, fluid movement, whipping it, backhanded, in a slashing arc across the other's shoulder and chin. With a shriek Pearce fell back, the gun dropping from his hands as they flew to the stinging wound. Not losing even the seconds it would have taken to retrieve the weapon, the Apothecary hobbled forwards, pressing his attack, knowing this to be his only chance.

Howling with shock and pain, Pearce stumbled back into the dense groundcover, raising one blood-stained hand against the oncoming blade as the other groped inside his jerkin. Then, to Greene's horror, the questing hand found what it sought, and with a triumphant cry Pearce pulled out the Apothecary's pistol. In the split second it took for him to locate and cock the hammer, Greene lunged forward with a strength born of desperation, the oncoming blade catching Pearce momentarily off balance. As he staggered back in a desperate attempt to avoid the Apothecary's thrust, he tripped and toppled helplessly, arms flailing in a vain attempt to save himself – just as the ground beneath him seemed suddenly to take on a terrible life of its own.

An appalling, metallic screech was joined instantly by a howl of bestial anguish, as Pearce's legs kicked out in a demented jig and a single arm clawed at the air above a grotesque mask of agony that only seconds earlier had been his face. Tottering forward, Greene came upon a vision of hell on earth: the mantrap's rusted jaws had sprung closed around the toppling man, crushing Pearce's shoulder in its monstrous teeth, all but severing an upper arm in one. Transfixed, the Apothecary swayed above the hideous tableau, numbed with shock and horror, a powerless witness as the final seconds of Pearce's life pumped away into the blood-sodden grass. Then a single shot rang out.

(46)

On the Wall on the left hand the ORGAN. A large pair of Ram's Horns. A pair of Horns of the Bald-Faced Antelope. A Cocoa Nut divested of its external covering. Several Tusks of the Hippopotamus.

Walhill. 16th May. The Seward's coach had arrived promptly at eleven, just as she had requested, its driver instructed that he was to place himself at the disposal of Miss Beasley for the remainder of the day. Never lacking in self-awareness, the elderly spinster had felt not the slightest compunction in calling upon her lifelong friendship with the Canon's daughter for the unexpected favour, knowing that she had never before made even the slightest demand upon their years of intimacy. In her letter she had explained briefly, that since her return to Staffordshire she had longed to revisit her childhood haunts – especially the countryside around her beloved Walhill – leaving discreetly unsaid the fact that in the light of her declining health, the opportunity for one last visit needed to be seized sooner rather than later.

With intuitive understanding, the Sewards had readily acceded to the request, being only too happy that they could offer some meaningful comfort to a suffering friend. Anna had tacitly acknowledged that this was to be a pilgrimage of a deeply personal nature, graciously suggesting that as she had a prior commitment, Grace should have the coach and driver to herself, if she would forgive Anna's absence.

In spite of the warming sun of a fine morning, she had emerged from the low porch of Milley's Hospital wrapped in a travelling cloak, hands thrust deep into a somewhat moth-eaten muff. She managed a wan smile of gratitude as the attentive driver handed her up into the small carriage, arranging a travelling rug across her knees while she gave him his route for the morning. As he climbed down and closed the door, she glanced past him at her home, eyes huge in a face as pale as dusted snow. He had been told that his passenger was an invalid who would require all his care. He could see that for himself, now, and set off at a gentle pace the better to negotiate the rutted lanes that lay ahead.

On Grace Beasley's instructions they had approached Walhill by a circuitous route from the north, through a maze of sunken lanes, with the driver having to seek directions from his passenger on several occasions. When they arrived beside the ruined lodge that she had described, the coachman helped the frail woman to alight, gazing across at the ivy-clad walls and gaping windows as he did. Seeing his attention drawn to it, she said: "This was home to a family of ten when I was a small girl. I would come to play whenever I could, though my brother was most disapproving. He shared my dear mama's proprieties, poor, stuffy boy. It burned down, years ago, I believe. Such a pity."

Embarrassed by the unexpected confidence, the coachman used the excuse of busying himself with a nosebag for the dappled mare, whilst the elderly woman strolled to and fro. She seemed, then, to arrive at a decision, saying:

"I recall the paths so well from here to the house that I believe I shall be able to find the wicket gate to their little orchard over there. It will take me into the woods above the house. Please wait here for my return. I do not intend to be very long."

Indicating that he was at her disposal, the coachman said he would be happy to wait for as long as the lady took.

"Everyone is so kind," she said with an absent smile, and walked slowly off through the overgrown garden to disappear into the dense woodlands beyond.

It was as if she had entered a giant's tent in some great, green encampment, lit with pale enchantment from the densely leafed canopy above. Her eyes roved away between the ancient trunks, the winter-fallen boughs that reared up like driftwood in a misted sea of bluebells, the sweetness of their scent borne upon a breeze that barely rippled through the woods. He was with her for a moment then. She heard his boyish laughter ringing through the chequered shade and seemed to glimpse her brother's darting figure as it played at hide and seek. Together, here, they'd sought the nests of nightingales: the press of dry oak leaves, their skimpy lining of a few horsehairs and fibrous roots, built down amongst the stitchwort and the woodspurge, or amidst the springing shoots of some old bole. Her eyes were drawn to where a shaft of light cut through and lit the turfy ruts, and thought she saw the tiny blur of hawk-moth wings against the waving blue of bugle spires.

Then, the sunlight faded and the woods beyond became a wall of serried trees, a palisade to keep her from her childish dreams. From the tallest of them all she saw a body swinging in the freshening breeze. She saw a twisted neck and bulging eyes, a purpled tongue protruding from a mottled face, slack arms hung down with lifeless fingers spread as if to grasp at air.

She halted, swaying, racked with sobs, knowing even as she stood that soon the storm-clouds massing in her head would break and sweep her will away. She gathered herself and turned towards the house whose chimneys peeped above the farthest trees. A path led off that skirted round the unseen lake. She knew that was her quickest route.

Now, as she plodded on, head down, scowling with resolve, not even the sight of a cormorant, wings spread wide to dry, distracted her as she made her way around the rush-fringed water that they had loved so well. Nor, when she passed the boathouse, sagging ever-lower on its green-scummed posts, did she permit a thought of all the times they'd rowed out from its musty berths. All of that was left behind her now. There simply was no time.

When, at last, she came to the gate into the ha-ha, she had to lay aside her muff and use both hands to wrench it open, wincing as its rusty screech. Heedless of the nettles growing in her path, she waded through them as she made her way round to the steps that led back to the lawns above. It was as she climbed them and emerged from the long-neglected topiary that hedged the deep-cut path, that she surprised a shirtless youth, scything grass around a lichened urn.

Gaping at the apparition, he backed away, scarlet with embarrassment as he groped for the shirt hanging from the branches near his tousled head.

"Did I shock you, dear?" she asked sweetly. "I am so sorry if I did. I have come to pay a surprise visit on your master. I know the way."

He nodded, awkwardly, obviously relieved at not having to engage the strange arrival and bowed her past.

"Do be careful with that, won't you," she added, "they can be most frightfully dangerous."

Smiling cautiously, he shrugged, and returned to his work.

Approaching the low, flagged terrace from the lawn, she saw the unmistakable figure she sought, heavily bandaged about neck and shoulder. He sat with his back towards her, papers spread across a stone bench, the leaves held down by a half-empty decanter and a single glass. Her slight footfall must have reached his ears, as, without turning, he barked:

"I said I was *not* to be disturbed! Do you dare to disobey me?"

"Oh, I think so," she said, quietly.

The effect was everything she could have hoped for.

ITEM:

On the Top of the ORGAN, in Glass Cases.
A Sky Lark. A Cock Yellowhammer. A Cuckow.

Walhill. 13ᵗʰ April. Left to his own devices, Tillett had decided to take matters into his own hands. He had delivered the Apothecary's sealed envelope to the Guildhall office around midday, knowing it would save Mr Greene time he could ill afford on his return. Whether his master would agree with that assessment, Tillett could not say, knowing only that in the mistress's absence the well-oiled machine that was the Saddler Street Apothecary was not running entirely to his satisfaction.

Aware that Mr Greene was frequently given to pursuing time-consuming tangents not at all connected with the business in hand, Tillett had decided to ensure – on this occasion at least – that, on his return, full and undivided attention be given to the replenishment of powders and nostrums that were the master's exclusive preserve. So it was that the prospect of a long luncheon and the briefest possible afternoon spent back in his stuffy office vanished in a trice as the Sherriff of the City of Lichfield read – then rapidly re-read – the Apothecary's missive:

> *...seeking conclusive evidence...directly or indirectly culpable of two homicides...earlier brutalities swept under the carpet... dangerously volatile...personal jeopardy...in the event that I have failed to return...evidence lodged with Ashton Lever of Alkrington, Rochdale...Reverend Blomefield holding further verifiable proof...all due haste...*

"Damn and *blast* the man," exclaimed the officer, reaching for his wig and endeavouring to recall whether he had brought his pistols to work that month. "Why the Devil can't he get on with what he's *good* at?"

Calling for his Clerk and the single Constable that was in earshot, he dispatched the former to The George, to cancel his regular lunch appointment with Sir Boothby Pagnell, the latter to summon whatever help was available from however many officers it was that were at his disposal. Detail had never been his strong suit.

Unable to locate his firearms, he was about to settle for a large, ungainly sabre when he remembered its baldric had been employed to tie something or other the previous year.

In disgust he seized his walking stick and sent for his horse, shouting down the now-empty corridor that the constables were to assemble and await his orders.

For as long as he lived, the Apothecary would never forget the sight that met him when he finally reached the source of the single, flat, detonation. Two figures appeared frozen in some theatrical tableau: one seated, staring out across the sunlit parkland; the other, kneeling, arms at its sides, head slumped forward as if in dejected submission. Light-headed with pain, gasping for breath, Richard Greene could make no sense of what he saw, even as he clambered the low steps and recognised the seated woman.

Seeming, for a moment, reluctant to tear her eyes away from the spread of the gardens, Grace Beasley finally registered his arrival, saying: "Richard! What a delightful surprise. But what *have* you done to yourself? You look as if you have been in the wars."

Before he could even imagine a response, she nodded at the kneeling figure, saying: "Even until the very last moment I was unsure I could do what was necessary, but when he realised that begging would do no good, he tried to kiss my feet. It was perfectly straightforward then."

She bent forward to rearrange the position of the small pistol on the bench between them. "It would appear he was doing his accounts when I surprised him." She picked up one of the closely written sheets, squinting at it and saying, conversationally: "Something to do with *Medusa* I believe. Who would have taken him for a Classicist?"

For the first time, the Apothecary saw the black hole between Bartholomew Hawson's lifeless eyes, and beyond him, the bobbing, fearful faces staring out from the windows of the fine old house.

"I should take you home, my dear," he said gently.

"Oh, Richard, *would* you?" she responded, with a pained smile of gratitude: "I really don't think I could face the walk back up to Orchard Lodge, where dear Anna's coach awaits. It's been *such* a day."

He caught her as she toppled from her chair.

Having finally taken time to draw breath and consult a pocket watch that read twenty minutes past one o'clock, Greene had reasonably assumed that, given Tillett's literal frame of mind, no assistance would be forthcoming until close to mid-afternoon at the earliest. Then, though, having rapidly reviewed all he knew about the city constabulary and its principal officer, he had to face the prospect that none might materialise at all, given the innumerable obstacles upon which its members were likely to stumble.

Consequently, he was faced with a series of dilemmas. How to summon the Seward coach from wherever it might have been left without leaving the still unconscious Grace Beasley? There being no conceivable way that she could be transported, otherwise? How to inform someone, *anyone*, that the erstwhile master of Walhill had been shot dead on his own terrace? Then, having no recollection whatever of quite how he had managed to stumble his way to the scene, how to direct someone, *anyone*, to where a murderous henchman lay dead in a mantrap, somewhere on the estate?

It was only as he found himself longing for nothing more than a good sleep that Richard Greene realised he had omitted his own condition from his review of problems. He raised a blood-caked hand to his brow and groaned.

After some time – he had no clue of how long – he became aware of someone standing close and jerked to attention. A tousle-haired youth, a scythe across his shoulder, stood gaping at the sight before him. "Alright, be she?" he said, at last, nodding towards the recumbent form of Grace Beasley. "Kind lady, 'er. Told me take care." Greene, realising he was in the presence of limited intelligence, replied gently:

"No, I am afraid she is not. She is most unwell."

"'Im an' all?" the boy said, nodding at the body of Hawson, still slumped on its knees.

"Worse, much worse," Greene said, solemnly.

The young face cracked into a lop-sided grin: "'Ates 'im, I do. Beat our Reuben bloody, 'im. Glad, me."

"Do you think you can help the lady, lad? We need to call her coach here; it's waiting somewhere close to a lodge?"

The grin widened, and he threw down his scythe on the lawn: "Orchard Lodge, that. Can run there quick for 'er, me."

With that he turned and sprinted away across the perfect lawn, disappearing down into the ha-ha within seconds. Greene sat back and drew in a shuddering sigh of relief, attempting, with little success, to come to terms with the grotesquerie of the situation.

His attention was drawn, then, to the sound of breaking glass, around the corner from the terrace where he sat, and he sprang to his feet, reaching into his coat for his own, reclaimed, pistol. He need not have alarmed himself. This was not a counter-attack in the making; it was the spectacle of various members of the Walhill household busily looting portable objects from the house, scarcely pausing at the sight of the small, solitary figure regarding their frenetic plunder. The source of the sound had been a mirror, now lying, smashed upon the cobbles of the stableyard, as they ran to and fro, arms full of as much as they could carry to a dairy cart.

Utterly unconcerned, Greene turned away, returning to where the unconscious woman sat, slumped, her breath coming in shallow gasps, her skin a sickly grey in the bright afternoon light that bathed the terrace.

Glancing reluctantly at the kneeling corpse, Greene realised – for the first time – that throughout the weeks and months that Bartholomew Hawson had assumed the role of nemesis in the Apothecary's affairs, they had never exchanged a word. Here, now, that unseen, vengeful presence was a shrunken husk, banal in its indignity, its threat dispersed like some bad odour on the wind. Greene sat and pondered on the nature of hatred, coming to no comfortable conclusion.

Within what seemed a miraculously brief interlude, he saw the familiar orange and grey livery of the Canon's coach, approaching at speed along the tree-lined drive. He descended the grand steps and waved it to a halt. Jumping down, even before the coachman could apply his brake, the grinning youth called: "Told you so, told you so!"

Greene waved back in gratitude as the youth skipped away.

As the Seward's coachmen hurried forward, Greene met him, speaking urgently: "There has been an appalling tragedy here. I have no time to explain, and must ask only that you concentrate on the urgent matter in hand, do you understand?"

The coachman saw the furious concentration in the Apothecary's face: "Of course, Mr Greene. Whatever you say."

Nodding gratefully, Greene hurried on. "Miss Beasley is grievously afflicted and must be taken home without delay. I shall help you with her but cannot accompany you yet. I shall follow on as soon as I may. There is not a moment to lose. If I have not caught up with you, then seek the Warden's *immediate* assistance at Milley's. Is that clear? I shall be unable to leave until the constabulary arrives."

He would wonder, later, how the Seward coach could have passed the Sherriff, unnoticed, on its way back to the city. Though, reminding himself of the warren of lanes by which the isolated estate could be approached, it would have been entirely possible for a regiment of Foot to pass by with less fuss than marked the eventual arrival of the city officers.

While he waited, he spent some time leafing through the spread account sheets wondering, idly, who the recipient of Hawson's fortune might turn out to be, and whether they would ever know – or even care about – the sources of their new-found wealth. Looking at the perfectly kept accounts he could see that the *Medusa*, alone, had made two Africa voyages within the twelve months; voyages whose human harvest totalled more than six hundred nameless souls: men, women and children: ...*all sound in limb and wind...bought of Ibn Saud, factor for Dahomey.*

He scanned the itemised columns, relating to the expenses of *the enterprise*: the cost of salt-fish and flour *not of the first quality*, of shackles, powder and ball, until he came upon the neatly calculated total from the sale of those that had survived ...*the rigours of their transportation to the Indies.*

He dropped the sheet as if it were tainted, needing, suddenly, to distance himself from the lifeless husk still bowed, submissively, at his feet.

Whatever horrors Greene had witnessed earlier, they had now ceased, to be replaced with an eerie calm that could have been mistaken for normality. He walked across the deserted stable yard to where he could see the blue livery of the magnificent coach through an open door, though it was what lay propped beside it that drew his eye. A pair of hacked marble figures *half of life-size* leant against a whitewashed wall whose pristine pallor gave them both an air of sour, yellowed drabness, as if they were abandoned refugees from some forgotten rout: unnamed, unloved guardians of a treasure long-since spent. He couldn't bring himself to examine them with any interest. Whatever magic they might once have held for him had fled, brutalised and spoiled, just like the now-meaningless hole from which they had been wrenched. He had not the slightest doubt that *the sun in splendour, a hands-breadth across* would have disappeared without trace. Not that it mattered, now.

He could see, from an occasional darting glimpse from upstairs windows, that not all the staff had decamped. There would be maids and the like, with no other place to go, he supposed – soon to be turned out, no doubt, when all this was closed and shuttered up by those who understood the value of capital investment.

He felt such a weight of desolation fall upon him, then, that he swayed with nausea and would have fallen where he stood, had not the sound of hooves upon the drive announced the arrival of the Sherriff and a half a dozen men, all lathered from their headlong ride. He offered up a silent prayer of gratitude for a shopman who must have shown the first spark of initiative in his long and undistinguished life.

"What's to do now, Mr Greene? What's to do?" puffed the Sherriff, clambering clumsily from a winded horse, the state of both rider and mount attesting to extreme circumstances. "Can't have this you know, calling us out, willy-nilly. Heaven only knows what Mr Hawson will have to say about it, riding up to a gentleman's door like yeomanry in battle-order!"

Looking past the flustered officer to the straggling, ramshackle troop in his train, the Apothecary simply said: "Why don't I take you to him, now? You'll find him quite unconcerned."

(48)

On some Shelves next the ORGAN. Several Roman Paterae, found near Colchester and Deal Castle, in Kent. A fragment of the Tusk of an Elephant found near eight feet below the surface of the Earth, in the Parish of Alderminster, in the Lands of Thos. Partridge, Esq. of Clopton, near Stratford upon Avon, Warwickshire.

17th May, 1776. Theodosia was too shocked to be angry, needing, instead, her wan and bruised spouse to repeat much of what he was patiently endeavouring to explain. The apportioning of culpability and recrimination would wait for some other time –a decision tacitly announced by the desperate concern she had shown for the bandaged, limping figure who had greeted her return – all that mattered to her was the why and wherefore, upon which he had manfully embarked.

"Frankly, my dear, poor Grace was, by then, so completely distracted, she might still have been sitting on Walhill's terrace, had sheer coincidence not placed me in the grounds."

"From whence you almost failed to emerge, alive," added Theodosia, her reserve fraying the more the sorry tale emerged.

"*Mm*, there was a hideous though unmistakable irony in the means of Pearce's death," he admitted, "though my sword-stick served me in good stead."

"And would have continued so to do in the face of your own loaded pistol?" she enquired, tartly. The Apothecary took the point and hurried on, describing the looting of the house and the Sherriff's arrival:

"That man is incompetence personified. He was actually fool

enough to demand that *my* pistol be surrendered for examination, in case it turned out to be the murder weapon, when the firearm in question had been pointed out as lying beneath his very nose." *I shall thank you to permit me to make up my own mind where any such matters are concerned, Greene* he said, *when I have assembled the entire staff and put them to the question.* The fact that I had also informed him – only minutes before – of the household's mass desertion seemed somehow to have passed him by. He and his buffoons then proceeded to spend so much time striking judicial attitudes all around the house and grounds, that by the time they got around to questioning them, even the last of the upstairs maids had made themselves scarce. But then what else would any sentient being *do*, faced with the prospect of answering to those clod-hoppers?"

"Don't rant, Richard, it is unbecoming," she said, lifting a handkerchief to his perspiring brow in mitigation, its scent of *eau-de-cologne* filling the overheated room.

"So, once even they had satisfied their morbid *curiosity* into the deaths – and I swear that most of the time it is little more than that – I was harangued for abetting the escape of *the murderess*, as our Sherriff now insists upon calling poor Grace. If it is to be believed, I was forced to invoke my role as her physician, and describe how I had dispatched an insensate, terminally ill woman to her home rather than leave her dying beside her victim– which, it must be said, may well have been her intention all along."

"But, Richard, like it as little as we may, the wretched man's referring to Grace in that manner is the simple truth," said Theodosia, biting back tears. "Dear Lord, if only I had understood the extent, the *depth*, of her outrage, I might have…"

"You could have done nothing, nor, in fact, could anyone, my dear. Of that I am now completely certain. It is one of the less palatable traits of our species that dislike can become loathing, then loathing transmute into a ravening growth that will destroy its host as surely as that host seeks to destroy the object of its hatred. I fear that the dear lady was prey not only to the cerebral tumour which was killing her but also to a force infinitely more malign."

"She was dead by the time that you reached Milley's, then?" murmured his wife, unable to hold back her tears.

"She was, my dear, though seldom have I seen one so recently deceased at such peace. She had regained sufficient sensibility to insist she be placed in her chair by the open window, and there we found her."

"*We*, Richard? I thought you returned from Walhill alone?"

"Far from it," he scowled. "I was accompanied – if not actually *shepherded* – by our Sherriff in all his pomp, there to claim for himself all credit for the seizure of *the murderess*, and, presumably, to be certain I did not cut and run and in belated acknowledgement of my own role in what he is now insisting on calling *the conspiracy*."

"Oh, my dear, as if you have not paid sufficient price for your generosity – for that is what has brought this wretchedness to our door – and not for the first time. You have already done their work thrice over?" she exclaimed." What more can the city authorities expect of you?"

"A short memory would, I think, top their list, the Sherriff, his Coroner and the constabulary being presently engaged in the rewriting of recent history: most importantly, of their own cack-fisted role in its handling."

"Those verdicts still rankle, Richard, I am well aware of that, but surely now is not the time to compound their misjudgement and embarrassment?"

"Embarrassment!" he cried. "*Their embarrassment?*" She attempted to restrain him, but he jumped to his feet and began an angry pacing: "First," he enumerated, furiously, holding up a finger, "the Coroner brought in a verdict of *Misadventure, whilst the balance of his mind was disturbed* on poor, murdered, Joe Crede – in spite of our conclusive forensic evidence to the contrary. Then, to compound the criminal idiocy," – he held up a second finger

– "a verdict of *unlawful killing, by person or persons unknown* in regard to Lemman's murder– without one single question being thought worth the asking of Pearce, any of Walhill's other men, or their *gentleman* master. And as for Aggie's death, out there on our street..?" He shook his head, continuing,

"As if *acting in self-defence* and *justifiable homicide* even begins to tell the tale of black wickedness that brought her to her death." He raised his hands in a gesture of hopeless impotence: "Don't you *see*, Theodosia? The deaths of those folk, good, bad or indifferent as they may have been, were simply not considered worth the time of the Sheriff, the Coroner or God help us, those bumbling morons of Constables." He came back to his seat, and sat, head in his hands. "But when the murderous, slave-driving bastard of a *gentleman* gets his just desserts on his own terrace, there is the Sheriff, himself, personification of all civic virtues, poised to seize the malefactor and drag her off to justice. Do you know what his parting question to me was? He enquired whether there might not be some *distemper,* some *contagious susceptibility* to which both Agnes Crede and Grace Beasley could have fallen prey?

"I swear, Theodosia, that had I but concurred – and called it *murderitis* or some other such nonsense – he would have the Constables scouring clean the scenes of both crimes as we speak, lest some hint of contagion remain to infect yet another member of the weaker sex."

She was shocked to see tears coursing down the cheeks of the round, unremarkable face she loved so well. "I just don't know what makes sense anymore," he said. "I just don't know."

49

ITEM:

A Manuscript Missal on Vellum, bound in Crimson Velvet,
with Clasps and Plates of Silver, on which are engraved, on
the front side, within an ornamented Shield, "Museo Ricardi
Greene, Cic. Lichfeldensi," on the other side, "Hunc Librum,
D.D. Teresa Wakeman de Aldridge, in agro Staffordiensi,
A.D. 1769 This book is in fine preservation, the Initial
Letters illuminated with burnished Gold and Colours.

Saddler Street. 2nd May, 1776. In the recurring absences of
Theodosia Greene 'on apothecary business' and on the third
occasion of his being told, that Mr Greene was 'not receiving',
Lionel Blomefield decided to take matters into his own hands.
Knowing better than to try forcing his way past either a spindly
but adamant shopman, or the far more intimidating prospect of
a guardian housekeeper, he decided, instead, upon a moderately
simple subterfuge.

Knowing of the long-standing friendship between Margery
and his own presiding sentinel at Breadmarket Street, he
suggested to that personage that an invitation to take afternoon
tea – extended in the direction of Saddler Street – would not, he
divined, go amiss.

With a degree of ingenuity that impressed even himself, the
Reverend Blomefield defused the immediate glare of suspicion
that met his suggestion by commenting that, as everyone in the
apothecary household had been, of late, under such intolerable
pressure, it could come as no surprise that her long-suffering

counterpart had, quite naturally, borne the brunt of it all, and was exhausted by the constant demands being placed upon her ever-generous nature. Knowing an unspoken cry for help when she heard one, the invitation had been sent.

At precisely five past four the following afternoon and having confirmed that the mistress of the house was out *in loco Apothecarius,* the elderly cleric presented himself at the street door. With a winning smile he brushed past the housemaid, pushing a shilling into her hand, and exclaiming that although received at short notice he was responding to Mr Greene's summons with all due haste.

"But Sir, the Master…" she began, helplessly

"…will be only too pleased to see me, dear girl! Up in his Museum, one presumes?"

The nervous nod was all he required. "I shall find my own way up. I should know the way by now, after all." With that he was past her, to the stairs.

Wheezing from the long climb to the third storey, the sight of an untouched tray of food and drink, left on a windowsill at the top of the stairs, should have alerted him, but he was too busy puzzling over the closed door to the Museum rooms. He had not even known there to *be* a door, it never having been closed in all his long years of visiting. In the circumstances, he ruled out knocking and walked in, unannounced.

The stench of brandy, stale air, and a wigless, bedraggled museum-keeper – staler by far – assailed his nostrils. He flinched back, barely stifling an oath, though the object of his visit would not have cared. Richard Greene lolled at his desk, head on a table strewn with a variety of equally soiled and neglected sheets, a toppled glass the principal culprit, an empty, unstoppered, decanter the obvious source. At Blomefield's feet was Ashmole's box, upended, looking as though it may have been kicked across the room.

"Well, if this is how 'not receiving' looks, my friend," he announced, briskly, to the insensible figure: "We shall just have to see what 'not putting up with anymore of this nonsense' looks like, shall we not?"

Sometime after five o'clock, as Theodosia was wearily returning from what had seemed like ever-longer rounds, she was surprised – to say the least – at the sight of the unmistakable figure of Margery, in best bonnet and under full sail, preceding her towards the shop. A creature of habit so inflexible that the word might have been coined for her, Margery's forays into the city could be predicted, and timed, with military precision – yet here she was defying convention. The answer would only be revealed some moments later when both women, in varying stages of incredulity –and in the case of Margery, outraged affront at her proven gullibility – learned that the Reverend Blomefield was presently upstairs with Mr Greene 'making certain Master eats his supper now that he's had his bath.'

Unsure whether to be jubilant that her husband's black depression might, somehow, have been lifted, or, furious at the usurpation of her wifely role – one which, admittedly, had proved wholly ineffective for the past three days – Theodosia took the stairs at a pace which belied both her years and the present state of her aching feet.

Entering their parlour, she took in the sight of two elderly gentlemen – one engaged with a plate of ham and piccalilli, the other apparently content to watch.

"Lionel," she said, "it would appear that you are both a conniver *and* a man of hidden talents."

"Guilty on both counts," he replied, grinning smugly, "though I have been vainly attempting to persuade Elspeth of the latter throughout our marriage."

"How did you effect the miracle cure?" she persisted: "I must know, for future reference."

"What *miracle cure?*" interjected her husband, tetchily. "I was a little out of sorts is all. Is one to be harried unmercifully at the first sign that one might be a trifle off colour?"

With magnificent forbearance, she came and sat beside him. "Welcome back, my dear, we've missed you."

Raising his eyebrows in mock exasperation, he turned to Blomefield, but was met with a raised finger, wagging in stern admonition.

"I have often had occasion to say that your levity is all-too frequently misplaced, Richard. This is one such occasion. Give thanks for this good lady's saintly patience in the face of your shameless self-indulgence."

"Amen to that, Lionel," replied Greene, in apparent solemnity, "though in one's own defence it should perhaps be added that in a marriage of such venerable antiquity as our own, a certain give-and-take has been required in that direction."

"Richard Greene, are you *suggesting..?*" Then she saw the twinkle that, for far too long, had been so lacking in his eyes. Laughing with relief, she reached out for his plate and before he could stop her, took the pickled onion he had obviously been saving for last. Before popping it daintily into her mouth, she said to the convalescent: "If you are to share my bed once more, husband, we shall at least do it on equal terms," before turning and adding: "Now Lionel, kindly unburden yourself while I enjoy this,"

Blomefield smiled benignly at their reaction to his stratagem and after cupping one hand to an ear with a theatrical flourish, rose to leave. Seeing the puzzlement on both faces he explained: "I was simply attempting to ascertain whether a certain domestic presence might be otherwise engaged before making good my escape." As if on cue, a distant clatter of pots from the scullery, below could be heard. "I do believe the coast is clear," he added, though not, Theodosia thought, without a degree of nervousness.

"Have no fear, Lionel. Margery is under strict instructions not to cause unnecessary bloodshed on the premises," said Greene, straight-faced.

"It is the good woman's interpretation of *necessary* which gives one cause for concern," replied the cleric, about to take his leave.

"Oh Lionel, there was something else. It had quite slipped my mind," said Greene, putting aside his tray, and coming a mite shakily to his feet. Blomefield stopped, curious, as the Apothecary turned back to his wife: "If you would, perhaps, excuse us for a short while, my dear? There is something upstairs that I think, perhaps, Lionel will be interested to see."

He was unprepared for his wife's reaction. Jumping to her feet, Theodosia said brightly: "I have done nothing *but* excuse you these three days – and many, many more – past, Richard. I know you and your *interests* better than do you, yourself, husband, and I will not stand by as you go off into another of your arcane huddles. As you are about to share this *something upstairs* with an elderly clergyman of only slightly tarnished reputation, I shall assume there is nothing improper involved and join Lionel in the revelation."

"So there," said Blomefield, grinning at the abashed husband "Perhaps now you should unburden *yourself!*"

"Well," began Greene, as if uncertain where to start: "It's just that unless I dreamt it, I believe I have stumbled upon the solution to Ashmole's riddling."

"Hence an upended box, apparently kicked half-way across the Museum?" enquired Blomefield, innocently, unable to miss the opportunity, though already feeling his anticipation burgeoning like a living thing.

"Um, no. That would probably have occurred sometime *before* the discovery. I did get rather vexed, I must admit. Something to do with my being a little indisposed, no doubt."

"No doubt," responded the other, nodding gravely to Theodosia. "So..?"

"Well, as I was *trying* to say," said Greene with as much asperity as he could manage, "I really need to show you, both of you, what I've found, upstairs."

Not without a certain embarrassment, the Apothecary took several moments to reassemble the erstwhile contents of the box, stooping to retrieve various items from wherever they had landed during *the indisposition*. When he had laid out certain of them on the opened leaves of his writing table, he stood back, saying: "It was actually Caisley's plan of the vanished medieval Palace that finally dropped things more or less into place, though not before Canon Seward inadvertently provided me with the reminder that Saint Peter – so prominently featured in the text – had been crucified head-down in mockery. I realised that..." – he upended the cruciform illustration with its strangely set text – "...what we had supposed to be an image of some sort of reliquary, was in fact a schematic plan of our Cathedral. Beneath, and within, the base of the drawing, what we had read to be the record of an archaic cartouche was simply Ashmole reiterating the cryptic aphorism of his accompanying letter:

As above, so below, 'tis perception wherein fortune lies...

So, here it is, again: 'AASB'. With old Elias saying: 'Read the image that I've given you upside-down.' Couldn't be simpler, could it?"

Blomefield suppressed a snort, but fascinated, joined Theodosia as together they bent over the evidence before them:

"So, all these dots..." she began.

"...Are columns," Greene volunteered.

"And this large one, here..?" began Lionel.

"...Marks the position of where the great Shrine once stood," said Greene.

"I can see that," replied Blomefield with a snort of annoyance, glaring at the oblivious apothecary.

"What a clever man," Theodosia murmured. Her husband

unsure to whom she referred, continued: "Quite apart from that, though, was this graceless, oddly laid text beside it. The blessed thing had us both foxed until..." Grinning triumphantly he laid out the borrowed plan beside the illustrated page for their inspection: "Though this antique plan does not show the relationship of the now-vanished palace buildings to the Cathedral itself, *this* does." He pointed at the three columns of text. "Look! Their layout conforms precisely to the foundation plan of the palace. This long paragraph here corresponds perfectly to this east-west range that stood along the church's northerly side, whilst these two paragraphs grouped here so oddly, match *exactly* the principal quarters of the palace proper: the Bishop's Hall, and so on."

"So, above that, this empty space that occupies so much of the right-hand side of the sheet..." began Blomefield, excitedly, only to be cut off once more:

"...must have been the palace garden, bounded by The Close wall and the palace buildings on two of the remaining three side, obviously."

"I think Lionel might have been about to say that, Richard," interposed his wife, who had seen the flush of annoyed frustration starting in the cleric's scrawny neck.

"Thank you, Theodosia," responded Blomefield, stiffly. "He is at his most impossible when over-excited." He turned back to Greene and said: "So, must we *invite* you to continue? The floor, regrettably, would appear to be yours."

Undeterred, the Apothecary continued: "Now, though, is where I started to become... vexed, for try as I might I could not, as yet, discern any means of proceeding, though by now I knew that the solution was all there in front of me."

"Much as it has always been, one supposes," interjected the cleric, with airy aspersion, shrugging at his friend with an unspoken: "So?"

"It came to me, finally, in the strangest way, as I was having a rest, with the side of my head laid upon the plan..." – he appeared

not to notice as his listeners exchanged a wordless glance – "…
with my cheek there." He pointed down. "I suddenly noticed the
coincidence between the position of the shrine and the centremost
of these three oddly broken lines:

…for flesh and blood hath not revealed it unto thee…

"It was as if the shrine and those particular words were marking
out a line, a meridian of some sort, off to the right of the page and
heading into the empty space."

They were hanging on his words by then. He continued with
a wan smile: "I suppose, in the circumstances, that at least the
first line of the final part might have been quite amusing, had I,
perhaps, been in a more jocular frame of mind." He shrugged,
continuing: "You know how these things can be: All of a sudden
my eye was being led to the layout of the other paragraphs: to
two separate things, in fact. Why, I asked myself, were *these* lines
centred above, and separated from, the rest of the following text?

Incline thine ear unto wisdome, and apply thine heart to
understanding yea if thou criest out for knowledge…

"And secondly, why had the remaining text been split into two
paragraphs below, like that? Then I saw it, plain as a pikestaff." He
sat back, palms spread, smiling broadly, as if his task was finished.

"Richard," said Theodosia sternly, "you are being uncommonly
trying. I might allow poor Lionel to throttle you, after all."

"No need, no need at all," responded the cleric, breezily. "It's
there for any fool to see. One simple draws a vertical line, upwards,
precisely between the two paragraphs – as so clearly indicated –
and where it crosses one's horizontal line, is *the spot*, so to speak.
It's that simple, is it not, Richard?"

Crestfallen, the Apothecary nodded, knowing he had been
played – and beaten, this time at least – at his own game. Enjoying

every minute of the fencing match between such old adversaries, Theodosia clapped her hands and exclaimed:

"Lionel, that was *magnificent*! Such deduction, such intuition!"

Seeing the stricken mortification on his face, neither could contain their mirth any longer, dissolving into helpless laughter, until Greene managed, ruefully, to join them.

"So," she finally managed, "where does this leave us, erudite husband of mine?"

"In the middle of Canon Seward's beloved rose garden, unless I am mistaken," he replied, "You know, my dear, those arbours to which he has devoted his every botanic hour, these many years past?"

"How very unfortunate," she replied. "In that case, your greatest challenge may still lie ahead, Richard."

"*Mine?*" he responded. "Only moments ago, it was *us*."

"Ah, but that was before the Canon's roses entered the picture, Richard. We both know to what your dear wife alludes," added Blomefield.

She came and placed her arms tight about him then, regardless of their old friend's amused presence: "You *know* the extent of our admiration for you, my dear, for everything your persistence, your intuition, has achieved. To rediscover what, indeed, must lay hidden there, will be the crowning achievement of your life as an antiquarian. No-one will ever be able to take that away from you."

Beyond his wife, the Apothecary could see his old friend pulling a face and making swelling motions around his head, but for some reason, could not find the humour in it.

"We shall just have to see, I suppose," he said, disengaging himself. "Suddenly, I feel very tired, will you both excuse me?"

Without waiting for a reply, he hurried out.

50

ITEM:

The lower part of the Window. Is wholly occupied by a
collection of artificial Magnets, viz. the compound Horse-Shoe
Magnet. – The Staple Supporters. – A set of Magnetic Bars,
with Brass Armour, for communicating the magnetic Power
to other bars of Steel. – The Annular, or ring Magnet; its
weight four ounces and a half; has raised a five pound weight.
– A staple Magnet. – The dipping Magnetic Needle, &c.
The Magnets have tin buckets to each, properly weighted.

The Cathedral Close. 23rd May, 1776. The palace garden was
laid out with a degree of classical perfection that only a truly
dedicated plantsman can achieve over many doting years. Whilst
Canon Residentiary Seward would describe its creation as
coming second only to his beloved family, both wife and surviving
daughter might have debated the point, allowing that, for as long
as anyone could remember, domestic horticulture had been the
driving passion of a busy life. That would not be to say, however,
that this had been a life deficient in all those other qualities that
made for the most cultivated of scholarly gentlemen. Had it not
been he who had inspired such memorable precocity in his own
young daughter's poetic and literary development, and could, no
less, claim authorship of *The female right to Literature*?

It had been, in fact, the very span of his interests that had first
drawn Darwin, Edgworth, Johnson and an ever-expanding variety
of the Midlands' literary luminaries to the Seward residence these
ten years past. Whilst, by now, the *aesthetic* aspects of Darwin's
own polymathic interests had long been devoted to nurturing the

poetical blossoming of his acolyte, Anna, he reserved his botanical enthusiasms for sharing with her father.

So it was that on the perfect, early summer morning when Lionel Blomefield arrived, unannounced, at the palace's garden gate, he was met by the sight of not one but two of the city's luminaries, absorbed in what appeared to be a particularly delicate graft in the stifling heat of the Orangery. Shirt-sleeved, wigless and perspiring freely, both rose, courteously but with a degree of reluctance, to greet the newcomer.

Earlier that morning, the Reverend Blomefield, acting in a manner that could only be described as furtive, had been spotted by Theodosia Greene from an upstairs window. Though long accustomed to the various comings and goings of friends and acquaintances through the Bore Street gate at the end of their long, narrow garden, this morning's visitor – instantly recognisable though he was – could be seen casting nervous glances at the back of the house and employing what sparse cover the various flowering shrubs had to offer.

Intrigued, Theodosia went down, and quietly let herself out through the scullery door, both housekeeper and maid being engaged elsewhere. Noiselessly she approached the gawky figure, standing with his back to her and straining upwards to the lower branches of their hazel tree.

"If it is the label you seek, Lionel, the tree is *Amentaceae*, though you are too late for catkins and rather too early for birds' nests, lest they be wrens. Perhaps you were just going to climb it?"

A paroxysm seemed to galvanise the straining man. Turning to the source of the voice and looking as if he had narrowly avoided a seizure, the cleric sagged against the trunk, his long features registering a mixture of shock and relief: "Oh, dear Lord, it is you, Theodosia! I had thought for one dreadful moment that I was set upon by *She with whom one trifles at one's peril*."

"Dear me, are repercussions still resounding at Breadmarket

Street?" Theodosia enquired, already knowing the answer from the look on Blomefield's gaunt features.

"You are the very mistress of understatement, Theodosia. I am only surprised the sound of detonations has not reached you here. As its nominal master, I am attempting to inhabit a household wherein a withdrawal of goodwill is regarded as no less than my due by all female staff, accompanied by the largely unspoken – though no less effective – recriminations concerning my role as husband and sole instigator of domestic turmoil."

"So, you were going to hide in our hazel tree. How silly of me not to realise it at once," responded Theodosia, relishing the rare discomfiture of the arch mischief-maker. The extent to which their old friend had been wrong-footed was revealed only then, by the almost comically crestfallen expression on his face. She relented with a laugh, laying a fond hand upon his lichen-stained arm. "Just so long as you are not in search of firewood, I shall enquire no further, Lionel, and in Richard's absence you will need to make no further explanation. I shall leave you to whatever scheme you are presently hatching, though do be mindful of the price still being exacted by the last one!"

She turned to leave the relieved cleric, but then, as if recalling something, turned back to him, and said: "Oh, and have no fear of recrimination from *our* domestic quarter, Lionel. I feel almost certain that Margery will have forgiven you by the turn of the century."

She walked away, still laughing.

When he had regained some composure, and having assured himself of no other watchful eyes, Lionel Blomefield opened his clasp-knife and returned to his task.

The Canon and the Doctor strove to contain their curiosity as a variety of polite small talk was exchanged, though none of it beginning to explain the folded camp stool clamped beneath one of Blomefield's arms, whilst the other attempted to control what appeared to be a collapsible easel and a lace-fastened portfolio. Finally, giving up the unequal struggle with gravity, he simply dropped them all on the cinder path, saying: "To explain this intrusion, Seward: our Apothecary, having donned his curatorial hat, has taken a fancy to exhibiting some illustrative record of what remains of the ancient fortifications of our Close." He gestured with his now-freed hands to the long expanse of walling that formed the northern boundary of the palace garden: "In spite of my exceptionally modest watercolour talents, he is particularly keen that I should record this, and, of course, what remains of the Bishop's Tower – it being, so he assures me – the last vestige of The Close towers."

"Rather more than a vestige, Lionel, though I am surprised Richard did not mention his interest to me when last we met." murmured the Canon. "Roofless and floorless though it may be, it is still a redoubtable monument."

"*Redoubtable*... Oh, very good!" responded Blomefield, to an increasingly puzzled Canon who wished for nothing more than a speedy return to their work in the Orangery.

"You are, of course, most welcome to capture our prospects," Seward said, "though I would ask you to be careful of newly seeded edges, and, of course, not to venture onto any of the borders themselves. The lawns should provide sufficient vantage for your studies. We shall await their outcome with interest."

"Oh, I doubt they will bear scrutiny before I have had the chance to work them up at home," said Blomefield, thinking on his feet.

"Nonetheless," the Canon persisted, "I am certain Anna will be as interested as am I. It is not every day one's garden wall is recorded for posterity. Now though, if you will excuse us, Doctor Darwin and I really must get on." Darwin waved his acknowledgement from the farthest fringes of the conversation, a position he had adamantly occupied since the interruption.

"G...Good p...painting, dear fellow," he said, turning for the

Orangery, rapidly to be joined by the Canon.

"So far, so good," breathed Blomefield to himself, rapidly checking his bearings against the huge outline of the Cathedral church that rose off to his left, beyond the high brick wall. "Now we shall see…"

When he had oriented himself to his satisfaction and simultaneously set up the easel well beyond the sightline from the Orangery, he gave one furtive glance to left and right before unlacing and opening his portfolio.

Within, lay a single, freshly cut hazel fork, tucked between sap-stained sheets of best linen-rag. Withdrawing it, he grasped its ends, and darted glances to and fro before extending it in front of him, arms bent, the single remaining prong extending like some questing antenna – for that was precisely what it was, though the Reverend Blomefield had not used a dowsing-rod for more years than he cared to remember.

What he did recall, though, was the uncanny degree of skill he had possessed as a youth, a fact attested to by the number of local landowners prepared to part with hard cash in return for the locating of a new well or a buried watercourse. The twitching rod had never let him down. Its use, as he knew well, was not limited to a watery search: with it he had located lost wedding rings, an undiscovered chalk void perilously close to newly dug foundations, and, basically, most things he had ever set his wand to search for.

The problem with that most *particular* skill, though, had emerged only later, when his theological studies had become a burgeoning vocation. With it had come the dawning realisation that –perhaps unsurprisingly – dowsing, along with crystal-gazing, the casting of runes, and the reading of palms, cards and tea-leaves, simply did not sit well with a tightly straight-laced clerical hierarchy and the ever-present likelihood of a congregation who could remember the last occasion when an ancestor had burned the local witch.

Hence, after the best part of forty years' neglect he would

resurrect a *rusty* talent, though one, he knew, that would confirm – or convincingly deny – the *something* that they believed to lie beneath the Canon's arbour. After due consideration he had thought it prudent not to mention his intention to the Apothecary; he could be so touchy about things. Checking his position one last time, Lionel Blomefield began to pace, slowly, deliberately, across the impeccable lawn.

(51)

On the left Hand the WIND-DIAL. A model in Plaister of Paris of the monument in Westminster Abbey; erected by Roubiliac, to the memory of George Frederick Handel, born Feb. 23rd. 1684, died, April 14th, 1759.

The shaking had been what woke him, with at first no more than a groggy awareness of a seismic tremble that he could feel across even the thick horsehair mattress. Then, though, peering about the familiar, still confines of the room revealed in the first light of a bright morning, to the unruffled surface of a waterglass on his night-table, he discerned to his growing consternation that its source lay not *beyond* the chamber but within his own bed. Thoroughly alarmed, he turned to the sleeping figure beside him, only to realise that the source was his own wife.

She lay rigid, convulsed, shivering to such an extent he could hear the chattering of her teeth – teeth revealed by drawn back, purple lips in a deathly-white face. With a shout of alarm, he scrambled out of bed to run to her side, pulling back the counterpane to reveal hands clenched about her wrists, her knees drawn up in a foetal crouch, her whole body shaking, uncontrollably, as if in the terminal grip of some unrelenting seizure. Reaching frantically for her shoulders, he lifted the rigid body into his arms, amazed, appalled, at its chill. Clasping her to him as if life depended upon it, he bellowed for assistance.

Within moments, both Margery and their maid had rushed to the scene, arriving dishevelled from sleep, wide-eyed with apprehension, to take in the sight of their apparently unconscious mistress in the Apothecary's arms. Both were sent scurrying away for hot water from the scullery copper, flannels, hot water bottles, brandy and whatever else the frantic husband could summon to a reeling mind.

Suddenly, as he clung to her in his desperation, chafing frigid limbs and clenched fingers, Theodosia's eyes opened, at first staring, wild, lost, until, second by agonising second, she began to return to him. As he watched in speechless relief, she seemed to drag herself up from some abyss, away from the nameless horror that had engulfed her.

"C…C…Cold, s…so c…cold," she managed through drawn lips: "So c…cold."

"Oh, my dear, thanks be to God you are restored to us," he whispered into her hair, just as the servants returned.

"You must drink this, but only sip by sip," he instructed, holding a spoonful of brandy to the quivering lips. After several spluttering attempts, she managed to take a full spoonful, and he watched as a single spot of colour burned back into her ashen cheeks. To left and right the womenfolk rubbed and chafed, warming with steaming flannels then briskly rubbing her dry, until, after what seemed to have been a trembling eternity, her agonised panting and shivering began to ease. On his instructions, Margery rubbed a capsicum and camphor balm into Theodosia's back, beneath a nightgown now sodden with rank sweat, as Greene continued to cradle her in his arms, rocking her, whispering words of love and comfort as she trembled against him, her body still visited by shudders and twitches that only gradually diminished as the moments passed.

Finally, with some colour back in her drawn features, and with bedding and nightclothes discreetly changed whilst the Apothecary mixed up a draught, below, Theodosia was able to collapse back against her bolster and await her husband's return.

From the moment he re-entered their chamber he could tell that she wanted them to be alone, so, with fulsome thanks to both their staff, he finally managed to persuade even a most reluctant Margery that the Mistress could be entrusted into his care for the moment. He would call for them as soon as he may, he promised, so that both could reassure themselves of her continuing revival. He could tell from their housekeeper's departing snort that he was only partially trusted in that area and knew that he would shortly be fending off the arrival of *coffin soup* – the particularly nauseating stewed-bone and offal broth that was Margery's sovereign remedy in times of crisis.

For several moments after they were left alone, Theodosia simply lay back, eyes closed, drained, holding her husband's hand in hers. When she did open the pale eyes that had always entranced him, they seemed to hold a question, a deep appraising search of his face, as if to reassure herself that all was as it should be there and could be counted upon.

"If I were to tell you that I have only barely escaped from something that was more than a dream – worse than ever the vilest dream could be – would you believe me, Richard?" she said in a voice barely more than a whisper. "I must know."

"My dearest girl," he responded, stroking the hand that held his: "you must know that I will. Have I not always taken you at your word, and never doubted you in any way?"

She seemed about to respond to that but paused, eyes closed for a moment, before she said, "This was no fever, no crazed imagining of some silly woman; it was an experience the like of which I have never known. And pray, *pray*, never to know again. I do not know that you – or anyone – can even begin to comprehend its awfulness. I was in a place beyond this world, this time, a place inhabited by Death. By Death and something, *someone*, else."

"Oh, my dear," breathed Greene, horrified to hear such awful words upon his wife's lips.

"There was a rhyme, too," she continued in a sleepy drawl. "A sing-song rhyme like children sing, yet no mouth sang it out. I simply heard the words and had to watch the dance."

She cocked an ear, and seemed to stare off, far away, as if straining to hear some distant echo, recall some fading sound: *Now ye'll dance...*

"*Theodosia!*" her husband's voice, sharp, peremptory, shook her back to her bedchamber, to her man, eyes bulbous with concern in his round face.

"He scraped and bowed, all ribboned curls beneath a black-plumed hat, though by the grace of God I was spared the sight of a face – if one there was – it was so dark, and yet..." She paused as if to search her memory. Greene tried to interrupt her reverie, but was ignored as she continued, wonderingly: "...and yet I could see what I was meant to see, *only* what I was meant me to see: the dance – that's when it began: *legs bent...legs straightened...legs stretched...and parted...and together...feet joined. Then, kicks to the left, kicks to...*"

"No! My darling girl, stop now! You must not return to that place!"

She took a moment to recognise her husband's voice, a moment more to somehow shake off the utter blackness that clung to her like wisps of some befouling fog.

"Oh Richard," she whispered, "there was but a pair of legs, *only* legs, moving as if they swam in air. All else was lost."

He pulled her to him as the tears welled up, but before they fell, she held him off and said in an imploring voice: "And they were *his*, I know they were, left kicking, dancing in that dreadful place. So cold, it was so cold..."

With frightful intuition Greene knew at once the 'he' to which his wife referred: the shadowed watcher in the vanished tower, the figure pointing, staring up at her and her alone, a spectre in a flag-draped transept.

She wept as if she would never cease, and he held her with a passion fierce as life itself until she slept.

ITEM:

A small Glass Case with folding Doors. A variety of Sea-shells, of the larger sort, in front of which stands a neat case, with a glass and burnished gold Frame; within, a piece of Shell work, representing a Cottage, Dove-court, &c presented by Mr Ryland of Birmingham. On each side two glass jars, in which are seen a variety of Shipping, Barracks, Centinals, &c the work of some French Prisoners.

13th May, 1776. Lionel Blomefield's early afternoon had been spent in a barely concealed delirium of excitement. Upon entering the bustling Apothecary premises in Sadler Street, later in the day, not even the blunt injunction that *neither Mr nor Mrs Greene are receiving*, could deflate his heady elation. Without enquiring into the reason, which he knew would not be forthcoming from the magisterially taciturn Shopman, he scribbled a note to the effect that he would expect Mr Greene, without fail, at a time of his convenience that same evening.

He departed, leaving Tillett to wonder how a retired clergyman could manage to get so much paint splattered about his person without, apparently, either noticing or caring.

If, several hours earlier, the Shopman had been a fly upon a certain wall in Breadmarket Street, however, he would have witnessed that gentleman attempting the doomed task of redeeming his garden daubs to an extent that would not provoke outright mirth in the viewer, because viewer there would shortly be, the gentleman knew with a dreadful certainty. After an hour's worth of inept pretence at artistic industry, he had been about to make good the escape from his self-imposed role in the sunlit garden, with easel and paintbox stowed neatly away, stool folded and portfolio tightly laced, when the Canon's daughter came limping into view, with a friendly wave.

"Oh, I am so glad to have caught you, Reverend, dear. Papa tells me that our garden has been immortalised. We are both thrilled, though he would never admit so!"

He gestured helplessly towards his providentially packed equipment:

"I regret that not only am I packed away, Miss Seward, but also – as I did say to your father – my poor daubs will not be fit for viewing without conspicuous industry behind closed doors! In fact, you caught me about to hurry home to do just that. I should not want to disappoint our antiquary."

"Well, by the happiest of coincidences, both the delightful Mrs Greene and I are invited to take tea at Breadmarket Street tomorrow!" A beam of delight illuminated her plump features: "What more perfect opportunity could there be to view your creations, if you will permit us?"

Knowing when he was hopelessly outmanoeuvred, Blomefield had capitulated as gracefully as rising panic permitted: "Of course, how perfect, as you say. Until then, Miss Seward, I shall look forward to your visit. Your interest is most... *unexpected*. I shall endeavour not to disappoint you."

Not even the prospect of what lay in the immediate future could have removed the spring from his step as he made his eventual departure from the palace grounds. The dowsing rod had performed beyond his every expectation: it had taken him no more than minutes to confirm their wildest hopes.

At the very moment when he had virtually finished his quartering of the target area of his search, and had been standing with his back to the great church and facing the ancient Close wall, the first movement of the hazel twig had been tentative. As he moved forward, however, the pull upon it strengthened with his every stride. It was as if he were above a linear void of some description – *a diggers' tunnel*, said a voice inside. "Or some ancient drain," he heard himself say, out loud, and was glad he had no listeners. An elderly man wandering about with a twig in his hands was one thing, one that was heard talking to himself, quite another.

He concentrated on the job in hand. And then it happened, as it had a hundred times before yet never with a power such as this. It took all his strength to keep stretched forearms from buckling with the sheer force of the downward pull. From where he stood, he sensed, he *knew*, it ran from left to right and further on ahead.

He could feel it was a man-made void, a place of stone, a place that held... He almost reeled with the sensory flood that threatened to overwhelm him then. He dropped the twig, that much he knew, but stooping, felt a growing reluctance to employ it once more, telling himself that he had all they needed to know. The confirmation of every hope lay there, deep down beneath his feet. Even without the wand, he felt its power, a radiant force from far below that he had never experienced until that moment.

"Oh, my Lord," he breathed: "What now?"

He hurried back across the lawn to pack away, before remembering his elected role. "Oh, dear me," he murmured, quietly peering into his material box at the unused brushes and the serried ranks of untouched paints that had sat, undisturbed, since the memorable day of their presentation at the dinner to mark his retirement.

The results, achieved over the following hour, failed utterly to demonstrate even the modest talent to which he had so self-effacingly laid claim, lacking – as far as he could see – a single redeeming feature. So it was that the further attempts at any form of salvage behind a firmly locked door in Breadmarket Street snatched catastrophe from the jaws of mere disaster. It was as he stood looking at the rumpled rag-sheet with the hole rubbed through its centre, where he had vainly tried to scrub away several trapped aphids, that he knew this, his last best hope, would be joining the three other ruined pages scattered at his feet. There was only one solution, he decided.

For all his pre-occupation and bone-weariness, the Apothecary had recognised the monosyllabic urgency of his summons, and duly presented himself at the door opposite St Mary's after sharing a quiet supper with his wife. Though still obviously shaken by the extremity of her experience, she had listened to her husband's carefully ordered thoughts, on that and other matters, before nodding unspoken agreement with all he had said, then announcing that an hour or so of painting would be all the medicine she required before they both sought their bed.

With some relief, Richard Greene took her at her word, and had left her happily ensconced in her workroom with the spectacular flower of one of the Dutch tulips she cultivated in the sheltered garden below. Looking up from her study of the astonishing striations of colour in its extravagant unfolding, her parting words had been: "It is not difficult to understand how these inspired such madness. It is as if every wile and fancy of Mother Nature were concentrated in a single flower. They are enough to take one's breath away."

She would never know how much he loved her then, as he bent to peck her cheek and lay a hand upon her shawled shoulder.

"You mean more to me than any Dutchman's fancy ever will," he said, smiling, and took his leave.

Even as the street door was opened by a harried-looking maid, he smelt the fire. Ushered into the hall and relieved of his light frockcoat, his nose wrinkled at the sour tang that hung in the air, only to have the question forming on his lips preempted by the arrival of the equally harried lady of the house.

"Oh, Richard, thank heavens it is only you!" she exclaimed with relief. "I feared it might be someone unaccustomed to Lionel's accelerating lunacy."

"What on *earth* has he..?" began Greene.

"A fire, this time," she replied, before he could finish. "And the next? Who is to say? An attempt at flight from the chimney pots, perhaps? He is quite capable of it."

He was about to speak once more when Elspeth Blomefield's eyes suddenly narrowed and she said: "Though why am I confiding in *you*, Richard Greene? It was upon one of *your* wretched paintings that *my* wretched husband was engaged, so he tells me. When the turpentine spilt, and the candle was upended."

"I do not begin to…" he attempted, helplessly.

"Oh, apologies are neither here nor there, Richard," she interjected, briskly. "Let us simply be thankful that the damage was limited."

"To *what*, may one enquire?" he managed, weakly.

"Well, I am afraid you must wave goodbye to your commission, though why you ever dreamt Lionel to be capable of delivering it, is, frankly, beyond me. All four pictures, at least two of my floorboards and a prized rag rug are scorched beyond redemption." Misreading what she saw in the Apothecary's face as contrition, her tone softened as she added: "Though, as we both know, anything involving Lionel could have been far, far worse. So that, at least, is a saving grace. You had better go out to him, Richard. He knows better than to show his face in the house this evening."

Without attempting another word, Greene bobbed acknowledgement and hurried into the garden, to where the glow of a lamp in the potting shed announced his quarry. The low door opened to the sound of his approaching footsteps on the cinder path, and a surprisingly happy countenance was revealed in the spill of soft light.

"I urge the most serious caution as to how and where you begin, Lionel," Greene hissed, as the door closed behind them.

He listened in a welter of emotions which seemed to replace one another like soldiers on a firing line, the entire gamut of speechless incredulity eventually giving way to simple outrage. "No, let me be certain I have this aright, Lionel: not only did you *choose* not to tell me of your intention to act, unilaterally, on *my* discovery, but you then used *my* name as the means of bamboozling an old and valued mutual friend, trespassing upon both his beloved garden and his trusting nature? Am I correct so far?"

The question being purely rhetorical, he continued, heedless of Blomefield's faltering attempts to intervene.

"So, we are left with a situation, entirely of *your* making, wherein to proceed in any shape or form with the confirmation and revelation of *my* discovery, this old and trusted friend of ours must be approached with the glad tidings that the subterfuge conceived and executed by *you* in *my* name was but a prelude to my asking his gracious consent that we – and however many labourers the task demands – destroy the centerpiece of a garden it has been his life's work to create. I think I am correct, thus far?"

Blomefield, by now unable to meet the Apothecary's red-eyed glare, stared intently out of the cobwebbed windowpane to the dusk beyond, as if seeking a means of escape.

"Right, let us move further into the realm of hypothesis, shall we Lionel, to that most unlikely of future days when a betrayed and heart-broken canon accedes to our request? *Presto!* Not only is an antiquarian cornucopia revealed, but also the most miraculously important *papist* cornucopia ever to survive in our post-Reformation land, complete with the bones of its very own patron saint! Hidden, in the first place, incidentally, so best to preserve it – and him – from protestant monarchy triumphant!

"So, what joy, what a challenge, eh, Lionel? The choices are dizzying: shall the Dean and Chapter petition the Head of the Church of England for his royal permission to rebuild a gilded, bejewelled High Church Shrine guaranteed to become the envy of all and the focus of every papist pilgrim who chooses to emerge from centuries of well-considered concealment in the woodwork? Shall they, instead, quietly rebury their own patron saint with a minimum of fuss and consign the greatest ecclesiastical treasure remaining from our despoiled medieval past to dusty display cases? Or might they still tuck him away, but sell it off, melt it down, and spent the proceeds on *more* cement-render to deface what little still remains of Poor Old Chad's great church? I could go on and on, the permutations are endless and most – depending upon one's perspective – worse than the next. Do we really believe an embattled Hanoverian king will wish to be the patron of a Catholic revival? – because, make no mistake about it, Lionel – the rediscovery of one of England's greatest shrines, *intact* – could bring about the beginnings of just that. George's memory of the Pretender, scarcely thirty years ago, might serve to remind him just how close a Catholic Stuart actually came to achieving the whole point of his march on London. That being to try out the throne for size."

"Oh, spare me the history lesson, Richard," said Blomefield, finally breaking his dejected silence, "Though I may have acted hastily, unwisely even, it was in a cause I believed we both espoused, a cause which, you may care to remember, elected to cheerfully ignore the moving spirit behind the whole original enterprise." He paused, as if to recall: "Now how does it go? Oh, yes: 'Seke him not he sleeps agen til brazen trump shal call men forth to glorie'."

"You have changed your tune to something I fail to recognise, Richard, and now seem, conveniently, to forget the enthusiasms that have driven us both, these months past. And, I might add, high-horses really do not suit your stature."

Greene rallied, though not with his earlier vehemence: "Oh look, Lionel, we know each other far too well to allow personal recriminations to cloud waters of this depth! I know I have been speaking in anger, but dammit, man, there are times when it is *not* misplaced!"

He held up a hand to forestall Blomefield's response, continuing: "You have just used the word *convenient* to describe my change of stance in this. No word could be further from the truth. The place in which I find myself is one I never expected to occupy, but one brought about by being party to a degree of such anguish, such waste and destruction, that I had never thought to witness in my life.

"In past weeks, *days* even, I have become so appalled by my own equivocation, my own failure to make a difference, to stand against the mindless greed and self-seeking which stalk our world, that I have come close to utter despair at a time when resolution has been most called for."

To the amazement of his old friend, as the Apothecary came, finally, to sit beside him on the piled sacks, the tears in his eyes could be seen glistening in the lamplight. "This must never go beyond these walls, Lionel, but now I have to tell you what Theodosia has endured. It is part and parcel of this dark and eerie legacy, though I have been blind to it until now..."

"And you believe that this... *visitant*... was somehow connected to Ashmole and the discovery?" Blomefield asked finally, having listened in complete silence to the Apothecary's evocation of his wife's ordeal.

"Far more than simply connected, Lionel – *instrumental* is my best guess. Look here." Without ceremony he pulled Ashmole's original letter to the Reverend Harrison from a capacious pocket, running a stubby finger down the lines until he found what he sought and read aloud:

For he you will doubtless meet, employ your Best Offices that he may be given the decent repose I could never bestow.

"I believe this says it all, if I am correct." He began to enumerate points on his hand. "Firstly, how was the crypt, the cache or whatever it may be, discovered at all? The answer, given the circumstances, must surely have been due to excavation or subsidence. If the latter, what was down there would most likely have remained buried, unseen; so: excavation. But for what purpose? *Rampiring?* No, there is plenty of remaining evidence for that elsewhere around the walls but not there. *A gun-pit?* No, too low. A *Counter-mine?* Far more likely, there are good records surviving about Prince Rupert's mining against the northern Walls, and the garrison's measures taken against." He paused, drawing breath.

"So, a garrison Trooper, involved we know not how, somehow locates the hidden void but, self-evidently – unable to access it, or its contents, unaided–manages to conceal its existence for several years during which the fortunes of war swing back and forth.

"Given the fact that both the Cathedral and The Close had already suffered grievous damage during the *first* of three sieges, the entire area within the walls would have been one vast spoil-heap. Hence, one must presume, the comparative ease by which our man could have disguised his excavation. Somehow, when Parliament subsequently reoccupies The Close, he meets Ashmole. By my reckoning, this must have been before the last garrison left The Close and during Elias's known return to Lichfield, briefly, after the fall of Worcester. A window of time measured in days or weeks, rather than months. Charles confirmed that for us through the Ashmole diaries – diaries which graphically record his broken-hearted wanderings around the ruined scene of his schooldays. Are you still with me?"

Blomefield nodded and waved him on.

"Why, then, obviously believing himself to be in possession of the exact location, did Ashmole not claim everything for himself – thus achieving the Apotheosis of a young, fortune-hungry opportunist? I shall tell you what I have concluded, Lionel."

His listener sighed and raised eyes, theatrically, heavenwards: "Richard, just get it over with. The suspense is more than I can bear, though I fear I have guessed your conclusion."

Greene continued as if he had not heard: "I am certain he, *they*, did find whatever they sought, but that something – something terrible beyond words – occurred to frustrate their plans. I believe that the Trooper, Theodora's *visitant*, lies down there still. Might it have been a cave-in, a murderous argument – dishonour amongst thieves? –we shall never know. We *do* know that Elias escaped, apparently uninjured, in body at least, but for whatever reason could neither return nor proclaim his discovery without revealing that he had abandoned – or worse – the dead accomplice who would inevitably be found below."

Blomefield nodded, pensively, then looked away, murmuring: "…doomed for a certain term to walk the night, and, for the day, confin'd to fast in fires, til the foul crimes, done in my days of nature, are burnt and purg'd away."

Then, brisk and businesslike, he came to his feet, dusting off straw and loose soil from his breeches: "So, we know what's got to be done then."

(53)

Third SHELF. An ancient piece of Sculpture in Ivory, being a representation of a Man on the back of an Eagle. A smelling bottle supposed to be made of Rice. A Bifrons, cut in Ivory, one Face represents that of our Saviour, the other a Scull.

The Cathedral Close. 24th May, 1776. A dozen clean spade cuts delineated the first turf, and willing hands set to the task of rolling back the lush, cropped grass, then lifting and laying it aside with all the care of handling an infant child. In the early dusk, the loamy tang of fresh-dug soil joined with the evening scents of a sun-warmed garden cooling to its nightly rest. Overhead, against a backdrop of the stately drift of orange clouds, the darting pipistrelles had joined the arabesques of sky-high swallows, feeding as if upon the substance of the air itself.

The diggers paused, straightening to savour a moment when the tolling of the city's hour rolled out across the Minster Pool, then bent to their task once more until their work was done.

Earlier that day, when breakfasting was scarcely done, the well-scrubbed pair that presented themselves, unannounced, at the palace door, were ushered in without demur. Their barely concealed surprise was only heightened by the servant's murmured: "I am to show you into the Dining Room, gentlemen; Canon Seward is at table and will receive you there."

Whilst the Christian charity and boundless courtesy of their host were, both knew, beyond question, his tolerance of interruptions at mealtimes was most certainly not. Unscheduled visitors had been known to spend the entire duration of a lengthy Seward meal, unrefreshed, unattended and left to twiddle thumbs with every opportunity to regret their sense of occasion – or lack of it. Hence, with extra trepidation, Richard Greene and Lionel Blomefield entered the gracious Dining Room.

Rising to meet them, Canon Seward beamed at the Apothecary, saying: "Richard, it is always a pleasure," and to Greene's companion: "Lionel! How nice; it is as if you never left. Did your *prospects* prosper? Anna is counting the hours until their unveiling."

Accepting the offer of chairs and the service of coffee, pleasantries of a slightly strained nature were exchanged until the servants left. As the doors closed behind them, and their host was on the verge of posing the obvious question, Greene seized the moment:

"Canon Seward, although I can only apologise for our untimely intrusion, the reason for it, will, I trust, become rapidly apparent. Before any proper explication can be made, though, Lionel has something of a pressing nature he wishes to explain to you."

"Indeed?" the old man responded: "I am intrigued," and laying aside his napkin, sat back with what Greene could have sworn to be a glint of amusement in his rheumy eyes.

The Apothecary was forced to conclude, later, that the sheer frequency with which Lionel Blomefield must have had to make groveling apologies and ever-more elaborate explanations for ill-conceived actions over many years, had made possible this morning's bravura performance. The sheer elegance of his display of ducking and diving did not, however, diminish the obvious sincerity of his contrition, though such was the sheer eloquence of its delivery that the Canon's benign forgiveness seemed a foregone conclusion even before the details of the previous afternoon's desperate fire-raising brought tears of mirth to their host's eyes.

"*When we practise to deceive…*, eh, Lionel?" he managed, at the end, then continuing: "It would appear, however, that you are now sufficiently untangled from the web of your own weaving to present yourself today. I not only accept your apology but also applaud your resilience." On that calculatedly ambivalent note, the Canon turned to Greene: "So, my friend, from what Lionel has so elaborately explained, you believe yourself to be upon the verge of a most momentous discovery in my garden, do you? Perhaps you will kindly elaborate?"

Through a largely sleepless night, Greene had struggled with the task of where to even begin on the maze-like explanation of everything that had brought them to this point, this place. Now though, after several sips of coffee, he found the words.

"Our lost Gospel, too?" Seward breathed, when the telling was done. "You are certain of that?"

"I can be *completely* certain of nothing, short of complete excavation," the Apothecary replied, "but, yes, I believe it to be with the Shrine – where it belongs, in fact."

"Indeed, indeed. Oh, my word, what a prize that would be, indeed." mused Seward, staring out of the long windows: "And all so close."

Abruptly, he turned back to Greene, seeming to stare at him, *through* him, with a fierce new intensity:

"So, my antiquarian friend, what are you now proposing? Shovels at dawn?

The silence that followed his question seemed to stretch longer than Blomefield, raptly attentive, would have believed possible, until, finally, wearily, Richard Greene replied. "Not long ago, Canon Seward, you expressed a sentiment which has stayed with me ever since." The old man cocked a bushy, interrogative eyebrow, waiting for him to proceed.

"Talking of the surviving fragments of the Shrine you said: Though what interest they would hold for our increasingly secular times, one can scarcely imagine; perhaps some things are best left undisturbed'."

Seward nodded in recollection, his intense gaze never leaving the speaker.

"As I explained at some length, last night, to Lionel, trying his patience even more than usual," continued Greene, giving a weary smile, "a combination of tragedy and circumstances of which I could never have dreamt has brought me to the same conclusion." He shook his head as if in wonder but continued: "Even now I can scarcely believe I am saying the words, but, although I am utterly convinced that the greatest antiquarian discovery of our age awaits excavation mere yards from where we sit, I am now of the wholehearted conviction that it must remain undisturbed; an absolute secret as it has been these two hundred and fifty years past."

The Canon stared into space, as if seeming to consider his reply before he finally spoke: "My dear friend, you are absolutely right, though in more ways than one. Whilst both your belief in the Shrine's survival and the inordinate lengths to which you have gone to *arrive* at such a conclusion are most admirable, permit me to remove any lingering doubts you may have about your conclusions." He turned to include Lionel Blomefield in his next words. "Its survival, gentlemen, is a simple fact, though there can be few more jealously guarded ones on this earth. The knowledge – the secret – of its existence, and its location, has been passed from generation to generation with a discretion you could scarcely imagine. The arrival – or should I say the very *existence* – of 'The Ashmole Box', as you call it, could never have been foreseen. It would have been, shall we say, caused to *disappear* had it ever come to the notice of any one of my predecessors. Your revelation of the hither-to unknown fact that Ashmole himself came within an ace of discovery is quite simply astonishing, as is the knowledge that the site somehow escaped detection after its initial rediscovery. Providence does, indeed, work in the most mysterious ways.

"To return to the business of the Shrine itself, though. Not surprisingly, details of all that may accompany it do not exist..." –

he smiled, wryly – "…due, no doubt, to Rowland Lee's prescient understanding of human frailty. An infamous history of our response to the seductive lure of buried treasure does little to recommend our human nature in the sight of the Lord. Here, though, at my own dining table, gentlemen, you have severally demonstrated a generosity and a greatness of spirit that leaves me humble. I salute you and applaud your decision with all my heart, though I suspect, Richard, that there may be some other thing still on your mind..?"

Once the few turves were stacked and the hole dug, Richard and Theodosia Greene knelt together to lay the box into its shadowed depths, watched by the lanky form of Lionel Blomefield who had taken the arm of his frail companion. Both Seward and he opened the books they held, once the Greenes had risen from their task, a gusting breeze ruffling the fine pages as they found their markers. Clearing his throat before he began, Lionel Blomefield stepped forward, whilst Theodosia moved, unobtrusively, to take his place beside the Canon.

"Man born of woman hath but a short time to live…"

As the day dimmed about them, together they spoke ancient words of parting and forgiveness, until, as if by tacit agreement, the Canon smilingly disengaged himself from Theodosia's arm and stood alone by the small excavation. He continued, remembering by heart the passage of the *New Testament*.

"Lay not up for yourselves treasures upon earth, where moth and rust doth corrupt, and where thieves break through and steal, but lay up for yourselves treasures in heaven where neither moth nor rust doth corrupt and where thieves do not break through nor steal. For where your treasure is, there will your heart be also." Finally, he added, "Soldier, known only to Our Saviour, may you find eternal rest."

"There," he said brightly, stepping back and turning to his companions, "that will have done the job. Once the turf is replaced, I believe we could all do with a drink."

Postscript

4ᵗʰ June, 1776. The ostensible purpose of the brief visit to Oxford had been the return of the borrowed map, though neither Blomefield nor the Apothecary had taken much persuading. Caisley had been proved entirely right in his assumption that the very existence of such a map would delight the Canon, and it had been duly delivered to the palace some days earlier. Enthralled by the loan and having completed a painstaking copy, annotated in his perfect, scholarly hand, Canon Seward had invited the two of them to view his 'pale imitation', and, though taking obvious pleasure in their approbation of his penmanship, had soon arrived at his principal purpose.

"As it would appear that you are both on more than nodding terms with this Bodley fellow…" he'd begun.

"*Sir* Charles Caisley," Blomefield had interjected.

"Indeed, indeed," murmured Seward, unimpressed: "It struck me that we might be of mutual service in the manuscript's return."

He had proposed that if they would accept his reimbursement for all expenses incurred, both Greene and Blomefield should visit the great library with a view to cataloguing those items identifiable as once having belonged to Lichfield Cathedral. Thence, if circumstance permitted, to embark upon some serious negotiation – "Horse-trading, you mean," Blomefield had interrupted with characteristic bluntness, "for their return?"

Seward had not deigned to reply, simply raising bushy

eyebrows as if in prayer. "I do not rule out purchase," the Canon had sniffed, "though it rankles even to say the word; you may inform your Bodley fellow that I have reluctantly concluded that the restitution of a once-great library takes precedence over such niceties as natural justice."

Their departure, a week hence, had been agreed, giving both men leeway in which to make necessary arrangements. The Canon had nodded sagely in response to Blomefield's certainty that there would be no problem in the making of his.

"I suspect Elspeth might purchase a coach outright if it means getting rid of me for a few days." Greene, avoiding eye contact with the Canon, had simply nodded.

As they had made their farewells, Seward's final words had been: "You might consider breaking your journey at that coaching-place near Warwick; the name eludes me, but I remember it as being quite acceptable."

"I'll wager the name does not elude Charles," Blomefield had laughed as they made their way back across The Close together. "Still, in my own case, even a few dozen flea-bites would be light relief at present."

Their days in Oxford passed all-too rapidly, in a welter of sightseeing, dining and, for the Apothecary, hours spent in heaven. The Bodleian collection exceeded his wildest imaginings, and, with the Canon's small catalogue soon completed, his waking hours were spent, entranced, among the stacks and shelves and cabinets, delving into an inky universe of wonder.

During the course of a blissfully uneventful coach journey, they had agreed that, if required, an appeal to Caisley's discretion would have to be made; otherwise though, a harmless fiction maintained: that their Ashmole-related search had gone so far and no further and was now consigned to the realm of unsolved mysteries.

Their host had seemed strangely unsurprised by their news,

though, Greene wondered, had there been a glint of something more than polite acceptance in its reception? Dreading that he might enquire into the fate of the antiquities in the box – not least the extraordinary manuscript fragment – both had been fervently grateful when the topic of conversation had moved gracefully on to the Canon's proposal.

"The issue at stake here, my friends, involves a debate that will, I fear, continue for as long as there are museums and collections such as this. Namely: when – and how – does *de facto* ownership become legitimate?"

"We have, on the one hand, the time-honoured convention of *caveat emptor*, enforced, if you will, by both law and usage, wherein the unwary buyer forfeits goods that can be proven stolen, with no right of financial restitution. Purchases of any moment for institutions such as this are, however, invariably the subject of discussion with one's Trustees, Steering Committee or the like; curators – in the main – not being encouraged to do business of a *market ouvert* nature, dealing with characters that prefer the hours of darkness for their transactions. However, on the other hand lies a murky realm of sanctified theft, whereby the spoils of war, the plunder of Empire and Colony, become somehow sacrosanct, above that same law – and most certainly beyond the reach of injured claimants. Can you begin to imagine, Gentlemen, the hundred and one loose ends that dear old Soane must have bequeathed to us along with – what was it? – seventy odd thousand items gifted to the Nation? One could spend an eternity of sleepless nights imagining the queues around Montagu House, composed of vengeful spectres and plundered Maharajahs! No, my friends, I fear that once unprincipled rascals such as I lay curatorial hands upon items, we are unlikely to be persuaded to part with them. *Lord*, Richard, you of all men should appreciate that!"

Nodding absently, Richard looked thoughtful before replying: "Do you do swaps?"

It had been a measure of how much she missed him, that Theodosia had entered the Museum rooms at all. Closed to the ticket-buying public for the brief duration of his absence, the pristine displays, the cabinets, the shelves of exhibits, seemed to have become meaningless trophies in a world of temporarily suspended animation. A world lacking its demiurge, its catalytic spirit, in the Apothecary's absence. Only the clocks, each ticking away its perfect measure, all combining in a gentle symphony of chimes, seemed to offer any promise of continuity, she thought. She found herself counting the hours until his return.

As she caught a passing glimpse of her own reflection in the dappled glass of a display, she saw a wraith-like figure gliding through the dust-motes of an empty room, and she remembered, once again, another figure, glimpsed against the dying light.

In the dimming of that sunlit evening, as they had stood, finally, beside the newly restored turf on the palace lawn, up on the ruined parapet of what they called the Bishop's Tower a figure – seen by her and her alone – had raised an arm and waved it, once, before she'd blinked, and it was gone.

About to leave, she saw an object loose upon the table that served as Richard's desk, a gleam of silver-gold that caught her eye. Knowing it for what it was, she picked up the perfect little head and gazed in fascination at the passion in the sculpted face. A full-lipped mouth grimacing at the bloody act engaged upon by long-lost hands, a pair of staring, sightless eyes that only saw a world within.

Rolling it in her palm, she felt the weight of gold and wondered at its worth. Yes, that was it, she knew now what was left to do.

They would take a trip to Walsall, just as soon as he returned – to buy a hat, no less. She saw it now, a rolled brim and an ostrich plume, or even two; the creation of a milliner who knew her craft.

Together they would seek out such a one.

He would be glad, she knew.

finis

Artist, academic and sometimes bluesman, Michael Anson lives in Norfolk, England.

Notes and acknowledgements

The genesis of this, the final part of the Lichfield trilogy, is due in large part to a serendipitous discovery. When I happened across the print of Lichfield Cathedral featured on page 68 I had no idea how remarkable it would turn out to be. Most appropriately, in view of its obvious rarity and great age, it shares with its subject the distinction of being a near-miraculous survival. John Hacket, Bishop of Lichfield 1661–70, had embarked upon the grimly daunting task of beginning clearage of the roofless, spireless, war-ravaged ruin he had inherited, the sight of which – almost twenty years earlier – had so horrified Elias Ashmole on his return to the city of his birth. The traumatic impression it made upon Ashmole would remain so powerful that with the new dawn of The Restoration, he would not only commission this print as a poignant *memento mori* to what he must have supposed would remain as lost splendours but would also become a persuasive voice for the wholesale restitution of this 'loyal and ancient' monument that had suffered so grievously in the royal cause.

I am indebted to my friend Nick Bundock, not only for his eagle-eyed scrutiny of the manuscript in general but also for his particular suggestion that TF – the subject of Ashmole's dedication – is most likely to have been Thomas Fairfax, distinguished soldier and parliamentarian, whose subsequent influence became pivotal in the return of Charles II to the throne. It was the thrill of coming into possession of that resonant, dishevelled page that set me out on the path of creating two parallel timelines, wherein the veil of time, the years separating Ashmole and Greene, would become ever thinner.

In the course of writing, I shared several notable experiences with Theodosia. The first involved our ascents of the Cathedral's immense tower beneath the restored Great Steeple. Guided by a cooperative Verger who had seen it all before, I entered the eerie, unseen roof spaces above the south transept leading towards the alarmingly narrow corkscrew staircase that climbs to the Ringing Chamber below the tower battlements. The chamber, as described in the text, is monumentally spectacular but as nothing to the sight that meets one's emergence out onto the platform above it.

Here, where vertigo and agoraphobia had dealt the poor lady such a devastating blow, I was simply transfixed by the height and the vista of city and surrounding countryside revealed. Way down to my right, to the northwest, the surviving gun-emplacement earthworks of Prince Rupert's royalist Battery, whilst across the Bishop's Pool and far down to my left, the Dam Causeway to the now-vanished South gate from whence the Parliamentarian cannon had brought down the vast spire whose replacement today soared above me. Up here too, beside me, the embrasure from which 'Dumb' Dyott – a local man with a duck gun – had shot and killed Lord Brooke, commander of the besieging Roundheads, far off down on the distant Dam.

Returning, reluctantly, to the huge chamber below, alone now since the Verger had pleaded a more pressing engagement, I began the ascent down what I fondly supposed to have been the stairs of my ascent. The further down I climbed the darker, dustier and hotter it seemed to become, until, to my genuine alarm, I finally came to a locked door at the stair's foot. Through its cracks I suddenly realised that, like Theodosia before me, I had mistakenly descended a second stairwell in the tower's walls whose existence had passed unnoticed on my ascent. I was spared the spectral vision down in the transept far below that had met the lady's gaze but regained the upper chamber drenched in sweat with no little relief.

Upstairs, at Milley's Hospital, some weeks later, I had been allowed to visit the ancient chapel from whose window Theodosia had experienced another of her uncanny visions, of walls and towers destroyed almost 150 years earlier. Here, today, the view had been blameless, with nothing to be seen but the houses of Vicar's Close opposite and the traffic below on Beacon Street. I did, however – just like my unfortunate predecessor – manage to almost brain myself, cracking my head on the low lintel of the chapel doorway.

Retracing Richard Green's climb – whilst in the company of Canon Seward – up the steep stairs to what has subsequently become the Cathedral Library now situated above the Chapter House, I was shown the site of the little-known Chapel of St Peter – with its vestigial wall painting of the inverted crucifixion – by the librarian. In the space of a short visit that lady managed to make very clear the centuries-old rancour shared by her and her generations of predecessors concerning Oxford's renowned Bodleian Library: that august institution knowingly held priceless volumes recognised by all as civil-war plunder from Lichfield Cathedral whose restitution they steadfastly refused to consider.

Some months later, and involving a small financial transaction and no acrimony, I did manage to locate, and have photocopied, one of the Bodleian's vast collection of the so-called Cotton Manuscripts. Its faint, spidery lines and annotations provide the only extant ground-plan of the long-vanished, medieval Bishop's Palace in Lichfield Close and also determine the mysteriously awkward textual layout wherein Greene's final discovery is perceived. I have no idea what can have happened to Canon Seward's assiduous copy of Sir Charles Caisley's thoughtful loan.

The Bishop's Tower at the north-east corner of the Close walls is the best of the few remaining defences that rendered the Cathedral as 'this great fortress', and, whilst in restricted school grounds, can best be viewed from Dimbles Lane beyond the eponymous dry moat. Close by, some years ago, an alarming void opened in the garden of one of the bungalows lining the lane, revealing what was confidently described as the entrance to one of the many siege tunnels excavated during the years of the Civil War. It was quickly filled in without further exploration!

I am most grateful to Robin, at Little Walsingham's Holt Antiques, for providing Ashmole's Box, to Bob Yeatman of Eastern Lightcraft for his photography and to Sue Knox for her graphic assistance. My thanks to swarthy Mercian friend, Keith Rowley, for endless patience in his reading of numerous iterations, and to Nick Bundock for his forensic eye, his judgement and his unremitting defence of the English language.

Once more, a most particular 'thank you' to Tom O'Reilly of Page d'Or who has provided unfailing support, advice and encouragement in the face of authorial foibles and typographic transgression.

The Burning Zone

Little knowing that the unearthing of a medieval grave slab will propel him into the realm of waking nightmare, Richard Greene, apothecary, antiquarian and museum-keeper extraordinaire, is the sole witness to a sadistic murder.

Badly injured in the doomed attempt to save the victim of a fire universally believed to be a tragic accident, Greene emerges from lengthy convalescence only to be drawn into the coils of a demented and murderous search for vengeance enacted from beyond the grave and across generations; a pitiless ritual of retribution inflicted upon all who had sat in judgement upon England's last heretic – the victim a crazed Anabaptist – sentenced to die a hideous death in the last judicial burning to stain English history.

Now, as the century of Enlightenment gathers pace around him, the terrors and obsessions of an earlier, darker time reach out to claim one final victim: the woman at the heart of Greene's own life.

A final offering to sate the ravening hunger of 'The Burning Zone'.

The Bishop's Grimoire

Richard Greene, apothecary, antiquarian and museum-keeper extraordinaire, witnesses the chance find of an ancient book, an arcane symbol partially visible on its cover identifying it as a work of ritual magic: A Grimoire.

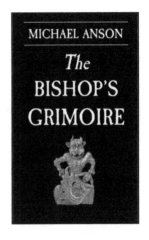

The provenance and authenticity of the age-old book identify it as an incredibly rare survival – a 'Black Legend', stolen five centuries earlier from the Vatican library, owned – and hidden – by Walter de Langton, a bishop of Lichfield who had stood trial for witchcraft around the year 1300 in Rome.

No one can envisage the approaching cataclysm: the collision of a demonic, stygian past with the presence of the prophet of Reason and the Nobility of untainted Mankind. In Greene's desperation that the book must somehow be destroyed, he unwittingly sets that scene.

As demented obsession turns to poisoning and murderous abduction, Greene must fight for more than life itself, burdened with the terrifying knowledge of what 'The Bishop's Grimoire' contains … and seeks.

An extract from

The Burning Zone
by Michael Anson

(3)

ITEM:

In the shallow case against the wainscot: an ancient crucifix of
bone with, still attached, sundry beads of its rosarie. Likely of
mendicant Greyfriars origin, whose grant of *liberum sepultum*
assured that those buried in their cemetery or in the habit of
their order would be secure from the attack of evil spirits.

17ᵗʰApril, 1746. On that bright afternoon, as the desperate
remnants of Bonnie Charlie's highlanders were being hunted
with dogs and bayoneted in the budding heather for miles around
Culloden Moor, Richard Greene was taking a bowl of tea in Mr
Rawlins's parlour and discussing the cultivation of musk roses.

Scarcely four months earlier, within the self-same oak-panelled
walls, the Duke, now busily earning the title of *Butcher*, had also
taken tea in the briefly commandeered house. On that day, though,
the talk had been of a *tactical* rather than horticultural nature, as
Cumberland and his senior staff had discussed a strategy to hold
the ever-nearing army of the Scottish Pretender at Derby. Today,
though, heedless of the old room's echoes, or of far-off events, the
young Mr Greene had been summoned to record a discovery.

It lay propped against the kitchen garden gate, still glistening
from the bucketsful of water employed to sluice the heavy loam
from its surface, and after social niceties had been briefly observed,

his aged host had hurried him out of doors, hobbling ahead through the warrenous house.

"It's a grave slab, most certainly," agreed the Apothecary, peering closely at the inscription which ran around the edges of the slab, framing a deeply incised cross.

Pointing at its decorated head: "A *cross fleurie*, I believe a herald would call it," he added, turning to his host; a spare elderly man, stooped attentively at his side.

Writing rapidly in a precise hand he copied the archaic letterforms. After pausing to brush off the worst of the remaining mud, Greene continued: "I fear my Latin is not of such an off-the-cuff variety that will permit anything approaching an immediate translation. I can say that it is a memorial to one 'Richard the Merchant' and that there is mention of his generosity to the Church, but the rest must await assistance from a lexicon, and as much inspiration – and patience – as I can muster."

The elderly face creased in quiet appreciation of the younger man's modest disclaimer, as he went on: "Surely one of the Reverent Gentlemen of The Close could oblige with far greater facility than mine?"

"Most likely, Mr Greene," responded Michael Rawlins, drily, "but to be quite frank – and knowing of your interest in all things pertaining to our ancient City – I felt that your drafting skills and, shall we say, your *discretion*, might spare me from the effusions of those learned gentlemen and their particular enthusiasm for my sherry wine. I do get so weary of being talked at, if you will permit me such unchristian candour?"

Nothing, in fact, could have surprised the Apothecary more

than the request, delivered just past opening time, that he attend upon this, the reclusive owner of The Friary. The messenger, a boy with an alarmingly swollen cheek, stood by, fidgeting miserably, as Greene squinted at the note – only as a postscript reading:

The boy would appear to have a gumboil; if it may be relieved for sixpence, kindly proceed.

He had met Rawlins only twice, when – on both occasions – the elderly man had happened upon him out sketching. His work had been politely admired and several suggestions regarding curiosities tucked away in the city's nether courts and alleyways had been made by the sparse figure, with brisk economy. Not now wishing to overstay what he sensed to be a somewhat finite welcome, the Apothecary completed his observations in the well-tended garden and promised to relay the translated text as soon as it was complete.

"I shall look forward to it, Mr Greene." The bony head in its sparse wig bobbed once as the massively studded door in the garden wall was closing.

"It is not every day one comes upon tombstones in one's tulip bed."

That it was to be more than two months before a raw-scarred and alarmingly gaunt young man would be able to return with the task complete entered neither head on that spring day in Holy Week.

Richard Greene was spared the knowledge that a season in Hell awaited him.

(4)

ITEM:

In a drawer within the Bureau, marked A: Twenty-
one specimens of small writing hardly legible without
a glass, amongst which the Creed, Lord's Prayer and
Ten Commandments, in the compass of half a guinea.
Some writing by Matthew Buckinger, born
without hands and feet, in Germany 1674.

18th April, 1746. The following day being Easter Saturday, there
was a brisk trade in the costly powdered pigments which the
Apothecary stocked. Like camphor for mid-winter, blue-bags for
the wasp days of August and, today, paints for eggs, much of the
shop's business ebbed and flowed with the currents of the year: the
trick being, as the Shrewsbury apprentice-master had reiterated
with numbing regularity, to foresee in order to *flourish*.

The shop in Saddler Street had been established little more than
for a half-dozen years and was indeed flourishing. Its proprietor
set out on his rounds leaving a competent assistant, his own
apprentice, and a keen-eyed wife to preside over the toothpaste
manufactory newly set up in the garden potting shed

Although there had been no time for a leisurely scrutiny of the
notes and drawing made the previous afternoon, a small scheme
was hatching in his head as he returned from his last patient, in
The Close.

He had crossed The Millrace and was passing between the high
old houses in Dam Street as the attractive stratagem formed: *Why
not? Why not, indeed? A careful redrawing of the grave slab with
its gothic inscription nicely rendered, accompanied by a succinct and
scholarly observation on its antiquity and sense. After all, had Cousin*

Johnson not invited a contribution to 'The Gentleman's Magazine' on several occasions? This would neatly fit the bill.

The scream took a second – several seconds – to fully punctuate his reverie, and he had to jolt his attention back to the moment to properly register its source.

"Fire! Fire! Oh God help us – he's still abed and helpless!" A distraught figure burst from a porchway behind the Apothecary, her mob-cap flying from dishevelled hair as she rushed towards him. Greene reached out instinctively, but she stopped and screamed again, a dreadful ululating wail, as she pointed up. As if conjured by her hand, a great gout of black smoke burst from beneath the eaves of the house she had fled. She stifled another wail with blackened hands pressed to her mouth as Richard Greene grabbed her by shawled shoulders.

"Your Master? *Quick*, girl, is it your Master in there? Mr Neille? Old Mr Neille?"

Though not one of his patients, the Apothecary knew the stiff and proper occupant of the house to be a retired man of means, one of the city's racing fraternity, not long arrived from the North.

"Yessir," gulped the terrified girl, "Oh God, for pity's sake don't let him burn."

By now, all within earshot – a dozen or more – were running towards the wild-eyed girl, but before any could approach for further explanation, Greene pushed the maid to one side and launched himself into the darkened entrance to the high house.

Already, an acrid skein of smoke roiled down from above, fogging the hallway and the narrow stairs, all but choking Greene in his first unguarded breath. He knew from bitter experience that every second counted in the confines of these tinder-dry dwellings – crammed with the horsehair, lathes and wattles which partitioned their age-old wooden frames. Without hesitation he dragged off his neckerchief and, pressing to his nose and mouth, ran for the stairs.

As he breasted the first landing the sound of crackling seemed to fill the air above, and dense smoke billowed about him as he flung open the nearest door. An upstairs parlour, quite empty, met his streaming eyes as he crouched ever lower to avoid the suffocating fumes.

A muffled crash from the floor above jerked his attention away from the mocking emptiness, and he knew with awful certainty that his goal lay at the heart of the conflagration that was now roaring on the top storey. As he stumbled towards the stairs a shower of huge sparks cascaded down the stairwell and onto the landing, flames leaping in response from the thick Turkey carpet at his feet.

Pausing only to haul his moleskin coat off and over his bent head, Greene ploughed up the remaining flight into a wall of heat that snatched the air from his lungs. Even as he approached the nearest bedchamber door he knew he was too late – as the sound of exploding glass cracked out through the all-enveloping roar.

He flinched violently back from the appalling heat, an arm bent hopelessly across his face as he fought towards the planked door. Ducking to one side, he kicked with all his might, cowering back from the flaring gust that belched from the blazing room.

As his half-blinded eyes caught a glimpse of what the chamber held, a window into Perdition itself opened to the reeling man. Spread-eagled upon a blazing tester, arms and legs lashed to its posts, a hideously blistered figure writhed in the last extremities of agony on a bed of flame. In the instant of vision that remained to Greene, his quailing mind registered one last, abominable, comprehension: a bloody void framed a silent scream beneath melting eyes, *in a mouth possessed of no tongue*. Even before the realisation could numb his very soul, a concussive blackness smashed down upon the Apothecary's barely protected head and he stumbled, fell and tumbled like a cast-off bundle of smouldering rags down the staircase. Above, an incandescent gale raged across the collapsing ruin of roof and walls.

Praise for Michael Anson's *The Burning Zone*:

"...a well-crafted, well-constructed novel ... could do for Lichfield what Cadfael did for Shrewsbury."
— Ralph James MBE, *The Lichfield Mercury*

"The interesting balance of fact and fiction make this a great read and a real page turner."
— Alison Smith, *Express and Star*

"Period drama at its best"
— Amazon customer

"...kept me riveted from beginning to end"
— Amazon customer

Praise for Michael Anson's *The Bishop's Grimoire*:

"This is one of the most enjoyable and unputdownable books I have read in a long time ... I can't recommend this book enough."
— Marilyn Pemberton,
Historical Novel Review (Editors' Choice 2022)

"A thoroughly engrossing historical thriller – A must read!!!"
— Amazon customer

"...an extremely well-written, exciting and absorbing read"
— Amazon customer

"Anson has created another thrilling page turner that you won't be able to put down!"
— Amazon customer

Lightning Source UK Ltd.
Milton Keynes UK
UKHW040609161122
412283UK00001B/98

9 781913 825584